D0049318

A Miracle
for
St. Cecilia's

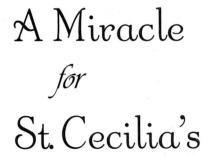

A Miracle
for
St. Cecilia's

Katherine Valentine

VIKING

VIKING

Published by the Penguin Group

Penguin Putnam Inc., 375 Hudson Street, New York, New York 10014, U.S.A.

Penguin Books Ltd, 80 Strand, London WC2R 0RL, England

Penguin Books Australia Ltd, 250 Camberwell Road, Camberwell, Victoria
3124, Australia

Penguin Books Canada Ltd, 10 Alcorn Avenue, Toronto, Ontario, Canada M4V 3B2

Penguin Books India (P) Ltd, 11 Community Centre, Panchsheel Park, New Delhi -
110 017, India

Penguin Books (N.Z.) Ltd, Cnr Rosedale and Airborne Roads, Albany, Auckland,
New Zealand

Penguin Books (South Africa) (Pty) Ltd, 24 Sturdee Avenue, Rosebank, Johannesburg
2196, South Africa

Penguin Books Ltd, Registered Offices: Harmondsworth, Middlesex, England

First published in 2002 by Viking Penguin, a member of Penguin Putnam Inc.

Copyright © Katherine Valentine, 2002
All rights reserved

ISBN 0-670-03113-5

Printed in the United States of America

I wish to dedicate this book to my dearest friend, my husband for thirty years, "St." Paul.

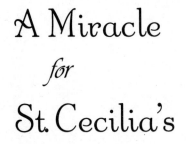

A Miracle
for
St. Cecilia's

Chapter 1

On the Monday of the last week of February, warm air from the south met the snow-covered hillsides of Dorsetville, creating a heavy fog that settled over the Connecticut River Valley town until the high roof peaks of the abandoned woolen mills along the river's banks rose, disembodied above the fog, like a spectral apparition. By Tuesday, the fog was so thick that the driver for Marcus Dairy, who had personally delivered milk, butter and cream to Main Street's Country Kettle for over twenty-five years, passed the restaurant twice in the pre-dawn darkness, and Sheriff Bromley's new deputy, Frank Hill, who had only been on the job for a little under two weeks, made a wrong turn onto Bates Rock Road and ran the town's police cruiser into Ted Platt's pond. Throughout that week, men in town cursed the fog that had the interstate just north of Dorsetville backed up for over forty miles.

Dorsetville's womenfolk, however, didn't mind the fog—even when it kept the schools closed for two days in a row. It was the mud they cursed. It turned driveways and pathways into troughs of viscous soup and left embossed patterns of rubber-soled shoes from one end of their homes to the other. The women knew that it was useless to try to prevent the mud from seeping in. Instead, they became masters at preventing damage while the mud lay siege.

Hooked rugs were rolled up and carefully tucked away as they were the women's most cherished possessions. Each had been painstakingly created from recycled pieces of woolen cloth, most took several years to create. First the wool had to be dyed, then cut into strips small enough to hook through a piece of burlap, but the effort was worth it, the results dazzling. These bright florals patterns, bold geometric designs and intricate landscape scenes were famous throughout New England and eagerly anticipated each year at the state fair. The women called themselves Dorsetville's Happy Hookers and won a blue ribbon every year.

Since the rugs were so highly prized, the areas by the front, side and back doors, which once sported these clever creations, now were adorned with bath towels purchased at Kmart during its January white sale for $2.99 apiece. Treasured quilts were draped in old sheets to protect them from dirty-footed children and muddy-bellied dogs. And when they visited, in a great show of solidarity against this evil agent, the women always left their brown-caked boots on the side porch and donned the pair of clean socks they had tucked inside their purses.

But by the first of March—which happened to fall on Ash Wednesday—a dramatic change took place as an arctic wind coursed into the valley, adhering to the countryside like a wet sponge to a freezer wall. It caught the residents of Dorsetville by surprise, residents who, under the February thaw, had sat by open windows, seed catalogues spread out on worn kitchen tables, gazing dreamily into the barren landscape envisioning summer's rich crops.

This morning's cold front vaporized the fog and froze the mud into brown molds of tire tracks and roadside glaciers comprised of half-melted snow where encapsulated chunks of granite, broken limbs and litter lay captive. The cold front had frozen Dorsetville solid.

It was only by true Yankee grit, ingrained in New Englanders for many generations, that the citizens of Dorsetville were able to rouse themselves from sleep this morning to face a sky domed in deep, charcoal gray clouds, a harbinger of heavy snow. Their only solace was in the old adage "March comes in like a lion and goes out like a lamb," which was oft repeated this morning as women throughout the valley searched hall closets for misplaced ear muffs and lost mates of gloves while the men braved the numbing cold outdoors trying to coax reluctant car batteries into life.

By six-thirty A.M., kitchen cabinets were ransacked in search of oatmeal canisters—their contents to be mixed with milk still delivered in glass bottles with paper caps left each morning in the square tin milk box by the side door. While the oatmeal was left to bubble at the back of the stove in a cast iron pot, homeowners would begin to make frantic calls to George Benson, heating and air-conditioning specialist as well as Dorsetville's fire marshal, to come and reset their furnace pilot lights, which had gone out unnoticed during the thaw.

George was needed most at St. Cecilia's Catholic Church, a monolith of gray granite and marble that sat along the town's square on a parcel of land much too small for the imposing structure. Morning Mass began at seven A.M. and the church's furnace—which was installed in 1941 to replace the original coal furnace—could be counted on for only one thing: it couldn't be counted on.

St. Cecilia's was an aberration among the white-steepled, clapboard houses of worship as indigenous to New England as its rolling countryside and its trees' spectacular autumn foliage. In fact, St. Cecilia's was the proverbial white elephant and a bane to its parishioners who had never been consulted on its design.

The church's benefactors, Irish immigrants who traveled up from the meanest poverty on the streets of Dublin to the lofty heights of leading citizens in their roles as mill owners of this valley town, had commissioned the building following a trip to Italy, lending testimony to Emerson's statement "Some men wear wealth like an ill fitting suit." In their quest to distance themselves as much as possible from the humble wooden structures in which they had worshipped as youths and to reflect their newfound status, they imported a host of Italian artisans along with some Italian marble in their plan to rival the great churches of Rome.

The result was a gaudy pseudo-cathedral of Italian marble, hand-painted friezes, gilded ceilings and fine wood carvings crammed into a building poised on a postage-stamp-size plot of earth. Many who saw St. Cecilia's for the first time commented that it looked as though it were suffering from gas.

St. Cecilia's extravagant style was the reason the church had been left to slowly disintegrate over the years. No one in all of New England possessed any of the skills needed to execute the repairs. Since the mid-1960s, the parish council had debated razing both the church and the rectory and replacing them with a structure more in keeping with the New England landscapes and the available skills of local tradesmen. But that would have required an enormous sum which the parishioners could ill afford.

Since there was really little the church fathers could do to prevent St. Cecilia's from unraveling, they elected to do nothing, and it was this lassitude, coupled with the last ten years of dwindling membership due to the closing of the woolen mills, that had reduced St. Cecilia's to a state of near collapse.

Thoughts of George Benson came to mind as soon as Father James Flaherty's bare feet touched the cold wooden floors of St. Cecilia's rectory. The furnace, which serviced the church and the rectory annexed alongside, was out again, evidenced by the tooth-chattering cold and the absence of rattling pipes and hissing puffs of steam. Father James bounced from foot to foot, quickly plowing through the pile of clothes he had strewn on the floor the night before in search of his favorite sweatshirt, which bore the message HELP STOP WORLD HUNGER . . . FEED A PRIEST. He gave it a quick once-over, checking for any stains, then quickly pulled it over his head, struggling only briefly over the small paunch that, since his fortieth birthday, had begun to inflate like a rubber raft around his middle. A few seconds more of scavenging uncovered a pair of black woolen socks that he pulled on with breakneck speed. A pair of sweat pants was retrieved from the laundry hamper by the side of the chest of drawers.

Grabbing the quilt from the bottom of his bed and wrapping it around his shivering limbs, he headed downstairs toward the phone, saying a silent prayer for his housekeeper, Mrs. Norris. Mrs. Norris, who had seen to the needs of St. Cecilia's priests for more than forty-five years and made all her decisions based on the state of her arthritis, had foreseen the incoming cold front.

"Winter's not done with us yet," she had declared. "The knuckle on my right pinky finger hurts something awful. Could only mean there's a snow storm coming," she said, rifling through the linen closet where handmade quilts of every design and calico—gifts from dozens of parishioners over the years—had been retired in concession to the mud. She heaped several into Father James's waiting arms.

Since Father James's arrival three years ago, he had learned never to question Mrs. Norris's arthritis and was most happy to help her distribute the bedding between the only two usable bedrooms in the entire rectory whose ceilings did not leak or plaster flake from badly cracked walls.

He had to admit, he liked the look of the beds piled high with hand-sewn patchwork quilts. His grandmother was a quilter who used old scraps of fabric to make beautiful bed coverings. The shirt he wore one day might be part of a patchwork square the next. He still had the quilt she had made for him from pieces of his mother's wedding dress and his father's baby clothes. She called it a memory quilt and that it was. Every time he looked at it, the warm family times he and his parents had shared before their deaths came flooding back.

If he closed his eyes on a snowy night, he could still see his grandmother seated by the Franklin stove with needle and thread in hand; hear the wind against his attic roof; and remember his grandfather's favorite saying, "Spend more time thanking the Lord for your blessings than reminding Him of your needs and you'll always be a happy man."

Father James had always tried to live by that motto, although lately he found it harder and harder to comply as the needs of his parish far outweighed its blessings.

Still, he prayed, "Bless Mrs. Norris, Lord, and her arthritis to Your service."

The hallway was dark in the predawn light, but Father James didn't bother to turn on the 60-watt bulb that sat in an overhead socket that had fallen from the ceiling several months before and dangled several inches below the tin ceiling tiles. Father James feared the light might seep underneath the bedroom door and awaken Father Keene— shepherd and pastor of St. Cecilia's flock for more than fifty years. At eighty-two years old, Father Keene, like so many elderly, found sleep elusive and often roamed the halls until the wee hours of the night. That, coupled with the chilling cold, made Father James move soundlessly past his room en route to the back kitchen stairs.

Father Patrick Keene was just one on the growing list of worries that plagued Father James lately. Although the elderly priest was just as spry and agile as when he had come from Ireland decades ago to take charge of St. Cecilia's, it was the condition of his mind that most worried Father James.

Several months ago, parishioners began to comment on the "new way" Father Keene celebrated Mass. Wasn't it interesting, they said, that he interspersed the new English Mass with the old Latin. Not that the older parishioners minded. In fact, many of them thought it quite a nice break in tradition. Added a little spice to the Mass, they said.

More recently, however, Father Keene had begun to pause, then stare blankly over the altar, as though he had lost his place, before breaking into the most beatific smile. Those who had witnessed this strange happenstance said it was like watching one who stood gazing into the face of an angel. Fortunately, this only happened when Father Keene celebrated daily Mass on Wednesdays, Father James's day off, which was primarily attended by St. Cecilia's elderly. Plagued with their own foibles, they were most generous in defending Father Keene's eccentric behavior.

Father James had prayed over Father Keene's condition, uncertain how best to handle the delicate situation. He had elected not to solicit the bishop's help, certain that if he did, the diocese would make arrangements to admit Father Keene to a nursing home. Father James felt a strong moral obligation to the elderly priest who considered St. Cecilia's his home. He prayed relentlessly for a small miracle that would enable Father Keene to live out his days among those he'd come to love as family. So far, the Lord had been silent on the subject.

Gritting his teeth against the cold and dampness that felt like frozen slabs of marble beneath his feet, Father James hurried down the back stairs and into the kitchen that now also served as his office. George's number was taped to the side of the black rotary phone as it was used at least twice a week from October to Easter. Father James lifted the receiver and began to dial as George came stomping into the kitchen.

"Cold as a mortuary in here," boomed George, who always spoke as though he were addressing the deaf.

"Good morning, George. Am I glad to see you!" Father James tightened the quilt around his shoulders.

"Yeah, I thought you'd need some help this morning." George dropped a box of tools onto the kitchen floor, shaking the house, then slammed the back door. "Off again, hey?"

"Afraid so."

"I told you last spring that you'd need a new furnace," he reminded the priest, rubbing his nose with a wool-mittened fist.

"Yes, but . . ."

"If it wasn't for the fact that my father had a box of old parts, I wouldn't have been able to patch it as long as I have."

"We are eternally grateful George. . . ." Father James began to feel the first rumblings in the pit of his stomach, a reaction many people had when dealing with George Benson.

"Don't know how much longer I can do it, though. I ain't no miracle maker, you know."

"No, of course you're not. I'm not asking you to be," Father James faltered, wondering how George continually managed to put people on the defensive. He took a deep breath, willed himself to stay calm and tried to explain. "There isn't any money in the budget for a new furnace." Puffs of steam from his breath rose like a steam engine laboring to make it up a steep incline.

George stamped his feet against the cold. "Why don't you go tell those fat cats up at the archdiocese to help out?"

The twenty-foot-square room suddenly began to feel small and confining as George's opinions began to take up residence.

"Seems to me they could afford it. I noticed the kind of cars they drive . . . Cadillacs and Lincolns. What's wrong with a Chevy hatch-back or one of those foreign economy jobs? Money they saved could easily be given to the poor, like you folks. Isn't that what the Good Book says they're suppose to do?"

"Well . . . yes . . . but . . ."

"Another thing . . . aren't you priests supposed to do a lot of pray-ing and fasting? I saw those church officials when they came by here last year. By the looks of their physiques . . . pardon my French . . . I'd say they don't do a lot of abstaining, if you know what I mean." George was a master of malaprop.

Father James sucked in his gut. "God is our source, not the arch-diocese," Father James said without conviction, drawing the quilt closer, hiding his own abundant physique. "He'll find a way to meet our needs."

"Well, if I was you, I'd tell Him to hurry up," George concluded. "Look at this place."

Father James followed his gaze, trying not to wince.

"You've got so many fire and building code violations here that I'm getting a crick in my neck from looking the other way. If this place ever burns down to the ground, I'll have a hard time convincing the fire commissioner that I never noticed any of this when everyone in town knows that I'm here servicing your furnace at least twice a week." George's eyes followed the length of extension cord threaded over heating pipes that ran power to Father's desk lamp.

Father James had moved his office into the kitchen last week when the roof over the study had begun to leak. He was still trying to get sorted out.

Focusing on the cord, George asked, "Didn't the church run a fundraiser last year?" He ran his hand over yesterday's stubble with fingers that were perpetually oil stained, then answered his own question. "Yeah, you did. You had a carnival. Rides, petting zoo."

Father James was incredulous. "Don't you remember, George? You shut us down."

"I did? Oh, yeah. I guess, I did. Those carnival people, you just can't trust 'em," he said, pedaling down a new lane of thought. "I went to inspect the site as soon as I finished changing Mrs. Bridney's air conditioner's filter. Got there about six thirty. Went to take a look at the fuse box that ran the whole shebang and nearly had a stroke. All their electric was running off one old, rusted fuse box. Thing was so ancient that I was surprised it worked at all. Sort of like yours, Father."

Father James's face flushed as he looked the other way.

"I says to one of them, a foreigner, 'This thing is a fire waiting to happen. It violates every electrical and fire code in the book.' They looked at me like I was speaking some strange language. But I knew they understood. Those foreigners are always pretending not to understand when it suits them.

"Then I opened up the box, and said, 'Mary, Holy Mother of . . . ,'" remembering where he was, he cleared his throat. "Never mind what I said, but the point is you wouldn't believe what I saw. They had put pennies inside the sockets where the fuses belonged! Can you imagine? And that wasn't all! You know what else I found?" George's indignation was gaining momentum as was the fever pitch in his voice.

"George, *please* . . . lower your voice. Father Keene is still sleeping."

"Sleeping? I thought you priests got up at sunrise to say vapors."

"That's *vespers* and they're said in the evening at . . ."

"Whatever. As I was saying . . ." George continued at full volume, "The lead wire to the Ferris wheel was frayed. Lying out there in the open, on the ground for anyone to step on and get electrocuted. Not to mention the danger of it starting a fire. Nearly gave me a coronary right there on the spot. I marched right back to my truck and put on my fire marshal jacket, so those people knew they were dealing with a city official, then rapped on the manager's trailer door. The guy looked like he had just gotten out of bed. Had him temporalily wrap those wires with some electrical tape while I shut it down from the main box. And let me tell you, I held my breath when I threw that handle.

"Darn carnival people. No telling what might have happened if I hadn't seen it. Mary Pitchett's Brownie troop had just bought tickets for a Ferris ride. The whole lot of them could have been electrocuted if it weren't for my keen observation skills. But does anyone thank me?" George was shouting now and Father James's stomach was beginning to pump acid. "No! They call me up and yell, 'Why are you trying to ruin our kids' fun?' Ha! I saved their little ass . . . er . . . behinds, that's what I did."

"That's true," Father James said, frantically searching for a way to divert George's attention from his own electrical shortcomings, the memory of last year's ill-fated carnival and George's dislike of all foreigners, but he just couldn't fathom where to begin.

"So what happened to it?"

"To what?" Father James had lost his place.

George rolled his eyes toward heaven. "To all the money you made for the building fund? You must have made something."

"Oh, that. There wasn't a lot of money left over. We had to pay the carnival people."

"You paid them? For what? I closed them down. There was no carnival!" George bellowed.

"We had a contract. It said if they showed up and set up, we owed them a fee."

"Even if the whole thing was a traveling fire hazard?" George couldn't believe what he was hearing. "If I live to be a hundred, I'll never understand the clergy. Poorest people on God's green earth and you always throw away what little you have."

"Apparently, no one thought to put in a clause about the need to pass the fire marshal's inspection," Father James said defensively. It really was too early for this.

But George wasn't finished. He folded his arms, settling his weight against a kitchen counter and asked, "You make anything?"

"About three thousand dollars."

"What did you do with it? You sure didn't put it into this place."

Father James smiled. "No, there were other needs that seemed more pressing."

"More pressing than this place? That's hard to believe."

"Well, let's see. The church purchased a new back door for Mrs. Halloway. Hers blew off during that summer storm last August. We bought some new school outfits for the Petersons' daughter."

"Damn shame a young family man like that getting leukemia. How's he doing?" George asked in a rare show of compassion.

"The doctors still haven't found a bone marrow match."

"Too bad. Nice family." George waited for Father James to continue, never divulging that he'd been tested as a possible donor.

Father James took a breath and plunged ahead. "I paid the vet bill for Mrs. Johnson's golden retriever, Honey."

"I don't believe it." George shook his head.

"That dog is all Ethel Johnson has since her husband died last year," Father James said, his patience waning. "And if St. Cecilia's didn't help with Honey's hip operation, Mrs. Johnson would have had to put her down. I just couldn't let that happen."

"No wonder this church is in such a mess," George grumbled.

George's ability to make Father James feel he should justify every expenditure outraged him; yet, for some unfathomable reason, he felt obliged to go on. "Then I gave fifteen hundred dollars to Mr. Rosenberg for new dentures. He lost his when he took them out at the Dairy Queen. Forgot them on his tray. If I remember correctly, he was eating something with raspberries in it and, you know how those seeds get caught under . . ."

"Rosenberg? What in heaven's name did you give him money for? He ain't even one of your own. Why, he's . . . he's a Jew!"

"So was our Lord," Father James answered softly, wondering if Mrs.

Norris still kept a bottle of Tums in the left-hand cupboard beside the sink.

Not the least bit chastened, George shook his head in disbelief, "You certainly take the cake, Father James. You're living in a place that's about to fall down upon your ears, ceilings leak, plumbing all shot to . . . well . . . you know. And instead of fixing up the place, you give what little funds that come to you all away."

"It's a matter of priorities, George. The needs of our parish were more important than those of this building."

"Some of us would argue with you about that."

"Now George Benson, didn't I hear a rumor that you're holding off buying that new van so you can sponsor the Little League baseball team that lost their sponsorship when Parsell's Garage closed down last spring?"

"That's different," he said gruffly. "Baseball teaches kids how to work together as a team. Teaches them leadership skills. Important stuff if these youngsters are going to someday lead our town."

"The Church believes that all people are part of God's team."

George had no reasonable reply to Father James's retort, so he snorted, grabbed his tool box and headed toward the basement stairs. "Listen, I've got better things to do with my time than to stand here and debate religion. I've got to see what kind of sorry state that old relic of yours is in downstairs and hope that I can get it running before that bunch of mothball-smelling old biddies show up for morning Mass."

Mrs. Norris walked through the back door at the same time Father Keene emerged from the back stairs, also covered in a patchwork quilt.

"Good morning to you all," Father Keene offered cheerfully in his thick Irish brogue.

"Good morning Father James, Father Keene," Mrs. Norris said, steadfastly ignoring George Benson. With one fluid motion, she discarded her woolen coat, donned an apron, and headed toward the stove.

"George Benson, you're mucking up my perfectly good clean floors with those rubber boots of yours. Look at the tracks you're leaving!

Now I'll have to get down on my hands and knees with a Brillo pad to get them off the linoleum." Mrs. Norris was the only one who could silence George Benson.

"Well, don't stand there gaping," she continued. "Get yourself downstairs and fix that furnace before we all catch pneumonia." She cracked two eggs into a small bowl and quickly whipped them into a yellow froth. "I suppose you'll want some breakfast since you're here."

"No, I had some toast before I left the house," George said petulantly. Since his wife Gertrude had left him several years ago, he often arrived on jobs at mealtimes. Although most of Dorsetville might find his opinions caustic and his behavior offensive, he was one of their own and needed looking after.

But his pride would not let him admit he had come to the rectory in hopes of having Mrs. Norris's famous cornmeal pancakes which she made every Wednesday morning. "Besides, I wouldn't want you to put yourself out on my account."

"Three servings or four makes no difference to me," Mrs. Norris said as she measured flour and baking powder into another mixing bowl.

"Shall I get the kettle?" asked Father Keene. He stood with only his bald head sticking out of the quilt, giving him the appearance of a single pea left in a pod.

"I already have it over an open flame. Your tea should be done in just a minute. If you want to help, why don't you go set the table, Father? I'll get things in order in here."

Father Keene eyed her suspiciously, still not convinced after nearly forty years that any American was capable of making a proper pot of tea.

George hadn't moved fast enough down the cellar stairs for Mrs. Norris's liking. "George Benson! Get a move on or our breakfast will freeze on our plates and those sitting in the pews during Mass will congeal like bacon grease on a marble slab."

George gave her a look that was meant to freeze molten metal, but was steadfastly ignored. He turned and banged his way down the basement stairs, mumbling as he made his descent, "People should just stay home when it gets this cold. Going to catch pneumonia and die. It will serve them right! Don't have the good sense God gave them. Never could understand why Catholics can't go to church just on Sundays like normal Christians."

Father James smiled, remembering that the people who presented the biggest challenges in life were also the ones who brought the greatest lessons. *"Increase my patience, Lord,"* he prayed silently.

"Can you handle all of this while I get ready for Mass?" Father James asked Mrs. Norris. Father Keene was standing over the sideboard, staring into space, with a beatific smile. His mouth was silently moving as though he were speaking to someone.

Mrs. Norris looked up and followed his gaze. "Don't you worry. You go up and get ready for Mass. I'll make certain that George stays in the basement until that furnace is fixed." Then, more softly, "I'll keep a close eye on Father Keene."

"Thanks, Mrs. Norris. I don't know what we'd do without you."

"Neither do I," she said with absolute certainty.

He was just about to go upstairs when the phone rang. Glancing at the kitchen clock, he noticed it was only a little after six-thirty A.M. His already unsettled stomach grew more queasy. Calls this early in the morning were seldom good.

"Good morning, St. Cecilia's. Father James speaking."

"Father, this is Father Richard Jerome."

"Good morning, Richard." Father Jerome was the archbishop's assistant. "What might I do for you this morning?"

"The archbishop wanted me to catch you before you left for Mass. Since it's Ash Wednesday, we know it's a heavy liturgical day."

"I was just about to get ready," Father said. "I don't have much time."

"This won't take long. The archbishop would like to see you this afternoon. He needs to discuss a matter of some importance. Do you think Father Keene could handle the three o'clock Mass alone?"

Uneasiness escalated to foreboding. "I . . . suppose so. Is there something wrong?"

"It would be better if you came and spoke with him," Father Jerome said quietly.

"Richard, we've known each other since seminary. If there's something wrong, I'd like to know."

There was a long pause.

"The archbishop wants to speak to you about closing St. Cecilia's."

The words of Job rang in his head: *"For the thing which I greatly feared is come upon me."*

Since the last woolen mill shut down five years ago, St. Cecilia's membership had drastically declined as families moved out of the area in search of work. When the archbishop had given him the post, it had been made clear that he had only three years to turn the parish finances around or the archdiocese would be forced to close the church. The three years would be up in six weeks.

Father James had come to dearly love the people of St. Cecilia's, who were poor in worldly goods but rich in faith and compassion. He knew the pivotal role the church played in most of their lives and had prayed, against all hope, that God would send a miracle. One had not yet arrived.

"Tell the archbishop that I'll be there around one o'clock," he said with a heavy heart.

The kitchen radiators began to rattle and ping under George's alchemy below. A burst of steam hissed through an open valve, sending out a cloud of warm, moist air, but Father James never felt its warmth. In his spirit, he felt as though someone he dearly loved and cherished had just been told they were about to die.

Chapter 2

T he Country Kettle's windows were covered in steam, a com-
bination of owner Harry Clifford's inability to properly vent
the dishwasher and the breath of dozens of patrons as they happily
chatted over the best cup of coffee in the entire river valley.

The restaurant had been built by Harry's great-grandfather in 1902
with an initial investment of only one hundred dollars and a wife
whose legendary cooking had kept customers focused on the culinary
delights they sampled and not on the dirt floor or the impoverished
decor. From the beginning it had catered to the mill laborers, blue-collar
men and women who sought an affordable place to take their families
out for a meal. It was largely ignored by the Dorsetville elite, who referred to it only when giving directions to their mansions on the hill.

The restaurant had continued to grow and prosper along with the
town; yet, the interior—except for the replacement of the dirt floor
with oak flooring—had remained much the same. Furnishings and ac-
cessories were never bought with a central theme in mind; instead,
they were gleaned from myriad sources. Tables came from tag sales or
were rescued from the dump; chairs, of varying designs, heights and
widths, were bought in lots and stacked in the rear barn for future use.
Customers even donated their old china services. Because none of the
plates or dishes matched, customers sipped coffee from an odd assort-

ment of china and stoneware and ate meals from plates of which no two were ever alike.

Over the years, the restaurant took on the feel of a grandmother's well-worn, yet cozy, kitchen. The oak flooring was now worn in spots under the tables from thousands of pairs of feet; so, too, was the paneling underneath the front counter from the knees of nearly a century's worth of customers.

Calico curtains, sun-bleached tangerine from their original cherry red and fashioned with ruffles, framed the two picture windows that looked out onto Main Street. Matching valances hung over the four windows along the building's east side that flanked School Street and gave a partial view of the side entrance to Linden's Funeral Parlor.

The tin ceiling lay mummified under dozens of coats of white paint; and an off-white wallpaper with tiny red hearts covered the walls over the wooden chair rail. The paper was several shades darker in the corner where Eyepatch Joe had sat for more than thirty years, smoking dozens of unfiltered Camel cigarettes. Joe had died from emphysema in 1997. In his honor, Harry had refused to repair the smoke damage and had placed a NO SMOKING sign on the front door the day after Joe's funeral.

Patrons' handmade needlepoint pictures covered the walls, and doorways and window casings were festooned with floral sprays, many purchased from the Dorsetville Garden Club. Craft items—a black-and-white cow, a chain-sawed carved bear wearing a blue and white handkerchief, and several hand-painted objects—filled all the available space on the window sills and floor.

For nearly a century, each generation shared special moments within these walls, until the Country Kettle became a time capsule filled with memories of couples' first dates over shared ice cream sodas or football victories celebrated with fat, juicy hamburgers and crisp golden fries. Enter the restaurant and the memories would greet you like cherished old friends.

The Country Kettle was also the place where many of Dorsetville's citizens started their day. This morning, the three-man highway crew sipped coffee while waiting for the fire department's hook and ladder trucks to arrive. The departments were scheduled to take down the Christmas lights still strung along Main Street. The forecast of snow, however, might hamper their plans so they lingered over second cups of coffee.

Al Bromley, Dorsetville's sheriff for more than thirty-five years, had joined them. Bromley stood six feet four inches tall and weighed nearly three hundred pounds, an imposing figure by those standards alone. But add to this a perpetual scowl and a voice that often sounded like the growl of an angry rottweiler and there was little doubt why Bromley was both feared and revered. Feared by the high school boys who believed that one steely gaze from the sheriff could possibly impair a young man from ever fathering a child; revered by those who felt it a privilege to have earned his respect.

This morning, Bromley and his deputy, Frank Hill—a thin, nervous young man recently graduated from the police academy and eager to please his new boss—had joined the town crew. The men sat at the round table under the front window, each more intent on being heard than on listening, as they debated the mayor's recent cost-cutting decision to sand only intersections from now until the season's last snow. As the talk grew more intense, some pounded the table to emphasize a point.

Sheriff Al Bromley sipped his coffee, only half listening to the conversation around him. He was more intent on the Main Street traffic outside as he kept watch, like a guard dog, over his town.

As the clock neared eight A.M., waitress Lori Peterson put a clean paper filter in the coffeemaker and poured a premeasured bag of decaffeinated coffee inside. St. Cecilia's parishioners, mostly elderly, would be arriving after morning Mass and they normally went through two pots of coffee and several cups of tea.

Lori poured the water through the top of the coffeemaker and placed the empty glass pot underneath the stream of hot, aromatic liquid that quickly appeared. She took a clean wet cloth and wiped up the coffee grounds that had fallen onto the Formica counter, then rinsed the rag in the pan of hot sudsy water she had just placed underneath the counter.

The hot water felt so good. She had never liked New England winters, could never seem to get warm; and the sudden shift in temperature from the balmy days the previous week to this arctic cold had chilled her to the core. Even the heavy cardigan sweater (a recent find at Second Hand Rose) and Harry's grill, pumping 120 degrees of hot steam against her back, couldn't relieve the numbing chill she felt.

Should she turn up the heat? She decided against it. Last time she'd fiddled with the thermostat, it had started a tropical heat wave that had bathed the entire restaurant in 95-degree-plus for over a week. George Benson worried that he might never get it back under control.

Instead, she made a cup of tea, placing a Salada tea bag in an Easter Bunny mug. With one quick glance, Lori's gaze swept the restaurant filled with morning regulars.

Mildred Dunlop, a retired elementary school teacher, was still working on the *Dorsetville Gazette* crossword puzzle, occasionally asking, to no one in particular, the name of this or that. "What's a three letter word for 'Cleopatra's bosom buddy'?"

Cowboy Joe, who had never actually been a cowboy but who always wore a cowboy hat and black alligator boots, sat at his place along the counter next to Danny Plumber, who actually was a plumber. Both were busy with their egg sandwiches and their coffee cups were still full.

She wondered if there might be time to give her husband, Bob, a call. For the moment, none of her customers needed a refill. All the checks were out. Probably no one would even notice her being gone.

She'd call and ask Bob if he had remembered to sign their daughter Sarah's permission slip for school. Seven-year-old Sarah's first-grade class was scheduled to visit the nineteenth-century Eureka schoolhouse in Springfield on Friday. It was to be the children's very first field trip and they were eagerly counting down the days. Their teacher had them make period hats for the occasion and one of the fathers had provided pieces of slate which would act as their writing tablets for the day. Sarah could hardly wait for Friday.

Bob would know, of course, that she wasn't really calling about Sarah's permission slip. Lori just needed to know that her husband was all right.

She blew on the steam rising from her mug as she headed toward the back rest room area, a small alcove to the left of the back kitchen, where a pay phone hung on the wall. Balancing the tea on top of the black console, she fished in her apron for a quarter, found one, then dropped it into the slot.

Although Harry had repeatedly urged her to use the diner's phone up front, Lori didn't want to abuse her boss's kindness. What if someone was trying to call in an order? She didn't want Harry to lose any business on account of her. She would use the pay phone and reserve favors for the times they were needed. Like when Bob was so weak he couldn't stand, or when he had to be driven to the hospital over in Woodstock for a blood transfusion. She dialed their number.

Bob picked up the phone on the first ring. "The coast is clear. My wife is at work. Come on over."

"Hi, honey," she said. The warmth of his voice offset the cold morning chill. "You know, if you keep joking like this, I might begin to believe there really *is* another woman."

"Now, who else would have me? Chemo has left me as bald as an American eagle and I can no longer bench press 150 pounds."

"You *never* could bench press 150 pounds," she laughed, "and as far as being a bald eagle, some of the sexiest men alive are bald. There's Sean Connery . . ."

"All right. All right. I can see that I'm not going to get any sympathy from you today, am I?"

"No, you're not," she teased, then grew silent.

Bob answered without being asked, "I feel fine. In fact, I think I'll put on a jacket and take a little walk outside. The fresh air will feel good."

"You won't go too far in case you get tired, will you?"

"No, I promise. Just down to Mrs. Santropietro's house and back. Scout's honor."

"All right, but please dress warmly. It's bitter outside. My hands nearly froze to the steering wheel on the way in to work."

"Speaking of work . . . don't you think you'd better get back to your customers? I'll be fine."

"They'll be a little late this morning. It's Ash Wednesday."

"Yes, I know. Father James called and said he'd bring the ashes around later this morning with Communion," Bob said.

"I love you and miss you." A lump rose in her throat.

"I love you too, honey," he said lightly.

"I'll call before I come home to see if you need anything from the store."

"I'll be waiting by the phone."

"See you later."

The tears came as soon as she hung up the receiver. Life was so unfair. What had Bob done to deserve cancer?

He was a good man. A great father. He had so much to give, so much he hadn't yet accomplished. Why should he have to battle with this deadly disease while other men who didn't deserve to live—rapists, wife beaters, murderers—lived to be sixty, seventy, eighty years old?

As she walked back to the front of the restaurant, she began to pray. She prayed a lot lately. In fact, it seemed as though she never stopped, often waking up in the middle of the night, placing a gentle hand on Bob's back and asking God to help him get through the night free of pain.

She prayed while she drove her car. While standing on line at the supermarket. While folding laundry late at night. Mostly, it was the same prayer. *Please, God. Don't let Bob die.*

But she wasn't the only one praying for Bob. Once a week, Father James offered a Mass for Bob's healing, and all the faithful at St. Cecilia's were praying just as fervently.

"Don't give up on Bob or the Lord," Father James kept urging her.

"The Lord might still have a miracle tucked away just for him. He, who did not withhold His only Son from dying a horrible death so we might live, will do everything He can to ease your pain. Just have faith. The Lord heals in many different ways."

Lori tried to have faith, but sometimes in the midst of the grim prognosis, it was hard. If only God would send a little hope, just a little hope, she might be able to maintain her faith. But what little hope she was able to conjure was quickly waning. Bob's chances for survival hinged on finding a compatible bone marrow donor and so far neither the National Bone Marrow Registry nor the hundreds of friends, St. Cecilia's parishioners, or relatives who had been tested matched. Even their small daughter had stoically endured the procedure in hope of saving her father. Sarah's bone marrow hadn't matched either. Time was quickly running out.

"Lori," Harry called. "St. Cecilia's here."

"I'm coming, Harry," she called back, folding up her anguish and tucking it away along with her Kleenex.

Chapter 3

The small group of St. Cecilia's elderly parishioners began to enter the Country Kettle one by one, carefully negotiating the wooden step that led in to the front door, wearing a small thumbprint of ashes in the center of their foreheads. All were over seventy, except for Ben Metcalf's sixteen-year-old grandson, Matthew, who bounded into the restaurant with youthful zeal, a blast of cold air trailing closely behind.

Matthew, a junior at Dorsetville High School, was spending the week with his grandfather after being suspended from school. It was a fact that his grandfather was still having difficulty assimilating. Troublemakers got kicked out of school, not smart A+ students like his Matthew.

Matthew was a brilliant young man but like so many who are inordinately gifted, he did not wear the mantle of genius well. His peers considered him awkward, a geek, someone to be made fun of.

So it came as a mega-volt shock to the students at Dorsetville High when it was discovered that Matthew was the prankster who had accessed Dorsetville's high school teachers' performance records from the school's computer, causing them to be flashed on the baseball scoreboard during halftime at the season's last game.

Although Dorsetville High School had witnessed hundreds of

pranks throughout its 150-year history, none had ever had such lasting and far-reaching consequences.

Since Matthew's stunt, several teachers had threatened to sue for defamation of character and parents were banding together, demanding an immediate investigation as to why the school board continued to employ teachers with chronically poor performance records.

Much to the Dorsetville school board's chagrin, Matthew's prank continued to make front-page news.

Sheriff Bromley leaned over and grabbed Matthew's coat as he passed. "Matthew, the principal over at the high school tells me you've been suspended from school. That right?"

Matthew froze. The sheriff knew his name! He swallowed hard. "Yes, sir."

"That's not good, boy."

Matthew stood, frozen in place, uncertain what he was suppose to do. Should he leave? Go sit down? Stay and wait? The sheriff's penetrating stare was unnerving. By nature, Matthew was a quiet, shy boy and was still having difficulty with all the notoriety, a consequence he had never considered.

It had begun as a simple test of skills. Could he access the school's main frame, override their security system? It was a challenge that had proven much easier than he had ever imagined.

Matthew began by creating a contest on the Web designed to attract school administrators. "Win Lots of Free Stuff for Your School," the Web site said. Then he posted information about the site inside school administrators' mailboxes. He didn't have to wait long for a school official to access the site and once they clicked on it, a cookie was launched that retrieved the information Matthew needed to gain access.

If he had stopped there, no one might ever have learned of the break-in, but Matthew just couldn't resist the urge to play around. He moved data from one teacher's folder to another's, uninterested in what was contained inside. He figured it would only be lesson plans, homework assignments and other stuff. But the principal's folder had held a lot more. Inside were the teachers' performance records, which Matthew unknowingly replaced with the baseball coach's team roster and that was how the records had found their way onto the scoreboard at halftime. Who would have ever thought a guy could get into so much trouble from just messing around with some office files?

The only bright side to this whole mess was that Matthew's peers now considered him a very cool dude.

Classmates who had steadfastly ignored him throughout his freshman year now wanted to be his best friend. "Rock on!" they cheered as they passed him in the halls.

Glory was giving way to panic, however, under Bromley's penetrating stare. Finally Bromley spoke. "So how long are you suspended for?"

Matthew's mouth went dry. "A week, sir."

The sheriff rubbed his chin. "And what are your plans for the week?"

"Sir?"

"You don't plan to loiter around the streets, now do you?"

"Oh, no, sir."

"Good." Bromley nodded in the general direction of the elderly St. Cecilia's crowd. "Go sit down with your grandpa and keep out of trouble. You screw up one more time and I'll personally cart your sorry behind down to juvenile hall and lock you up myself. Understood?"

"Yes, sir."

Matthew turned quickly to go and overturned a chair. He swiftly righted it then fled to join his grandfather and friends, crashing alongside and disappearing, like a turtle, deep inside his oversized winter jacket.

Sheriff Bromley covered a smile with a hand before turning back to the road-sanding debate. The boy was a good kid. He just wanted to scare him into staying that way.

Lori watched Matthew fall into a chair as she opened another bag of coffee, poured the grinds into a paper filter, shoved the filter in place inside the coffeemaker and then threw the switch. Hot coffee streamed into the Pyrex pot.

Mornings were Lori's favorite time of the day at the Country Kettle. She looked forward to the group of regulars who arrived straight from the seven A.M. Mass. They seldom ordered anything more than a mug of coffee, but Lori didn't mind. She knew they hadn't come for the food. They came for the friendship and good conversation which helped to take the edge off the loneliness and near-poverty they endured. For one or two hours each morning, they could forget their homes in disrepair, the aches that wracked their bodies, the children who never called and the fear of a life quickly drawing to an end, and find renewal of spirit and warmth for their souls in the company of dear friends.

They always sat in the same place, the large round center table. Harry never minded. In fact, he usually went out of his way to welcome them.

"How is my favorite group of senior citizens this morning?" he called out from behind the grill. "Glad to see the cold didn't keep you at home."

It was a sentiment that Lori Peterson deeply shared. She had come to depend on the group for encouragement and a sense of hope.

"How's Bob doing?" they'd asked each morning, their faces eagerly waiting for an answer, their eyes filled with concern.

"I've elicited the help of St. Teresa," Ruth Henderson would remind her. "She's never been known to fail."

"Neither has St. Jude," Ethel Johnson added tartly. "I've started another novena in Bob's name."

Lori always smiled. Harry called the contest between the two women "dueling saints."

Others brought rosaries and prayer cards and slipped them into her apron pocket. "These are for Bob," they'd say shyly.

But the elderly St. Cecilia parishioners also brought laughter and good-natured ribbing, filling the restaurant with stories of their youth and the history of their town, often inviting others to pull up a chair and join in.

The group's usual, jocular banter, however, was missing this morning. Even Ethel Johnson's dog, Honey, who led the contingent through the front door and who normally hurried back to where Harry kept her bowl of scraps, hung near her mistress, appearing anxious. As soon as Ethel was seated, the golden retriever quickly slid under the table and nuzzled close to her feet.

Bundled in wool scarves, most made from cloth milled in town several decades ago, and heavy topcoats and hats, they began to peel off layers of clothing and pile them on an empty chair. Arthritic fingers made the task slow and laborious.

Fred and Arlene Campbell, the only couple left in the group, helped each other off with their coats, then sat down without a word as Lori eyed them quizzically from behind the counter. She looked at Harry who only shrugged his shoulders as if to say, "I haven't a clue."

The Henderson sisters, Ruth and June, maneuvered their walkers around the table with the aid of Timothy McGree, who dressed like a man who lived alone and badly needed a wife and whom the sisters proclaimed was still "full of vinegar." Today, however, he was uncharacteristically quiet.

Ben Metcalf pulled a chair close to Matthew then sat down with a hard thud and hung his head low over clasped hands.

"Hot chocolate this morning, Matthew?" Lori asked.

"Yeah," Matthew said between blips and beeps of an electronic hand game.

"Turn that darn thing off," said Ben, annoyed.

Matthew looked up in surprise. His grandfather seldom spoke sharply. Matthew shut off the game and reached inside his back pocket for the new copy of *Computer Graphics* that had come in the mail only this morning. He caught Sheriff Bromley looking his way and slid deeper into his chair, hiding behind the magazine cover.

Sam Rosenberg, part of the morning regulars, always waited for his friends to return from Mass. Normally dressed in a polyester windbreaker and chinos, today he looked out of place in a sport coat and tie. He had just returned from Woodstock where he had dropped Harriet

Bedford off at the travel center for her yearly pilgrimage to Manchester. She was not due back until Saturday and for the next few days, Sam would seem like a ship without a rudder. Sam moved his coffee over from the counter and pulled out a chair. No one greeted him.

"Have they announced the end of the world?" No one laughed.

"They want to close St. Cecilia's," the Henderson sisters said in unison.

"Close St. Cecilia's?" He sat down slowly like a boxer who'd just been winded by a blow. "Why?"

Harry, who always kept his ear tuned to his customers' conversations, shot out from behind the grill with a spatula still filled with home-fries. "Who says they're going to close St. Cecilia's?"

"Father James announced it at Mass this morning," Timothy answered. "Just before he and Father Keene gave out the ashes."

"No one told me and I'm on the parish board." Harry walked over to the town crew and dumped the mound of home-fries onto their plates. "On the house."

"Thanks, Harry!"

Harry pulled up a chair alongside the group. "Lori, pour me a cup of coffee, will you?"

Ethel looked up. "Apparently the archdiocese called early this morning with the news. Father James asked us to pray. He has an appointment with the archbishop this afternoon. It doesn't look good."

Lori's hand shook slightly as she poured Harry's coffee. If they closed St. Cecilia's, what would she and Bob do? If it hadn't been for Father James's encouraging words of faith these last few months and the support of the church community, her family would not have survived Bob's illness.

"Now, now," Ruth Henderson said, patting Lori's arm, sensing her fear.

"Somehow the good Lord will work this out," June Henderson added. "He knows how much St. Cecilia's means to all of us."

Lori didn't doubt that God knew of their problem, but would He intervene to help? She was still waiting for Him to send Bob a donor.

"If they close the church, will they send Father James away?" she asked.

"I suppose so," Harry said.

Her eyes began to water. "Father James comes several times a week to have tea with Bob. I don't know what he'd do if it weren't for those visits."

"We're not going to let them close St. Cecilia's!" Arlene Campbell said. It was the first time anyone had ever heard her raise her voice. "We're going to band together and fight it! That's what we'll do."

"That's right, honey," her husband, Fred, chimed in. "There's power in numbers. Remember when we banded together to have Grand Union restock our favorite cookies, Social Teas? They tried to say that no one bought them anymore. Well, we just came together and drew up a petition, then presented it to that young store manager and he caved right in under our demands. They've stocked them ever since." Fred smiled triumphantly.

"I think this might be a little more complicated than that, Fred," Harry said kindly. "In fact, I seriously doubt if the archdiocese cares what we think."

"What do you mean, they don't care?" Timothy said, his Irish temper flaring. "This is *our* church and the archdiocese has no right to try and close it down!"

"I'm afraid that's not true," Harry said.

Knowing that Harry was a member of the parish board and privy to official church business, the group grew silent.

"You see, St. Cecilia hasn't been able to meet its expenses for over four years now. The membership is dwindling. The building is falling down around our ears. We've tried to reduce costs to meet our income, but, well, that's gotten harder and harder to do since the woolen mill closed and so many people moved away to find jobs."

"What will happen to all the social programs if the church closes? St. Cecilia's sponsors the food pantry and meals-on-wheels." Sam, at seventy-five, still delivered meals to homebound seniors in his 1973 gold Plymouth Duster.

"They'll have to find another place or shut down," Harry conceded sadly.

"Shut down?" Sam couldn't imagine the dozen or so people he faithfully visited each day managing on their own. Without his visits they would starve and he couldn't let that happen. "How will those people be fed?" He once knew the pangs of hunger in Germany during the war and the kindness of strangers who had risked their lives to help a Jew. How could he do any less?

"Now, now, Sam. Watch your blood pressure," Ethel warned.

"If St. Cecilia's closes its doors, where will these programs go?" he asked no one in particular.

"I suppose they could rent a place here in town," Timothy offered. "We certainly have plenty of empty store fronts along Main Street."

"But who will pay for the rent?" Sam challenged. "Social programs are run on a shoestring. Always have been. Rent payments mean less money to buy food. Who will decide who doesn't eat?"

The sobering question hung in the air like a heavy fog.

"What about the town hall?" Ben Metcalf offered. "The town wouldn't charge for rent."

"It's already packed to the gills with offices," replied Harry.

"Maybe the Congregational church could take it on," Ethel said.

"I bet they'd just *love* to," said Timothy, his voice dripping with sarcasm, the result of a longstanding feud between the two churches. "Better still, I bet they'll throw a party when St. Cecilia's closes its doors for the last time. They've always hated having to share the town green with our church."

"Getting back to our church, how about running a fund-raiser?" Arlene Campbell asked.

"We tried that last year, remember, dear?" Ethel said, stroking her retriever's silky ears. Honey now lay with her head on her mistress's lap, looking up with sorrowful brown eyes.

"Oh, yes. The carnival. I'd forgotten."

"George Benson shut us down," Timothy reminded them. "Besides, the only people who might come are the people who live in town, and we all know they don't have a lot of extra money. Times are hard for everybody."

A pall fell over the group as they sat in thoughtful silence.

"Would anyone like more coffee?" Lori asked.

"No thanks, dear. I think we'll just go home," Arlene said.

"Me, too." Ethel reached for her coat. Honey scurried out from under the table, paws slipping on the wooden floor, and looked searchingly into her eyes. What about my scraps? she seemed to ask.

"Is everyone leaving?" asked Fred Campbell, who had started to doze off. "I was going to order toast this morning."

"I'll make you some when we get home, dear," Arlene said, helping him on with his coat.

Lori handed Matthew a Styrofoam container. "Pour your hot chocolate in here and take it home." He took it shyly.

"Thanks, Lori," he said averting his eyes.

Matthew waited for his grandfather to slip back into his woolen coat, then quickly followed him and his friends outside, steadfastly avoiding Sheriff Bromley's hard stare.

Chapter 4

The three older men and Matthew braved the bitter cold, tucking their hands deep into their coat pockets as they ambled along Main Street. No one really wanted to go home. Not yet. It was barely ten o'clock. What would they do with the rest of the day?

The three men and the boy walked silently, their reflections orbiting past the blackened storefront windows, separate planets with private thoughts locked together by their core concern for St. Cecilia's. No one spoke.

Sam Rosenberg wondered how the news of St. Cecilia's closing would affect Harriet Bedford, who had managed to survive a crushing heartache only through the comfort of her church, her priest and parish friends. Ben was remembering his years as an altar boy under Father Fanny's tenure. Timothy, St. Cecilia's head usher, wondered what would give his life purpose after the church closed, and Matthew wondered how long it would be before everyone in town forgot about his prank.

As they rounded a corner, St. Cecilia's stone facade loomed in the distance and unconsciously, they made a right onto Church Street, their thoughts acting as magnets. No one stopped until they had reached St. Cecilia's main doors.

"Dorsetville isn't going to seem like home anymore if St. Cecilia's closes," mused Timothy.

"We've been coming here every morning to Mass for over seventy years." Ben laughed. "Remember Saturday afternoon confessions when we were kids, Tim?"

Timothy's face broke into a wide grin. "Sure do. Father Fanny was pastor then and Father Keene had just arrived from Ireland."

"Poor Father Keene. Father Fanny treated him just like one of us altar boys," Ben said, stamping his feet to keep them warm against the cold.

"No one messed with Father Fanny," Timothy remembered. "All fire and brimstone."

"Which is why the line outside his confessional on Saturday afternoons was always empty and Father Keene's wound around the church."

That triggered another memory and Ben asked, "Remember when Patricia Murphy moved here from Bradford?"

"Ah, Patricia Murphy," Timothy mused. "Red hair, tiny waist, long legs and the biggest pair of . . ."

Ben cleared his throat and motioned to Matthew.

"Quite a hot number, hey, Gramps?" Matthew teased.

Ben placed his arm around his grandson's shoulders and confessed. "Let's just say that Timothy and I spent a lot of time at the altar rail doing penance for our impure thoughts."

"I'm glad I'm a Jew," Sam opined.

"Because you don't have to confess your sins to a rabbi, Mr. Rosenberg?"

"No, because Jews don't have impure thoughts," Sam said, tousling Matthew's hair.

The men burst out laughing. But the laughter quickly subsided as the small party stood soberly once again looking up at the church steeple whose cross seemed to touch the low hanging clouds.

"It's a shame to board up such a good building," Sam mused. "To lose a place of worship is like losing a part of God." He could still remember the deep pain in his father's eyes the night the Nazis burned down their synagogue.

A sharp wind cut through the small group. The sky grew more overcast and gray.

"Looks like snow," Timothy said, tightening his collar. "I guess I'd better be getting home before it starts to come down. You coming, Ben?"

"No, I think I'll go in and light a candle. That all right with you Matthew?"

"Sure, Gramps. It's not like I have any place to go."

Timothy thought a moment. "I might as well join you two. You know what the Bible says about when "two or three are gathered together." We make the quota, so let's pray together for a miracle and see what happens."

"A miracle is what we'll need to keep St. Cecilia's from closing," Ben mused. "You coming, Sam?"

Both Father James and Father Keene called Sam an honorary Catholic who seemed at times more involved than some of the parishioners were with the church. Sam called the numbers at their Thursday night Bingo games and played poker with the men on the parish council once a month in the back room at Kelly's bar. He also helped to establish an annual seder through his synagogue each Passover for St. Cecilia's parish.

"Sure, I'll come. Maybe He'll listen better to a Jew."

The three men and the boy entered the quiet sanctuary, the only sound their footfalls resounding against the marble floors as they marched toward the front of the church. The altar had already been reset for the afternoon Mass and a font of fresh ashes stood nearby.

The niche where the statue of the Blessed Mother had once stood was to the right of the altar. It was empty now. A spray of roses rested where the feet of Mary used to be.

To the left of the altar was a second niche where St. Anthony—patron saint of miracles—stood holding the Christ child in his arms and looking benevolently at the bank of candles beneath his sandaled feet. All but seven were lighted. Ben dropped several coins into the metal box, then removed four long tapers, handing one to Matthew, then to each of his friends. One by one they lighted a candle then bowed their heads in silent supplication.

Ben, Timothy and Matthew made the sign of the cross, walked to the center aisle, genuflected in front of the Blessed Sacrament, then slid into the front pew. Sam stood for several seconds gazing up at the face of the saint before walking over to join his friends and nearly colliding with Father Keene. The elderly priest had suddenly appeared from the sacristy dragging a five-foot wooden cross and looking as though he would topple over at any minute.

Father Keene, who was deeply troubled by Father James's announcement this morning, had decided to set up the Easter display a few weeks ahead of schedule as a panacea for his worry. Physical labor always made him forget his troubles. He hadn't calculated, however, on how tiring the project would be.

"Here, let us help you," Timothy offered, moving out into the aisle and taking hold of the cross.

"Thanks be to God who provides help before we call," said Father Keene.

The two men settled the cross in its holder by the right side of the altar. To the front of the crude cross, a small waterfall sat ready to cascade over plaster rocks. Several generic cactus surrounded the base completing the tableau. Father Keene had been working on it for hours.

"Glad to have the help, my son. We won't be needing any more accidents like that which so recently took the life of our Blessed Mother's statue." Father wiped his forehead with a handkerchief from his back pocket.

"How'd it break?" asked Sam.

"It's a sad story for sure," Father Keene said, slowly lowering himself onto the front pew. "Ah, that's much better now." He gazed mournfully up at the empty space where the Blessed Virgin Mary had once stood.

"The statue was removed so workers could repair the big crack at the base of the opening. One of the men lost his grip as they were lowering Our Beloved Mother to the floor." Father made the sign of the cross. "She shattered into a dozen pieces. 'Twas a mournful sight."

"There's no money to replace it, I suppose?" Timothy asked.

"No, I'm afraid."

"Didn't the men have insurance?" Sam asked.

"They were volunteers," Father answered, rubbing his bald head. "And if the truth be told, they weren't to be blamed. They're normally responsible lads but that day it was raining, and you know how slippery this marble floor can get when it gets wet. It was an accident, that's all. Still, 'tis a crying shame."

The men sat in quiet reflection.

Timothy mused, "Somehow, the church doesn't seem to be quite the same without her."

"Yeah, it was like she used to look out and watch over us," Ben added.

Father Keene leaned back in the pew, feet spread apart, his head tilted up toward the ceiling, an indication that he was about to embark on one of his many rich stories of life as a boy in Ireland. Matthew and the three men settled in as Father Keene's brogue began to lilt through the stillness like the strains of a finely tuned harp.

"In County Kerry, where I was born, there was a blessed little church in the village of Sneem where the most beautiful statue of Our Blessed Mother resided. 'Twas a treasure, to be sure. All hand-carved with these delicate folds in her gown. Her crown painted in twenty-four carat gold. Oh, she was as beautiful a sight as you'd ever wish to behold.

"The villagers all believed that she was the protector of their fair town and for two hundred years, since the day of her arrival, the town prospered and grew. Then one day, the parish priest went in to light the candles for Mass and discovered a horrible deed had been done. The niche was empty. Someone had stolen Our Blessed Mother."

"Did they ever find out who took it?" Ben asked.

"No. It was just gone. Without a trace. I suppose that someone stole it for the money it would bring. Times were hard back then," Father Keene reflected. "You did what you had to do to survive."

The men grew silent knowing that Father Keene would continue when he felt there had been a significant dramatic pause.

"Aye. No one ever did discover who took the Blessed Mother, but it soon became evident that the town would suffer because of it.

"Storms began to blow in over the Caha Mountains. Fierce, hard, cold storms that damaged the crops, and sunk many a small fishing craft at sea. The town was cursed, they said. People became fearful and moved away. Oh, it was a perilous time.

"Then one, by one, the grand little shops, ones that had so proudly lined the main thoroughfare, closed. Boarded up. Abandoned. And soon, even the sweet, blessed church had to close its doors. It was a sorrowful sight, to be sure."

"Sounds like what's happening to our town, hey Father?" Matthew said, caught in the spell of the story.

"Yes, it does my lad. Yes, it does." Father Keene reflected for a moment before concluding, "The world will certainly be a little dimmer should St. Cecilia's close her doors."

"That's the truth of it," Timothy agreed.

Father Keene sat up and slapped his knee. "That's enough of my storytelling. There's work to be done. Any of you lads want to help an old priest get this Easter display set up?"

"Isn't it a bit early?" asked Timothy.

Father Keene shook his head. "It's just the sort of thing this parish needs right now. Easter is the message of hope for moments when all seems to be lost."

"All right, Father," Timothy said, unbuttoning his coat. "Tell us what you need done."

Both Matthew and the men threw their coats over the back of the oak pew, then made several trips from the storeroom in the basement of the church to the main altar. They worked as an efficient team and, in no time, had the display up and working, complete with running waterfall.

Sam repositioned it to prevent water from spraying onto the marble floor and causing yet another accident, as Father Keene left them to "grab a morsel of lunch before I faint from hunger." He thanked them all before leaving.

Timothy slipped his arm into the faded navy blue Peabody jacket he'd worn for nearly forty years. The lining sagged several inches below the coat. "I was thinking about the story Father Keene just told us," he said. "Do you think that's why St. Cecilia's is closing?"

"Don't know." Ben pulled the woolen cap over his thinning white hair.

"Yes, but isn't it queer that the very same thing has happened to St. Cecilia's?"

"You think the fact that Mary's statue is missing has something to do with the archdiocese wanting to close down the church?"

"It's a thought," Timothy said, genuflecting at the end of the pew. "I'm not saying I believe it, but what if it *does* have something to do with St. Cecilia's closing?"

"I guess it *could* be possible," Ben hesitantly agreed.

"There's only one way to find out," Sam offered.

"How?" Matthew asked, silently having taken in the exchange.

"Replace the statue and see if your archbishop changes his mind."

"We don't have any money to replace it," Timothy reminded Sam.

"I suppose we could ask for donations," Ben suggested.

"Gramps, I don't think anyone would want to contribute."

"Why not?"

"Number one, if you told them that you wanted a new statue because you thought that its absence was the *real* reason St. Cecilia's was closing, they'd probably say it was time for you to consider an old-age home."

"The boy's right," agreed Sam. "It does sound kind of crazy."

"Number two," Matthew continued, "if people were going to give money, they would want it used to save the church from closing, not to pay for a new statue."

"Still, it's too bad we couldn't test our theory just to see if we're right," Timothy mused.

"Maybe you could borrow a statue?" Sam suggested.

"It's not the kind of thing you borrow," Timothy said.

Sam shrugged his shoulders. "Just a suggestion."

The men stood, hands in coat pockets, staring at the empty space.

"Gramps? Does Mary's image have to be solid?" Matthew pulled the magazine out from his back pocket.

"Solid? A statue is a statue."

"But what if we were able to replace the statue with an image?"

"An image? You mean like a poster?"

"No, no." Matthew riffled through several pages until he found the one he wanted. Pointing to the heading he said, "See here. This is all about holograms and how they can be produced."

"A holo . . . what?" Timothy asked.

"Hologram," Sam interjected. "It's a three-dimensional image created by the use of a laser beam which reflects off an image from a mirror reproducing an exact replica."

Matthew looked at him with new respect.

"I keep up," Sam smiled.

"You've lost me," Ben said.

"Look," Matthew pointed to the page where photos of holograms were being used in store displays. "See here. This jewelry store had a really expensive diamond ring that they wanted to display for customers, but they were afraid that it might be stolen. So instead of displaying the real thing, they had a hologram made, a three-dimensional replica of the ring, so customers could see what it looked like. But since it was just a picture and not the real thing, they didn't have to worry about its being stolen."

"They can do that?" Ben asked.

"Sure. It's easy." Matthew's excitement began to grow. "We can do the same thing with a statue of Mary."

"Make a hologram?" Sam asked. He thought a moment, then slowly nodded. "I suppose it could work."

Matthew was already making a mental inventory of the equipment he'd need. Most of it he had at home, but whatever was lacking he could borrow from an engineering student he had met at a computer camp at the state college this past summer.

Matthew looked up at the back of the church and then at the empty niche. "We could transmit from up there in the choir loft, then beam the image into the alcove."

"No, wires, no nothing?" asked Timothy incredulously.

"No need," Matthew beamed proudly. "What do you think, Gramps?"

"I don't know. Maybe we'd better ask Father James about this first."

"But what if the idea doesn't work?" Timothy cautioned. "We've got to give Matthew a chance to test it out and see what happens."

"Oh, it will work," Matthew insisted confidently. "I just need a little time to put it together."

"I hear time you've got," Sam reminded him.

Matthew blushed but bravely continued. "I'll need to get in touch with my friend over at the college. See if we can borrow their lasers. And I'll need some special film. The only place that carries it is the camera store over in Woodstock."

"We can use my car," Sam offered. "Right after I deliver the noon meals."

The group walked toward the back of the church.

"Do you think it'll make a difference?" Ben asked, his hand resting on the doorknob.

"I don't know," Timothy replied, turning up the collar to his coat. "But it's better than just sitting around and doing nothing."

"Well, one thing's for sure," Sam said, pulling on his gloves.

"What's that?" Timothy asked.

"Our idea certainly couldn't hurt."

"You're right about that," Ben replied.

Matthew pushed open the heavy oak door and they all stepped outside into a rushing wind that hit them full in the face. Hunching their shoulders forward, the three men and the boy began their descent down the winding road and headed toward Main Street and Sam's parked car, sparks fairly flying off the soles of their shoes.

Chapter 5

"You're saying that it would take an estimated two hundred twenty-five thousand dollars to bring St. Cecilia's up to building code with another three hundred fifty thousand to renovate both the church and rectory," said Father Dexter McCarthy, the archdiocese's executive financial director, who was seated in an Italian leather chair behind an eight-foot mahogany-inlaid leather-topped desk.

"I know that those figures seem high, but no repairs or updates have been done on the buildings in over fifty years," Father James explained.

Father McCarthy studied Father James, perched on the edge of his chair, an urgent glint in his eyes. Father McCarthy could probably recite the conversation that would follow verbatim. He had hosted dozens of similar meetings over the last ten years concerning older parishes—financially unstable with buildings that were relics, fire hazards, needing to be torn down—with priests, like Father James, who had come to plead for more time, more money, more patience on the part of the archdiocese.

Sadly, no matter what they said, the facts remained the same. Parishes that could not support themselves must be closed; antiquated buildings boarded up, properties sold, parish resources shared. It was the only way the Church could survive the new millennium. It was also a highly unpopular stance but the one that the archdiocese had decreed. Archbishop Simmons had no choice but to institute the reforms and Father McCarthy had been given the unpleasant task of putting those reforms into practice.

Father McCarthy peered over his glasses and watched the growing frustration being kept in check on Father James's face. How long would he be able to control it? Father McCarthy wondered.

Father McCarthy was tall in stature and short on grace, having spent years as the brunt of great animosity from priests who saw him as an impediment to their lofty missions; priests who acted as though parishes could be maintained solely by good intentions.

As far as Father McCarthy was concerned, faith was all well and good in matters of eternal redemption and overcoming life's many bumps and potholes. But it was good, hard cash, not faith, that paid the bills. Something St. Cecilia's did not have. The church would have to be closed.

Father McCarthy braced himself, like a fighter in the ring, and continued. "The high cost of renovating St. Cecilia's was one of the major factors in deciding to close the parish. The building is hopelessly outdated, that and with"—Father McCarthy flipped through the financial spreadsheets he had in front of him—"only fifty pledged parishioners, most of whom are elderly and without any means of supporting the church, we just cannot afford to keep it open."

"You can't afford to close it!" Father James hadn't meant to shout. He had hoped to persuade the archbishop to give St. Cecilia's more time, to implore him to continue to help maintain the church for just a few more months while they sought other avenues of support.

Father James had spoken to his parish council about holding a raffle. He had begun a building fund committee (although as yet no one could come up with a list of prospective donors whom they might solicit), and he had played with the idea of opening a Catholic bookstore in the church's basement. All he needed was some start-up money. Surely, something would work.

Father James lowered his voice. "Please, listen to what I am saying. The elderly parishioners of St. Cecilia's need that church, so do the poor in the parish—and there are many."

"The archbishop and I are well aware of these needs." Father McCarthy removed his glasses and massaged the ridge across his nose. "But the truth is, we cannot go on supporting parishes that do not or cannot pay for themselves. Although it greatly saddens us," he amended, "we have few options."

"Give me some more time, please," Father James pleaded. "Three years was not enough time to turn things around."

"I suspect that a decade would not be enough time to collect the money needed to repair the building alone," Father McCarthy parried.

Father James stood and began to pace, running a hand through his thinning black hair. "What about the church's obligations to its people? For over a hundred years, the people of St. Cecilia's have supported their parish and the works of this archdiocese. These are hard-working, lower- and middle-class people. They kept St. Cecilia's going during some of the hardest economic times in our country.

"Children went without new clothes and wore hand-me-downs and coats with mended linings and patched seams when St. Cecilia's needed a new roof. Men patched up their old automobiles, and worked double shifts so the women could stay home, teach religion classes, help out with programs for the elderly and the home bound. They faithfully tithed and took care of those who were less fortunate than they. They have been faithful in everything the Lord has entrusted to their care. They have fed and clothed the poor. Visited with the sick and . . ."

Father McCarthy threw up a hand, warding off any further litany. "I am very aware of your parishioners' faithfulness to the church, which only makes this decision that much harder."

"They were faithful in their tithes and in offering their many talents. How can you abandon them when they are old and poor and need the church more than ever?"

"We are not abandoning them. They can go to St. Bartholomew's in Burlington."

"You don't understand, " Father James tried to reason. "Most of my parish is either too old or too poor to make that kind of commitment.

Younger members have to work and can't drive all the way to St. Bartholomew's for daily Mass, turn around, and drive another twenty miles and then on to work. And the elderly either can't afford to drive the distance or are too infirm.

"If you close St. Cecilia's, they will be orphaned. They depend on our church for comfort and direction." He was reminded of Bob Peterson. "There is currently a young woman whose husband is dying of cancer. This is probably the hardest trial they will ever face. How can I ask them to travel twenty miles to a huge, impersonal parish?"

"St. Bartholomew's is *not* impersonal," amended Father McCarthy. "Father Vincent has instituted dozens of outreach and fellowship programs."

"That parish has more than fifty-five hundred families. How many of those people do you think Father Vincent knows personally?"

"There is a shortage of priests. Father Vincent does what he can and does it admirably."

"I didn't mean to imply he doesn't. But I know the needs of my parish and they *need* St. Cecilia's. Besides, St. Bartholomew's cannot provide the community services we do. We have a noontime meal program that's the only source of nourishment for hundreds of elderly people. We run a health clinic and food bank."

"The archdiocese can make arrangements to keep those going, perhaps renting a smaller, more cost-efficient building," Father McCarthy suggested.

"Fine. But what about their spiritual food? Many of our parishioners are over seventy. They're nearing the end of their lives. They're afraid and need the comfort of the church, the sacraments and the fellowship of our church community. These are the poor, the hungry, the lonely whom our Lord entrusted to our care. Are we to abandon them because we fear some numbers at the bottom of a ledger?"

Father McCarthy waited quietly for Father James to compose himself and said with unaccustomed compassion, "There is nothing the archdiocese can do. Your church is no different from the dozens of other small parishes that are being closed. They have similar needs and stories that are just as compelling. But there is nothing the archdiocese can do to maintain all of these parishes if they do not generate the monies needed to cover their expenses.

"I'm sorry, Father James. I really am. It's evident how much you care for these people and how they have grown to love and depend on you and your church. I wish there was something else we could do, but the numbers don't lie. St. Cecilia's must close."

Finding no perch for his arguments, Father James returned to his chair. "What will happen to Father Keene?" He held his breath, knowing the reply yet still hoping.

Father McCarthy avoided his eyes. "He'll be placed in a nursing home. I'm sorry, but the last Mass will be celebrated on Easter Day. You will be reassigned to another parish and Father Keene will be placed in whatever facility has room which, according to our records, will probably be somewhere out of state."

Father James looked up with tears in his eyes. "That means that no one he knows or has loved for over fifty years will be able to visit him."

"As priests, we agree to go where we are sent without debate. Father Keene has been a faithful member of our order. I know that it might be hard on him, but I am certain that he will accept it."

Father James leaned forward in his chair and placed his head in his hands. "Why doesn't God answer my prayers for this parish? I've prayed without ceasing for months."

How many priests had he met over the years? Father McCarthy wondered. Three, maybe four hundred? Few had impressed him enough for him to have remembered their names. They were just men intent on personal missions that had little to do with the beliefs they so pithily espoused.

Some came with evangelistic zeal, only to wane under the steady repetitive grind of daily parish work. Others bore political ambitions and quickly delegated parishioners' needs to underlings while they courted the rich and influential, large donations and tracts of land, assuring themselves ascendancy within the Church's hierarchy.

Father McCarthy had always been drawn to what he referred to as the quiet priests, those men who wore the robes of true humility and came with quiet obedience to God's will when called.

These were the men who came without personal agendas, wishing only to be made available to do God's bidding. They ministered, as Jesus ministered while here on earth, to all, condemned none, and trusted God to love everyone equally.

Few owned more than a smattering of personal belongings. Many drove older-model cars. They had learned that worldly goods often separate ministers of God from the people they most need to serve. While priests in power, those who might head the powerful diocesan offices, wore tasseled Gucci loafers and had condos in New York's posh East Hampton, God's true shepherds often found their needs met from much humbler sources.

These opinions did not mean that Father McCarthy wasn't a realist. He knew the importance of money and political power. Both were needed just as much as charitable works. Without money to effectively lobby for government reforms such as health care for children, prescription assistance for the elderly, or the rights of the newborn, society might neglect those who most need protection under the law in favor of corporate profits.

But Father McCarthy's personal intercessory prayers were always for those whom God had called to shepherd the parishes: the priests who bore their flock's sufferings as though they were their own; who diligently worked and prayed to meet those needs; the priests who fed the hungry, visited with the sick and kept watch for the lambs who had gone astray and whose prayers, Father McCarthy was certain, were given special entry to God's throne.

"We all suffer from time to time with a lack of faith, or feelings of great discouragement," Father McCarthy offered.

The role of counselor, comforter, was a new one for Father McCarthy and he shifted uncomfortably in his chair; yet, he spoke from personal experience. He had entered the priesthood, like all the other men, wanting to make a difference in the lives of God's people. He would never have chosen the church role he now played. It had simply been thrust upon him and, in obedience, he had complied.

It had been hard. There were many times throughout the years when he questioned whether his role could possibly make a difference for Christ. It was a theme that he often explored while on personal retreats. Recent years had brought peace as he realized that when we dedicate our lives to God's will we must learn to trust Him implicitly and not question the paths upon which we are led.

Father James stood, getting ready to leave. "So, that's it?"

"I'm afraid so."

"St. Cecilia's will close?"

"Yes, on Easter Day, unless you can find the"—Father McCarthy tucked all compassion under a mask of efficiency and business—"the five hundred seventy-five thousand dollars needed to renovate and a steady source of future revenue."

Leaden clouds domed the sky, sealing in the damp, icy cold air as Father James let the heavy oak doors close behind him; he drew his black topcoat up against his neck and walked across the quadrant to St. Joseph's Cathedral. As soon as he stepped through the doors, images of his ordination rose to greet him.

It was here, twenty-one years ago this May, that he had dedicated his life to the Lord's service. He had been so moved by the ceremony that when it called for him to lie prostrate before the cross, he feared he might not be able to get up. He wished only to lie by his Savior's feet and learn from Him and to share those lessons with others who could not discern the Lord's voice so clearly.

Father James headed toward the front of the church and the private chapel where he had often prayed as a seminarian, to remember a time when, as a young priest, he could pray prayers that lifted troubled souls out of their darkness and into the light of God's grace. It was a time when his words were filled with the power to comfort, to enlighten, to inspire when his own confidence in God's miraculous power knew no bounds.

But he hadn't felt that way in years. In fact, most of what he said or did now was by rote, like a school child's daily recitation of the Pledge of Allegiance: words, devoid of meaning. Sadly, he had lost his vigor, his zeal. It had been buried underneath the enormous daily load he carried as St. Cecilia's pastor.

He hadn't started out that way. In fact, when he had arrived three years ago, he was filled with enthusiasm, certain that careful planning could bring the church finances around. He had been wrong.

His first line of attack had been to reduce costs. Simple enough or so he had thought. First he closed the church during the week and reduced the number of Masses on Sunday from four to two. He also eliminated Saturday evening vigils. He figured he could save more than five thousand dollars a year just on heat and electricity. The parishioners endured the cutbacks but he found that he could not.

Several young couples stopped coming to Mass. When he investigated, Father James discovered that many, in order to support their families, had second jobs that often required working on Sundays. Father James rescheduled the Saturday five-o'clock Mass.

Then suddenly, the elderly parishioners began to take ill in record numbers with an assortment of ailments. These were normally spry and active individuals. Now, however, dozens were confined to their beds. What had happened? He paid Doc Hammon a visit.

"It's not their bodies that are in trouble. It's their minds," Dr. Hammon confided. "These people are depressed."

"Depressed? But why?" he asked.

"The elderly thrive on structure," the doctor explained. "Retirement is a two-edged sword. It means freedom from punching a time clock, but it also means their sense of importance has been removed. Up until this point, their lives were heavily regulated by their jobs. They had to get up each morning to earn a paycheck so they could support their families. Remove the job and they no longer have a reason to get out of bed. So in order to reclaim some of that structure, the elderly often seek an activity that restores their sense of being needed."

"Are you saying morning Mass gave our elderly parishioners a reason to keep active and that by closing St. Cecilia's during the week, I have somehow disrupted their sense of order?"

"Exactly," Dr. Hammon said. "Morning Mass is important to your elderly. They've structured their whole lives around the church. Timothy McGree gets up at six A.M. each morning so he can open the doors, set things up. Afterward, Harriet Bedford drives around with Sam Rosenberg to give out communion to the house bound, and Ethel Johnson and Arlene Campbell are needed to clean up. Then there's the Rosary Society that prays after Mass for all the sick in the parish and so on and so on.

"Now some of these things might sound insignificant to us, but to the elderly it's a place where people depend on them. Makes them feel as though they're still needed and have an important task to perform."

Father James reopened the church for morning Mass that very week.

Other cost cutting measures met with similar results. There was his plan to get the high school boys to cut the grass and shovel the snow, which would have saved the church an additional three thousand dollars, but Father James quickly discovered that sports and socializing took precedence in a teenager's life. By mid-July of his first year, the Congregationalists next door were giving him the evil eye every time he walked out of the rectory. At this point the grass hadn't been cut or the gardens weeded in nearly three weeks.

His biggest blunder was when he had tried to replace the costly beeswax candles with electric ones.

"How can you expect us to throw a switch instead of lighting a candle?" Ruth Henderson rebuked. "Candles, *real ones*, are a tradition in the church. You can't just replace them. Besides," she added, leaning forward on her walker, "asking us to turn on an electric candle and find any solace in it is like asking us to pray in front of a street lamp."

Perhaps he should have stood firm, refused to buckle under the procedures he knew must be implemented if the church was to be saved. But he had not. Instead, he had elected to put people before finances. It had proven to be St. Cecilia's undoing and his as well. Now, where once faith had grown, seeds of doubt took root. For the first time in his priestly career, he began to question God's faithfulness and caring.

How could the God of compassion allow St. Cecilia's to close when so many found comfort and solace within its walls? But maybe God had not failed. Maybe it was Father James who had failed. When was the last time he'd been able to discern God's voice clearly among the clamor of his own fears, guilt and shame at not being a better shepherd?

His flock had trusted him to guide them, help preserve what they held precious, and he had failed. He should have tried harder to save the church, find new revenue sources. Surely, there was something else he could have done and didn't?

Father James deeply loved his parishioners whose problems and pain he shared. He lifted them in prayer every morning—Bob and Lori Peterson, Mrs. Norris, Timothy McGree, Ben Metcalf and his grandson Matthew, Ethel Johnson, Fred and Arlene Campbell, the Henderson sisters, Harriet Bedford, Harry Clifford and the scores of others who faithfully gave of their time and talents. He even prayed fervently for George Benson—his personal "thorn in the flesh."

Father James knew that his love alone could not stop St. Cecilia's from closing; only God could do that. The priest had come to the end of his own strivings and knew there was no other way to the miracle he sought. At the bank of lighted candles by the altar, reminders of God's eternal light, Father James bowed his head with a penitent heart and prayed as he hadn't prayed in a long, long time.

Dear Lord,

Is there something that I have done which has displeased you? Have I been presumptive about our friendship? Do I secretly harbor any prideful thoughts that have placed me outside of your grace? I earnestly wish to know, Father. For if there is something which sep-

arates me from your love, I ask that it be revealed so I may confess my sin and restore my soul to your grace.

I became a priest so I could share your love, your gift of salvation, but I no longer feel that my talents are of any worth. I have tried to keep St. Cecilia's open, but I have failed. Maybe if I were a better administrator or fund-raiser, I could have succeeded. But, as you know, I was never one for facts and figures. I preferred fellowship to financial rosters. Was this a failing? Did I displease you with these shortcomings?

Whether it was my fault or not, the fact is St. Cecilia's is closing. I have failed the flock that you have placed in my care and for this I am heartily sorry.

Lord, I have joyfully been your servant for most of my life and with the Psalmist can earnestly say, "I have never seen the righteous forsaken nor their descendants begging bread." Therefore, I trust that you will turn this to good. Somehow, you will provide a place for Father Keene to retire that will make his last days more joyous than the past. That you will keep the Peterson family in the palm of your hand and find a donor for Bob or, should you take him home, provide the grace for his young family to get through.

My mortal mind wants to pray a selfish prayer—please find a way to keep St. Cecilia's open. But my spirit, your spirit that resides in me, would pray a more powerful prayer. The prayer that ushered into this world the greatest gift ever bestowed upon man—salvation. The prayer that says "Not my will, but yours, be done."

I am your humble servant and wish only to do your will. Please give me the ability, through example, to help your flock go on in faith and trust in your sovereign will.

Father James made the sign of the cross, then rose from his knees; it was dark outside and had begun to snow. In his heart, however, there was radiant light. Genuflecting before the host as he exited the pew, he felt a peace he had not known for many years.

Chapter 6

B y four-thirty that afternoon, the skies had turned an angry steel gray, but Lori ignored the ominous warnings, having taken off an hour early to attend the three-o'clock Mass. The small cross of ashes—now a light gray smudge—Father Keene had applied to her forehead had already faded from the humidity that pumped into the dining area from the poorly vented dishwasher in the back kitchen.

Lori rushed about trying to catch up on her chores in between waiting on the few customers who straggled in and out during the late afternoon. Coffee, hot chocolates to go. A piece of pie or dish of rice pudding eaten at the counter.

Lori worked quietly, efficiently, as though on autopilot, as she boxed the ketchup bottles, filling one from another; restocked the envelopes of sugar and Equal and containers of jelly, making certain that each had equal amounts of strawberry and grape preserves. She washed the sticky maple-syrup containers with hot, soapy water; cleaned one of the two coffee urns with a steel brush and cleaner; and brought up extra coffee filters, napkins and Styrofoam cups from the basement storeroom.

And as she worked, she compiled lists in her head. First, the grocery list: *dog food for Elmo, bread . . . do we need eggs?* If only she hadn't forgotten the carefully detailed list she had crafted last night. She'd left it on the kitchen counter in her hurry to get Sarah off to school and herself to work.

"If you hurry and finish your breakfast, I'll let you help Mommy string the Easter eggs on the lilac bush by the front door after supper," she had promised Sarah, even though it was several weeks too early to begin decorating for Easter. Her daughter's face had lit up with excitement, and the bowl of Cap'n Crunch disappeared within moments.

Lori would have to add plastic Easter eggs to her list. She'd also have to stop at Stone's Hardware and pick up the telephone jack Bob wanted to install in the living room. Did Stone's carry plastic Easter eggs?

She walked back to the kitchen and placed the empty creamers in the dishwasher, mentally charting her route along Main Street: first Grand Union, then the hardware store, then . . . one of the creamers slipped out of her hands and rattled onto the tile floor.

"Everything all right back there?" Harry called.

"Fine," she hollered. "Just dropped a creamer."

She pulled back the urge to rush though her chores. Try not to think about driving home in the snow, she told herself. Her husband's pick-up truck often fishtailed when the roads got slick, scaring her half to death.

She finished placing the creamers in the industrial-size dishwasher, which Harry called Dark Vader, reached overhead to the large sprayer nozzle, gave the creamers a heavy rinse, then threw on the switch. The metal rack made its way down the conveyor belt.

Harry yelled out again, "Lori, leave that for me to finish. You get on home before it starts to snow."

She walked back out front. "I'm almost through."

The customer who had sat under the side windows sipping a cup of coffee engrossed in the *Dorsetville Gazette* walked over and handed her his check with a five-dollar bill.

"Thank you and come again," she said, handing him his change. A lock of chestnut hair fell across her face. She really had to find time to get a haircut.

The man counted out five dimes and placed them on the counter before heading out under the thickening clouds.

"Go home before this storm starts up," Harry implored, staring out the front windows. "I tell you, it's going to be a whopper. Just look at that sky." The clouds were thickening in the west. "Radio says we're going to get at least six inches, but my guess is we'll get more like twenty-four." Harry could accurately predict snowfalls to within one inch.

"Sure? I'd like to get a head start on my grocery shopping before it starts coming down."

Grocery shopping in Dorsetville was always a major challenge whenever snow was forecast. The town's seniors quickly filled the Grand Union parking lot with their boat-size cars, depleting shelves with amazing agility, and acting as though there wouldn't be another food delivery until spring. Lori would be lucky to find any milk or bread left.

"Yes, I'm sure. Go on home." Harry turned the sign on the front door to read CLOSED. "I'm packing it in for the day, too."

He pushed a chair back in place, then looked up to see Lori hesitate. "Go! Before it starts to snow and the roads get slick. I'll close up. Heck, I only have to walk upstairs when I'm done. You've got to travel nearly five miles, all on back roads, none of which will be sanded until this thing really starts to howl, if I know our town's crews."

He walked over and gave her a gentle shove. "I can close up alone, now go."

"Thanks, Harry, you spoil me." Harry was like her surrogate big brother.

"Yeah, sure," he laughed. "I let you work for minimum wage, clog up your arteries with all the cholesterol you can eat, and let you wait on customers who leave you"—he counted the five dimes left as a tip on the counter—"pocket change."

Harry was thirteen years her senior. He had never married and seldom dated seriously, except for that one time he courted Heidi Farrell, whose father owned the Agway Feed Store. But they broke it off after eighteen months when Heidi, who had a crush on *Bonanza*'s Hoss

Cartwright—whom Harry resembled—discovered *Dr. Kildare*'s Richard Chamberlain, whom Harry most definitely did not.

It wasn't that Harry didn't like women. He did. It was just that he liked his life the way it was—uncomplicated. He could come and go as he pleased, unmindful of anyone else's demands. Harry was a very contented bachelor who, after twenty years, local matrons had finally stopped trying to fix up with a succession of nieces and distant female cousins.

Harry hadn't always worked in his family's restaurant. In fact, when his parents were alive, he had pretty much tried to ignore it during his high-school years. That was when he was the town's most famous quarterback—weighing in at 335 pounds and standing 6 feet 4½ inches tall—and the reason Dorsetville's football team had won the state championship three years in a row. In his senior year, there had even been talk of college recruiters and offers of scholarships. That was before Harry broke a hip during one of the playoff games. He remained benched the rest of that year, and his visions of a professional football career faded.

Harry seldom ever spoke about those years. He was a man who believed that happiness was a choice and the past was best forgotten. "You can't always pick your opponents," he would say whenever people told him their troubles, "but you can pick your plays." This philosophy was why he admired Lori so much. She didn't ask for special treatment or for pity like most people in her place would have done. She went about doing what needed to be done without complaint. In fact, you would never know that her husband was dying of cancer by her cheerfulness and sweet disposition.

Lori carefully folded her apron and began to slip into her coat. The lining had ripped along the shoulder seam and she had to be careful not to make it worse. Its repair was on her long list of things to be done.

"If I can get to the store before the shelves are picked over, I'll pick up the ingredients for a coffee cake. I'll have some extra time this evening to bake so I can bring it in for tomorrow's breakfast crowd."

Lori had begun to supply some of the restaurant's baked goods. Her grandmother's sour cream coffee cake, which was a favorite of the St. Cecilia's crowd, always sold out as soon as customers spied it sitting on the counter under a glass-domed cake dish, as did Lori's pumpkin and cranberry breads and her Haddam Hall gingerbread tea cakes—a special favorite of the Dorsetville Garden Club, and which they often ordered for their monthly meetings at the library.

Her baked goods were becoming so popular that Harry had toyed with the idea of installing a couple of big ovens in the back and starting a small bakery. He hadn't mentioned the idea to Lori, though. She had enough to handle with Bob's illness. Business propositions could wait.

❧

By the time Lori walked to her truck in the back parking lot, fat snowflakes had begun to fall and cover the windshield. She opened the cab door, grabbed the gallon of windshield wiper fluid that she had bought on sale at Kmart the previous week, popped the truck's hood, jumped back out and walked around to the front of the cab to secure the open hood. Bending over the engine, she found the dispenser and poured in half a gallon of fluid, screwed the cap back on, lowered the hood and jumped back inside. By this time the inside of the cab was dark, shrouded in a blanket of snow. Lori started the engine, giving it a couple of hard revs so it wouldn't stall, then jumped back outside and scraped the windows clean.

By the time she had finished, her hands ached from the cold. Where had she left her woolen mittens? She had them in her hands this morning when she was getting ready for work. Probably left them on the kitchen counter along with her shopping list.

Lately, she marveled at how much she could accomplish in a twenty-four-hour period and how self-sufficient she had become. Before Bob's illness, she had never balanced a checkbook, paid a bill or changed a ceiling light bulb—and she didn't have a clue what lay hidden under the hood of a car, let alone know what receptacle held windshield fluid. She had also never worked outside of the home.

Lori remembered the abject terror she felt when Bob's doctors had taken her aside a few months into his illness. It was impossible for Bob to continue to work, they had said, implying that she must take on the family's role of breadwinner. Bob's need for repeated blood transfusions and various therapies while he waited for a matching bone-marrow donor would leave him weak and susceptible to disease. Lori had nodded in agreement as fear began to chisel at her resolve to be upbeat and positive for Bob. But who would hire her? She had no skills.

She had put on a brave face as they drove home. It would be an exciting challenge, she told him. Sarah was in school full time now, having just started first grade. She no longer needed a stay-at-home mom. Besides, Bob would be there to watch Sarah after school.

Lori teased Bob. "It's about time you got a taste of just how difficult it is to watch a seven-year-old."

Later, she had quietly slipped out of the house, walked the mile to the running brook at the rear of their property, sat on a boulder and cried. She had never felt so terrified in her life.

"Where am I going to find a job and who will hire me?" she asked out loud.

She had no work experience. She had married Bob right out of high school and within a year was pregnant with Sarah. Bob was working at the mill and making forty thousand dollars a year. Although it was not a lot of money, Lori knew how to run a house on a tight budget. She'd done it as a youngster after her mother died. Similar budgeting had allowed her to stay home with Sarah.

Lori's life had never been easy. Her mother had died when she was seven years old, Sarah's age. Her father, an alcoholic, had been stern and verbally abusive her entire life. Lori had often thought that her mother had died because she saw no other means of escape.

She had two older brothers, Ted and John, who fled from the house before their eighteenth birthday, never stopping to finish their last six weeks of high school or bothering to write afterward. Lori had been fourteen when they left and their absence had thickened the dark pall that shrouded their home and intensified her feelings of isolation and loneliness.

Although Lori was popular at school—a trim-figured, chestnut-haired girl with a winsome smile—she was careful never to bring any of her friends home or give them her phone number. "My father doesn't allow me to talk on the phone. He uses it for business and doesn't want the line tied up," is what she said when they asked why they couldn't call her at home.

But the truth was her father was a mean-spirited, foul-mouthed drunk whose anger was like a minefield. She was never certain when an innocent word, phrase or deed might trip an explosion, and she certainly didn't want any friends around should that happen; nor did she want them listening on the other end of the phone when her father came home drunk after work, which he did more times than not.

Whenever she would leaf through those dark, teenage years, her thoughts would always come to rest on one particular evening, the way a well-studied book falls open to a particular page.

It was late June. Lori had ignored the hot, airless kitchen and cooked all afternoon in hope of pleasing her father. Irish stew, it was his favorite. Back then, she had still believed herself capable of earning his love through good deeds. She'd be a better cook, a better housekeeper, a better daughter. She had learned the great fallacy of that belief in later years.

She had just ladled the fragrant, rich stew into her father's dish and was returning to her chair when she saw him scan the table. Immediately, her heart began to pump faster.

"What is it, Da? Did I forget something?" she asked nervously.

"Where's the salt shaker? Did you hide it somewhere?" he scowled.

"No, Daddy," Lori ran to the counter, still hoping to avert an angry episode. The shaker was nowhere in sight. Why hadn't she checked the table before calling him in for dinner? she chided herself. She opened the spice cabinet. It wasn't there, either.

"You're such a stupid girl. Why did you call me to dinner when the table's only half set?" He picked up the bread bowl and looked around it. Not finding the shaker, he flung the bowl across the room. Next went the glass butter dish, striking the refrigerator, shattering, leaving a sickly, yellow smudge.

Lori could feel the muscles along her stomach tighten, like a contender awaiting a blow.

"You're worthless! No better than those no-good brothers of yours who left without as much as a 'thank you, Da.' Who do they think paid the rent all of those years? Put three square meals on the table each day? Santa Claus?"

The tinderbox of rage that had long ago replaced her father's heart had been set aflame and through past experience, Lori knew it would quickly consume him. She edged closer to the pantry door, ready to lock herself inside and climb out the window if need be, at the first hint of conflagration.

"I work my hands to the bone supporting your lazy carcass and do you care? Well, do you?" he screamed.

"Yes, of course, I do, Daddy. I know how hard you work." She never was quite certain if she should answer his questions, which seemed to further incite his rage, or remain silent and be accused of insolence.

"You do? You do? Then why don't you set the table properly, the way it's suppose to be set? Your laziness has ruined my dinner."

"I'm sorry, Daddy. I won't forget it next time. I promise."

"You promise? You promise? What good is *your* promise?"

He shoved himself away from the kitchen table, his chair falling over backward in his wake. Lori jumped, ready for flight. Now in a red rage, her father stomped toward the kitchen sink and threw in his dinner plate. Potatoes and carrots splattered on the wall and on the dotted Swiss curtains she had recently laundered; the statue of the Madonna and Child, which had been her mother's and which now rested on the window sill above the sink, dripped with gravy.

"I'm going out to find me a place that knows how to serve a man properly." He grabbed his cap, then took what was left of the household money out of the tin box kept on the china hutch. "This mess had better be cleaned up by the time I get back."

These scenes had increased with alarming frequency during her high-school years. Depression set in, although at the time, "depression" was not a word associated with teenage girls. Most would have called Lori's inability to concentrate during class or her lethargic responses a case of daydreaming; her weight loss a growing spurt teenage girls often go through; her refusal to accept invitations to dances, parties and high-school social activities, normal teenage girl moodiness.

Only once did a teacher ask if she was okay when she had come to class with a black eye. Lori responded with a forced smile. "Tripped on the stairs." Just as the teacher had thought.

While her classmates worried about SAT scores and college applications, Lori wondered if she would make it through another day at home. She had even called the state's social services department to inquire how one might be placed in a foster home. They asked why. She told them. The man on the phone said she should stop feeling sorry for herself. At least she *had* a father, a home. There were kids out there who had neither.

Lori suffered silently after that, feeling more and more like an observer of life, distanced from the trivial complaints of her peers whose parents were deemed too strict because they wouldn't lift their curfew, or too stingy because they wouldn't allow them to purchase the newest Bee Gees record. How she envied their childish complaints! How she envied them their parents!

She had met these moms and dads when they had acted as chaperones for class trips or dances. Gentle, soothing voices. Soft, caresses. Words of endearment. She used to close her eyes at night alone in her bedroom, anxiously awaiting the return of her drunken father, and try to imagine what it must be like to be loved.

Lori had never felt love of any kind although she had longed for it, romanticized it. If she had been asked to define it, she would have been at a loss for words. It was like someone being asked to define the moon or the stars, which were visible from a distance but that could not be touched or examined up close. So was love, until she met Bob Peterson.

Bob was two years her senior and although he was handsome in a quiet way, he never actively solicited girlfriends. Girlfriends meant dates and dates meant money and Bob came from a family where money was in short supply. Like Lori, he had lost a parent. His dad had died when he was only ten. But, unlike Lori, his mother was a bright ray of sunshine whose faith in God's grace was steadfast.

Mrs. Peterson—an optimist of the "if life gives you lemons make lemonade" variety—had responded bravely to the death of her husband and the loss of her means of support.

"God will provide. He always does," she professed.

Several weeks later, the realtor John Moran called to ask if she might consider boarding a man who had recently transferred from the Midwest. And, thus, the Peterson Boarding House was born and her faith reaffirmed.

Mrs. Peterson, however, still had to depend upon Bob and his younger brother, Joseph, to contribute in order to make ends meet. Each took an after-school job to help supplement the family's income.

Consequently, Bob didn't have a lot of pocket money to spend on ice cream sodas at the Country Kettle or tickets to the Palace Theater movie house. Unlike other boys who might have resented giving up high school sports or after-school clubs, Bob didn't mind. In fact, he felt proud to be contributing to his family's upkeep, a pride that was reflected in his mother's eyes each week when he handed over his paycheck.

Faith in God's rich provisions was a cornerstone in the Petersons' home. Mrs. Peterson consulted God for all of her needs and the needs of her sons, even going so far as to pray that God would provide both sons the perfect wives. So when Bob brought Lori home to dinner one Sunday and shyly announced afterward that he'd someday like to make her his wife, Mrs. Peterson was not at all surprised, knowing in her spirit that through this shy, gentle young girl God had answered her prayers.

Lori was starved for the type of home life and love that Bob's mother provided and, unlike other girls who might have clamored to be taken out for hamburgers and fries, Lori was content to visit Bob's on Saturday nights, sewing patchwork quilts with Mrs. Peterson around an old-fashioned quilting frame while Bob cleaned his hunting rifle or played with the family dog. Conversations and laughter filled the house, quieting only when Garrison Keillor's A *Prairie Home Companion* sounded on the radio.

The peace and tranquillity of those evenings sustained Lori during the turbulent hours at home and gave her a vision, where before there had been none, of what a happy home life could be like.

Before Mrs. Peterson's death, she had told Lori, "Make Christ the head of your home and it will always be a happy home. Talk to Him every day as you would your best friend; tell Him your heartaches, your burdens and fears. Let Him carry them. Place them completely in His capable hands, then step away and watch provisions come from places you never imagined. That's what I've done all of these years, and I can tell you that Jesus has never failed me."

Lori had never forgotten Mother Peterson's words and it was to Jesus she had gone when confronted with the challenge of becoming the family's breadwinner, although she couldn't fathom then how He would provide her with a job when she had absolutely no skills.

But what is impossible with man is possible with God, and the very next day, when she was walking along Main Street en route to Sam's Shoe Repair, she spied the HELP WANTED, WAITRESS NEEDED sign in the window of the Country Kettle. Although she had never waitressed before, Lori reasoned that it was something she could learn to do. Taking a deep breath and trying to steady her nerves, she walked into the Country Kettle and right up to Harry and asked if she could apply.

Harry was trying to work the grill and serve meals as she entered and it was easy to see that he was quickly falling behind.

"Which one of you ordered the grilled cheese with bacon and chicken salad sandwich on rye?" he asked the men at the counter.

"I ordered a hot pastrami on rye with Swiss cheese and my friend ordered a BLT on white toast," a construction worker said.

"Take these and I'll give you each a free piece of apple pie for dessert," Harry said, slamming the plates down in front of them.

"Excuse me," Lori said, quickly assessing there would be no good time to interrupt. It was now or never.

"My name is Lori Peterson. I saw your HELP WANTED sign in the window and I wanted to know if the position is still open?"

"It sure is," Harry said, wiping his hands on his apron and reaching over the counter to shake Lori's hand. "My former waitress, Louise, retired. Finally decided to take her kid's advice and move down to Florida." Harry cleared away a used coffee cup and wiped the area down with a wet cloth. "Fell on the ice last year and broke a wrist. Said that was the clincher." He looked into Lori's nervous young face. "You ever waitress before?"

"No, I haven't," she said, with downcast eyes. But then, remembering how much she needed a job, she broke though her natural reserve. "But I'm sure I can learn."

"I'm sure you can, too," Harry said, his blue eyes filled with compassion, his pudgy chipmunklike cheeks inflated with a smile. Dorsetville was a small town. Harry knew about her husband's illness. "How soon can you start?"

God had managed to do it! Find her a job without any experience and one that was only five miles away from home. It was heaven sent! If Bob suddenly needed her, she could be there in less than ten minutes. She praised the Lord all the way home.

The first few weeks were a hard adjustment for Lori, both at home and at the restaurant. She felt she was sleepwalking through the day. And when she would get discouraged, fearing she might never get it right, Harry would only laugh.

"You'll get the hang of it," he encouraged. "Just relax and think of these people as your friends, not your customers. The regulars are good, decent people. They don't mind if you screw up. Heck, if my cooking hasn't chased them away, nothing you do can hurt. You'll do just fine."

Harry had been right. The customers were wonderful even when she mixed up their orders, which she did a lot in the beginning. No one ever complained or grew impatient, especially not Harry, who only shrugged his shoulders when she returned to the grill with one of her mistakes. "Won't go to waste," Harry would say, dumping the contents into Honey's dog dish. "Mrs. Johnson's dog will love it."

Lori loved working at the restaurant and quickly decided that when Bob recovered (she always was careful to use the word *when*), she would continue to work for Harry. Working for Harry felt like working for family.

Chapter 7

L ori felt an inexplicable urge to stop at St. Cecilia's to pray for Bob as she slowly made her way toward the other end of town. She tried to disengage the thought as she carefully drove down the snow-covered street, hoping that Grand Union hadn't closed early due to the storm. The snow was already coming down hard. She switched the wipers to fast and hunched closer to the steering wheel to get a better view of Main Street.

As nerve-racking as driving in the snow was, Lori had to concede that it made the tattered shops and sagging Victorian homes along Main Street appear enchanted. As the snow quickly covered missing clapboards, fallen fence posts, and sagging porch steps, she could almost envision what Dorsetville might have looked like in its heyday.

In the late 1800s, Main Street was a stately thoroughfare, where carefully coiffured ladies, with servants in tow, leisurely strolled, gazing into the windows of Peitry's Emporium, the Palace Theater, Mrs. Wilson's Confections and Tea Room, Brown and Long's Milliner's Shop, and Sullivan's Jewelry Store. In 1889, the town was so prosperous that when the ladies complained that their long skirts became caked in mud when they went shopping, the town fathers commissioned the entire thoroughfare to be paved in brick. They set up a brick furnace at the edge of town and hired Chinese laborers at twenty-five cents a day. The project was completed in less than six months, costing the town treasury a total of $675, a bargain, even in those days.

Few of those women, however, were truly appreciative of the patterned brick street or the beautifully crafted architecture that housed their favorite shops; instead, their thoughts were on the newest musical playing at the Palace Theater, or the social tea to be given in St. Cecilia's newly completed basement or whether Dinova's Market would be able to deliver a rack of lamb for Saturday night's dinner party.

As the woolen mills began to close and people moved away in search of jobs, Main Street's elegant facades began to crumble. Peitry's Emporium now hosted the Salvation Army's Main Street mission. Its arched windows—cracked with flaking trim painted gunmetal gray—had once showcased dresses imported from Paris. Now the windows were empty, curtains drawn aside. Those peering in would see a cavernous space filled with metal folding chairs.

Other storefront signs now read KIM'S NAILS, BOB'S BASEBALL CARDS and SMOKE SHOP, GO VIDEO and SECONDHAND ROSE while many more remained empty or boarded up, bearing realtor signs: FOR LEASE OR SALE, CALL JOHN MORAN AT 555-1200.

Even Dorsetville's Town Hall was in desperate need of repair. The roof on the large square building, which housed the offices of the town clerk, tax assessor, building inspector, zoning commission, dog warden, health department, and the mayor, was more than twenty-five years old and leaked so badly that the municipality had begun to issue stainless-steel water buckets along with the town charter to all newly elected town officials.

A strong north wind rocked the truck, driving the snow hard against her windshield, as Lori turned off Main Street and onto Church Street. The yellow lines on the pavement were already obscured by swirling eddies of snow. She carefully circled around the town green and headed toward St. Cecilia's. Knowing that this urge to pray defied all logic, she pulled the truck alongside the curb where she had parked only a few hours ago while attending the Ash Wednesday service.

She turned off the ignition just as the truck's heater began to pump warm air. Did she really want to go out into this numbing cold? No. She'd much rather finish her errands and get home before the roads grew slick, but she seemed to be propelled by an inner force over which she had little control. Gathering her resolve, she opened the door and slid down to the street, pulling the hood of her coat up against the wind, but not quickly enough. Several icy flakes fell against the nape of her neck, and she shivered. The sidewalks were covered with a dusting of snow as she walked carefully in her white waitress shoes, trying not to slide, toward the church's main entrance. A strange sense of urgency drove her.

A welcome covering of warm air enveloped her shoulders like a woolen shawl as she stepped into the vestibule. Blessed warmth, she thought, dipping a finger into the holy water and making the sign of the cross. She unbuttoned her coat as she walked down the center aisle, heading toward her favorite pew at the front of the church. She paused only briefly to genuflect before settling in the pew.

She slid out of her coat. What was she doing here? The weather was only going to get worse and there were groceries to buy and the hazardous trek up the mountain to their home on a road that apparently didn't exist on any town map. She had to call after every storm to remind the town crews that it still hadn't been sanded.

Lori forcefully tried to quiet her mind, empty her thoughts of outside concerns. She was here to pray for Bob. She stared out onto the empty niche where the statue of the Blessed Mother had once stood. The church seemed somehow different without Mary. Empty.

She pulled the kneeler forward and knelt but words wouldn't come. What could she possibly say that she hadn't already uttered a few hours ago in hopes of convincing God to intercede on Bob's behalf? It seemed like such a hopeless exercise. The only words that came to mind were, *Please, God. Please, don't let Bob die.*

How do you know if God has heard your prayers? she wondered. She wished she possessed the faith Mother Peterson had had, a faith that just seemed to *know* that God was working for her. A faith that embraced a Heavenly Father having substance and form, not just some religious abstract.

"Father," she said out loud. The word conjured up an image of her earthly father. She shoved it away because at times it was hard to separate the two.

Mother Peterson had once said she believed that people found the God they went looking for. If they sought the God of vengeance, they would find Him. The Old Testament was filled with passages about God's raining down fire and brimstone. If they sought the God of compassion and love, they could find Him, too, in Christ. Christ was whom Lori now sought, but could she find Him? She pondered this, staring into the bank of candles, hundreds of tiny dancing flowers representing other prayers, other needs. What could make her prayers different from the rest, more likely to be heard?

She closed her eyes, taking in the smells of beeswax, incense, and the soft perfume of the flowers behind the altar. Suddenly she was seven years old again, getting ready to recite her lines as the angel in the Easter pageant, bringing good tidings of Christ's resurrection to the disciples who had entered the empty tomb (which in this production were the Sullivan brothers garbed in their father's bathrobes). It was her mother's last Easter. It had been a happy time.

Lori felt the stirrings of self-pity. She felt so alone. She missed her mother. She missed Mother Peterson. How she wished they were here to help her get through this Easter, which she feared might be Bob's last.

She angrily swiped at the fears. No! No! No! She would not allow herself to think that. Bob would be all right. The doctors had said that his youth and his otherwise strong good health were important factors in his favor.

They will find a bone marrow match. They must!

She remembered what Sam Rosenberg had once told her. "As long as there is hope, there is life." She thought of Sam, whose entire family had died in German concentration camps. How had he been able to go on?

Hope, Sam had said.

Hope. She turned the word over in her mind as a jeweler might examine a precious stone. Hope was the lesser cousin to faith. Whereas faith denoted a commitment, a firm resolution to believe no matter what the circumstances, hope demanded much less. A gentler companion, it barred none from its embrace.

That's what I need, Lori thought. *Hope.*

She had tried to conjure up faith for Bob's healing. It couldn't be found within her fear-locked mind. But she could hope. Hope that they would find a donor. Hope that Bob would recover and the cancer would be beaten. Hope that Bob would live a long life and someday dance at their daughter's wedding. Hope.

But seconds later, fear, always watchful from the sidelines of a searching soul, swooped down and snatched away this small morsel of comfort. What would she do if Bob was to die? What would happen to her and Sarah? How would they go on? Lori without the man she had come to love more completely with each passing day? Sarah without the father whose smile alone could heal any wound?

The snow fell gently outside covering the countryside in a garment of white while the church lay silent, unaffected by the storm. Lori shivered and looked up at the crucifix behind the altar. She had always averted her glance from Christ's mangled form, but now she gazed at it intensely, saw the cold metal spikes that had been hammered through His feet and wrists. Saw the blood dripping from the two-inch Jerusalem thorns that had been savagely driven into the crown of Christ's head. Tears slid down her cheeks as she continued to study the crucified form, tracing His body slumped against the cross in death. The tears flowed copiously.

Lori had sat before this image most of her life yet until this moment, she had never really seen it for what it was. Not a depiction of the dead Christ, but a monument to God's ultimate sacrifice of love. And for the first time she connected to that love, not as a Catholic, or even a Christian, but as a mother who has just learned of the death of another's child and how that child had been given freely in her stead. Lori covered her face and wept loudly.

How could anyone love another that much? she pondered. And with that question came an epiphany as a recent gospel reading resounded in her mind: "He that spared not his own Son, but delivered Him up for us all, how shall He not with Him also freely give us all things?"

The fears that bound her soul began to unfetter as she reached to grab hold of this new revelation as another woman long ago had once reached toward the hem of His garment, knowing that the healing of her spirit could be found within its folds.

Dear Lord, she prayed, *Bob is dying.*

She nearly choked on the words but stumbled onward, afraid of losing the momentum of this revelation.

The doctors are doing everything they can, but it might not be enough. I can't imagine my life without him. I love him so much.

I have prayed for his healing and I want to believe that you will answer that prayer, but if it depends on my faith, then I am in real trouble, Lord, because I haven't any. I want to believe, but I'm afraid. I feel like the man who came to you a long time ago to ask you to heal his child. Remember him, Lord? You asked him if he believed. He said, "Yes, I believe. Please help my unbelief."

I am like that man, Lord. I want to believe that you will heal my husband, that you will send a miracle, but I can't seem to find the faith to sustain that hope.

I don't know what you have planned for Bob. I want to believe that you will send him a miracle, but if you can't, I know that you will take him home to be with You in heaven . . . the ultimate healing . . . and that someday we will be reunited. But whatever you decide, Lord, I bend to your will. I only ask that you send me a little hope to see me through.

As soon as she finished praying, a quiet peace stole over her soul, replacing the heavy garment of fear she had worn. She could feel the tension in her shoulders release and the tightness in her chest from constant worry begin to dissipate. She suddenly knew that everything was going to be all right. No matter what the outcome, she no longer felt alone.

Lori sat quietly, savoring this new peace when the church doors opened, forcing her back from her reverie. A surge of wind blew down the center aisle, rushing toward the altar until the linen altar cloth rippled under its flow and the flowers shivered. An indefinable stillness seemed to settle over the church in its wake.

Soft footfalls sounded. An adult and a small child made their way toward the altar. Lori reached in her pocket for a crumpled piece of Kleenex, wiped her eyes, softly blew her nose.

She should be on her way. The snow was bound to make the roads slick and there was all that shopping to do, yet she felt compelled to stay. Five more minutes, she thought, and closed her eyes again in silent prayer.

A shadow fell across her face and she opened her eyes. The toddler with big, brown Asian eyes watched her soberly.

Lori smiled and the child smiled back, a huge crescent-shaped smile ringed in chocolate. She had raven hair arranged at odd angles, like chopsticks allowed to fall every which way in a wide-mouth jar. It made Lori's smile broaden; that, and the way the child stood, like a mummy stiff in her one-piece pink nylon snowsuit. The child glanced quickly at her mother who knelt in prayer by the side altar, refocused on Lori, then gazed up, past her shoulder, as though something or someone was positioned over Lori's head. Lori turned around. There was nothing there.

"Hello, sweetheart," she said. "What's your name?"

The child studied her for several seconds before withdrawing her thumb and answering. "My name is Hope." The child plopped her thumb back in her mouth.

A force like an electric current revved up inside Lori's brain. It couldn't be. Maybe she had heard wrong. She asked the child again. "What did you say your name was?"

The child removed her thumb again. "Hope," she said, then stuck it back in her mouth.

"Hope," Lori repeated. She could hardly believe it. God *was* listening. "God has sent me hope!" she shouted, then reached for the child as though to steady herself.

The child's mother turned just as Lori enveloped Hope in her arms. The woman rushed over, pushed Lori away and snatched her child free. Backing a safe distance away, she spoke rapidly in a foreign tongue while casting Lori a malevolent scowl.

"No, no, you don't understand," Lori rushed to explain. "I wasn't trying to take your child. You see, I was praying for my husband. He's been very ill with cancer. Leukemia." She was rambling but couldn't seem to stop herself.

"I asked God to send me hope. Then your daughter came and stood in front of me and I asked her name and she said it was Hope."

The woman's fears mounted. "No English," she said tersely. "No English."

Lori pointed to the child. "Can you tell me her name? Name?" Pointing to herself, she said, "My name is Lori. Lori Peterson." Pointing to the statue of St. Anthony, she said, "Saint Anthony." She pointed to the child, "Name?"

The woman slowly nodded with understanding.

"Her name Hope," she said, pressing the child more tightly to her breast. "Little Hope."

***

Lori was no longer cognizant of her surroundings. She drove the truck over back streets, oblivious to the slippery roads, unconcerned when the truck fishtailed at the traffic light at Whittemore and Main, causing several cars to drive up on the sidewalk. Horns blared. Tempers flared. She didn't notice a thing. Like Mr. Magoo, of cartoon fame, the truck somehow righted itself, and she continued on her errands as though nothing had happened, leaving a pile of disabled vehicles in her wake.

Lori walked down the Grand Union aisles, her body continuing in a forward motion while her mind, like a scratched 45 record, repeated the incident in the church over and over and over.

"Please send me just a little hope, Lord. Just a little hope."

"Her name is Hope. Little Hope."

Lori placed items in her shopping cart that she later would have no recollection of ever purchasing.

She stopped at Stone's Hardware Store.

"Hi, Lori," Mark Stone, the owner's son, called as she walked by. "What can I do for you this evening?"

She kept on walking without a word, then stopped in front of a display of garden gloves.

"Lori?"

"Telephone wall jack. Plastic Easter eggs."

"You all right?"

"Where do you keep them?"

"Keep what? Oh, the Easter eggs are by the register and the phone jacks are at the back of the store. Do you want me to get you one?"

"One what?"

"Telephone jack." *Bob's condition must really be taking its toll*, Mark thought.

"Oh, yes. My husband needs a telephone jack," she said, suddenly remembering why she was there.

"I'll get you one and be back in a jiff." He dove into a sea of customers who had come for emergency supplies. The weatherman had just upgraded the incoming storm to a nor'easter.

While Lori stood waiting for Mark to return, Timothy McGree rounded the aisle.

"Hi, Lori," he yelled, competing with a noisy debate between a husband and wife over a kerosene heater. "Doing some shopping before the weather gets bad?"

Lori didn't see Timothy, who stood expectantly waiting for a reply. Nor Sam Rosenberg. Nor Ben Metcalf. Nor Ben's grandson Matthew. Nor the cardboard boxes and cellophane bags filled with foreign-looking electronic pieces that they carried.

Mark returned with the telephone jack. "Anything else, Lori?"

"No, no. That's all." She walked past Matthew and the men. "Excuse me," she said as though they were strangers, grabbing several net bags of plastic Easter eggs as she passed by. She handed Mark a twenty-dollar bill, not waiting for the change, and walked out of the store.

"That was *real* strange," Matthew said, watching through the window as Lori climbed into her truck and eased out into traffic.

"She's a lady with a lot on her mind," Sam offered.

"You got everything?" Timothy asked Matthew. "What else did that friend of yours say we needed?"

"I think we have everything." Matthew counted the boxes and the cellophane bags. "Yep. That's it. We have the lasers and cameras in the back of Sam's car, and the rolls of magnetic film in my pocket. Seems like we've got everything."

"Good. I think we'd better hurry," Sam said, anxiously looking out the store's front window as the snow began to pile up along Main Street.

"I hate driving up that hill of yours, Ben. I want to be safely home before this storm gets any worse." He helped Matthew pile his purchases on the counter, urging Mark with his mind to hurry along. The last thing Sam wanted was to get stranded by the side of the road with a trunkful of the university's expensive equipment "borrowed" by Matthew's college friend.

"Will that be cash or charge?" Mark Stone asked, noticing for the first time that the cashier's line had wrapped itself around the store.

"Anyone bring any money?" Timothy asked.

Chapter 8

I t was as black as pitch and the roads were beginning to get slick when Father James arrived at the Petersons' house and confronted their driveway—a narrow, unpaved path with deep ruts that wound its way through a thicket of trees, over a small wooden bridge and straight up a sharp hill, which ended at the kitchen's side door. Making the sign of the cross, he prayed that the Jeep's worn tires, which he had planned to replace next fall, would be equal to the task.

The windows in the Petersons' home shone like golden beacons in the falling snow and Father used them like a compass to navigate the steep incline. Finally, with a grateful heart, he pulled the car safely in front of the old barn next to George Benson's van and turned off the lights.

As Father James opened the car door, a sudden burst of wind ripped it from his hand, loudly scraping the side of the parked van.

"Oh, no," he groaned. He was tired, cold and half worn out from the arduous drive, and now this.

He didn't relish having to confess to George Benson that he had just damaged his van. If he were a swearing man, he would have sworn. Instead, holding his breath against the cold—which he had always done since he was a child without knowing why—he got out to survey the damage. The door was tightly wedged between his car and the van and it took some effort to pull it free. Fortunately, it was the side that had been sideswiped by a FedEx delivery truck last month. It was hard to tell what additional damage, if any, Father James had done. Like a thief in the night, Father James quietly closed his car door and headed toward the house, deciding there was no need to mention this to George.

Father James hunched forward and began the dangerous trek across the driveway, which had frozen over with water seeping from a disconnected gutter spout near the porch. He made a mental note to call Chester Platt, a local builder, to send one of his men to fix it. Chester was one of the many people in the parish whom he could count on for charitable acts of kindness.

The house stood warm and inviting, its windows aglow, the smell of wood being burned in the fireplace. It was a stunning piece of Victorian architecture built in 1888 by one of Dorsetville's woolen mill supervisors—two stories high, with a wraparound porch liberally decorated in gingerbread trim, and a large turret with leaded windows. Bob's parents had bought the property in the late 1950s for five thousand dollars during a period when older homes were considered to be white elephants. Many were still standing vacant around the town's green. Bob and Lori had inherited the magnificent house from Mrs. Peterson.

Father James slid down the slight incline by the side of the porch, wishing he had remembered to put his L. L. Bean rubber-soled nor'easters in the backseat. The loafers he wore, which had been perfectly acceptable footwear this morning, were of absolutely no use now. Somehow, he managed to make it to the porch railing without taking a spill.

Thinking how hazardous the fallen snow had already made the wooden stairs, Father James grabbed a broom at the top of the landing and made quick work of dusting off the steps for Lori's return. After sitting most of the day, the simple exercise felt so good that he didn't notice seven-year-old Sarah peeking out from behind the living room curtains.

The side door opened, spilling a pool of light. "Hello, Father James," Sarah called out through the half-open door as she tried to hold tightly to Elmo, the Petersons' medium-size black-and-white dog of uncertain lineage that looked eager to be let loose to roll, like a confection, in a dusting of snow.

"I thought you were Mommy," she said with a slight lisp, having recently lost her two front teeth.

"No, it's just me, but I'm sure she'll be home any minute." He jogged up the stairs, replaced the broom and rubbed his hands together. "You'd better get back inside before you catch a cold. Hi, Elmo."

Elmo exploded in greeting.

"Elmo, get down! Bad dog! Get back inside!" Sarah chastened. Elmo pulled back his ears and sulked back inside.

As soon as Father James walked over the threshold, the house threw its warm air around him. *Praise you, Lord, for central heating, and all the George Bensons who keep it going on cold winter nights*, he silently prayed.

"Do you want me put your coat on the radiator? It's all wet."

"Why, Sarah, that would be very nice," he said, handing over his overcoat.

"Mommy always does that with my mittens," she chattered. "It makes them nice and warm when I put them back on."

Father James had never seen Sarah quite so polite. She was by nature a boisterous child, and the Petersons' house normally resounded with "Sarah, please sit still." "Sarah, stop jumping on the sofa." "Sarah, don't tease the dog." It must have something to do with the Easter Bunny's upcoming visit, he thought. She won't be disappointed, he mused. Father Keene, Mrs. Norris and he had pooled some money, planning to buy one of the large Easter baskets at Kmart filled with a three-pound chocolate bunny, several yellow sugared marshmallow chicks, an assortment of Cadbury eggs and a pink stuffed rabbit all wrapped in violet cellophane.

"Daddy's in the kitchen. He's making . . ." She was about to say that her father was making a mess and was going to be in big trouble when Mommy got home, but changed her mind. That might be considered tattling and she was uncertain if the Easter Bunny would frown on that. Mommy said he only left baskets for good little girls and boys.

She let the sentence hang in the air and led Father James toward the back of the house, her blond curls bouncing in her wake.

Father James could smell Bob's famous marinara sauce with fresh basil, white wine and Crimini mushrooms grow stronger as he headed toward the back kitchen. He prayed a dinner invitation would be forthcoming. It certainly would be just the ticket he needed to remove the dark pall that had dogged him all day. Sauce, pasta, a crisp green salad with freshly grated Parmesan cheese, black olives, and roasted red peppers—and a glass of Chianti. Ah . . . he could almost taste it!

He entered the kitchen, his soul raised in toast to Bob's culinary talents, when he spied the room and gasped. The imagined culinary feast instantly shattered like a glass goblet that has fallen to the floor. Every work space lay covered with dirty dishes, pots, pans, plates and cooking utensils.

Sauce ran down the front of several cabinet doors. The sink was stacked with a motley assortment of cooking instruments. An iron skillet filled with water rested to the side. Pieces of congealed fat now rode atop its surface. On the stove was a cutting board splattered with the remaining shards of onions, mushrooms, green peppers, carrots and basil, and smoke was escaping in a steady gray stream from the sides of the oven door.

Father James thought, *Poor Lori*, but said instead, "Looks like you've been busy."

Bob, seated in his wheelchair, was hard at work at the kitchen table. "I'm fixing some lasagna. Thought I'd surprise Lori." He ladled sauce, assembly-line fashion, into six casserole dishes and three 9 x 12-inch pans spread out in front of him.

"Expecting a crowd?"

"Looks that way, doesn't it?" He forced a laugh, which sounded tired. "I'm afraid my cooking is suffering from a case of the 'might-as-wells.' I was only going to make one pan, but then thought, since I'm at it, I might as well make two. Then I realized that I had gone a little overboard in making the sauce, so since there was so much extra, thought I might as well make another pan. Then I cooked too many noodles, so I thought I might as well keep going."

"At this rate, you'll be able to throw a church supper and invite the entire parish," Father James joked, sampling the sauce with a piece of bread. "Hmm . . . one of your best batches! My compliments to the chef."

"The credit goes to my mother. With a house full of boarders, I had to learn how to cook. Why don't you stay for dinner?" Bob offered.

"I'd love to." He tried to act as though the idea had never occurred to him.

"I'll ask George, too, when he comes up from downstairs."

"Furnace problems?"

"Lori found water on the basement floor this morning. I just thought I'd have George take a look in case it was something serious."

"Seems like all of Dorsetville has kept him busy today. He was at the rectory early this morning."

"That furnace still giving you trouble? How old is that thing anyway?"

"How old is the church?" Father James volleyed, not able to resist the temptation to sample Bob's sauce again. "Boy, that's good! Since I'm going to have the privilege of enjoying this feast, why don't I help clean up?"

"Happy to accept. I am getting a little tired." Bob rubbed the back of his neck. "I forget how quickly this illness can drain my energy. Apron is in the pantry."

Father James disappeared behind the pantry door.

"What's this I hear about St. Cecilia's closing?" Bob called after him.

Father James reappeared, slipping a floral apron over his head. "The rumor mill is already at work, eh?"

"And my wife's a charter member," he teased. "Lori said you were summoned to see the archbishop."

"I was there most of the afternoon. I'm afraid they want to close the church the day after Easter."

"Are you going to let them?"

"I haven't much choice," Father conceded sadly, tying the apron strings behind him. "The archdiocese can't continue to pay our debts, and the church hasn't been able to meet its expenses in over a year." He looked over at Bob and for the second time today wondered who would minister to this family when St. Cecilia's closed.

Father James tried to change the subject. "Did you get any updates today on the bone-marrow search?" There was no one left in Dorsetville who hadn't been tested, including Father James. So far, no match.

"Not yet, but we're still hopeful," Bob answered. "Got any ideas about what can be done to keep the church open?"

Father James began to scrub a large pot with Brillo. "No, but I'm still hopeful." Then quoting Romans, he added, "Who against hope believed in hope."

"I guess that goes for both of us."

Both men fell silent.

The wall clock ticked softly in the corner. Soft refrains of Barney's theme song wafted in from the television Sarah was watching in the other room. Elmo, seemingly bored, sauntered into the kitchen and threw himself down alongside Bob's chair, falling instantly asleep. Bob reached down and stroked his fur.

The back porch light illuminated the falling snow outside the tall kitchen windows. "I never get tired at looking at the snow," Bob said to no one in particular.

Father James heard a wistful note in Bob's voice as though he were contemplating how many more snowfalls he might see. A few months ago, Father James would have encouraged him to banish such thoughts, but now there was no denying that the disease had taken its toll. At its onset, Bob had weighed 258 pounds. Now he weighed 145, and the man Father James had once seen effortlessly pick up a hundred-pound bag of gravel and throw it in the back of his pickup truck could barely lift his small daughter.

Yet nothing could detract from the inner strength of this man. If anything, the disease had increased the sense of spiritual power in Bob's eyes. Poets called the eyes the windows to the soul. If true, Bob's soul was pure, radiant light.

Bob broke the awkward silence. "In the beginning, I used to worry that this might be my last snowfall or my last autumn . . . my last Easter. I don't worry about that stuff anymore. I figured as long as I had the ability to choose, I was going to choose to thoroughly enjoy *this* moment and not worry too much about what may or may not happen next. God has things covered."

"That's powerful advice for everyone," Father James agreed, drying his hands on his apron and pulling up a chair.

Bob sprinkled mozzarella over the lasagna. "Since the day I was diagnosed with cancer, God has continued to supply our needs. When I couldn't work any longer, God provided Lori with a job at the Country Kettle, and He couldn't have found her a better boss."

"I agree," Father James replied.

"Lori never had an outside job and although she tried to hide it from me, I knew she was scared about having to support our family. Then God sent Harry Clifford, who turned out to be one of our greatest blessings. If Lori needs time off to take Sarah someplace after school, Harry tells her to leave. No problem. If I have to go to the doctors, he loans us his van so I can lie down in the back. No other boss would do for us what Harry's done."

"I know," Father James said. "We are blessed to have him on our parish council."

"But God's faithfulness doesn't end there," Bob continued. "Six months ago, my health insurance ran out. I went to the Lord and told Him I needed some serious help. The very next day, a social worker shows up at our door and through her I was able to get connected to all the programs run by the American Cancer Association. She even found a way to get me into the free health clinic at the hospital *and* hooked us up with a fuel-assistance program that pays for all of our heating fuel. Talk about God's providing for all of your needs!"

"Praise the Lord!" Father James proclaimed.

"God has stocked our pantry with an overabundance of food. Someone is always dropping by with a pot of soup, loaves of bread, baked goods." Bob laughed. "Some days I have to plead with people to take food to the soup kitchen."

Then he turned earnest. "People often get it wrong when sickness or tragedy enters their lives. They become filled with fear or resentment, as though to say, 'I should be exempt from all of this.' Or they act as though God has turned His attention elsewhere. But that's not what the Bible says. Jesus said, 'In the world ye shall have tribulation: but be of good cheer; I have overcome the world.' We are not promised a life free from suffering. But we *are* promised that He will lead us safely through whatever trials life throws our way."

Father James reached over with tears running down his face and placed a hand on Bob's shoulder. In all of his years as a priest, he had never heard the role of suffering so eloquently yet so simply explained.

"My dear friend, you have made your life a living epistle."

Bob smiled, lightening the somber mood. "My point is, if God can provide for all of my needs, He will provide for St. Cecilia's. So, as I see it, you could approach the archbishop's decree to close St. Cecilia's in one of two ways."

"I'm all ears."

"You can see it as the end of the parish or the beginning of a new adventure."

"Adventure? I like the sound of that."

Bob wiped his hands on his apron. "Some might see this as an ending. But maybe God sees it as an opportunity to begin something new. My advice is to give it over completely to Him. Trust Him. He has a plan. Remember what you once told me? Trials are just God's way of furrowing the soil so saints and miracles can grow."

"I *do* give good advice, now don't I?" Father James laughed. "Too bad I have such a hard time using it in my own life."

Bob looked up and laughed, wiping cheese off his hands with a terry cloth towel. "Look at me! Giving sermons to a priest."

"Even priests need reminding once in a while. I've spent the entire day wondering what I was going to do. Rebuffing myself over how I had failed the parishioners. I seem to have forgotten God's role in this and His power to find solutions when we think none exist. Thank you, Bob." Father James suddenly felt ten pounds lighter in spirit.

George Benson clambered up from downstairs, the smell of fuel oil clinging to his clothes. "I wondered who Bob was talking to. What are you doing here?" he asked Father James. "Didn't know priests made house calls. Thought only Protestant clergymen did that."

"We go where we are needed," Father James said jovially. Even George Benson couldn't dampen his new spirit.

"Father's staying for dinner. You're welcome to stay, too, George," Bob said, sprinkling liberal amounts of Parmesan cheese over the pans of lasagna.

"Don't mind if I do." George watched Father James refill the kitchen sink with hot, sudsy water, and felt not the least bit inclined to help.

"Thanks, George. Lori went downstairs this morning to start a load of wash and saw the floor was covered with water."

George sank into an off-white cushioned chair in his grease-stained coveralls. "Just a leaky valve on the water heater. But I fixed it."

Bob balanced a pan of lasagna on his knees and rolled over to the stove. "Can't thank you enough for coming out in this weather."

"It's my job." George figured he'd let Bob think it was an inconvenience and that way nobody would expect him to get involved doing dishes.

"Give me the bill and I'll get Lori to write you out a check." Bob opened the oven door to a steady plume of smoke.

"I forgot my account book. I'll have to mail it to you."

Father James watched George's gruff reflection in the darkened window above the sink and smiled. George Benson might be one of the most opinionated, obstinate men he had ever met, but he was also one of the kindest. George would never send that bill. Just like he had never sent all the other bills for furnace repairs and maintenance checkups since Bob had taken ill.

The smoke detector went off with a deafening shriek. Elmo scrambled to his feet and began to howl. Sarah ran in from the living room with her hands covering her ears.

"Daddy, should I call 911?" she screamed above the din.

"No, no, it's all right," shouted Dorsetville's fire marshal. "There's no fire. Just smoke. Dirty oven, that's all."

George slid his chair across the kitchen floor, stood with dirty feet on the chair cushion, reached up for the alarm, took it down and pulled out the batteries.

The noise was just winding down when Lori walked in the back door laden with two heavy grocery bags. "Is there a fire?"

"Hi, honey." Bob was madly waving a dish towel, fanning the smoke out an opened window. "Nothing serious. Something spilled over in the oven, which made a little smoke."

"Hi, Mommy," Sarah said, still shouting. "Can we decorate the Easter tree tonight? Please, Mommy? Please?"

"Let Mommy get her coat off and rest for a minute," Bob said.

"But Daddy, Mommy said that we could put up the eggs when she got home. Didn't you, Mommy?" Sarah danced around the crowded kitchen.

"That's enough, Sarah," Bob warned. "Go into the living room, watch the rest of your program and I will call you when dinner is ready."

"But, Daddy!" She stood her ground.

"Go, I said!"

Sarah stamped out of the room, Elmo trailing close behind.

"Are the roads getting bad?" Father James asked, grabbing the grocery bags out of Lori's hands.

Lori unbuttoned her coat. "I really didn't notice." She threw her hat and muffler on the table, walked over to the oak hutch, opened the bottom doors and pulled out a bottle of Merlot. She poured herself a tall glass, then downed it in one quick swallow.

Bob looked on in complete bewilderment. They had known each other more than ten years and in all that time he had never once seen her touch a drop of liquor, a silent protest against the substance that had destroyed her family's lives.

"You all right?"

"I don't know." She poured herself another and ignored the phone as it began to ring.

George walked over and picked up the receiver. "Peterson residence. It's who? Oh, the hospital. Yep. Yeah. Yep. I got it. I'll tell them. Okay. Bye."

He hung up the phone. Well if that didn't beat all. He was just setting his taste buds around that pan of lasagna. After he delivered this message, those hopes would be dashed and lasagna was one of his favorite meals.

"That was Mercy Hospital," George said, grudgingly.

Lori carefully placed the wine glass on the kitchen counter. Her heart had begun to race.

"They said that they've found Bob a bone-marrow match. It seems they need you to come in tonight so they can get you ready to start the procedure tomorrow morning."

Lori screamed in joy, setting Elmo off, who charged in from the living room in a fit of barking. Sarah raced in on his heels.

Lori reached over and grabbed her husband, nearly tipping over the wheelchair.

"I can't believe it," he said, holding her tightly. "They've finally found a match."

Lori was sobbing so hard she barely could breathe.

Father James embraced the young couple, his tears mingling with theirs. "This is such wonderful news. The very best! All we needed was to trust God and have faith."

Lori looked up with a new brightness to her soul and whispered. "And a little hope."

Chapter 9

There was less than a month left until Easter, and Father James's list of matters needing attention before St. Cecilia's was to be closed had not grown any smaller. In an effort to try and catch up, he had taken to doing several things at one time. This morning, however, it was his undoing.

He had just dialed his best friend, Jeff Hayden, while taking a sip of steaming black coffee when his eyes fell on that weekend's church bulletin recently returned from the printer's. Under "Meetings" it read:

> *Thursday at 5 P.M., there will be a meeting of the Little Mothers' Club. All ladies wishing to be Little Mothers please meet with Father James in his study.*

Father James choked at the exact moment that Jeff answered his phone.

"Hello? Hello? Whoever this is, are you all right?" Jeff asked.

"Just a minute," Father James said, gasping for breath as he mopped up the front of his shirt where most of the explosion of coffee had landed.

"James? Is that you?" Jeff laughed. "You sound like you're about to die."

"From embarrassment, perhaps," he quipped. Father James's mind, which never worked properly without eight hours of sleep, was still muddled. He cleared his throat and tried to focus on why he had called. "Sorry. I've been up all night with a sick parishioner."

"Everything's all right, I hope."

"It appears so. His name is Bob Peterson and he's in the throes of one of the toughest fights of his life. Cancer. I'd appreciate it if you would keep him and his family in your prayers. He's beginning the procedure for a bone-marrow transplant this morning."

"Consider it done," Jeff replied, then added, "I hope you weren't calling to cancel next week's visit."

"God willing, I'll be there," Father James said with more enthusiasm than he felt.

This was the worst of all possible times for him to take time away from the parish, yet he and Jeff had planned this visit months ago—a visit that was to culminate in Jeff's engagement party. Jeff had asked Father James to be his best man, an honor the priest felt duty bound to perform. Still, he wished all of this could somehow be postponed until after St. Cecilia's closing.

"Great! I'm glad to hear it," Jeff said, then turned away to speak to someone in the room. "Sorry about that. I'm at work. Speaking of which, I've taken an entire week off. I figured we could spend some time walking down memory lane. Explore the city. Remember Mama Sophie's, the restaurant over by Canal Street?"

Father James started to salivate at its mention. Sweet-tasting calamari, deep fried with Sophie's secret cornmeal coating and served with linguine in clam sauce. His stomach rumbled, reminding him he hadn't eaten since yesterday afternoon.

"Do I remember it?" he said. "Are you kidding? The promise of a meal at Sophie's was the only thing that got me through that first year of science and plate tectonics." Father James had no head for things that could be measured or weighed.

"I was able to get us a couple of front row tickets for the Knicks game at the Garden," Jeff continued.

"I haven't been to a basketball game in . . ." Father James couldn't remember.

"The New York Public Library is having an exhibit on rare illuminated manuscripts that I thought you'd like to see and . . ."

"Wait a minute," Father James interjected. "I thought the purpose of my visit was to meet your fiancée, Allison, get fitted for a tux and talk about wedding plans? By the sound of this itinerary, I doubt we'll have time to do both."

"That, too," joked Jeff, whose voice grew soft at the mention of his future bride.

"I can't wait for you to meet my Allison," he crooned. "She's smart, talented. Runs her own business. She's drop-dead *gorgeous* and just a plain all-around great lady. You're going to love her."

"I've been looking forward to this for months."

"So, no excuses this time, then. You'll be here on Saturday?"

Guilt coursed through his veins. How many times had he been forced to cancel their plans? Twenty? Thirty? As a church pastor, Father James was always in the midst of some type of emergency. An unscheduled visit from the archbishop. The death of a parishioner. Not to mention the steady stream of marriages, baptisms and liturgical programs.

His schedule had grown even worse since coming to St. Cecilia's three years ago, where there seemed to be an emergency of epic proportions each and every week—leaky roofs, faulty electrical wiring, falling plaster. The list was endless.

But not this time, he resolved. Nothing was going to prevent him from sharing the week with his best friend.

"I'll be there. Scout's honor," Father James assured him. "Nothing short of the Lord's return can stop me, my friend. I'm eager to meet the woman who has the good sense to marry you. You've been a bachelor far too long."

"Look who's calling the kettle black."

"I'm already married . . . to the Church."

Jeff laughed. "Okay, you've got me there. So, what time do you think you'll arrive on Saturday?"

"Father Keene is taking over the morning Mass, so I can leave right after breakfast, say around six-thirty. There shouldn't be much traffic, so I should arrive around noon."

"Great! I'll plan a simple lunch, then we'll kick off our shoes and spend the afternoon catching up. How does that sound?"

"Sounds great. I honestly can't remember the last time I did absolutely nothing."

"Don't get used to it. Allison's expecting us for dinner at her place on Saturday night, then there's Sunday Mass at St. Timothy's. Monsignor Casio wants to see you. Says he misses your Tuesday night poker games."

It had been Father Casio, not monsignor, when he had attended St. Timothy's during college and it was the older priest who had helped Father James decide to enter the seminary.

"Then there's brunch with my parents afterward, hordes of old friends who have made me promise to tell them the moment you're in town, which pretty much fills up all of next week. And let's not forget the most important event of all—my engagement party next Friday night. In between all of that, we have to get you fitted for your tux. I don't suppose you own one, do you?"

"They're not exactly standard issue for the priesthood."

Jeff laughed. "I don't suppose they are. I'll make an appointment with my tailor for early in the week. Perhaps if I promise him a special dispensation from a priest friend, he might be able to get the alterations completed before you return to St. Cecilia's so you won't have to come back for a final fitting before the wedding."

Jeff's wedding was less than eight weeks away. St. Timothy's had been booked for the June fourteenth nuptials over a year ago, as had Tavern on the Green in Central Park, where the reception would follow. It was going to be a large and—if Father James knew the Haydens—very lavish affair. Jeff's father, Bradford Hayden, was a New York state supreme court judge, which meant that most of the state's and city's dignitaries would be in attendance. The governor and New York City mayor were both expected to attend.

"Sounds great. I'm counting the hours."

"You need directions?" Jeff teased.

"Very funny."

"It *has* been awhile since you've been to the big city."

"I think I can still remember the way."

"See you then. Oh, by the way, wear your collar. It will make it easier on all of my mother's matchmaking friends to know that you're already spoken for."

Father James hung up, his spirits greatly cheered. He missed Jeff. Why had he allowed other matters to take precedence over their friendship? Fifteen years in the confessional had taught him how common was the regret of allowing friendships to slip away and die. He resolved that in the future he'd spend more time with treasured friends.

The wind howled outside the kitchen. The snow had continued all night with blizzard force and the thermometer outside the window overlooking the kitchen sink read minus five degrees. He'd have to search for the wool-lined gloves Mrs. Norris had given him last Christmas. He had several parishioners plus the River Glen Nursing Home to visit today.

Dear Lord, he prayed, *please be with all of those who are without shelter and touch the hearts of those who have so much, to care for those who have so little.*

His stomach rumbled again and he glanced at the kitchen clock. Mrs. Norris should be arriving shortly to begin preparations for breakfast. In the meantime, he poured himself another cup of coffee and took a sip. He allowed the hot liquid to slip over his tongue and slide down his throat, bringing with it a comforting warmth like a flannel robe. He often prayed that when he arrived in heaven he would find the aroma of coffee wafting through its celestial halls.

He took another sip. When it came to visions of heaven, Father

James was a simple man. He wished for only two things: copies of his favorite, albeit obscure, Hal Borland books complete with the time to read them and mugs of dark, rich coffee.

As he savored his coffee, he watched the falling snow outside the kitchen window with as much fascination as he had as a child, never tiring of a winter storm's magical transformation of the New England landscape. It was as though Nature sent the snow to erase all evidence of man, his buildings and roads, leaving a blank canvas without blot or stain, forcing man to look out onto a new landscape and to ponder what he would do differently if he could begin again.

Father James's thoughts returned to Jeff. The two men had met in their first year at Columbia University and quickly became best friends and roommates. Both had come from strong Catholic families who emphasized duty to God through service to others. Father James had decided in his senior year to answer the call to the priesthood. Jeff had gone on to study law, later working as a city prosecutor. More than likely, Jeff would follow in his illustrious father's footsteps.

Father James swallowed the last of his coffee, thinking it was the worst possible time for him to be leaving St. Cecilia's. His parishioners needed him now more than ever. He felt as though he were abandoning them. Guilt flooded back in a tidal wave, which he tried to offset by remembering his recent conversation with Archbishop Simmons.

"You need this short holiday to help to replenish yourself," the archbishop had said. "St. Cecilia's closing and all that entails will take its toll. You have your parishioners to relocate, the physical closing of the church and rectory, placing Father Keene in a nursing home and the stress of Holy Week. Take the time off to provide some additional stamina to help you get through all of this."

The archbishop had arranged for a new priest, Father Dennis Osborne—only weeks out of the Boston seminary—to take over Father James's duties in his absence.

"Father Dennis is a little . . . er . . . exuberant, but he'll do fine. And there's always Father Keene to lend a hand if Father Dennis needs assistance," the archbishop had added.

Father James used the archbishop's words to assuage the guilt he felt over his defection, reasoning that he owed his friendship with Jeff as much attention as he did his parishioners. Besides, as Bob Peterson had so poignantly pointed out, there was nothing else Father James could do. Whatever was going to happen was already in God's most capable hands.

Father James threw caution to the wind and poured himself another cup of coffee, which he knew from experience would make his heart beat like a mouse's in a room filled with cats and his mind spin so fast that he would trip over ordinary words for the next twenty minutes.

He poured a half cup, then disengaged his better reasoning and filled the mug. He'd use the extra charge to work on the final report due to the archbishop within the next few weeks. It was a task he had been avoiding, but one that, if he could finish, would free him to better enjoy his time in Manhattan.

He began to feel the first tremors of caffeine, heeded the warning and dumped the rest of his coffee into the sink.

Father James had written only a paragraph when his mind wandered back to his impending trip and his excitement grew. He had almost forgotten how much he loved New York City. At times, Father James wondered where this love for Manhattan had originated. He had grown up on a farm in the middle of New England and had only visited the Big Apple once, on a field trip with his eighth-grade class. They had seen the United Nations and later had taken a ferry ride around the Statue of Liberty. He had never forgotten the charge of energy he felt that day. The very air seemed to crackle with excitement.

In his junior year in high school, as he sat filling in college application forms, Father James mentally circled Columbia University as his first choice and, to his great amazement, he was accepted. He would also have the great good fortune to have Jeff Hayden as his roommate.

Jeff was the sophisticated New Yorker, having grown up in the city, and James, the country boy all wide-eyed and full of wonder at the Big Apple, yet they had struck up an immediate friendship that had lasted for more than twenty years.

Father James was looking forward to going back.

Mrs. Norris walked in, snow covering her coat. "Good morning, Father James." In her hand she held two glass milk bottles left that morning in the milk box by the side door and whose paper caps had popped open as the cream at the top froze. She placed them on the kitchen table before removing her coat.

"Good morning, Mrs. Norris. How do the roads look?" Father James had barely made it home this morning at four A.M. Although the main roads from the hospital at Woodstock had been cleared and sanded, the secondary roads were slick as ice. Twice he had spun out of control as he tried to negotiate a corner. By the time he had finally made it to the rectory, every muscle ached from tension.

Wednesday was normally his day off, but he had decided to take over Father Keene's River Glen Nursing Home visit. The last thing Father James wanted was for the elderly priest to fall and break a hip.

Mrs. Norris lived two houses down from the rectory. "The sidewalks haven't been shoveled, but the roads all seem to have been plowed."

She struck a match and lit the flame under the tea kettle, then walked over to the cupboard and took down three cereal bowls.

"How does a bowl of hot oatmeal sound this morning, Father, with a little brown sugar and cream?"

Father James considered this. He really should watch his weight. All of his pants were too tight and his shirt seams were stretched to their very limits. "Sounds much too good to resist." He hadn't eaten dinner last night. A few extra calories at breakfast would only even things out.

Mrs. Norris measured oatmeal into a cast-iron pot. "Why don't you go up and see if Father wants some homemade biscuits this morning. Harriet Bedford sent over some of Father's favorite orange marmalade before she left on her trip. I know he's been dying to sample it."

A knock thundered against the kitchen door, making them both jump. Then a burst of cold air hastened the entrance of George Benson. "It's cold enough to freeze a man's eyeballs this morning," he said coming through the door and stamping his feet on the sisal mat. "Came to see if that furnace needed attention."

Father James smiled. It was more likely that he had come to see what Mrs. Norris was cooking for breakfast. He played along.

"Seems to be working just fine, George. But since you're here, why don't you stay for breakfast? I'm sure there is plenty of oatmeal and Mrs. Norris was about to make some biscuits so Father Keene and I could sample Harriet Bedford's orange marmalade."

George eyed Mrs. Norris like an anxious dog needing approval before stepping on the parlor rug. She looked up only briefly from flouring her pastry board. "You're welcome to stay, but you take off those wet boots before you walk across my clean kitchen floor. I don't want to have to go mopping up after you again."

"I need my boots on if I'm to take a look at the furnace," he sparred. "That dirt floor in the cellar is ice cold."

"Then take off your boots, walk across the kitchen floor in your socks, then put your boots back on when you get to the bottom of the stairs," she said, speaking as though to a petulant child.

George bent down and began unlacing his boots, mumbling heavily under his breath, "I don't see what the big deal is. It's just snow. Clean water. It's not like I'd be tracking in mud."

Mrs. Norris, whom Father Keene said could hear a feather fall to the floor, pointed the rolling pin in George's direction. "If you have something to say to me, George Benson, then say it out loud and clear."

"Nothing. Not a thing. I just want to check on the furnace before I wash my hands." George tramped across the linoleum floor, his big toe sticking out of a hole in his right sock.

"Don't you think you should see what's keeping Father Keene this morning?" Mrs. Norris asked Father James, taking a biscuit cutter and pressing a dozen perfectly shaped circles from the rolled pastry. "He usually has the tea kettle boiling before I get here. I hope he hasn't caught the flu from those Gallagher twins who were over here the other day."

"He just might have decided to sleep in this morning." Father James answered. "It certainly is a good day for it."

Still buoyed by thoughts of his upcoming trip, Father James bounced up the back staircase, taking it two steps at a time and knocked on Father Keene's door.

"Breakfast will be ready in a few minutes, Father Keene."

No answer. He knocked again.

"Father Keene, are you up?"

No answer. He felt the first flicker of concern.

"Father Keene?" He knocked again, then slowly opened the bedroom door.

Father Keene's bed had not been slept in. The pajamas and robe that Mrs. Norris always left at the end of the bed were still there, neatly folded, as were the full carafe of water and clean glass on his night table.

Where could he be? Had someone requested a priest and Father Keene been forced to go out into the storm? But surely, if that were the case, he would have left a note telling them where he'd gone. He searched the closet. Father Keene's kelly-green woolen coat was gone, as were his favorite woolen cap and the flannel-lined woolen mittens Mrs. Johnson had made him last Christmas. Apparently, Father Keene had gone out. But where?

Practicing what he often preached, Father James braced his mind against thoughts of despair and focused on a logical reason that might explain Father Keene's absence. Problem was, he couldn't think of any. He headed back downstairs.

"Mrs. Norris, did Father Keene mention having to visit with a parishioner last night?" he asked as he reached the bottom stair.

"No." Mrs. Norris stood in front of the oven door holding the charred remains of Father Keene's supper. "If he did go out, he forgot to turn off the stove. It's been on all night. Lucky it didn't start a fire." She placed the indiscernible mass on top of the range.

"He's not upstairs in his room and it looks as though he didn't sleep here last night. Where could he have gone? Do you know if any messages came in requesting a priest?"

Wiping her hands on her apron, she walked to the desk and flipped through the message pad. "No, there aren't any messages and Father always leaves a note when he's called away. There aren't any messages on the answering machine, either." Her voice began to quiver.

Father James moved like a linebacker to offset her fears. "I'm certain that there was an emergency and he didn't have the time to stop and write us a note. He'll probably call in any minute now and tell us that he's on his way home."

He could see that his words had had absolutely no consoling effect.

The cellar door banged open and George came trudging through. "Furnace is right as rain. Got a good fire going and the pressure is right on target. Should keep your parishioners nice and toasty this morning."

He untied his shoes and carefully placed them on the mat beside the kitchen door. "What's the matter with you two?" he asked en route to the sink to wash his hands. "You burn the toast this morning, Mrs. Norris?" He seemed oblivious to the fact that no one was laughing.

"Father Keene is missing," Mrs. Norris answered quietly.

"Now, Mrs. Norris, he's not *missing*," Father James said, trying to remain calm. "He's just . . . gone out and we don't know *exactly* where he's gone."

"I saw him late yesterday afternoon. Right before the storm hit," George said, lathering his hands under the kitchen faucet. "He was walking down Bates Rock Road. I stopped the van and asked if he wanted a ride back into town, but he said he was enjoying the walk. Said he was about to start back into town, so I drove away."

"You drove away!" Mrs. Norris cried.

"He said he didn't want a ride."

"Oh, sweet Jesus." Mrs. Norris reached into her dress pocket for her rosary. "If he was out in this storm, he couldn't possibly have survived. The weatherman said it was down to minus seven degrees at five A.M. this morning." Mrs. Norris's worry chugged ahead under a full head of steam. "He's probably lying on the forest floor. Cold, near death. Oh, poor Father Keene. What are we going to do?" she wailed, covering her face with her apron.

"Don't panic," Father James said, trying not to panic himself as he reached for the phone. "It's possible he returned here after his walk and was called out again and simply forgot to leave us a note. But even so, I think we should call Sheriff Bromley."

"Sheriff Bromley? Dear God, have mercy," she cried, fingering the first decade of her rosary. "Hail Mary full of grace, the Lord be with you, Blessed art thou amongst women and blessed is . . ."

"Just as a precaution," Father said calmly.

He dialed Sheriff Bromley's home number. The sheriff answered on the first ring.

"Bromley, here."

"Hello, Al. This is Father James at St. Cecilia's. We may have," he lowered his voice, "a problem."

"What kind of problem?"

"Father Keene is missing."

"What makes you think he's missing?"

Father James told the sheriff what they had discovered.

"Now, it's possible that he's been called to minister to one of our parishioners," he said, willing his words to be true.

"Have you called any of them?"

"No, not yet. You see, Father Keene usually leaves us a note and, well, there isn't any."

"I see."

Mrs. Norris's composure crumpled further as he continued. "George Benson's here and he said he saw Father Keene walking along Bates Rock Road right before the storm hit. We're worried that he might still be out there."

"I'll be right over," the sheriff said, then added, "don't buy any trouble until we have all the facts. Meanwhile, start making some phone calls and see if he can be accounted for."

"Thanks, Al. I appreciate your help."

The sheriff hung up without a good-bye.

"Al said he'd be right over."

"No need to worry," George said, sensing it was his job to lighten things up. "He's a tough old Irishman. He'll be okay. Like you said, he's probably with some parishioner." Looking around and quickly despairing about breakfast being served anytime soon, he offered to help. "Want me to pour some orange juice for breakfast?"

"Breakfast!" Mrs. Norris screamed as though all of this was entirely George Benson's fault for not forcing Father Keene to accept a ride.

"Who can think about breakfast at a time like this? Poor saintly Father Keene out there somewhere in this storm." And to emphasize her point, she stalked to the stove, turned off the jets under the oatmeal and the tea kettle and put the tray of uncooked biscuits in the refrigerator.

George's visions of warm bowls of oatmeal laced with heavy cream, hot buttermilk biscuits with Harriet Bedford's famous orange marmalade and generous mugs of coffee vanished with the velocity of the flick of a television remote.

Wiping his wet hands on his pants legs, he stormed across the cold linoleum floor, crashed heavily onto a small stool and stuffed his heavy wool-stockinged feet into his work boots.

He hoped that the Fergusons, who lived across town—and who had most fortuitously left a message on his answering machine this morning requesting repair of a faulty pilot light—hadn't yet finished breakfast. They were Baptists and, as far as George was concerned, a sight more dependable for a decent meal than these Catholics.

Chapter 10

Sheriff Bromley threw his Chevy Blazer into four-wheel drive to the strains of Patsy Cline's "Crazy" and headed down Dorsetville's unplowed back roads toward where George Benson had reported seeing Father Keene last.

The snow was falling as fast as the temperature with a current reading of minus 5 degrees and a wind chill factor of 53 below zero. It was a real nor'easter, he thought, something this part of New England hadn't experienced in over twenty years, a fact that greatly concerned him. He feared some citizens would mistake it for just another winter snowstorm, like the dozens they had experienced before. Problem was, they would be wrong. And if they weren't *really* careful, some, like Father Keene, could be dead wrong.

The back end of the Blazer fishtailed on a patch of black ice. The sheriff eased off the gas. Overconfidence, even with four-wheel drive, had landed many a winter driver in deep snow. He inched slightly closer to the steering wheel as he cautiously navigated a sharp bend in the road. This time the Blazer held its ground. He leaned down, turned off the CD player and turned on the radio, catching the tail end of the latest weather report.

Well, folks, this looks like a real nor'easter. We've got seventy-five-mile-per-hour winds reported to the north of us, heavy snows and record-setting low temperatures. Manchester reports minus seven degrees with a wind-chill factor—now are you ready for this?—a wind-chill factor, folks, of minus ninety-six degrees! We haven't experienced temperatures like these since the mid-1800s.

The governor has ordered the schools and town offices closed, advising that people stay off the roads unless absolutely necessary. Health officials are urging people to stay inside. With temperatures this low, anyone caught outside for more than ten or fifteen minutes could easily die. So unless you absolutely have to be someplace, stay at home. Make some hot cocoa, plug in a video or grab a good book; this storm is going to be with us for a while.

It will take the town crews a couple of days to dig their way out of this one, the sheriff thought as he drove under the state overpass. Plow trucks could be heard overhead. Coming out from under the protective structure, the Blazer started to skid slightly to the right. Bromley took his foot off the gas and slowly turned the steering wheel into the skid, gave it some leeway, then brought it back onto the road. He wouldn't be able to stay out here much longer.

The plowed roads were quickly growing impassable again, which worried the sheriff. Joey White, who lived out this way, had emphysema. Twice last summer, Joey had needed emergency services. The sheriff had just dropped off a handheld radio in case the phone lines went out.

God, I hate the idea of getting old, he thought, remembering the sight of Joey gasping for air as he clutched his chest with a bony hand. Looking down at Joey's suffering face, near blue from lack of oxygen as the paramedics strapped him to a gurney, reminded the sheriff of the stories his old man used to tell about him and Joey White beating the pants off the boys at St. Cecilia's. Looking down at him then, it was hard to believe that Joey White was ever young or strong.

Thank goodness Bob Peterson was still in Mercy Hospital. Harry had filled him in when he'd stopped at the restaurant this morning for a cup of coffee.

"Lori called around eight-thirty to say that the doctors had begun turning off Bob's immune system." Harry had poured the sheriff's coffee into a mug that read WORLD'S GREATEST SISTER. "They'll do the bone-marrow transplant in a couple of days, then he'll be in isolation for the next four weeks," Harry had said, waving aside the sheriff's dollar. "It's on the house."

"Tell Lori that my wife and I will babysit for little Sarah whenever she needs," the sheriff said, slipping off the stool.

"You and half the town," Harry laughed.

Another patch of ice. He slowed down and barked into his two-way radio at the town dispatcher, "Betty? Get those town crews up here. Where're Joe and Pete? They should have plowed this road hours ago."

"Joe's got the flu and Pete says his car won't start," Betty Olsen, who had been the town's dispatcher for twenty-two years, answered.

"You call them back and tell them *I* said I don't care how sick they are or if they have to *walk* to the town garage. I want these roads cleared pronto!"

Even though Sheriff Bromley had no jurisdiction over the highway department, Betty never argued protocol with him. She simply did what she was told and let the highway department head duke it out with Bromley later.

"I'll call them right away."

"Tell them I want the main roads to Joey White's place cleared and some sand up here on the north edge of town by the Metcalfs'. Anyone coming through this underpass by Bucks Hill Road is going to lose it."

"Sure thing," Betty replied, quickly adding, "Sheriff, Father James just phoned. He said he's called everyone in the parish, and no one's seen Father Keene."

Bromley swore. "Ring Tom Chute over at the radio station. Ask him to make an announcement about Father Keene's disappearance. Maybe one of his listeners has seen him."

Truth was, however, Bromley didn't hold out much hope of Father Keene's surviving if he'd been caught in this storm. Father Keene had taken a walk in the most isolated part of the township—only barren farmland and ramshackle farmhouses with gaping windows and empty door frames, long abandoned to the elements. Even if Father Keene had made it to one of those, they would offer no protection against the subzero temperatures.

Bromley crossed the one-lane bridge over Bee Brook and began the sharp incline toward the Metcalfs' house where Ben lived with his son and his family. Halfway up the mountain, Bromley spied a car by the side of the road hidden under a foot of snow. A black funnel of smoke rose out of the tail pipe.

"Damn fools." Bromley swore so loudly that Betty Olsen at the other end turned down the volume. He switched on his flashing lights, pulled alongside and wrapped his favorite blue scarf his wife had knitted across his nose and mouth before stepping out into the storm. The wind was driving so hard that it plastered the scarf across his face like a piece of shrink wrap. The sheriff leaned heavily into the wind and headed toward the car, thinking that some people have no common sense. Snow rolled over the top of his boots, falling into the lining that would turn to ice water later. It only increased his bad mood.

Using his elbow, he cleared snow away from the driver's window and peered inside. A thin-faced boy of about twenty with stringy black hair, a few dark chin hairs and thick black glasses looked back. Bromley rapped on the glass, hollering over the wind at the "damn fool idiot" inside the car. The boy rolled down the window. A girl of about thirteen or fourteen was seated next to him and tightly wrapped in an old blanket that hid most of her face.

"You trying to kill yourself?" Neither the wind nor the scarf covering his mouth could muffle the sheriff's threatening rottweiler growl to the boy.

"Ah, no, er . . . no, sir," the young man stammered, teeth chattering. The outside cold air had just siphoned off the small amount of heat inside.

"Are you the only fool on the planet who doesn't know that if you run a car with the windows closed, not to mention the tail pipe covered in snow, that the car fills with carbon monoxide?"

"I didn't know."

"Yeah, well you should. You've got a university parking sticker here. Doesn't that college teach you anything of use? You a student?"

"Yes, it does, sir. Yes, I am, sir."

"What year?"

"Sophomore."

"Sophomore?" Bromley spit on the ground. It froze into an ice crystal in midair. "You're a *sophomore in college* and you *never* learned that people can die from monoxide poisoning when they run a car with the windows tightly shut?"

"No, sir," the youth said. "I guess I missed that class."

"You missed that class," Bromley repeated. Was this kid being a smart mouth or was he just plain stupid? He decided it was the latter, which only emphasized what he already knew: Education in this country was going to the dogs. College kids these days didn't have enough sense to look both ways before crossing the interstate.

"Let me see your license and registration," he ordered. "And *turn off the engine!*"

Bromley opened the door and pulled him out. The kid fumbled around in his back pocket for a wallet; it was held together with rubber bands. It took him several more seconds as he nervously searched for his driver's license. It was stuck to the back of his Blockbuster card. He handed both over to the sheriff, who swore, then pulled them apart, sticking the Blockbuster card in his coat pocket. The sheriff studied the license closely.

"You're Dominic Costello and you live at Thirty-five West Ridge Road in Uniondale. That correct?"

"Yes, sir."

Bromley studied the picture against the shivering boy.

"I've grown a goatee since that was taken," Dominic offered weakly.

"Let's just say you've tried," Bromley quipped. "And the girl in the car? Who is she?"

"She's my sister, Stephanie."

"Your sister, hey? And what in blue blazes are you two doing out in this storm? Didn't you hear the warnings on the radio?"

"Ah, no, sir. My radio's broken."

A burst of wind caught Dominic's cap and hurled it into the road. He looked imploringly at Bromley, his oversized ears turning an angry red.

"Go on. Go get it." The sheriff's feet had just turned into ice blocks.

Dominic slipped and fell several times grabbing for his cap. It finally snagged on a low bush. He walked back toward the sheriff, who was looking none too happy standing covered in snow.

"There's no way I can pull you out of that ditch with my Chevy," Bromley said, inspecting the kid's car. "You'll have to wait until the town crews plow and sand. Then we'll call a tow truck."

Bromley bent into the front seat of the car. "Gather up your things, young lady. You're going to have to come with me."

The girl reached into the backseat, retrieving a large canvas tote; she slid over to the driver's side and out the door without uttering a word.

"You two get into the Blazer."

Dominic and his sister hunched down into the wind, scurrying into the backseat. A metal partition separated them from the front of the SUV and there were no handles on the inside of the back doors.

Climbing in, the sheriff knocked the ice off his boots against the running board, then swung his feet into the cab and closed the door. He pulled his scarf off and examined his face in the rearview mirror, happy to note there was no sign of frostbite.

"You two warm enough back there?" He turned on the heater fan to high.

"Yes, sir."

"Hey, kid," he said to the boy, "there's an ice scraper underneath your seat." All the windows were covered with snow and he wasn't about to go back outside. Bromley released the back door locks. "Hop out and clear off the windows."

Dominic jumped out and quickly began to clear off the snow. The sheriff watched the pencil-thin youth having difficulty standing erect in the blizzardlike wind. He wondered if he shouldn't have first anchored the kid to the car. Somehow, Dominic maintained his balance, making quick work of the snow, then hopped back inside. Bromley could hear his teeth chattering from the front seat.

He put the Blazer in drive. "Where were you two headed?"

"Matthew Metcalf's," the boy answered; his sister was again hidden beneath the blanket.

"You a relative?"

"No. Just a friend."

"Friend? Aren't you a bit old to have a sixteen-year-old as a friend?"

"We met last year at computer camp at the college."

Bromley looked sharply at him in the rearview mirror. "Computers, eh? You wouldn't have taught him how to access privileged information in our school system's computer, now, would you?"

"No, sir," Dominic insisted, his face turning ashen.

"Good," Bromley said, concentrating again on the road. "You want me to drop you off at the Metcalfs' or do you want to come back into town with me?"

"If it wouldn't be any trouble, sir, we'd like to go to the Metcalfs'," Dominic said.

"Far less trouble than getting a county mortician to come up here and place the two of you in body bags. Which, by the way, is exactly what would have happened if I hadn't come along."

The backseat remained quiet.

Bromley reached for the radio. "Betty," he shouted, loud enough to be heard without it.

"Yes, Sheriff."

"I've got a twenty-year-old Dominic Costello and his sister, Stephanie, in my car. Rescued them from the side of the road. They live at

Thirty-five West Ridge Road in Uniondale. Give their folks a call and tell them they're all right and that I'm dropping them off at Matthew Metcalf's place."

"Right, Sheriff."

"Any new developments with Father Keene's disappearance?"

"No, sir. Deputy Hill is contacting all the downtown businesses to see if anyone's seen him. Harry from the Country Kettle said Father was in earlier in the day for a cup of coffee and some pie, but left around one-thirty before the storm started up."

"Tell Hill to meet me at the station when he's finished. I think it might be time to call in the state troopers."

The Blazer's wheels found purchase in the snow and steadily made its way up the mountain to the Metcalfs' place. In less than twenty minutes, Bromley had pulled up safely by the back door.

"All right, you two. We're here." He noticed Julie Metcalf in the house, standing in front of the kitchen sink. He waved and she waved back. "You two stay here until this storm is over. You got that?"

"Yes, sir. Thanks." Dominic and his sister tore out of the Blazer, slipping and sliding their way toward the side door.

As an afterthought, Bromley rolled down the window and yelled out into the storm, "Either of you see an elderly man walking as you drove along the back roads?"

"No," they answered in unison.

"All right. Go inside," he said, rolling up the window as snow rushed in, depositing in his lap. He brushed it aside.

"Betty," he said, ejecting the Patsy Cline CD and inserting Conway Twitty, "tell Deputy Hill that I'm on my way back into town and that I've decided not to wait. Have him alert the state police now. Tell them we have an emergency situation and we need their assistance."

"Right away, Sheriff."

"And call Father James. We'll need a command post and the town hall's too crowded. Tell him that we'd like to set it up in the church's basement. Oh, and have him tell Margaret Norris to set up a couple of those large coffee urns, the ones they use at church suppers. It's going to be a long haul."

"Right away, Sheriff."

He turned the volume up on the CD player as he began the long, slippery descent into town to the strains of Conway singing, "You've Never Been This Far Before."

Chapter 11

The travel center, wedged like a piece of cheese in Woodstock's business district hub, was filled with an assortment of people in various stages of indecision as they awaited the arrival of several Trailway buses, all long overdue.

The buses were trapped in a fifty-mile backup along the interstate, just outside of Pittsfield, the result of an overconfident Jeep driver who lost it on a patch of ice, causing a forty-car pileup. It was going to be a long wait for the relatives and friends, many of whom had begun to wonder if they should risk the trek back home along roads still slick with ice and snow or hunker down and wait it out.

Most of Woodstock's stores remained closed, waiting for side streets and sidewalks to be cleared, so there was little to distract those inside. Some napped, reread yesterday's newspapers, and feasted on Cheez Puffs, barbecue potato chips, Milky Ways, Mounds bars and tepid coffee from vending machines lined in a row by the restrooms. The hot-chocolate dispenser, which had run dry—much to the chagrin of several rumpled youths—appropriated all manner of coins and crisp dollar bills with no intention of delivery. Someone had attached a handwritten note, IT'S OUT OF ORDER AND YOU'RE OUT OF LUCK.

Those waiting had divided into two groups like metal shards polarized by some invisible magnet. One group in sweatpants and Kmart-issued clothing was seated close to the reception desk as they waited for the Manchester bus. This was the talkative group, sharing gossip, recipes and local politics. The other half, awaiting the arrival of the Manhattan bus, sat in stoic silence, occasionally peering with impatient glares over old copies of the *Wall Street Journal* or *Forbes* magazine.

The only employee of the Woodstock Travel Center, a short, stocky, middle-aged woman with the fashion sense of a fifteen-year-old, seemed unconcerned by the delays or the looks of impatience directed her way. She was more absorbed in her copy of *Soap Opera Digest*, posting a two-inch, red-lacquered fingernail, so as not to lose her place whenever someone asked when the buses would arrive.

"How would I know?" she would say, then return to her reading.

As the morning waned, the first group formed an easy alliance as strangers will when, by fate, they find themselves part of an unexpected event. Lounging on blue plastic chairs, legs crossed to reveal a myriad of winter footwear and fanciful socks, they shared stories of similar storms and the havoc they had wrought—like when the governor closed the state in 1978 after a three-day blizzard, traffic pileups on I-91, cases of frostbite, frozen pipes, stalled cars, dead batteries, the best and worst of all-weather snow tires, hot toddies and cold remedies.

The other group, congealed with annoyance, sat in what they perceived to be New England fashionably correct L. L. Bean outfits, peering in stony silence through Eddie Bauer tortoiseshell glasses, interested only in reestablishing old routines after three days of blizzard conditions. The arrival of the Saturday, eight A.M. Manhattan bus was a firmly entrenched part of that routine. Several times a week, this bus brought all manner of supplies and hired help that most Woodstockians—the majority of whom were transported New Yorkers—seemed incapable of living without. Three days of impassable roads was one thing. Three days without au pairs, cooks and copies of the *New York Times* was quite another.

Sam Rosenberg arrived at seven forty-five and quickly settled into the chair closest to the door. Beside him sat a Stew Leonard shopping bag—gotten on his last trip through Danbury—that contained a Thermos of hot coffee and two buttered cranberry muffins. Sam had stopped at Harry's en route with his hopes set on Lori's famous coffee cake, Harriet's favorite. But Harry said Lori was still at the hospital with Bob.

Bob's bone-marrow transplant had gone smoothly, with no signs of rejection. If all continued to go well, he would be home in a month. Sam planned to stop at the hospital for a short visit if Harriet wasn't too tired from her trip. Bob was in isolation and they would have to visit through a glass partition, yet Sam felt just seeing their smiling faces would give Bob a lift.

It was nearing ten-thirty and Sam had already read the *Bargain News* twice, making a mental note to pull the rusted push mower out of the back shed and clean it up. Apparently it was now considered a "collectible" and worth five hundred dollars.

After another quick trip to the men's room, Sam took a walk along the small portion of Main Street that had just been shoveled. Within twenty minutes, both the cold and boredom forced him back inside the travel center. He reclaimed his seat, wishing he had remembered his book—David McCullough's *Mornings on Horseback*, the story of one of Sam's heroes, Teddy Roosevelt—which was still on the kitchen table.

At times his faulty memory really irked him and it seemed that it grew worse with each passing year. Only yesterday, he had driven to Grand Union twice for margarine, forgetting it both times. He had recently started writing himself notes. Problem was, he forgot those, too.

Sam wondered if there was any news about Father Keene, who had been missing since Wednesday afternoon. Thinking he might give St. Cecilia's rectory a call for an update, he reached in his pants pocket and brought out a fistful of change. He counted out seventy-five cents, then noticed the long line at the pay phone and decided to wait.

It had been a few tense days as Sam, Timothy, Ben and Matthew had sat vigil in the basement of St. Cecilia's while state search parties combed the countryside. The only break in the monotony had come on

Thursday morning when Sheriff Bromley had pressed Ethel Johnson's golden retriever into service. The state's canine search and rescue unit was held up on another call in the western corner of the state.

"Ethel, didn't your husband train Honey to track?" Sheriff Bromley asked as he sipped coffee.

"Why, yes, Sheriff. How kind of you to remember." Ethel bent down and petted her beloved retriever. "She was trained to track small game—rabbits, possums. Henry said she was the best tracker he'd ever trained."

"More coffee, Sheriff?" Mrs. Norris asked.

Father James, who had just gotten off the phone with the local radio station, joined them. "Any news?"

"Nothing yet," the sheriff replied. "Thanks, Mrs. Norris." Turning back to Ethel, he asked, "Do you think she'd be any help in tracking Father Keene?"

Ethel Johnson's eyes sparkled. Imagine the sheriff asking if her Honey might be of use in the rescue effort! "Oh, I think she'd be a tremendous help! Wouldn't you, girl?"

The twelve-year-old retriever lying by the side of her chair raised her head questioningly and began to thump her tail.

Deputy Frank Hill, who stood next to the sheriff trying to appear less expendable than he felt, gave a wry smirk, turned away and mumbled under his breath, "That dog is ancient and about as useful as a pair of tennis shoes in a snowstorm."

One of Sheriff Bromley's eyebrows arched, a warning quickly heeded by the more experienced of his men. His new deputy, impervious to such signals, continued to enjoy his own cleverness. "I bet that dog's eyesight is so bad that she has trouble just finding her way home," he mumbled further.

"Excuse me for just a moment, Ethel, Father James," Bromley said politely. He grabbed Hill's elbow and towed him, like a dysfunctional piece of equipment, toward the other side of the room and out through the emergency exit.

Deputy Hill assumed that the sheriff wanted to speak to him privately on a police matter of great importance and offered no resistance. Bromley stopped just outside the back door. Hill struck a relaxed (but what he perceived as a professional) pose, hitching his thumbs into the belt of his service revolver like he had seen cops do on crime shows, and waited.

"Something come in?" he asked with a swagger.

Bromley looked at him and shook his head. What had possessed him to hire this clown? "What the devil were you mumbling about in there?"

"Huh?"

"I heard your smart aleck remarks."

"I . . . er . . . I just thought that . . ." Hill's hands slid off his belt into his pants pockets.

"Hill, did I ask you to *think*?"

"Er . . . no, sir . . ."

"Did I *ask* your opinion?"

"No, sir."

"Do you know how long I've been sheriff in this town?"

"Thirty-five years, sir."

"Thirty-five years. That's right. And do you think that in my thirty-five years of sheriffing, I might just know a tad more about what goes on around this town than you do?

"Yes . . . er . . . yes, sir." Hill felt a twitch develop above his left eye.

"Did you know that Henry Johnson was one of the best hunters in this area?"

"No, sir."

"And did you know that people came from all around to have him train their dogs?"

"No, sir."

"It's been awhile since Henry died and maybe that dog has forgotten most of what she's been trained to do. But, then again, she just *might* discover something that could be useful while we wait for the state's canine unit to arrive. And since time is of the essence, don't you think that's a rather good plan?"

"Yes. It's a . . . good . . . great . . ."

"In the future, Hill, I want you to keep your opinions to yourself because, you see, those opinions are about as useless as you are. It's experience, not opinions, that count in law enforcement and as far as I can see, you're running on empty in that department."

The sheriff tromped back through the heavy metal door, leaving Hill open-mouthed and wondering how he had managed to land on the other side of Sheriff Bromley's good temper. Possessed of a Teflon personality, however, Hill spent less than a minute pondering this quandary. *The sheriff is under a lot of pressure and he probably didn't mean anything personal,* he thought. *Pressure. That was it.* Good thing the sheriff had him to blow off some of that steam. Feeling better now, Hill hitched up his pants and walked back inside where he was needed.

"Anyone interested in helping out with the search?" Bromley asked those gathered around Ethel Johnson's table.

"You thinking of using Honey?" Father James asked. The dog opened an eye at the sound of her name.

"I was thinking along those lines. That is, if it's all right with Ethel here."

Like a mother whose child has been chosen to star in the school play, Ethel beamed with pride. "Of course, Sheriff. Honey would be happy to help."

"Every minute counts in weather conditions like this, and Honey might give us the edge we need," said the sheriff. "The state's canine unit won't be here for quite a while yet." Looking around the table he added, "I'll need some of you to volunteer. Someone to drive. Another to act as a handler. No, not you, Ethel," he said, as she rose from her chair. "That hip of yours couldn't stand another break." She reluctantly sat down.

"I'd be willing to go," Father James offered.

"I think it would be better if you stayed here," he said. "I was hoping that maybe Timothy, Sam and Matthew might help. I know Sam delivers those meals-on-wheels. How's your car in the snow? I don't need any more trouble than what I've got."

"I just put those Sears all-weather tires on. So far, so good," Sam said, already slipping into his fur-lined coat. Timothy, Matthew and Ben were buttoning up as well.

Bromley thought a minute. "All right. Just stay off the back roads and if the search looks as though it's headed that way, give me a call and I'll send some of my men."

He handed Sam a two-way radio. "You know how to work one of these things?"

Sam looked at it as though it were a Rubik's Cube. "No."

"I do." Matthew grabbed the radio out of Sam's hand and turned it on. "Testing, testing, one-two-three."

The sheriff frowned. "Yeah, it figures *you'd* know how."

Matthew stepped back behind Father James.

"I don't know if this is a good idea," Father James said. "These men are . . ." he faltered for a word that would not offend them but would convey his concerns for both their age and their health.

"Old fogies," Timothy offered.

"That's not what I was about to say." He tried to rephrase his concerns. "It's awfully cold and icy out there. One fall and you'd be in the hospital for weeks."

"It's nice of you to worry, but we'll be all right. We have Matthew to do the fetching. We'll keep inside the car where it's warm."

"They'll be all right," Sheriff Bromley said. "They've got the radio if they need any help."

Like players taken off the bench, a current of excitement charged through the old men. They no longer felt like useless appendages. Like their younger virile counterparts, their services, too, were now needed.

Mrs. Norris, who had been sent in search of a piece of Father Keene's clothing, now returned with a pair of his dirty socks wrapped in a Grand Union plastic bag, feeling they were of too personal a nature to be displayed in public. She handed the bag discreetly to Ethel.

Ethel thrust her hand inside the bag. "Want to go tracking, girl?"

The question triggered an immediate reaction in the golden re-triever, who metamorphosed in a flash from a sleeping old dog to a frisky pup. Honey scrambled to her feet; her nails clicking, trying to find purchase on the linoleum floor; her eyes filled with light; her tail thumped hard against the table leg. She gave a sharp bark.

Ethel patted her head. "That's a good girl. You still remember everything Henry taught you, now haven't you girl?"

Much to Mrs. Norris's chagrin, Ethel withdrew Father Keene's socks and dangled them in front of Honey's nose. "Take a good sniff, girl." Mrs. Norris demurely turned away.

The dog nudged the socks with her nose, then waited expectantly for further instructions. The group of men watched this exchange in quiet fascination.

"Good girl, good girl." Ethel patted Honey on the head. Normally, the retriever would have pulled back her ears and begun to wag her tail at this sign of affection. Instead, she sat as still as a marble statue waiting for the next portion of the game.

"I want you to go with Matthew, here . . ." Ethel continued.

Matthew stepped out from behind Father James and stroked the dog's fur. "You remember me, don't you girl?"

The dog looked up at Matthew to register who he was, then turned back to her mistress.

"He's going to take you in Sam's car . . ."

The tip of her tail twitched slightly at the mention of the word *car*.

". . . to the place where Father Keene was last seen. Then I want you to pick up Father's scent and show Matthew where he's gone. All right, girl?"

Honey tilted her head to the side, as if in question.

Ethel puzzled for a moment, then laughed, "Oh, dear. No wonder you're looking at me so confused. I've forgotten to give you the proper command. *Fetch*, Honey. *Fetch.*"

That was the word she had been waiting for. Honey barked several times, jumped up and ran back and forth to the basement door as if to say, "Follow me!"

"Well, she *seems* to know what you're talking about," Deputy Hill said.

Bromley glared at him. "Don't you need to be someplace *else*?"

"Where's that?" Hill asked hopefully. Maybe the sheriff wanted him to set up road blocks, or act as the department's spokesperson for the media.

"Go ask the men outside if they want any coffee."

"Sure, thing, Chief," Hill said, his shoulders slumped in disappointment.

"Don't call me *chief*," Bromley yelled after him as he watched the older men march out with Honey happily prancing alongside Matthew. The chances of their finding Father Keene was a long shot. But at present, he'd take any odds he could get.

The older men piled into the 1973 Plymouth Duster, with the Sears all-weather tires, while Matthew took a scraper to the windows. Honey, having played this game many times, took her assigned seat in the front by the driver. Timothy sat in the passenger side. Ben and Matthew climbed into the back.

The town crews had plowed and sanded most of the night, making the streets passable, but still hazardous. Sam was an experienced driver in these types of road conditions, having delivered meals to Dorsetville's elderly shut-ins for over fifteen years. He carefully turned the Plymouth off Main Street and headed toward the outlying countryside.

With four people and a hundred-pound dog, the car windows completely fogged up before they had driven out of town. Sam switched on the defroster and within minutes created two distinct temperature zones. The front seats sweltered with near tropic temperatures as hot, molten air pumped against the windshield while the back shivered under an arctic freeze.

Normally, it was a twenty-minute ride to where Bates Rock Road and Route 172 intersected, where George Benson had last seen Father Keene. But with the steadily falling snow and patches of black ice, it was an hour before they arrived at the turnoff.

"Here it is." Sam turned the wheel.

"Wait," Timothy warned, "Don't turn in. See there? A tree's come down and taken some electrical wires with it."

Sam stopped and leaned over the steering wheel.

"Any way we can go around it?" Ben asked from the backseat.

"No, the road is completely blocked," Timothy said.

"Anyone got any ideas?" Sam asked.

"We could go around to the other side of town," Ben suggested, "past the interstate, then circle around Harriet Bedford's nursery and come in by way of the north side of Bates Rock Road."

"I don't know," Timothy said, looking up at the sky through the windshield. "That's on the far side of town. What if the roads haven't been plowed? And the weather looks like it's going to turn mean again. I don't want to get stuck up there. You know how the winds rip through that part of town."

"I say we give it a try," Sam said, putting the gear shift in drive. "If it looks like it's going to be hazardous, we'll turn around and come back."

Timothy mumbled more warnings, but Sam ignored him as he made a three-point turn and headed in the new direction.

"Roll down a window, will you, Tim," Ben said, settling back against the seat. "That dog's breath would kill a horse."

Sam and Timothy opened their windows a crack, which further lowered the backseat temperature. Ben and Matthew huddled closer and said nothing.

Except for the extra moisture, the men had almost forgotten that Honey was in the car. She moved only occasionally, to lift her nose into the air and sniff, sorting through the hundreds of scents blowing in through the partially open windows, matching them against the one she had been told to track. But all that changed the instant they drew near to Harriet Bedford's nursery. Suddenly Honey inched forward and placed her front paw on the dashboard.

"You think that means anything?" Timothy asked.

"Maybe she sees something," Ben mused.

"What's to see?" Sam said, wiping the moisture from his side window with his sleeve. "There's nothing out there."

"You think Father Keene's been by here?" Timothy asked.

"That's not possible," Ben offered from the backseat. "George saw him on Bates Rock Road, a good seven miles from here. Even in good weather, Father Keene could never have made the walk."

Matthew unbuckled his seat belt and leaned over the front seat. "What is it, girl? Something out there?"

In response, Honey began to bark.

"What's she barking at?" Sam asked, trying to keep his attention on the curve up ahead.

Honey barked louder and more insistently.

Sam's eyes were glued to the road. "See if you can get her to stop that racket."

"Maybe she smells the old rabbit hutches at Harriet's place," Ben offered. "Her son Peter used to raise rabbits for the 4-H Club. Remember, Tim?"

"Yeah. He won a couple of blue ribbons at the Goshen Fair."

"You sure Father Keene hasn't been around here?" Matthew shouted above Honey's repeated barks.

"No. That's impossible, " Timothy said.

Sam had just started past Harriet's driveway when Honey seemed to explode, leaping from Timothy's lap to Sam's.

"Get her off!" Sam yelled, panicking. "I can't see the road."

Timothy grabbed Honey's collar and yanked but he was no match for the strength of the dog, who was determined to keep up the racket until she was set free outside. Chaos ensued. Sam hollered at Honey to stop. Timothy pleaded for Matthew to find the dog's leash. Ben invoked St. Christopher for protection.

Honey, who could not get the humans to understand that she needed to be set free to track the scent she had caught on the wind, threw herself on Sam's lap and began to lick his face.

Sam screamed as the car veered sharply to the right and bounced hard over several blocks of plowed snow and ice before landing, with a sickening thud, in a ditch inches from Harriet's favorite red maple tree.

Silence. Honey immediately stopped her barking and resumed her position in the center of the front seat and waited.

"Is everyone all right?" Sam asked, taking quick inventory of his own condition. Nothing hurt. Everything seemed to be working. He sighed with relief. The car could be fixed, he reasoned. Him, well, he was not so sure.

"I'm all right," Timothy said. "Ben? Matthew? How are you in the backseat?"

"We're all right."

"We'd better get out and see how bad it is," Sam said, putting the car in park and turning off the engine. "Matthew, put the dog on the leash. We don't want to lose her up here."

The men piled out of the car and stood shivering in the wind as Matthew jumped down into the ditch to examine the damage.

"It looks like the tire blew when it hit the ditch, Mr. Rosenberg," Matthew said, clinging to Honey, who strained against the leash.

"There goes one of my Sears all-weathers," Sam lamented. He wondered if this was covered under his warranty.

Honey pulled hard on the leash, responding to a set of rules the group knew nothing about. According to what she had been taught, she was now supposed to be set free to track. She resumed barking.

Matthew tightened his hold. "Should I call the sheriff on the radio?"

"You might as well." His grandfather reached inside the car and handed the radio to his grandson. While Matthew fiddled with the dials, Ben sighed, "What a sorry bunch we turned out to be. We go out to help rescue Father Keene and we end up needing to be rescued."

"Things happen," Sam said. "We're all unharmed. That's what really matters."

"Granddad, would you hold on to Honey?" Matthew turned the radio knobs to the sound of high-pitched static.

Ben watched his grandson fiddle with some dials. "Stand still, you blasted mutt! Haven't you caused enough trouble for one day?"

Timothy stood next to Honey and looked in the direction of the house. "You think something's wrong up at Harriet's place? Maybe someone's broken in? The dog seems to smell something."

"I doubt if anyone's been around in this storm," Sam offered. "And I checked the house just before the storm began."

"My guess is that she smells a rabbit or a possum," Ben offered. "Like Timothy said, she probably smells the rabbit hutches out back. After all, that's what she's been trained to track. Not humans."

Matthew rapped the black box with his hand. "I can't get a clear signal. This storm seems to have caused some interference."

"Oh, great!" Timothy said.

"Well, we can't stand out here," Ben said. His teeth were chattering so hard that he feared his Poli-Grip might not hold. "We'll freeze to death."

"Do you have a key to Harriet's place?" Timothy asked Sam, blowing into his cold hands. "Maybe we could make a call from there."

"I have a key, but the phone lines have been down since the freeze on Monday."

The group was now covered with a fine dusting of snow, like old furnishings retired under white sheets. The wind had picked up and the temperature had begun to drop.

"Timothy is right," Sam said. "We'd better get out of this storm. Let's go inside, start a fire, keep warm."

"I agree," Timothy said. His hands were turning purple.

"That sure is a long driveway," Ben said. It was covered in nearly three feet of snow. It would be hard going.

The group braced themselves against the wind for the arduous walk down the long drive. Honey was the only one enthusiastic about this turn of events, barking more frantically now as she pulled Matthew.

"Hey! Look at this, Granddad," Matthew yelled, as he locked his feet together and allowed Honey to pull him like a sled.

"What's that?" Ben asked, turning around.

The men stopped to listen. The sound of sand trucks, their plows scraping along the road, could be heard rumbling in the distance. The group walked back to the road just as a town sand truck began its first sweep past the driveway. They waved their hands and shouted for the driver to stop.

The driver backed up and rolled down his window. "You guys stranded?"

"Car went off the side of the road. Landed in the ditch," Sam said, pointing to his Plymouth. "Can you give us a ride back into town?"

"Sure thing," the driver said. "I can fit three of you in the cab here with me. The kid will have to wait for a ride with the other sander. He's right behind me. Should be here in a few minutes."

"You go ahead," Matthew told the men, who were beginning to shiver. "Get inside the truck. I'll wait here with Honey."

Matthew didn't have to wait long before the other sander arrived, driven by a man who looked as though he hadn't slept since the storm began. "You climb in," he told Matthew, leaning across the seat of the cab and opening the passenger door. "You'll have to put the dog in the back. I've got allergies."

Matthew walked around to the back of the truck. "Up here," Matthew said, pointing to the pile of sand in the back. Honey jumped on. "Sorry, girl. It looks like you'll have to ride out here." Matthew tied her leash and climbed into the welcome warmth of the heated truck.

Honey watched Matthew and whimpered as he disappeared inside the truck, all hopes of the game's continuing suddenly over. Honey lay down on a soft pile of sand and leaned her head on the cold metal tailgate, watching forlornly, the scent of the game she had been sent to track fading as they drove back into town.

Honey, wet and shivering with cold after the forty-five-minute ride in the back of the sand truck, entered the church basement and froze.

Seated in a line in the center of the floor were five hundred-pound German shepherds. She adhered herself to Matthew's pant leg and whimpered.

Ethel Johnson spied her beloved pet the minute the small group entered through the door. "My poor girl! Just look how cold and wet you are."

Ethel climbed over the shepherds, ignoring an occasional growl, her arms filled with warm blankets.

"Come here darling, and let mommy wipe you off." She clamped her arms around Honey's neck. The dog began to lick her face.

"There you go. What a good girl!" Ethel's voice was filled with a mixture of pride and sympathy, having already heard of the failed rescue attempt. "Now don't you worry, my darling. You did your best. That's all we asked. Let me have your paws. Poor dear, all full of sand."

Ethel completely ignored Sam, Timothy, Ben and Matthew who were looking just as cold and forlorn.

"Would my Honey like a bowl of warm milk?"

The shepherds' ears perked up and their eyes looked hopefully in her direction. "Leave it!" one of the dog handlers commanded. The shepherds, crestfallen, looked the other way.

***

Outside, the state police and their unit of snowmobilers and cross-country skiers, heavy beam flashlights strapped to ski masks, were lined up outside St. Cecilia's. Sheriff Bromley towered over the head of the state police, Captain Charlie Halstead, as they referred to a map of the surrounding area.

Deputy Hill stood several paces behind, speaking to another state trooper who stood stony-faced and silent as Hill rambled on about the newest search techniques being used by the state rangers at Yosemite National Park. Hill had read about it in a recent issue of the *National Law Enforcement Gazette*.

The ground search continued most of Thursday night. Local radio and television news programs issued updates throughout the day, even though there was little to report.

By late Friday morning, the snow had tapered off enough to begin an air search. The sound of helicopters flying their patterns across the fields and mountainside and along the river's bank reminded many villagers of reruns of M*A*S*H. Neither air nor ground crews, however, uncovered any clues to Father Keene's whereabouts and with each hour, the chances of finding him alive became all the more slim.

Law enforcement units, however, were not the only troops marching to Father Keene's rescue. An army of prayer warriors had been unleashed at the first report that their beloved elderly priest was missing.

Father James conducted a special prayer vigil. Even with the storm still raging outside, St. Cecilia's pews were quickly filled with both Catholics and non-Catholics alike. The Rosary Society petitioned the intercession of the Blessed Mother on Father Keene's behalf. The Altar Guild kept a supply of fresh candles and tapers under St. Anthony's statue—the patron saint of lost articles—and the Knights of Columbus invoked the intercession of St. Jude—the patron saint of hopeless causes. Even the Dorsetville Congregational Church and the Salvation Army lent their support. The Congregationalists offered their guest rooms to those involved in the search and the Salvation Army provided blankets.

Women rallied from every denomination to collect in St. Cecilia's kitchen to provide urns of fresh coffee, sandwiches of every variety and enough cakes, cookies and pastries to rival the output of Entenmann's Bakery. The state police later rated this one of the best search operations they had ever been on.

George Benson also did his part, making certain that the furnace didn't fail. And while he would occasionally saunter down to the dirt basement to check on his charge, mostly he reenacted the last conversation he and Father Keene had shared by the side of Bates Rock Road.

"I told Father Keene that a terrible snowstorm was on its way and that he should let me drive him back into town. I even cleared off my front seat in the van. But I just couldn't convince him to come. I may never forgive myself."

George would then cast his eyes down toward the ground and sigh. "If only I had forced him into the van none of this would have happened."

These histrionics were not without reward for they brought words of consolation from those who insisted that George mustn't blame himself and took pity on George's remorse. Dinner invitations greatly increased. George treated these invitation as his due, having missed so many other meals at the hands of the town's Catholics.

Sam's pants had stuck to the plastic chair. He stood up and stretched wishing the bus would hurry along. It was nearing twelve forty-five. He had been here for more than four hours. Most of the conversations had subsided, people seemingly anesthetized by the monotony of the wait, which made the announcement over the P.A. system all the more jarring.

"Everybody, may I have your attention," the woman at the counter shouted into the P.A. system, assuming an air of importance as all eyes turned her way.

"The travel center has just received word that the buses will be arriving here within the next thirty minutes. The Trailways bus from Manchester will be here within twenty minutes, followed by the Boston bus, and the Providence bus."

Several people applauded.

"The bus due in from Manhattan, however, has experienced technical difficulties. I think they said it was a fuel pump. They will be further . . . er . . . furtherly delayed."

The L. L. Bean group stormed out.

Chapter 12

Harriet Bedford was dreaming as the Trailways bus stood motionless in traffic on Interstate 91. Her head lay against the slightly reclined seat, tendrils of gray hair falling from the old-fashioned upsweep she had worn for more than half of her seventy-five years.

Occasionally, a frown would cross her face and a single tear would escape from beneath a closed lid, then another, and another, until a rivulet formed, coursing down cheeks covered in a network of wrinkles, like fine fault lines on a piece of marble.

It was the same dream, carrying her along a pathway well worn through the years, a shroud of memories that threw itself over her soul, blocking all light, sealing in grief and pain first experienced on that fated day when news of the tragedy had arrived.

It had occurred twenty-five years ago, on a cold, winter's morning in December, bleaching her life of the radiant colors that once had made it glow and, for a long time afterward, leaving the inner landscape of her life as colorless and as barren as a countryside blanketed by an ice-covered snow.

From the shadows, Christmas of 1973 emerged complete with its package of torment. An involuntary cry escaped her lips, making the woman seated beside her turn slightly from the book she was reading to gaze in her direction.

Behind Harriet's closed lids, the picture formed of two caskets, one small, one large, where lay her two-year-old granddaughter Melanie and her daughter-in-law, Elizabeth.

The choir sang softly. She could still hear the refrains of the hymn . . .

King of might and splendor,
Creator most adored,
This sacrifice we render
To thee as sov'reign Lord.

How valiantly the choir, filled with friends and neighbors, fought not to break down. Even Father Keene had difficulty maintaining his composure. Several times his eyes misted so heavily with tears that he could no longer read the prayer book the altar boy held before him. He recited from memory.

Lord,
be merciful to your servants Elizabeth and Melanie.
You cleansed them from sin in the fountain of new birth.
Bring them now to the happiness of life in your kingdom.
We ask this for Elizabeth and Melanie forever and ever. Amen.

Through the prayers and hymns were woven the conversation with Sheriff Bromley who had delivered the tragic news.

"*An eighteen-wheeler lost it on the interstate,*" he had said. "*We think he was drunk. Your daughter-in-law's car was in his path when he jumped the divider. She and your granddaughter were killed on impact.*"

Dead? she repeated that word again. And again. And again.

It was as if the word could not penetrate her mind. How was it possible? If they were dead, surely the world would have stopped. But somehow people continued to go about their ordinary lives even though these two wonderful souls were no longer among the living.

No. It had to be a mistake.

But it wasn't.

The sheriff drove Harriet to Peter's work. *Should I deliver the news?* he asked. *No, it will be easier for Peter to hear it from me,* she said. Peter's boss led her son into his office, quickly disappearing behind the closed door.

It was the hardest thing Harriet had ever been asked to do. A strange sense of detachment gripped her. It was as if another delivered the tragic message. She heard her voice, but she was not behind it. Instead, she stood as an observer, watching from some distant place as her son's eyes filled with unspeakable pain.

Peter entered the darkness but, unlike Harriet who still had to function and take care of the myriad details, he seldom emerged, just occasionally to respond to his three-year-old daughter Allison's outstretched hand.

Harriet walked through the rituals of death, making arrangements from a distant place that lay on the fringes of grief. She chose two caskets, gathered the last set of clothing—Melanie's new pink jumper and the hiking shoes she wore each Saturday morning to follow her father into the woods; and a soft, cashmere sweater set for Elizabeth that brought out the blue in her eyes, eyes that would never look upon Allison's or Peter's face again.

At times, Harriet felt as though she might drown from grief, yet she stoically fought on. If she caved in, who would help the survivors find their way out of the darkness?

Later, she walked the cemetery with the caretaker, finally choosing two plots nearest the woods and the wildflowers that Melanie and Elizabeth had so dearly loved.

The caretaker asked if she was all right. She smiled bravely and waved him on, then watched as he entered the small aluminum building at the edge of the cemetery before falling down in the snow to cover the plots with the warmth of her body as though she could somehow take the stinging chill off death and impart warmth to this unyielding patch of dirt that would soon become the repository for those whom she so dearly loved.

She grieved openly for some time before getting up, brushing herself off and squaring her shoulders. There was still Peter and Allison, she reminded herself, and they would need her to be strong.

The church was filled the day of the funeral with friends who wept as though they personally had lost a child, a wife, a daughter, a mother. Father Keene presided; an altar boy, shy in the presence of death, kept his eyes cast down, trailing close behind. Father intoned:

> I hope in the Lord, I trust in His word,
> Out of the depths I cry to you, O Lord;
> Lord hear my voice!

Then Peter screamed.

Its deep, guttural pain seemed to separate the very air, creating a chasm. Peter now stood upon a distant plain. No one dared to move, fearing that to do so would be to plunge Peter into an abyss so deep he would be lost forever.

"Trust in the Lord! How can I ever trust Him again?" he shouted, his body shaking with the force of his grief.

Father walked around the coffins, his cheeks stained with tears, his eyes heavy with compassion and reached out a consoling arm.

"Peter, my son, I know your sorrow and so does Jesus."

Peter flinched at his touch.

"How would you know how I feel? A priest who has never had a wife or a child?" Peter pushed Father's arm away.

"Peter, please," Harriet pleaded. "He's only trying to help."

"Really?" he snarled. "Then have him pray to his God and tell Him to bring back my daughter, my wife."

"Daddy." Allison, seated next to Harriet, began to whimper and cry.

"Peter, please, darling. I know how hard this has to be on you, but you're scaring Allison."

"Don't cry, Daddy," Allison pleaded. A tiny voice. "Grandma says that Mommy and Melanie are with Jesus. He will take care of them now."

Peter raised his fists, tilted his head and shouted to heaven, "How could you do this to me? How could you take both my wife and my child and expect me to believe in your love? Damn you!"

Harriet reached out and tried to draw him close as she had done a thousand times before when he was a child.

"My poor, dear, dear, Peter." She groped for his hand, unable to see through the blinding tears. "Don't damn God. He loves you, Peter. He knows the pain you're feeling. He, too, once lost a child."

"If that was true, why didn't He save me from this pain? What kind of loving Father would want his child to suffer as I am suffering? Why didn't He stop the man who killed my family from taking those drinks or from getting into that truck or from passing out behind the wheel?"

"I don't know why He chose not to avert their death anymore than I understand why He didn't stop the crowds from crucifying His only Son. But this I do know, Peter. God loves you. And He is grieving right along with you. Look behind you, Peter. Look out over the pews. See the army of saints He has sent to help us carry this burden."

Peter threw off her hand, fixing her with a menacing stare. "I would rather He had sent protection to my wife and daughter."

"We both would have preferred that, but God's ways are often mysterious and what we can't understand we must accept on faith."

"How can you defend Him? He took my wife! He took my little daughter! *Your* granddaughter. My sweet, sweet, Melanie." He began to crumble under the weight of her name.

Harriet reached out. He angrily pushed her away.

"Every morning, I came to Mass and prayed that He would watch over my family. Keep them safe from harm. I trusted Him!" he screamed. "And He betrayed my trust.

"If you loved them as much as I did, then you could not defend Him. You could not possibly love a God who was indifferent to my prayers. If you love me and Allison, you must hate Him as much as I do." His words were tipped in poison aimed at her heart.

"God did not do this," she cried. "A drunken driver did this. God gave us free will. Elizabeth used her free will when she decided to travel to Woodstock with Melanie to do some Christmas shopping. The truck driver used his free will to drink and drive. Our Lord said that He did not come so we would no longer suffer, for even He had suffered. He came to empower us to overcome suffering. Peter, He's doing that today by filling this church with people who love you and Allison and me. He's here, Peter, just as He promised He would be. He's present in the spirit of everyone in this church."

Peter's pain, anger and hatred had sealed off his soul. Harriet's words bounced off with no effect.

"Choose," he demanded. "You can love your God or you can choose to love me and Allison, but you cannot love both."

Harriet fell back against the pew as though physically struck. Allison quickly slid over and slipped a tiny hand into hers.

"Grandma," Allison whimpered.

Harriet gathered her granddaughter in her arms and held her close, savoring the sweet smell of her. For Harriet, there could be only one answer.

"I cannot abandon God," she said softly with firm resolve. And with those words, she understood for the very first time what St. Paul had meant when he wrote "For it is granted to you on behalf of Christ not only to believe in Him, but also to suffer for Him."

"Then you choose to live your life without us." Peter snatched Allison from her arms. "You may come to the cemetery. But after that, I will consider you buried with them. You will never see your granddaughter or me again."

Involuntary bursts of grief and pain filled the church. Some openly wept. Ethel Johnson reached across her husband's lap and grabbed hold of Peter's arm. "You can't mean that. You're just overcome with grief. In a few weeks, things will seem much . . ."

"I do mean it." He turned and stormed out of the church to wait in the black limousine.

Over the next several weeks, Harriet called and wrote letters, to which Peter never replied. She sat by the phone all Christmas Day hoping that Peter would bring Allison by. Their presents remained un-opened under the tree. The next day, she drove to Peter's.

As soon as Harriet pulled into the small cul-de-sac, she spied a FOR SALE sign posted in front of the three-bedroom Cape, which Peter and Elizabeth had bought before the children were born. The windows were without curtains, just gaping black holes. The trash cans were over-stuffed with discarded boxes and other packing debris. It looked as though they had left in a hurry.

Harriet drove to John Moran's realty office. "I have no idea where Peter has moved," John said. "The sale of the house is being handled through a lawyer in Woodstock." With a look of deep compassion, he gave Harriet the lawyer's name.

It took several days for the lawyer to return her call and when he did, he made it very clear that he would not divulge any information about his client, no matter how much Harriet pleaded. Even a later visit from Father Keene could not move him.

With the help of friends, like Sam and his wife, the prayers of the faithful, like Father Keene, Harriet slowly healed. She still felt a deep sadness when a birthday or holiday rolled around. Christmas was espe-cially hard, for it signaled the anniversary of Elizabeth's and Melanie's deaths and another year without Peter and Allison. Easter was another difficult holiday.

Some who experience heartache travel down a road of self-pity and grief. Others choose the higher road, preferring to believe that God is in the midst of all pain, not outside of it. Harriet chose the latter.

But as the years rolled by, some would feel the need to make ex-cuses for God's delay.

"At least you have those three years with Allison and Melanie," or "It's not wise to hope for things that can never be."

Harriet, however, needed no false platitudes. She knew in whom she believed and was confident that He would someday heal her heartache. She knew God's word needed no addendum, just quiet confidence and trust. She had learned the dynamo of spiritual power available in the prayer of relinquishment, its power manifested in the greatest gift ever given to mankind—the gift of salvation. "Not my will, but Thine be done." A child of God need only *choose* to believe and not let doubt enter in. Her faith had never wavered.

As Harriet maintained her steadfast belief in God's power to save, God increased her gift of faith and a ministry began to bloom from the barren landscape of her pain—a powerful ministry of intercessory prayer.

She kept a small brown leather prayer journal, easily fitted inside her purse or an apron pocket, filled with the hundreds of prayer requests she had received through the years. Written on its ruled lines were petitions for renewed health, better jobs, financial assistance or the myriad needs people encountered along life's way.

People asked her to pray, not because her prayers were more powerful than theirs, but to help them uphold those prayers before God's throne, as Aaron once had held up Moses' arms as the battles raged. And so she prayed.

She prayed as she waited in line at the Grand Union, at traffic lights, in her doctor's waiting room and while walking down country lanes. Most people in town knew exactly what she was doing with eyes fixed, gazing straight ahead, her mouth moving silently in prayer. No one would dare disturb her, not even with a soft hello or a gentle pat on the arm. Almost everyone in Dorsetville at one time or another had a prayer request listed in the pages of her prayer journal; many could recite the story of a miracle or two.

The bus stopped in front of the travel center and opened its doors. Several passengers squeezed by while Harriet reached into the overhead rack and pulled out her coat, hat and gloves. She had pushed her small overnight bag underneath her seat and had to give it several tugs before she could pull it free.

"Harriet! You're finally here." Sam's smiling face was the first thing she saw as she stepped off the last metal stair. Her heartbeat increased slightly, her cheeks blushed, as he swept the carrying case from her hands and extended an arm for her to grasp.

"Watch your step. It's still icy in spots." Carefully, he led her through the crowd of passengers who waited for the driver to open the luggage bin as though she were the most delicate of creatures needing assistance. "It's nice having you home again," he whispered softly, patting her gloved hand.

"And it's good to be home. I'm completely worn out," she said, taking comfort from Sam's firm grasp as they sidestepped a leather traveling case someone had carelessly abandoned on the walkway.

"Now, I love my younger sister," she continued, "but my visits to her convent wear me out. Ever since she was made mother superior we barely get a chance to talk when we're together. Something or someone always needs her attention and for some strange reason, she thinks I should be just as busy. I try to convince her to let me read quietly in my room or take a walk in the woods while she's attending to the convent's affairs. But, oh, no. Not Mary Veronica. She has to drag me along."

They waited for the light to change to cross the street even though there were no cars in sight.

"While I was there, I helped serve over five hundred meals a day. Can you imagine! I thought my feet were going to fall right off."

"Why so many meals?" Sam asked. "I thought it was a small convent."

"It is, but the soup kitchen at St. Ann's was being renovated and Mary Veronica offered the convent's facilities until they were back on line. Unfortunately, she also offered my services."

Sam gently laughed. It was good to be with Harriet again. He'd missed their conversations.

"I'm glad to be home to get a rest," she joked, quickening her pace as they neared Sam's car eager to get out of the cold.

"I am so sorry about the bus's delay," she said, watching Sam unlock the passenger side. "I imagine you've been waiting for hours."

Sam shrugged. "What else do I have to do? When you're gone I have no one to direct my day. 'Sam can you change that lightbulb on top of the stairs?' 'Sam, can you drive over to Ethel's and pick up a quilting frame?'" he mimicked.

"You make me sound like Mary Veronica," she laughed.

"It must run in the family," he teased.

"But it is nice to know that I've been missed."

Sam patted her arm. "That you have, my dear. That you have."

Harriet found herself blushing as Sam helped her inside the car.

"But I have to admit, since you left, there's been plenty enough to keep me busy."

"Like what?" she asked as he closed the door. She had to wait for an answer as he circled around and slid into the driver's seat.

"It's hard to know where to begin," Sam said, settling behind the wheel. He paused briefly. There was never an easy way to share bad news.

"Harriet, I'm sad to tell you that your archbishop has ordered St. Cecilia's closed. The Easter service is to be the last." Sam started the engine.

"Close St. Cecilia's? Why would he want to close our church?"

"Father James says it's lack of money."

Through habit, Harriet looked over her shoulder as Sam began to back out onto Main Street. "All clear my way."

They headed down the street.

"I know that lately the collection baskets have been emptier than usual, but the archdiocese has always helped out in the past," Harriet continued.

"There's also the condition of the church and rectory to consider," he reminded her. "If it weren't for George Benson acting as fire marshal, St. Cecilia's would have been condemned years ago."

The dark pall that had accompanied Harriet's dream and which she had managed to shake off until a few minutes ago closed in again.

"Where will we go if St. Cecilia's closes?"

"Your archbishop has suggested St. Bartholomew's," Sam said, allowing another car to pass.

"St. Bartholomew's! Has he gone mad? Why, that's all the way over in Burlington. Who's going to travel to Burlington every day for Mass? Hardly anyone of our friends drives any longer. And, as you know, many of us depend upon the few who still have cars to pick up groceries and medicines. Why, if it weren't for you, Sam, many of our friends would have to go into nursing homes."

Harriet grew quiet before adding, " I can't imagine not attending Mass at St. Cecilia's. There must be something we can do to change the archbishop's mind."

He hated to see her so distressed. "Father James has already tried but apparently, the matter is closed."

Harriet reached into her purse, searching for her rosary beads, which were tangled around a cellophane packet of tissues, her eyeglass case and a small change purse. She went to her rosary like some go to a box of chocolates during a crisis. She carefully untangled the strand and laid them across her lap.

Sam reached into the shopping bag for a cranberry muffin. "Here, this will tide you over until we can stop at the Country Kettle for some lunch. There's a Thermos of coffee in here too, but I'm afraid it's a little cold."

"I'm not really hungry, Sam. But thank you anyway."

"Nonsense. You haven't eaten in hours. Do you want to get one of those sick headaches? You know how your blood sugar drops when you get hungry."

Harriet couldn't help but smile. "Sam, you are always so thoughtful."

"It's my pleasure."

"Thanks for keeping such a good watch over me," she said with a touch of shyness.

He looked across the seat and smiled. "Someone has to."

"A muffin will do just nicely." She reached into the Stew Leonard bag not wanting to appear ungrateful. As she undid the plastic wrap, she noticed they had just sailed past their turnoff. "Sam, you've missed the road to Dorsetville."

"We're not headed home. Not just yet. There is some good news mixed in with the bad."

"Oh?"

"They found a donor for Bob Peterson. He received a bone-marrow transplant yesterday."

"A transplant! How wonderful! How is he doing?"

"I thought we'd stop at Mercy Hospital and see for ourselves. That is, if you're not too tired from your trip."

"Not at all! I think that's a great idea," she added. "I've been praying that God would send a perfect match."

Sam laughed. "Well, apparently, God has answered your prayers. I spoke to Harry this morning when I stopped to pick up the muffins and he said that the doctors are amazed at how well Bob is doing."

"Praise God." Another answered prayer she could enter in her prayer journal. "As soon as I'm settled in at home, I'll make up a couple of meals and you can deliver them to the Petersons."

Sam nodded, happy to have Harriet resume planning his days.

As they traveled along the back roads headed toward the hospital, Sam grew unnaturally quiet, prompting Harriet to ask, "Is there something else?"

He hesitated, "Harriet, it's about Father Keene."

She clutched her rosary beads tighter.

"Father Keene is missing."

"Missing? What do you mean he's *missing?*"

"He took a walk late Wednesday afternoon, right before the storm, and no one has seen him since."

"Oh, sweet Jesus." The car suddenly felt as though all the air had been sucked out. She partially rolled down a window. "You mean he's been out in this weather since Wednesday?" She glanced out at the countryside. Moments ago the fields and mountainsides covered in snow were beautiful; now they appeared menacing.

"Apparently."

"Father Keene," she whispered. Tears glistened. "He's been like a brother to me . . . always there . . ."

Sam reached across and took hold of her hand. "I know."

"Even when . . ."

"Now, now, Harriet," Sam consoled. "Let's not think the worst. Maybe he's found a way to get out of the storm."

"Anything is possible." She prayed, *Let Father Keene be found safe.*

Later over lunch at the Country Kettle, Sam related his part in the search efforts including the use of Ethel Johnson's dog.

"You said that Honey wanted to investigate up by my house?" Harriet asked between spoonfuls of minestrone.

"She was pretty persistent about it. Insisted that we let her out of the car. That's the reason we landed in the ditch outside your driveway." Sam broke off a piece of bread and dipped it into his soup. "Timothy and Ben figured she must have smelled Peter's old rabbit hutches. You know, the ones behind the barn."

Harriet wiped her mouth with a paper napkin. "I got rid of those things years ago. I can't imagine what could have piqued her interest but it couldn't have been Father Keene." She took a sip of water. "He could never have walked from Bates Rock Road to my farm in good weather, let alone during a blizzard." She shook her head, "No, Honey must have smelled something else."

"I guess." Sam reached for the check. "It's been awhile since she went hunting with Harry. Maybe she's just out of practice."

It was nearing three-thirty by the time they pulled into Harriet's driveway and met Chester Platt, who had just finished plowing. Sam pulled the car alongside the pickup truck as Chester rolled down his window.

"Welcome back," Chester told Harriet. "My wife reminded me that Sam had gone to pick you up and that I had better get over here and plow you out. I hadn't bothered before, since I knew you were gone to visit your sister." Chester flipped a cigarette out the window. "By the way, how is our Mary Veronica?" he asked with a twinkle in his eye. They had dated in high school.

"Busy as always, Chester."

"That's our girl." Even after all these years, his eyes became pools of warm light whenever he spoke her name.

Their courtship had lasted throughout high school and most folks in the town assumed someday they'd get married. But in their senior year, Mary Veronica found a social conscience, a discovery that often landed her in hot water with the local businessmen. Chester's uncle was one of them.

The summer of their senior year, Mary Veronica had helped to organize a boycott against the local clinic. The clinic refused to treat welfare recipients or the indigent even though it received state funding. Up until that moment, the clinic's policy had been a well-guarded secret. But suddenly it was front-page news when Mary Veronica persuaded a state senator to demand a full-scale investigation. Chester's uncle was later jailed.

Chester's parents were completely ignorant of the clinic's policies, but were, nevertheless, extremely embarrassed by the whole incident and managed to shift most of the blame from the uncle and to Mary Veronica. After all, wasn't she the one who had made this whole mess public? Chester broke off the relationship two weeks before their senior prom.

Mary Veronica left Dorsetville right after graduation, first joining a Catholic ministry in the Appalachian Mountains of Kentucky, then later as a postulant to the Daughters of the Immaculate Conception of the Blessed Virgin Mary. She had recently been made mother superior.

Chester lighted another Marlboro with the truck's lighter. A short burst of wind blew the smoke back into his face.

"Thanks for plowing, Chester," Harriet said, leaning into Sam's side of the car. "You make living out here in the winter possible."

"My pleasure, Harriet," said Chester. "CL and P said the electricity won't be restored for some time. A lot of trees are down. But I checked on the firewood box by the back door and you've got plenty to get you through for a while."

"Sam filled it before I left for my trip." Harriet said.

"I can chop some more, if it's needed," Sam offered.

"Well, I'd better get going. I have to fetch my grandsons from a Scouts' meeting over in Uniondale." He revved the truck's engine. "Now, I shoveled the front walk but I didn't have time to clear a path by the back door. I'll come back early tomorrow and finish it up before I go check on my crews." Chester owned a construction business.

"No, need, Chester," Sam said. "I'll grab a shovel out of the shed and clear it out before I leave."

"You sure? I really don't mind coming back."

"Sam, you needn't . . ." Harriet protested.

"I don't mind at all," Sam said. Sensing their concern, he added, "I'll take it slow. Besides, you don't want to deprive me of a hearty bowl of Harriet's soup afterward, do you?"

Harriet laughed, "Oh . . . Sam."

"All right then. I'll leave the back porch to you." Chester shifted the truck into first gear, waved his good-byes and was gone, leaving a slight spray of snow in his wake.

Sam pulled alongside the front walk, got out, then opened the trunk to remove Harriet's overnight bag. Chester had sanded the front path well but it was still slippery going. They trod carefully toward the front door.

Harriet placed her key inside the lock, but the door was open.

"Now that's strange," she mused. "I could have sworn I checked it before I left."

"You did. I saw you do it," Sam confirmed. He began to feel uneasy. "Maybe we'd better go back to the car. Call the sheriff."

Harriet ignored him. "Ssshh. What's that?"

"What's what?" Sam dropped her suitcase on the porch.

"It sounds like someone snoring."

Harriet slowly pushed the front door open into the living room and stared, frozen in disbelief.

"Oh, dear God!" she exclaimed.

"Great Father of Abraham! I'll be!" shouted Sam joyously.

Father Keene was fast asleep on the living room recliner with Harriet's Walkman earphones covering his ears, the muted strains of Andrea Bocelli singing "Panis Angelicus" seeping through. In his lap lay her dog-eared copy of *At Home in Mitford*. The priest was snoring loudly.

"Well, if that doesn't beat all!" exclaimed Sam. "The dog *was* right!"

Chapter 13

Father James stared at his image in the mirror over the bathroom sink as though it were a stranger. During the night, his face had somehow stretched downward as though it were made of Silly Putty, producing jowls. The upper portion of his features had fared no better, especially his eyes, which now bore the tired look of an elderly man.

"When Jeff gets a load of this face, I hope he'll still want me as his best man," Father James sighed morosely to the stranger.

With little conscious thought, he turned on the tarnished copper faucets and prepared to shave.

It had been a roller-coaster week, one he hoped he'd never have to repeat. It all began when the archbishop announced St. Cecilia's was to be closed, quickly followed by the news that Mercy Hospital had found a bone-marrow donor for Bob Peterson and concluding with Father Keene's disappearance during one of the region's fiercest snowstorms and then his miraculous return. It made him dizzy just thinking about it all.

In addition was the weight of all the items that needed quick resolution as the closing of St. Cecilia's loomed nearer. He had barely slept a wink last night. An inner voice had continued to tick off problems like the seconds hand on the nightstand clock. Was it any wonder he felt so exhausted?

The water in the sink overflowed its porcelain edge and soaked his slippers.

"Good grief!"

He yanked the metal chain attached to the stopper. The water rushed out the drain in a funnel. He started all over again.

Keeping a sharp eye on the water this time, he searched the medicine cabinet for the container of shaving cream and the packet of Good News disposable razors. He was down to the last one. He'd better add it to his list of items that needed to be picked up at the Dairy Mart before he left for Manhattan.

It was five-thirty on Saturday morning and he planned to leave for Manhattan at six-thirty to begin his weeklong visit with Jeff Hayden. The problem was that although he desperately wanted to spend time with his best friend, Father James did not want to leave St. Cecilia's. Not now. Not in the midst of all this turmoil. Of all the times to take a vacation, this was the worst.

His elderly parishioners still would not consent to attend Mass at St. Bartholomew's in Burlington when St. Cecilia's closed, even though Father James had made arrangements with the archbishop to purchase a bus that would take Dorsetville parishioners back and forth to daily Mass.

"We've attended St. Cecilia's our entire lives and we don't intend to switch churches now," they stubbornly insisted.

In between working with the rescue efforts to find Father Keene, Father James had canvassed his parishioners door to door, consuming dozens of slices of cake and pie and quarts of tea as he tried to change their minds. It had been to no avail. The only thing that had moved during these visits was his midriff, by several inches, reducing his selection of pants down to two.

It was apparent that other than his expanding waistline the campaigns were having no effect. He switched tactics and began to tuck short pitches into each of his homilies.

"We are many members, but one body," he sermonized on Thursday morning, paraphrasing St. Paul's epistle. He paused to let the words take effect while looking out over the sea of faces who appeared no more moved by the words of the Lord's apostle than they had been by Father James.

On Friday, he continued, holding tightly to his patience. "St. Bartholomew's is the same church as St. Cecilia's. It may be a different shape and in a different location, but it is the *same* church." He pounded the podium for effect. His parishioners pursed their lips and shook their heads, unconvinced.

Finally, the Henderson sisters felt it their duty to voice their strong opposition to Father James's campaign. The elder, seventy-three-year-old Ruth, a retired English teacher who had a penchant for the non sequitur, stated, "To say that St. Bartholomew's is the same as our beloved St. Cecilia's is like saying that store-bought bread tastes the same as homemade soup."

"Brilliantly stated," said her seventy-two-year-old sister June, filled with pride at her perception of her older sister's mastery of the English language. June had never finished high school. She was too "delicate," her father had said.

Father James remained confused over this analogy, but Ruth had that effect on most of her listeners. He issued a noncommittal response. "I will lift that insight up to the Lord in prayer."

The sisters left for their home across the town green, satisfied that they had done their Christian duty.

Father James held the button down on the Colgate shaving-cream canister several seconds too long, producing enough white foam to shave the winter fur off a Morgan horse. But he didn't notice. Instead, he smeared it on until his features were completely obscured by a three-inch white beard. He picked up his disposable razor and began to shave, mentally listing all the issues yet unresolved.

He still needed to find a nursing home for Father Keene. He paused and hung his head in prayer. *"Dear Lord, please give me wisdom and lead me in this matter."*

As he resumed shaving, his heart swelled with both compassion and grief for Father Keene. It seemed so unfair to move the priest to a new home miles away from everyone he knew and loved. How would he feel to live out the rest of his life among strangers?

"Surely, Lord, there must be another tactic that I simply haven't considered," he prayed.

He chided himself. It was too early in the morning to be depressed and that was just where these thoughts were leading. He forced himself to think of more pleasant images. He envisioned Jeff's smiling face when he arrived. The excitement of New York City . . . the sounds . . . the great food. . . . But his thoughts, like magnetized shards, jumped right back to the needs of his parish.

What was to become of the social programs housed in the basement of the church? Each one would need a new home. The community food pantry, meals-on-wheels, the senior center. His spirits sank again.

As soon as the archbishop had decided to close St. Cecilia's, Father James had consulted John Moran, whose real estate firm held the leases on most of Main Street's storefront property. John had finally agreed to donate an abandoned building next to the town hall for a period of six months. After that, he said, he would have to charge rent for the space. Father James knew that no matter how insignificant the rental fee was, it would be more than many of the programs could afford to pay. He hoped Father McCarthy would follow through with the archdiocese's offer to subsidize some of the programs.

He looked through the open bathroom door toward the clock on his nightstand: 5:40 A.M. He could feel a headache beginning at the base of his neck. If only he could just turn off his mind, declare a moratorium on worry until he returned. On the brighter side, however, there were still three weeks left before the church was to close. That was enough time to do what was needed to be done, wasn't it? There was absolutely no reason he should feel guilty about taking a holiday. Right? He reminded himself that St. Cecilia's was going to close regardless of whether he stayed or went, and there was nothing he could do to change that fact.

These were God's people, too. His children. And He had promised to provide whenever there was a need. Father James was not alone in this. Thinking about God's provision reminded him how God had provided Father Dennis to help while he was away. He thoroughly enjoyed the young priest whose childlike enthusiasm for God and for his new role as a priest had helped renew Father James's flagging spirits.

Father Dennis had been ordained only a week before he was given this assignment. Although it was only temporary, the archbishop was grateful for it. It gave him time to ponder what was to be done with Father Dennis, who stood 5 feet 10 inches tall, weighed over 350 pounds and was filled with so much evangelistic zeal that the archbishop feared he would do more to offend than to convert. This, however, had not proven a problem at St. Cecilia's. The parishioners greatly enjoyed him.

"First time I haven't fallen asleep during a homily in years," Fred Campbell told Father James after Father Dennis's first sermon. "I like his fire."

Timothy happily pointed out other benefits of having Father Dennis onboard. "When Father Dennis speaks, we don't need to turn on the P.A. system, or our hearing aids for that matter. Look at all the money he's saving us. The church saves on electricity and he's saving us seniors a bundle on batteries!"

Father James wished that he and Father Dennis hadn't met in the midst of St. Cecilia's closing. He would have liked to have spent more time with this passionate young priest. Fortunately he believed Father Dennis was one person he didn't have to worry about while he was gone. He had both the Lord and the Henderson sisters to keep him in line.

A small section of skin under the white shaving cream turned pink.

"Dear St. Joseph!" he exclaimed, wiping away the foam, revealing a two-inch gash. "Great! This is just great!" He'd arrive in New York with bandages all over his face.

An inner voice taunted, *"It's an omen. You're cutting your own throat by leaving at a time like this."*

Father James swatted at the thought like a noisome bug. "I will not allow fear or trepidation to steal my joy. This week's visit with Jeff is a gift from the Lord, *who—by the way, in case you've forgotten, Father James Flaherty*—often separated Himself from those He loved when He was about to face a crisis. And the Lord knows, there is an abundance of crisis at St. Cecilia's, and I'll need every bit of strength I can garner if I am to get my flock through it all."

It was nearly six-thirty by the time he headed down the back rectory stairs and toward the church annex. He stepped into the church, still slumbering in the quiet morning light. The stained-glass windows threw a prism of color across the whitewashed walls and along the marble floors polished to a soft patina by the thousands of feet that had trod over it.

He knelt to pray, beginning with praise and thanksgiving for Father Keene's safe return, although it was still unclear how Father Keene had managed to walk the seven miles from Bates Rock Road to Harriet's farmhouse in a blinding snowstorm.

Father Keene's disappearance had shaken the entire community. After the second day, most had presumed the elderly priest was dead, frozen beneath an icy blanket of snow. It was a miracle that he had survived the ordeal and many, including Father James, were eager to hear the details of his story, but Father Keene wasn't offering any. Every time someone asked for an explanation, he became vague or changed the subject.

Father James smiled as he remembered Harriet Bedford and Sam Rosenberg marching through the rectory doors with Father Keene in tow.

"That which was lost has now been found," Harriet proclaimed cheerfully.

It had taken Father James several seconds to recover from the shock and find his voice. "Praise the Lord and all his saints! Father Keene, you're safe!"

Mrs. Norris had flown across the linoleum floor, locked the elderly priest in an embrace and sobbed uncontrollably into his woolen coat.

"There, there, Mrs. Norris," Father Keene said, patting her head. "I'm fine. Just fine."

Over the older priest's protests, Father James threw his arms around them both. "You're going to smother me to death," Father Keene quipped.

"You had us worried near to death," Father James countered, giving him one last hug. "The entire town has been out looking for you. Where have you been?"

"I've been waiting out the storm at Harriet's," he said nonchalantly.

"Harriet's? How did you manage to land there?" Father James asked. "I thought George Benson last saw you up by Bates Rock Road. That's a good seven miles in the other direction."

Father Keene ignored the query. "Sorry to have caused everyone so much anguish, but as my dear, departed father used to say, 'The good Lord keeps watch over children, drunks and old men.'"

"We thought you were dead," Mrs. Norris cried, pulling a crochet and linen handkerchief from her apron pocket.

"Dead? Why, my dear Mrs. Norris, don't you know that it takes more than a snowstorm to kill an Irishman?"

"That's not funny," she scolded. "I haven't slept a wink in days."

"It was just a wee bit of a snowstorm that came up quickly as I was taking my walk. But the Lord provided, as He always does. I found my way to Harriet's house where I've been as safe and warm as a field mouse in a thatched roof."

"I'm still a little confused." Father James pressed on for an answer. "How did you walk that far in the storm?"

Father Keene ignored the query as he went in search of his reading glasses. "I see my mail's been piling up. Now where did I put my spectacles?"

"You could have at least given us a call to tell us that you were all right," Mrs. Norris said, pulling the wire-rimmed reading glasses from the pocket of his woolen coat.

"The phone wasn't working." He settled the glasses on the tip of his nose and picked up his mail.

"Lines are still down outside the town," Harriet confirmed, unbuttoning her coat. "In fact, most of the county is out. I don't expect many of us will have service back before late next week."

"We would have called as soon as we discovered Father Keene asleep on Harriet's living room recliner," Sam laughed. "What a welcome sight that was!"

"We could hardly believe our eyes," Harriet attested.

"I'm surprised that the sheriff didn't check your house," Father James mused, watching Father Keene shuffle through the mail as though he had been away on vacation.

"I had told Sheriff Bromley that I would be away visiting with my sister and since my house is on the opposite side of town from where Father Keene was last seen, he probably saw no reason to check." Harriet laid her coat on an empty chair.

"I'd still be interested knowing how you managed to make it all the way over to Harriet's house in the blizzard," Father James told Father Keene.

"I walked through the woods," replied Father Keene. "I didn't realize how bad the storm was until I came out."

"Still, that's an awful long way," Father James continued. "How *did* you make it through several acres of forest, over a steep mountain and then down to Harriet's place in a blinding snowstorm?"

"I just flew above it," he joked.

"No. Seriously, I'd like to know," Father James persisted, not to be waylaid this time from getting an answer.

"Oh, it's a long story to be sure, and not one I'd be wanting to tell on an empty stomach," he replied. "Now, my dear Mrs. Norris, what do you say to a nice cup of tea and some of your famous scones? And to add to that delicacy, we could spoon on some of Harriet's orange marmalade." He saw her hesitate, and added with a twinkle in his Irish eyes, "Isn't it proper to celebrate the return of the prodigal son by killing the fatted calf? And since we've no calf, I am certain that your scones will do just as nicely."

Mrs. Norris gave him a sound kiss on the cheek and said with mock sternness, "Don't you ever go wandering off again without first telling me where you're going." She wiped the tears from her eyes with her handkerchief as she went to fetch the tea kettle from the back of the stove.

"I'll be making the tea, if you don't mind," Father Keene said, taking the tea kettle from her hand with an agility that was surprising for a man who had just been through such an ordeal.

Chapter 14

Father Keene heard Father James walk downstairs. He knew he should get out of bed and bid him a safe trip to New York. Instead, he rolled over and threw the covers over his head, wanting desperately to avoid any further inquire as to how he had made it safely to Harriet Bedford's house in the midst of the worst snowstorm in more than twenty years. How could he tell them the truth?

He had pondered for three days how to explain the miracle as he sat snug and warm inside Harriet's home with a fire crackling in the fireplace, a pot of soup warming on the open hearth and watched the storm as it raged outside. But try as he might, he could not come up with a plausible story that would explain how he had traveled seven miles over the small mountain range separating Harriet's nursery from Bates Rock Road in the midst of the blizzard that covered the countryside in snow, sleet and subzero temperatures.

From the moment he had entered the rectory door, everyone had clamored to know how he had done it. Harriet, Sam, Father James, Mrs. Norris. Even George Benson had stopped at the rectory later that afternoon and quizzed him.

"Men half your age would have died out there. How did an eighty-two-year-old manage to survive?" George had asked, in between slurping spoonfuls of clam chowder—a late afternoon snack he had finagled out of Mrs. Norris by telling her he had worked through lunch.

"Would you pass the rolls?" he asked Father Keene. "So, how did you walk that distance in a blizzard?"

Father Keene evaded a direct answer by launching into a tale about his great-grandfather who had once walked all the way from Dublin to Killarney at age ninety-five. Fortunately, when he had finished telling this story, with as many embellishments as he could possibly inject, hoping to distance himself as far as possible from George's query, Mrs. Norris had appeared with a three-layer chocolate cake, redirecting George's interest.

Father Keene remained in his room, the door firmly shut against any further inquiries while Mrs. Norris and Father James tried to bridle their curiosity.

After all, they said, Father Keene had just come through a harrowing experience. He needed to be alone. Time to regain his strength. There would be plenty of time later to discuss the miracle of his survival.

But Father Keene had no intentions of discussing any of it with anyone. After all, what could he say? That he had been rescued by two angels and told that God wanted him to play a part in His plan to save St. Cecilia's? He would have to tell them something, but what would they believe? He searched and searched for a feasible story.

One involved a newly found shortcut through the woods. Father Keene had abandoned that idea when he realized that most folks in Dorsetville knew every pathway and tree stump within a forty mile radius.

Another version centered on the priest's ability to convince George Benson that he had been mistaken about where they had met. Father Keene could insist that it had been Poverty Road—three miles from Harriet's farm—not Bates Rock Road. But the improbability of this plan was clear. George had lived here all of his life. He was also the town's fire marshal. If anyone knew which street was which, it was George Benson.

As people continued to squeeze him for a plausible explanation, the pressure resulted in a severe case of hiccups, which even Mrs. Norris's tried-and-true remedy could not stop.

"I don't understand it. A tablespoon of sugar moistened with a drop of water has always cured hiccups before," she told him, completely perplexed. "I don't know why it won't clear up yours."

By late Friday night, he lay exhausted on his bed, staring up at the pattern of branches outside his window silhouetted against the ceiling. Every now and then he'd hiccup and the metal bed would shake slightly on its coasters and the springs beneath the mattress would creak.

It was a bright moonlit night and a soft, lemon-coated beam suffused through the bedroom window. He could hear the wind whistle and whine as it chased eddies of snow around the building, periodically sending a shower of soft white granules past his window, where they'd meet with the moonlight to sparkle like glitter.

Soon the sound of the wind outside, the familiar creak of the house as its floorboards and wooden lattice behind plaster walls swelled and contracted in soft groans, and the steady warmth of the patchwork quilts piled high on his supine form made his eyes grow heavy with sleep and the voices that had clamored at him all day fade.

His thoughts, no longer fettered by a heavy load of worry, began to drift aimlessly over the landscape of recent events and finally alighted on the moment he lay in the snow—the blizzard raging around him—realizing that he was about to die.

"You sure you don't want a ride home?" George Benson asked, from inside the warmth of his van.

"Thank you so much for your kindness, George, but I'll be turning back shortly," Father Keene replied, his cheeks rosy from the cold. "I just need a wee bit of a walk after saying this afternoon's Mass. Helps me to wind down."

"Weather forecasters are all saying that a real nor'easter is on its way. Just look at those clouds." George craned his head out of the window to look up at the sky. "You sure you don't want a ride back to town before this thing starts?"

"I'll be just fine. As soon as you leave, I'll turn around and start back."

George hesitated, wondering if he should insist. "Maybe you'd better come with me. I'd hate for you to get caught in this thing."

"No, no. You be getting along, now. I'm certain there are folks needing your services."

"I do need to get to the plumbing supply store before they close," George remembered.

Father Keene insisted. "You get along, then. Don't worry about me."

"All right. If you think you can make it back to town before it starts." He put the van in drive then adjusted his side mirror with a gloved hand.

"See you tomorrow for breakfast," Father Keene said with a smile of devilment just as George began to pull away.

George hit the brakes. "The furnace acting up again?" he asked hopefully.

"You know how it is when the weather's bad."

"Maybe I'd better stop over before I start my other jobs. Check things out."

"That would be greatly appreciated, George."

"It's my job. No need to thank me." George rolled up his window.

As soon as the van had disappeared over the rise, the snow began. Fat, leafy flakes fell, then disappeared as soon as they hit the ground, the type of snow that never amounted to much. Father Keene ignored it.

He crossed the small stream that separated the road from the Platts' farmland and felt his spirit begin to flutter like a bird sensing an updraft upon which it could soar. Father Keene needed the quiet balm of nature. It was as central to his soul as water or air was to his body. He savored these moments, which was why he stubbornly walked on, ignoring the threatening skies above and George's dire warnings.

Today, the elderly priest was greatly burdened by the archbishop's announcement that St. Cecilia's was to be closed, and the aggrieved looks on the parishioners' faces as Father James had delivered the news during the Ash Wednesday service. He needed to speak to God alone, bereft of noise and distractions. *Surely, God will not allow His people to suffer the loss of their beloved church,* he mused, bending forward as he climbed the steep embankment and headed toward the woods that lay just above the ridge.

A herd of dairy cattle grazed on top of the small rise; the sight of their black bodies ringed with a center of white made him laugh. The locals called these cattle Oreos. The herd was busy nipping at what little grass still grew underneath the rocks and around fence posts. They barely gave him a glance as he began the rise and headed toward the small ridge of mountains that separated the north and south portions of the town just behind the farm.

As he walked, his thick-soled boots sank into spots the manure had heated. The earthy smell of pasture and cattle rose up to meet him, transporting him back to the fields that had surrounded his boyhood home in Smeen. Echoes of his mother's voice reverberated across the corridors of time. "No matter what prized plot of land you build your house on, cows always seem to have the better view." The memory made him laugh out loud. One of the cows lifted her head as the sound of his laughter carried across the silent meadow.

Father Keene entered the path that wove around the fields and into the woods in search of the small clearing that boasted a twenty-mile unobstructed view of the valley and town below. It was his favorite place in all of Dorsetville.

Standing high upon the mountain ridge, Father Keene could make out the town green—a cluster of church spires and century old oak and maple trees all competing for their share of the sky. Encircling the village was a maze of stone walls that quadrant off the many farms, appearing to the priest like seams in a patchwork quilt, separating scraps of different patterned fabrics. And scattered here and there throughout the valley were dozens of rooftops, from whose chimneys smoke rose, then curled and thinned to disappear on the wind like apparitions called back to the netherworld.

With eager anticipation, Father Keene entered this favorite spot, ready to savor the beauty from high on this perch, relishing the first rush of jubilation the scene always brought. He had positioned himself in the center of the clearing—the spot that provided the best vantage point—when the weather took a sudden and angry turn. Within minutes, the scene below was completely obscured by raging currents of snow and ice.

He stood as still as a city pedestrian waiting for traffic to abate, believing that it was just a snow squall. He had seen many since coming to New England and knew they died as quickly as they came. He waited but the snow only thickened and within minutes his coat was covered in a thick layer of icy granules.

He turned back toward the path in the direction he had come from but could no longer decipher north or south. Which was the way back down? Sheets of ice and snow had severed the landscape, obscuring familiar landmarks.

He stepped forward and stumbled over a fallen log. For several seconds, he lay in the snow, too stunned to move. The wind increased, urging him up. He rose slowly, thankful that nothing had broken in the fall.

Finally on his feet, another gust roared through the clearing with the speed of a runaway train. It caught him off balance, slamming him down hard against the frozen ground. He heard a *pop*, felt an enormous jolt of pain as he landed hard on his left side. A rib had broken.

His breath came in short, labored puffs. Deep breathing intensified the blinding pain. Tears rolled down his face and instantly crystallized. He tried not to let his mind fill with fear or panic, knowing that to survive he must get up and keep walking. Suppressing the rising terror that threatened to immobilize him, Father Keene rolled over onto his hands, screaming in pain but refusing to stop until he was once again upright.

Another burst of wind carried the traces of chimney smoke, and for just a moment hope was revived. Chimney smoke meant shelter. He turned, heading in its direction but had walked only a few yards when his foot caught on a hidden boulder now slick with ice. Arms flailing but finding no purchase, he crashed to the ground again.

His cry seemed to shake the very snow off the branches. He had landed on his back. His face was quickly dusted in a fine coating of icy granules. A black tide rushed up, pulling him down in an undertow of darkness. He struggled like a swimmer against a strong current, refusing to allow his mind to slip below the surface of consciousness. To do so would mean certain death. The barrage of ice pellets that stung his face helped him to resurface.

In a strange way, the pain now became his best ally, like the sharp, pointed finger of a friend egging him onward. Together they groped their way along the ground, over the boulders and toward a small niche under a tall pine tree. Grabbing hold of a cluster of low branches, he inched his way up, then leaned exhausted against its bark, pondering his next move. *Perhaps the thicket of pines deeper in the woods will provide shelter,* he thought.

The broken rib prevented him from standing erect. Bent with pain, he inched forward, feeling his way through the low underbrush and around tree trunks until his hands and feet turned to heavy frozen masses without feeling or form.

Another gale ripped through the forest, bending twenty-foot trees in its wake as though they were mere twigs. The entire forest began to creak like the sound of a ship's hull giving way under a full gale. The elderly priest kept walking, devoid of any plan. He dared not stop.

The wind's speed increased and grabbed at tree limbs and branches as it charged through the forest. A succession of explosive snaps followed, sounding as though a madman with a rifle had been let loose. Next came the muffled thud of heavy limbs crashing to the forest floor.

Father Keene looked up into the whitewashed sky and saw a portion of a limb—several yards round—bouncing overhead, then heard the wood snap and break. Using what little reserves he still possessed, he raced out from under the limb, only to have another crash down at his feet. He twirled around, then darted, first one way then another—like a squirrel crossing the highway—trying to seek safety; his boots filled up with snow.

The wind paused and he stood anchored until a large dark shadow charged out in front of him. He turned sharply to avoid collision. A family of deer leaped past. If he could just rest. Regain his strength. Think of a plan.

You can't stop, he admonished himself. *Keep going. Keep going.*

By five o'clock, Father Keene knew that he was not going to survive. What little daylight had not been obscured by the snow was rapidly fading. Within twenty minutes, it would be dark and the temperatures would plummet further. No one could survive these temperatures for more than a few minutes. He slid to the ground, savoring a strange sense of peace in the knowledge that he no longer had to go on, or fight, and began to slip under the blanket of cold, ready, at last, to sleep.

Dear Lord, he prayed, postponing the rest he so craved until he finished this last prayer. *Thank you, Father, for the gift of life that you so graciously have given me. I've had a blessed life and eighty-two is a fine age to have lived to.*

I have tried to live my life as Christ, my Savior, would have lived it if He had walked in my steps. I know that there were times that I have fallen, sinned by using a harsh or unkind word. Or worse, I have not given a word of comfort when I could have. For this, I ask your forgiveness.

If you are inclined to grant a dying man one last request, this is mine. That you will save St. Cecilia's. That you will find a way to keep the church open. It's a blessed church, Lord, filled with good people. But then I wouldn't be telling you anything that you don't already know, would I?

So, there it is. I'm ready now to finally leave this bag of bones and travel home. I hope that I won't fare too poorly when I finally see You face to face. Amen.

At first, he thought that the cold had affected his mind, creating a vision, like a mirage witnessed by those in the desert of things hoped for but not really seen. The snow began to separate, like a curtain drawn open to reveal the brilliant rays of the sun. He could actually feel the heat radiate outward and warm his limbs. He sat up and watched with fascination as the golden light began to move toward him, and from its center he could hear a voice say, "Fear not. We are messengers sent from God."

He rose to his feet, surprisingly free from all pain and watched with fascination as the light was transformed into two huge angels. Their faces shone like sunlight reflected off polished gold. Their white garments radiated a luminescence that glowed like the corona around the sun. They stood nearly nine feet tall, with broad shoulders and biceps the size of hams, and as they moved nearer, Father Keene could see the cords of muscle along their arms and necks.

He felt a shiver of fear as he looked up into their faces, uncertain how to act in the presence of these heavenly bodies. Should he kneel down? Bow?

He remained standing as he asked, "Have you come to take me to heaven?"

"No. It is not your time, Patrick Keene," they answered simply.

"Not my time?" Disappointment filled him. Having glimpsed a portion of heaven, how could he rejoice in having it withheld? "Then why have you come?"

"There is still work for you to do here on earth."

"What is it that God would have me do?"

"You prayed that God would save St. Cecilia's and He has favored your request."

Father Keene fell to his knees. "Praise be to His Holy Name." Hot tears traveled down his weathered cheeks. "You have no idea how grateful the parishioners will be when they hear this news." Then he paused. "But what would God have me do?"

"God needs your presence at St. Cecilia's as He brings this promise to pass."

Without conscious thought, the words once uttered by the Blessed Virgin Mary fell from his lips, "I am the Lord's servant. May it be as you have spoken. "

The angels walked toward him. Father Keene looked up into their faces, suddenly unafraid.

They leaned the priest's torso upon their chests then picked up his legs and carried him into the raging storm. Surprisingly, Father Keene no longer felt any discomfort. He was neither cold nor in any pain from the broken rib. Even his frostbitten feet and hands appeared perfectly normal.

It seemed as though he had only blinked once before the angels were placing him in front of Harriet Bedford's farmhouse. Father Keene turned to comment how quickly they had arrived, but they were gone, and within seconds of their disappearance, the storm began to rage again.

He made his way to the back door of the house and knocked, but Harriet was not home. He fished for the milkman's key she kept hidden under the metal milk bin, quickly found it and let himself in.

And for the next few days, as search parties combed the countryside looking for his frozen remains, Father Keene stared into the flames of a roaring fire as though it held the secret to what he was going to tell everyone when he was found.

Chapter 15

The bustle of New York City after the quiet of a small New England town had Father James as frazzled as a cloistered monk at a bake sale. He was exceedingly tired, his feet hurt from pounding against the unyielding concrete and he missed his own bed. Where was the stamina of his youth? he wondered.

Though he still loved New York and the memories it evoked of his college years, he loved Dorsetville more and the thought of returning tomorrow was bittersweet. How would he find the strength to say his final good-byes to all the good people of his parish—Mrs. Norris, Timothy, Ben, Harriet, Harry, the Petersons, to name just a few? He would even miss George Benson.

As a priest, he had been transferred many times before and, undoubtedly throughout his career, he would be again. But this was different. A priest normally leaves a parish knowing that the church will remain. When he leaves St. Cecilia's, the church community would end.

St. Cecilia's parishioners had become his family over the last three years, as lasting relationships were forged through the valleys and the mountaintops, the trials and the blessings scattered throughout parish life. He had joyfully baptized their newborns and cried with them as he committed their loved ones' bodies to their final resting places. He had heard their confessions and they had discovered his foibles, and like any family, they had learned to love regardless of the flaws.

But this parish possessed something more. It was a church community that walked the talk, as a friend of his often said. Never before had he witnessed a congregation place such heavy emphasis on faith in action, and it seemed as natural to them as breathing.

Time and time again, Father had seen the poorest in his parish give the most generously in times of need. Just recently, the Campbells gave their 1985 Dodge Omni to a poor family that lived down the street, when they discovered the family's only car had broken down and could no longer be repaired. Neither of the Campbells, whose eyesight had deteriorated badly, could drive any longer.

The Campbells lived on social security without pensions or savings, and Father James knew that they sorely needed the cash the sale of their car could have generated; yet their compassion would not allow them to withhold help from someone in need if it was in their power to help.

Dorsetville was filled with these types of stories—people helping neighbors and friends quietly and without fanfare. Father knew that at this very moment if he was to look inside Lori and Bob Petersons' home their freezer would be stocked with food, their house cleaned from top to bottom and a list of baby-sitters for Sarah would be waiting next to their phone. St. Cecilia's was like that.

It would be a heart-wrenching task to finish the preparations to close the church, but even more difficult would be the committal of Father Keene to a nursing home. Throughout his stay in New York, it had been the first thing he thought about when rising in the morning and the last he thought about before drifting into an uneasy sleep at night.

During the week, alone in Jeff's spare bedroom with the city sounds just outside his window, Father James fantasized that he would run away, get lost in all the noise and bedlam of the city. He pondered what would happen if he elected not to return or took sanctuary in a monastery. Let someone else—someone emotionally detached—go about the task of closing the church and committing Father Keene. Father James feared he wouldn't have the stamina to endure the finality of shutting those heavy oak doors to the sanctuary for the last time.

The words of our Lord fell like a gauntlet across his self-pity and despair. *"If this cup can be taken from me, not my will, but Yours be done."*

Christ had not promised an easy life or a life without heartache. He himself had been known as the "Man of Sorrows." But He did promise to lead Father James and his church through the darkness, to turn that which seemed an impossible trial into a great blessing, if only Father James would learn to trust in God implicitly and not lean unto his own understanding. To stand fast and persevere.

His friend, Monsignor Casio from St. Timothy's, whom Father James had visited early in the week, had helped him to find new resolve not to question God's plan. Their visit had been a balm to Father James's troubled spirit, lifting him up from despair and back toward soul-confidence and faith.

As soon as the monsignor spied Father James, he pointed to his old friend's stomach and laughed. "Jimmy, I see you've finally joined the Catholic brotherhood of portly priests. A welcome change from that twig of a college student I once knew."

Father James mumbled something about there not being time to exercise, but when his old mentor laughed louder, he gave up the pretense.

"Consider it an occupational hazard," the monsignor said. Jeff had gone to pick up the wedding invitations which left the older priest and his former prodigy alone.

"In fact, I think a parish likes to see its pastor with a little paunch." He took a box of Cuban cigars off his desk and offered one to Father James. "A well-fed priest is a sign of a prosperous parish."

Father James bit off the end of the cigar. "In my case, that couldn't be farther from the truth." He told his friend about St. Cecilia's imminent closing.

"If the archbishop has ordered your parish closed by Easter, I'm surprised that you're here in New York. I know that the Haydens are good friends, but your duties must always take precedence."

Father James moved the ashtray on the desk closer. "I had my qualms, but the archbishop insisted. He said it might help to strengthen my resolve for what has to be done."

"Who's watching your flock while you're away? That elderly priest, what's his name?"

"Father Keene? No. The archbishop sent over a young priest, Father Dennis Osborne, to watch over things while I'm gone." Father James shared Father Keene's newest adventure, then ended with the archbishop's decision to place him in a nursing home.

The monsignor silently worked his cigar. "Sounds like you have quite a lot on your plate right now."

"I'm not looking forward to going back. In fact, I've been fantasizing about staying here in New York until it's all over."

"No, not you. Some other of my former candidates, perhaps, but not the Jimmy Flaherty I know." Monsignor Casio leaned back in his chair.

"Remember the time I sent you over to the tenement house on Forty-ninth Street where some of our parishioners lived? It was in the dead of winter. You went to help Father Grimm." This jarred a memory that made him laugh. "Poor Father Grimm. How the children did tease him about his name. Anyway, I sent you to give Father Grimm a hand and you came back without any shoes."

Father James blushed. "There was an immigrant father who needed to go to work and someone had broken into his apartment that morning and stolen his shoes. It was no big thing."

Monsignor Casio smiled. "I was hungry and you fed me. I was naked and you clothed me. I was in prison and you visited me. A priest with such compassion could never abandon his parishioners when they need him the most."

The two men sat silently, puffing on their cigars, a halo of blue smoke forming over their heads.

"And there's nothing left to be done to keep the church open?" the monsignor asked, studying the tip of his cigar.

Father James shook his head. "If there is, I don't know what it could be. I've tried everything I know how to do. I wrote letters. Applied for grants. Held fund-raisers and actively worked on upgrading our membership, but when the mills closed so many of our parishioners moved away."

"And did you pray?"

He looked with earnest eyes. "Without ceasing."

"Then you have done all you can."

"Then why do I feel as though I've failed God, His people, the Church?" He bent over in the chair as one does who feels faint.

The monsignor rested his cigar in the glass ashtray, got up and walked over, placing a hand on his shoulder. "If your heart is centered on the welfare of your parish, then you cannot fail God or His Church or His people. Sounds like He has something else in mind for your parishioners."

"Like what?" A ripple of light began to shine through his darkness.

"I don't know. But then, I'm not God."

The light disappeared. "While I wait for God's plan to be revealed, what can I do to help the elderly parishioners who refuse to attend Mass at St. Bartholomew's? I'm fearful that many may die outside the sacraments of the Church. Then there's the issue of Father Keene. If we place him in a nursing home, we will be abandoning him at a time when he needs us most. Is that the way to repay a faithful servant of God?"

"But that's just it, Jimmy. You've forgotten that Father Keene is God's servant, as are your parishioners. They are God's responsibility, not yours. You're there to lead them, not to provide for them. That's God's job. Allowing God to prove His faithfulness is the most important lesson a priest can teach his flock. My advice is to step back and see what God will do." The monsignor walked back and stubbed out his cigar.

"I know you're right, but still," Father James said, "that doesn't stop the heartache I feel at watching this wonderful parish, rich in good, kind people, become spiritually homeless."

"Nonsense," the monsignor said as he opened a window to air out the room. A horn blared outside. "God will not abandon His people, or you or Father Keene. As with all great trials, there is a powerful lesson hidden in this seemingly rocky path. But to discover it, you must walk it. You can't go around it, or pray yourself out of it.

"You see, Jimmy, that's the trouble with our society. We're conditioned to hop in a car, a plane or some other mode of transportation and get where we want to go. We've almost forgotten the art of the journey and its importance. You and your flock are interpreting this as a time of deep sorrow. Turn it around and see it for what it really is—a time of great revelation of God's faithfulness. A time of miracles." Monsignor Casio watched Father James raise an eyebrow.

"That's right. I said *miracles*. God still provides them for those who dare to believe. Why just recently I read about a church in Massachusetts that had a similar problem as yours. Their building was falling apart and they didn't have any funds to repair it. Then one day, the pastor happened to pull out a painting that had been tucked in a church basement closet for years and wondered whether it might be worth something. So, he took it to an appraiser. Guess what? The painting turned out to be an Andrea del Sarto, a famous Renaissance painter. It sold last week at Christie's Auction House for $1.1 million dollars."

The light was returning to Father James's spirit.

"God has a plan," the monsignor said with confidence, settling again behind his desk. "Now, granted, it's one you don't know about; but then we don't need to know. God has asked us to go by faith, not by sight. So change your perspective. Stop viewing St. Cecilia's closing as a disaster. Instead, see it as golden opportunity for God to reveal His faithfulness to His people. And don't be afraid of the word *miracle*. It's always been my experience that when people have no resources of their own, God steps forward in some of the most extraordinary ways."

"You sound like a parishioner of mine," Father James said, thinking of Bob Peterson.

"Seems like you should take his advice."

"It's hard to maintain faith when you don't see anything happening," Father James confessed humbly.

The monsignor pointed to a painting of a glorious sunset above the fireplace mantel. "See that? See the open space around that sunset? See how it's just empty sky? Artists call it 'negative space.' Now look at how it's used to hold up the main elements of the painting. The colorful shards of light breaking across the sky. The dazzling gold of the setting sun. That negative space is the filler the artist uses to support his subject. Without those spaces, the painting would collapse into a mass of indiscernible colors and shapes."

He leaned forward, looked Father James straight in the eye and brought his point home. "That painting is a lot like prayer. The answers to our prayers are the clearly defined elements, like this sunset. But the moments in between—the negative space, if you will—are just as important. Those moments, that space, frame the answers to our prayers. Without the waiting, there can be no miracles.

"God has not turned His face away from your needs, Jimmy. Neither has He refused to provide for those needs. His silence is simply the backdrop used to highlight the gifts He will surely bring."

⚜

The Haydens' home was filled with the soft sounds of jazz, overlaid with lively conversations, bursts of laughter and exuberant greetings. The three-story townhouse on New York's fashionable Upper West Side was filled from the ground level to its rafters with friends and associates who had come to celebrate the engagement of Judge Hayden's son.

The people who jammed the various rooms represented the A list of New York's society. The men—dressed in tailor-made tuxedos—and the women—in expensive designer originals—were titled, dignitaries, movie stars or political heavyweights. In the library Donald Trump, Mayor Rudolph Giuliani and Barbara Walters were engaged in a heated discussion about the new alternate side of the street parking laws. In the front parlor, Princess Fergie was seated on a Brunschwig chair chatting politely with Eileen Fisher. Across the hall, Stephen Spielberg lobbied for a celebrity's right to privacy with a New York senator. The men stood next to a signed Al Hirschfeld of *Cats* that the Haydens had bought at a benefit auction for the restoration of Grand Central Station that had been hosted by Jacqueline Kennedy.

Father James watched from a discreet distance, greatly intimidated by it all, wishing he could be more like Monsignor Casio, who apparently had no such qualms. Standing to the left of the Italian marble fireplace, the prelate was engaged in animated conversation with Diane Sawyer.

"Enjoying yourself?" Judge Hayden asked Father James.

"It's not exactly like the functions I normally attend. No casseroles or cheese dips in sight," he joked.

The judge laughed as he handed the priest a glass of champagne. "If this isn't to your liking, there's a bar set up in the corner. I can't abide that stuff, myself. I'm strictly a bourbon drinker. Champagne's my wife's idea."

"This is just fine," insisted Father James, taking a sip from the long-stemmed Baccarat glass. The liquid slid down his throat like velvet. It must have cost a small fortune.

"Looks like a great party," he mused, the wine taking the edge off his party jitters.

"It's not every day your youngest son announces his engagement, now is it? Have you met Allison?"

"Yes. Jeff and I went to visit her shop. What a great place," he said in earnest. "And what an education I got!"

"She knows her stuff, that's for sure."

"I even got to watch her create some incredible arrangements for an affair the British Embassy was hosting. They were like works of art."

"She's a great little businesswoman, too," the judge said proudly. "Started with a small shop three years ago. Up on 110th Street."

"Kind of a risky location," Father James said, taking another sip of his champagne.

"That's what I would have thought, but Allison made it work. She was smart. Started right out specializing in just exotic flowers, unusual bouquets. It was a real hit from the get-go."

"Care for an hors d'oeuvre?" a waiter asked the two men.

Father James chose the paté on a thin crust of pastry; the judge salmon mousse piped on a cucumber wedge.

Judge Hayden took a sip of bourbon to clear his palate. "Allison learned all about plants while traveling with her father when she was a kid. You'll meet him later on. Name's Peter. Interesting man. Worked as an energy consultant to some major oil companies.

"Anyway, Allison went with her father to all these exotic locations and got interested in botany at an early age. Started to major in botany at college but left after her junior year. Spent her tuition money instead on a small floral shop. Used her connections overseas to help stock the shop with all kinds of exotic and unusual flowers and plants. New Yorkers loved it! Last year she moved the business to its present location over on Seventh Avenue, and the rest, as they say, is history. One of the fastest growing businesses in the city. Most of New York's high society shop exclusively at Allison's. She even has her own Web page."

"I saw Martha Stewart while we were visiting," Father James said, scanning the room for the waiter with the hors d'oeuvre tray.

"She's a regular. In fact, Allison's done her show a couple of times. Doesn't do it any longer, though. Doesn't have the time." The judge replaced his drink with another as a waiter passed by.

"How's your drink, Jim?"

"Fine."

Both the bourbon and the excitement of his son's engagement propelled him forward. "She's a talented woman, no question there. A good sense of civic duty, as well."

This was an important characteristic, according to the judge's opinion. He had plans for Jeff to follow in his political shoes, and a wife involved in charity work would be a great asset.

"Allison's interested in programs that help children overcome a loss—loss of a parent, a sibling. That's how she and Jeff first met. She had helped launch a pilot program for children who had lost family members to street violence. Allison petitioned the city to lease small plots of land so the children could plant memorial gardens. Jeff heard about the plan and volunteered to help write up the leases."

"Sounds like you're besotted by your future daughter-in-law, Judge."

"We all are. As far as I'm concerned, Jeff couldn't have found a better partner to share the rest of his life with." Judge Hayden looked around the room. "There's her father talking to the monsignor. Let me introduce you."

"Peter, let me introduce you to Jeff's best man," Judge Hayden said. "This is Father James Flaherty. Father, this is Peter Bedford, Allison's father."

"Hello." Peter extended a warm handshake. He was a slender man with salt-and-pepper hair and the leathery complexion of one who has worked most of his life outdoors. He was deeply tanned for this time of year.

"Charles, Charles," Mrs. Hayden called. "There's a phone call for you in your study."

"Excuse me," the judge said. "You two get acquainted and I'll be right back."

While the judge disappeared into the crowd, Father James said, "The judge tells me that you've traveled to some rather exotic ports."

"I've spent most of my career scouting sites for oil companies."

"Sounds like interesting work."

Peter took a sip of scotch. "It is when you're on the trail of a major find. Other times, it's just legwork. Hot and boring."

"Allison seems to have liked it. The judge tells me that's where she discovered her love for botany."

Peter smiled, his eyes softening with a father's love. "Allison has a special gift, the ability to find happiness wherever she is."

"That is a rare gift, indeed," he agreed. "But I suppose if the Lord hadn't sent you to those exotic ports, Allison would not have uncovered this particular talent."

"She's a lot like her grandmother. Both seem to have a natural gift with plants."

Peter began to look a little pale. He set aside his drink.

"Are you feeling all right?"

"Just a little jet lag," Peter explained. "I got in late last night from Istanbul. Think I'll lay off the booze, though. That should help." He rubbed his left arm. "The judge says you're from a small parish in New England."

"Dorsetville. It's about midway up the state, alongside the Connecticut River. Do you know the area?"

Peter's color faded further. "What's the name of your parish?"

"St. Cecilia's. Are you sure you're all right? I could call someone."

"No." Peter sounded winded. "I see Allison coming this way. Let's not make a fuss. I don't want to ruin her party."

"Maybe if you just sat down," Father James scanned the room. "There's a chair over there."

"That's a good idea."

Peter walked two steps before collapsing on the Persian rug. A woman standing nearby screamed. Conversations stopped in midsentence.

"Someone call 911," Father James shouted. He knelt down. "Peter?"

"Daddy! Daddy, what's wrong?" Allison rushed over.

Mrs. Hayden—who often said that raising five sons had taught her to be equal to any emergency—saw Peter crumble and immediately grabbed a cell phone from the pocketbook a guest had slung over her arm and dialed for an ambulance while waving a servant on to fetch Dr. Billings.

Seconds later, the doctor came running into the room. "Move back. Let me through."

Mrs. Hayden grabbed for Jeff's hand as he tried to rush past; his father, the judge, followed close behind. "What's happened?" the men asked.

"Looks like a heart attack," Dr. Billings said. "Someone get me an aspirin and make it quick."

"Here, I have some in my purse," Barbara Walters said.

Father James looked up from where he was kneeling and realized the star no longer seemed intimidating.

Peter motioned for Father James to bend nearer.

"Father, I think he wants to speak to you," Allison said, working hard to retain her calm.

Father James leaned forward.

"Do you know a Harriet Bedford?" Peter's voice was just a whisper.

"Yes."

Peter looked into his face with mournful eyes. "Harriet Bedford is my mother."

"We need to get this man to the hospital STAT," Dr. Billings said, rising to his feet.

"I've called an ambulance," Mrs. Hayden said.

"If we wait for an ambulance this man will be dead. Mr. Mayor, is your limo outside?" the doctor asked.

"At your service."

"Can you get us a police escort? Every minute is crucial."

Mayor Giuliani nodded to his bodyguard standing unobtrusively in the corner, who relayed the request through his headset. The bodyguard nodded back, indicating that everything was in place.

"They're ready to go as soon as we get him into the car," the mayor assured Dr. Billings.

Several muscular men, who Father James assumed were bodyguards of the other elite gathered in the room, appeared. He noticed their holstered guns as they lifted Peter up off the floor and began to carry him outside.

Peter grabbed hold of Father James's sleeve. "I want you to come."

"There's plenty of room, Father," the mayor offered.

"Thank you."

Allison and Jeff followed closely behind.

Monsignor Casio thrust something at Father James as he raced by. "Here. You'll need this."

Father James quickly climbed into the limousine amazed to discover that it contained a gurney and medical equipment. Peter had already been placed on the stretcher and the doctor was adjusting an oxygen mask. The priest assumed this was not how the car had appeared when the mayor had arrived at the party a few hours ago. Apparently it was designed to instantly convert into an emergency medical vehicle.

As they rode through the city streets, the siren blaring, Father James peered inside the bag Monsignor Casio had given him. It contained a prayer book, a vestment and a vial of oil. Everything he would need to administer the last rites. He prayed that it would not be needed.

Chapter 16

The hospital waiting room was shrouded in silence. Seated opposite Father James were Allison and Jeff, hands tightly clasped, still clad in tuxedo and sequined gown, which seemed out of place in this setting, although Father James conceded he couldn't imagine what might be the proper attire in a situation like this. The couple had run out of conversation hours ago; now they stared fixedly at the floor, awaiting news from Dr. Billings and his staff who had been working on Peter Bedford for nearly three hours. There was still no word.

Father James held a dog-eared copy of *Newsweek* in his lap and stared at the same page as he had done for hours, the text obscured by a continual loop of the evening's events that replayed again and again in his mind—his arrival at the Haydens' townhouse, whose brightly lit windows had cast pockets of warm light onto the dark sidewalks; the rooms filled with conversation against the strains of a live jazz quartet; the soft scent of tropical flowers wafting in the air; the dining room table and sideboards groaning under the weight of such delicacies as poached salmon, Beluga caviar and thin slices of prime steak—a gift from a Texas senator who had flown in that morning—in a rich Madeira sauce; his first meeting with Peter Bedford and the double shock of the man's collapse and the discovery that he was Harriet Bedford's lost son.

Father James glanced across at Allison. What were the odds that his best friend's fiancée would turn out to be Harriet Bedford's lost granddaughter? Now that he knew of the relationship, it was easy to discern Harriet's features in Allison's face—wide brow, nicely spaced green-gold eyes, high cheekbones, sharp, well-defined nose and a long thin neck.

He glanced back down at his magazine, pages obscured by a new tangle of thoughts. What did Allison know, if anything, about her grandmother? What had Peter told his daughter? Perhaps that Harriet was dead? As much as he wanted to tell Allison the truth—that her grandmother was very much alive, living in Dorsetville, and had never stopped praying that someday they'd be reunited—he could not, especially now. Allison already had enough to deal with for one evening.

His thoughts were interrupted as Dr. Billings walked in the room, his tuxedo replaced by surgical scrubs. Allison and Jeff jumped to their feet as though the weight of the news the physician was about to deliver could be better carried if standing.

"I'm afraid it's not good," Dr. Billings told Allison before she could ask.

Allison inhaled sharply, steeling herself against Jeff whose face was drawn with fatigue.

"Your father has had a massive heart attack," Dr. Billings told her. "The left ventricle has been severely damaged."

Jeff gripped Allison's hand tighter and asked, "And the prognosis?"

Dr. Billings's eyes darted around the room like a bird, refusing to rest on Allison's face. "Not good. Few patients in Mr. Bedford's condition live more than a few hours. I'm sorry."

"Oh, please, God, no." Allison cried. Jeff drew her closer.

"I wish I could offer you more hope, but we've done everything we can do. The damage to your father's heart is too massive to repair."

"Allison . . . " Father James began.

"Can I see him?" she asked.

"Certainly. He's a little groggy from the pain medication, but he'll recognize you. However, Mr. Bedford wishes to see Father James first."

Father James looked at Allison.

"It's all right," she said. "I'll wait until you're through."

Father James nodded, then gathered his things from a side table, patting Allison's hand as he walked by. He followed Dr. Billings out of the waiting area, through hospital corridors that smelled strongly of antiseptic and around yellow plastic signs that read CAUTION, WET FLOORS. Finally, they stopped in front of a set of double doors leading to the intensive care unit. Dr. Billings pressed an eight-inch-round steel button on the right side of the wall and the doors swung open.

"He's in here," said Dr. Billings, pausing by the open door of a room directly in front of the nurses' central monitoring station.

Father James glanced inside the glass paneled room where Peter lay, ashen, swathed under white sheets, connected to a network of tubes, wires and monitors. It was a stark contrast to the rugged, deeply tanned figure Father James had met for the first time only hours ago.

"I'll leave you alone," Dr. Billings offered. "If you need anything, just ring the buzzer."

"Thank you," Father James said, then walked in the room.

The lights had been dimmed in deference to the patient's need to rest, but the bank of machines that pumped and hissed with heartbeats of their own were still visible, their monitors casting a soft, diffuse light. Peter's eyes were closed. The priest walked over to the bed and touched his hand.

"Peter," he said softly, "it's Father James."

Peter looked up, his eyes unfocused from the painkillers. It took him several seconds to focus. "Father . . . James . . . I need to . . . talk . . . to you." The words were thickly spoken as though Peter's tongue was coated in cotton.

"I'm listening," Father James replied. "Take your time."

"I don't think . . . I have much . . . time left," Peter whispered. "And there's something I have to confess . . . before . . . I die."

"You wish the sacrament of reconciliation?"

Peter nodded.

Father James reached inside the leather satchel Monsignor Casio had given him, withdrawing a linen stole, a prayer book and the holy chrism. Father James kissed the stole, placing it around his shoulders, rested the prayer book on the bed, then slipped the ring attached to the holy chrism on his finger. Making the sign of the cross, he told Peter he was ready to begin.

"Bless me Father for I have sinned," Peter recited.

"The Lord be on your lips and in your heart that you may properly confess all your sins, in the Name of the Father and of the Son and of the Holy Spirit."

"It has been many years since my last confession," Peter began. He paused. "Do you know what happened to my wife and daughter?"

"Yes. Your mother told me about the accident. I'm sorry."

Peter focused on the ceiling, forcing his voice to remain steady as he grimaced in pain. "When it happened, I was angry at everyone. The drunk driver who killed my wife and daughter. At the highway crews who didn't have the right equipment to get them out fast enough— they lost precious moments. But mostly, I was angry at God. Where was He during all of this? Where was the compassionate, loving Being that I had trusted? How could He have let this happen? He could have saved them and He didn't. I hated Him for it.

"When my mother wouldn't join me in my anger, I lashed out at her. I told her that she had to choose. Me or her God, that she couldn't have both. I don't know . . . I wasn't thinking clearly."

"That's understandable," Father offered. "Few could have gone through that type of tragedy and not have felt anger."

"At the time, perhaps, but I had no right to let it go on and on for years. It just seemed that once it started, I couldn't undo what I had done. I felt there was no going back. So I chose to submerge myself in my work and forget there ever was a Dorsetville, or a St. Cecilia's, or a God, or my mother. I've hurt her terribly. She didn't deserve it and now it's too late to make amends."

Peter wept.

A nurse quietly stole into the room. Seeing Father James vested, she quickly left without comment.

"If I could only ask my mother's forgiveness," Peter lamented, his breathing more labored. "She didn't deserve the kind of punishment I inflicted. She was a great mother. An even greater grandmother. How could I have been so cruel as to take her only grandchild away? I know how deeply she must have suffered, but I was too self-absorbed to care about her need for comfort. I was focused on my need for revenge against her God."

"I've known her for years and I've never once heard her utter an unkind word against you or what you did," Father James offered.

"You've talked about what happened?"

"Many times, and I can assure you that she has always spoken about you with a mother's love. She harbors no unforgiveness. She loves you and Allison very much and never stopped praying that someday you would all be reunited."

"Except that it's not going to happen now, is it?" asked Peter.

Father James desperately wanted to assure Peter otherwise, yet he could not. Instead, he counseled, "Perhaps not in this life, but most definitely in the next."

"If only I could believe that." Peter turned to the priest, his face contorted in a pain rooted not in a damaged heart but in a damaged soul. "Oh, Father, I want to believe what my mother and the Church have taught me. I want to believe in a heaven. I want to believe that there is more than just this, but I can't. I've tried."

Tears formed again in the corner of his eyes. "I keep thinking about death and how my mother was always so confident that there was a God. I wish I had her faith. I'd like to believe that Elizabeth and Melanie are waiting for me." Peter grimaced in pain.

"Do you want me to call the nurse?"

Peter shook his head. Father waited.

The pain began to ebb. Peter's face relaxed as he drew in a slow breath then continued. "My heart's been in bad shape for about a year."

"You didn't tell Allison?" Father James asked.

"No. There wasn't anything the doctors could do. I didn't want to ruin her wedding plans. I thought I might be able to make it through. Tell her after the honeymoon. It's one more thing that I've put off until it was too late," he confessed, then added, "but I don't want to put off making things right with God any longer. I'm not sure how to begin, especially when I'm not at all certain that I really believe that He exists."

"You want evidence, proof, before you choose to believe?" Father asked, not unkindly.

A soft smile played across Peter's face. "That's a fair assessment."

"Peter, there is proof."

"There is?"

"You act surprised. Do you seriously think that our Christian faith could have survived for more than two thousand years if it was merely based on a myth?"

"Go on," he asked, intrigued.

"The Christian faith is based on factual, eyewitness accounts of what happened when Jesus Christ walked among men. The Apostle Peter wrote, 'For we have not followed cunningly devised fables, when we made known unto you the power and coming of our Lord Jesus Christ, but were eyewitness of his majesty.' These men who personally knew Jesus believed him to be the Messiah."

"But, Father, how do I know that *they* were telling the truth? Couldn't they just have made up these stories?"

"That's a good and honest question. Let me see how I can explain why their testimony has always been considered truthful." Father James paused for a moment.

"Two thousand years ago, a group of men we call the Apostles joined a ministry headed by Jesus Christ, who professed to be the only Son of God, the Messiah for whom the Jewish race had long awaited. But did they believe him just because he said he was the son of God? No. They demanded proof." Father James hesitated. "Did you ever meet some of the fishermen who work along the South Street piers?"

"I've dealt with them when I had to ship equipment overseas."

"What kind of men are they?"

"Rough. No-nonsense kinds of guys," Peter answered.

"Easily duped?"

"No. They're pretty street smart."

Father James angled closer. "Those were the same kind of men Jesus choose as his followers. Rough characters, nobody's fools; men who used their hands and risked their lives out on the open seas to make a living. They were the kind of men that just wouldn't believe Jesus because he said he was the Son of God. They would have wanted proof. So Jesus invited them to follow him.

"For three years, these men ate, slept and journeyed with Jesus up and down the countryside and during that time they got all the proof they needed. With their own eyes, they watched as Jesus commanded the seas to be calm and saw him obeyed; saw Jesus reach out a hand and restore sight to the blind; command a legion of demons to remove themselves from a poor tortured man, then saw how that man was wonderfully restored; watched awestruck as Jesus took just a few loaves of bread and a couple of fish and fed a multitude of people; stood in open amazement as Jesus commanded the spirit of Lazarus to come back from the grave.

"Then came Good Friday and like you, Peter, the Apostles began to doubt. How could Jesus be the Messiah, the Son of God? The Jews believed that when the Messiah came he would come in power as a king to reestablish Jerusalem. But that hadn't happened. Instead, they had seen Jesus crucified. Laid his beaten and broken body on that cold slab of stone inside a tomb, then watched as Roman guards rolled a heavy stone across the entryway and sealed it with a Roman seal. Their faith wavered. They doubted. Had they believed a lie?

"But on Easter morning the Risen Lord appeared and over the next forty days, Jesus was seen by hundreds of people. Not as some ghostly form, but as flesh and blood. In the gospel of Luke, Jesus asks, 'Why are ye troubled? and why do doubts arise in your hearts? Behold my hands and my feet, that it is myself: handle me, and see; for a spirit hath flesh and bones as ye see me have.'

"To prove this point, he asked if they had anything to eat. They gave him a piece of broiled fish which he ate in their presence.

"Suddenly all the words that Jesus had spoken throughout his short ministry came to life, and they understood that all that he had proclaimed was true. Jesus *was* the true Son of God. The grave could not contain him and through the blood he shed on Calvary, he had ransomed man from sin.

"For the rest of their lives, these simple fishermen traveled from the shores of Galilee and around Asia Minor sharing with others what they had personally witnessed and knew to be true. Salvation had finally come to mankind though Jesus Christ. They faithfully gave testimony in these firsthand accounts even though their message was fraught with pain and suffering and immeasurable hardships. They were beaten, imprisoned, tortured and finally most were killed. Peter was crucified. James and Paul beheaded. But no matter how they suffered, not one of them ever renounced his testimony."

"And if their story was a lie, someone would have cracked under that kind of persecution," Peter conceded.

"Exactly," Father said. "These eyewitness accounts, these *facts*, are recorded in the New Testament and are the basis of our Christian faith. But the validity of these claims does not end here. Down through the ages, there have been countless other reports from reliable witnesses testifying to the transforming power inherent in Christ; lives that once were filled with darkness and despair have been given new meaning and empowerment.

"No other faith possesses the transforming powers inherent in salvation through Jesus Christ. His ministry is just as powerful today as it was two thousand years ago."

"Father, I want to believe, but . . ."

"I know. You're still trying to reason it out, why would a loving God allow your wife and daughter to die such a tragic death? I can't answer that. I can't tell you why God might pull someone out of a burning building completely unscathed, and yet not intervene for your wife and child. I can only trust that His wisdom is far greater than mine.

"You see, Peter, faith does not come by reasoning. It comes first by choice. You must *choose* to believe, to exercise your free will. In return, God gives us the faith to appropriate His promises for salvation.

"In John 11:25 Jesus says, 'I am the resurrection and the life: he that believeth in me, though he were dead, yet shall he live.' You have the Lord's promise that when your spirit leaves your mortal body it will be reunited with the Father. But this cannot happen unless you *will* it to happen by making a choice. Will you believe or not? Will you accept Jesus Christ as your savior?"

A curtain of silence fell, separating the two men. The decision that Peter was to make must be made alone. Father James bowed his head in prayer, allowing Peter the privacy of his thoughts. Finally, Peter said softly, "I choose to believe, Father."

Father James felt a hot flash of tears run down his cheeks. He smiled.

"Would you pray with me?" Peter asked.

"It would be my honor." Father James made the sign of the cross and began to pray out loud.

Dear Father: Peter is preparing to enter Your Presence, dear Lord. He knows that his life has not always reflected your grace and for that he is humbly sorry. For a long time, Peter has harbored unforgiveness toward his mother that Satan has used as a wedge to separate him and his daughter from a loving mother and grandmother. We renounce this sin in Jesus' name and ask that it be washed away by the blood of the Lamb.

Like the prodigal son, Peter wishes to come back home, Father. Back to the fold. He believed once as a child, but as a man he has allowed the world's reasoning to block out Your light. He repents, Father.

Your Holy Word says that if we confess our sins, you are faithful and just to forgive us our sins. We stand on that promise, Father, knowing that we have the full assurance that You stand ready to welcome Peter back with open arms through the gift of salvation your Son provided through His suffering at Calvary. Thank you, Father, through Jesus in whose holy name we pray. Amen.

Father James concluded the sacrament of reconciliation. "*May Our Lord Jesus Christ absolve you, and by His authority I absolve you from your sins in the Name of the Father and of the Son and of the Holy Spirit.*"

"Amen," Peter said.

Father James lifted the cover of the holy chrism where a piece of cotton lay soaked in anointing oil. Dipping his finger into the vial, he anointed Peter in preparation for his final journey. Peter closed his eyes. His body relaxed, tension ebbing away. He looked at peace.

Allison and Jeff were standing outside the door as Father James closed his prayer book. He motioned them in.

Allison rushed over and took her father's hand. She brought it up to her lips and softly kissed the spot where the IV was taped, as a mother might try to kiss away a child's hurt. "How are you feeling, Dad?"

"Not too good, baby," he whispered.

"Why didn't you tell me you were so ill?" she asked, sliding onto the bed to run a hand along his cheek.

"There was nothing you could have done."

"I could have postponed the engagement party. You were on a plane for more than thirty hours just to get here. The trip must have put a terrible stain on your heart."

"Don't do this, Allison. Don't blame yourself. There is nothing you could have done."

"But . . ."

Peter reached up and silenced her protests with a finger placed on her lips. Then he glanced over at Jeff, standing at Allison's side. "I know that I'm leaving my little girl in good hands."

Jeff nodded. "You can count on me, sir."

"Leaving? Don't talk like that." Allison struggled hard against the tears. "You're going to be fine."

"No, I'm not, Allison." Peter's voice was growing weaker. "We both know I'm dying."

"No!" The word was spoken as a command not a denial. "You can't die. I won't let you. You're all I have."

"No," Peter said, growing weaker. "You have a wonderful fiancé and a grandmother who loves you very much."

"Grandmother?" She studied his face as tears rushed down her cheeks. "You haven't spoken of her in years."

"I know. It's something I deeply regret. Please forgive me, dear. Father James tells me that she is still living in Dorsetville. Father James is the pastor there."

"Father, you know my grandmother?"

"Quite a coincidence, isn't it?" he smiled. "She's going to be overjoyed to see you again."

Peter arched his back, the pain intensifying. He labored to speak. "I want you . . . to promise me . . . something."

"Anything. What is it, Dad?"

"Promise me . . . that you will tell your grandmother how sorry I am for all of these wasted years. Tell her . . . I'm so sorry for the pain I brought her. Will you . . . do that for me, Allison?"

She nodded, clutching her father's hand harder. The EKG monitor began to flat line. A nurse rushed in.

Allison sobbed. Her body trembled as Jeff threw his arms around her shoulders as though trying to impart some of his strength. Dr. Billings walked back into the room and studied the monitors. He looked their way with compassion. "I'm afraid he's going now."

"Oh, Dad, please don't leave me," she cried, reaching out to him as she had as a child. "I need you. You're supposed to be here on my wedding day. You have to walk me down the aisle. Remember? I can't get married without you here to give me away."

"I'll be there," he said. "I . . . promise." His gaze shifted from Allison to the foot of the bed. He rose slightly off the pillows, staring into empty space.

"Dad? What is it?"

"Could it be?" he asked, his voice a mere whisper, then his eyes flew open wide with recognition. "Yes, it is!" His face flooded with joy. "Oh . . . Elizabeth! Melanie!"

And with those words, Peter Bedford fell back against his pillow and closed his eyes for the last time.

The waiting room was empty except for Father James, who had started to doze off in a chair while waiting for a return call from the rectory in Dorsetville. He had left a message for Father Dennis on the answering machine. "Call me at (212) 555-1345 as soon as you get this message," adding, "it's urgent."

He hung up the phone, removed the stiff white collar and took a chair opposite the television mounted on the wall high above a set of chairs. It was spewing out late-night infomercials. He watched a man pour some white powder on a rusty sink. Within seconds the rust melted away. He wondered if he should write this information down. The rectory's upstairs bathroom could certainly use some magic, then he remembered that the church was closing in a few weeks; the rectory would be boarded up. He leaned back, closed his eyes and waited for the return call from home.

His thoughts centered on the impact the news he had to deliver would have on Harriet Bedford. She would soon learn she had lost a son, but she would also discover that she had regained a granddaughter. His emotions over the news he had to share were as mixed as the message itself.

He tried to phone Harriet directly, but the phone lines were still down from the storm. *Perhaps it is better this way,* he thought. He'd have Father Dennis drive Father Keene over to Harriet's and tell her personally. They were old friends. It would give Harriet comfort to have him there.

Father James leaned down and untied his shoelaces then stretched out his long legs, crossing his feet at the ankles. Why is the answering machine on at the rectory? he wondered. Parishioners only called late at night when there was an emergency. They needed to be comforted, not to be told to leave a message and someone would get right back to them as soon as possible. Strange. Both Father Dennis and Father Keene knew how strongly he felt about this point, yet they had disregarded his wishes. Why?

He pushed the thought to the back of his mind along with everything else that had happened and tried to rest. In a few hours, he would have to begin the long drive back to Dorsetville and he had no desire to fall asleep at the wheel.

He and Jeff had talked it over. Father James would stay until Allison had completed the arrangements to have her father's body taken back to Dorsetville, then he would leave. When he arrived at the rectory, he would contact Harriet and begin the funeral arrangements from there. Jeff would arrive with Allison later.

He had just begun to drift off to sleep when he heard St. Cecilia's name mentioned. He looked up and something on the television screen caught his eye.

"Holy Mother of God," he gasped, trying to shake himself awake. He had to be still dreaming!

The camera had just panned onto George Benson, resplendent in his official fire marshal uniform, posing uncomfortably against the backdrop of St. Cecilia's stone façade with what appeared to be hundreds of people milling around outside the church.

"What in heaven's name?" Father James walked across the room and stood on one of the chairs beneath the television, then reached up, turning the volume louder, ignoring the taped sign that read DO NOT TOUCH THE CONTROLS.

The camera swung away from George and back onto the studio. CNN's predawn anchorwoman recapped the segment.

"Wasn't that a great inspirational and, what I might add, seasonal Easter story.

"As you've just seen, thousands of people have begun pouring into the small town of Dorsetville where the faithful say the Blessed Virgin Mary has appeared in the sanctuary of St. Cecilia's church.

"The vision was first reported four days ago when George

Benson—Dorsetville's fire marshal and full-time heating and air-conditioning repairman—was conducting some work in the church and saw the image. Mr. Benson quickly called the parish priest, Father Keene, who also saw the vision.

"Oh, dear God . . ." Father James groaned, nearly falling off the chair. He jumped down.

"When interviewed, Father Keene stated that he believes Mary's appearance is an answer to the prayers of his parish for a miracle that would prevent the church from closing. Apparently the archdiocese has ordered the church closed after Easter services due to declining membership. But by the crowds that we saw stationed around St. Cecilia's tonight, that will not be a problem any longer.

"That's it for this report. Jack, what's up next?"

"A Marian apparition?" Father James asked the empty room.

Why hadn't anyone called him about this? And where was Father Dennis while all of this was taking place? Although Father James had cautioned the young priest not to call him unless it was absolutely necessary, a reported Marian apparition should have qualified.

Father James bent down and tied his shoelaces. He had to find Jeff. Tell him that there had been an emergency back in Dorsetville and that he needed to leave immediately.

His stomach churned. If only he had a roll of Tums. What was Father Dennis thinking? How could he have allowed something like this go public before it could be investigated by Church officials? What would the archbishop say? Should he call him? No, he'd better wait until he had all the facts.

Father James sailed out of the city. Traffic was light this early in the morning. It was barely four-thirty. He did eighty all the way, reaching Exit 9 off Route 684 in just over an hour. From there, Dorsetville was only another hour and a half away.

The sun's first rays broke over the soft New England hills as he passed the sign for Waterbury along Route 84. It was still too early for commuters. It was just him and an occasional eighteen-wheeler. With few distractions, there was plenty of time to think.

There was only one thought, however, that kept pounding through his head like a jackhammer, filling him with an odd mixture of excitement and dread. What would he do if the Virgin Mary really *was* appearing at St. Cecilia's?

Chapter 17

Father James was completely unprepared for what he encountered as he turned off the interstate onto the exit ramp, five miles outside of Dorsetville. Throughout the long ride, he had hoped and prayed that he would be able to contain news of the reported Marian vision long enough to have the incident properly investigated by Church officials. But what he discovered as he began the drive along Route 7, however, was that it was already too late.

On either side of the small two-lane highway was an assortment of vehicles—RVs, trailers, SUVs and station wagons with blankets and pillows pushed up against their back windows, sporting license plates from as far away as Nebraska. They lined the dusty back roads on the outskirts of town like sardines in a can.

A makeshift sign outside Chris Dotson's chicken farm advertised campsites for fifteen dollars a night. From the number of tents, it appeared several dozen campers had taken Chris up on the offer. Father James drove on wondering how this could have happened. How had so many people arrived so quickly? And as he drove on, things only got worse.

The village of Dorsetville had been invaded by what appeared to be a traveling road show. Booths of every design and color, some with canvas tenting, others just aluminum card tables, lined every available sidewalk and alleyway. Some sold rosary beads, others crucifixes. The sale of daily missals vied for attention with statues and pictures of Mary with Child, the Sacred Heart of Mary, Mary of Guadeloupe, Mary of Medjugorje, Mary of Fatima, and Mary of Lourdes. A collection of religious paintings on velvet leaned against the front of the town hall.

He spied Ben Metcalf and Timothy McGree haggling with a vendor outside the Country Kettle. Ethel Johnson, walking Honey, was in animated conversation with a woman holding up a microphone while a cameraman walked backward filming. The threesome wove in and out of hot dog and pretzel vendors, a man selling holy water from a five-gallon plastic jug labeled POLAND'S WATER and a pushcart filled with helium balloons reading OUR LADY OF ST. CECILIA'S.

Above the main thoroughfare, Christmas lights twinkled brightly, like a gaudy rhinestone necklace. The town crew had been unable to remove the lights due to the February fog followed by the March blizzard. Apparently some town official had gotten the bright idea to throw the switch.

A young child ran in front of his car. Father James stood on the brakes. Where were the parents?

The Toyota Avalon in front of him had also come to a screeching stop. He stared at the bumper sticker as he waited: MY WIFE'S A HOOKER . . . GREEN MOUNTAIN RUG HOOKING SOCIETY. Normally it would have made him laugh. Instead, he waited in silence. Finally, he realized that there was a whole line of cars up ahead of him that weren't moving either. He stuck his head out the window. Amazing! Imagine a traffic jam in Dorsetville! To his knowledge, it was the first one the town had ever experienced. Several horns blared with impatience. Father James inched his Jeep along to where Deputy Hill was directing traffic. He pulled alongside and rolled down the window. Hill peered in suspiciously, then smiled as he recognized Father James.

"Oh, it's you. I didn't recognize the car. Thought it was just another tourist complaining about the traffic," Hill said. "Welcome back." He reached inside and shook the priest's hand. "I suppose you've heard about everything that's happened here since you've been gone?"

"No, not really," Father confessed. "What *is* all of this?"

"Is that the priest from St. Cecilia's?" someone yelled from out of the crowd.

"Yep. Father James Flaherty, himself," Hill yelled back with an air of importance. "People have been asking since dawn when you'd return. But I suppose you want to get right back to the rectory before you start meeting with people."

"Meeting people?"

"No problem. I'll get you right through."

The deputy took the whistle strung around his neck and blew so hard his face turned red. The priest rose several inches off his seat.

"Stop!" Hill shouted, raising his hand even though no one was moving. "Everybody stop! Let the priest from St. Cecilia's pass through."

"It's the priest! I told you so!" someone shouted.

Father James winced. They were acting as though he were the pope, and with that thought pandemonium ensued. He watched with a strange sense of detachment as the sidewalk full of people moved, like a mudslide, in his direction. Within seconds, throngs of people surrounded his car. Everyone seemed to be shouting at him at the same time.

"Father! *Padre!* Bless me, please! May I have a private word? I saw the Blessed Mother also, Father. She appeared to me in my son's room the day after he married that Lutheran. *Pray for us.* Are you going to hear confessions privately? Father, I really need to speak to you alone. Father James, I am a reporter with the *Today* show; we were wondering if you might give us an interview. Please ask the Blessed Mother to bless my son, he's dying of AIDS."

Suddenly above the melee boomed Sheriff Bromley's voice. "Hill, you damn fool!" The sheriff elbowed his way through the crowd. "Let me through. I'm the sheriff. Move aside." The crowd began to part like the Red Sea. Finally the sheriff made it to Father James's car and snarled at Hill. "What are you trying to do? Get Father James killed?"

"I was . . . er . . ." Hill stammered.

"You people get back!" Bromley ordered but no one moved. "I said get back!" Still, no one moved. Calmly, as though he did it every day, he removed the gun from his holster, pointed it straight into the air and fired. The crowd screamed. Some ran to the sidewalk for safety. Others cowered, their hands over their heads.

Deputy Hill could see that the sheriff needed help. He gave several more sharp blasts with his whistle. "That's it now, folks. Back up! Quiet down! Let the sheriff talk."

"Give me that whistle, you moron," Bromley barked.

Deputy Hill handed it over looking slightly confused. He was just trying to help.

"Now, listen here, you folks," the sheriff yelled into the crowd. "Dorsetville is a peace abiding town. Folks around here mind their manners. We don't go around accosting people, and I won't allow you to either. So if you want to talk to Father James, then send him a note, give him a call or make an appointment. But don't let me ever see you gang up on him again or anybody else for that matter. If I do, then I'll close down this town and throw you all out on your ears. And as sheriff of Dorsetville, it is my official right to do just that if I feel that your actions are putting others at risk. Now all of you, get along. Get out of the street and mind your manners."

The crowd quickly receded like flood waters, melding back into the throngs who had already sought safety on the sidewalks.

"You all right?" the sheriff asked Father James, ignoring the long line of cars behind him whose motors idled quietly, waiting. No one dared to blow a horn.

"I'm fine, but what is happening around here?"

The sheriff shook his head. "Damnedest thing I've ever seen in all my years of sheriffing. Started last week when George Benson said he saw the Virgin Mary appear in your church. He was bleeding the radiators in the sanctuary when it happened. The people who saw him afterward said he looked whiter than Chester Platt's albino heifer."

"George Benson?" Although it had been George's television interview that had initially caught his attention last night in the hospital waiting room, Father James still could not believe it.

"Yeah, George Benson. Ain't that a rip?" The sheriff spit on the ground. Seeing the driver in the car behind Father's Jeep stick his head out the window and look like he was about to complain, he shouted, "You got something you want to say to me?" The man hastily ducked his head back inside the car and said something short and testy to his wife, then closed the car window.

The sheriff continued. "George ain't exactly religious, now is he? Hell, he ain't even Catholic. You ever heard of the Blessed Virgin Mary's appearing to someone who ain't Catholic?"

"Can't say that I have," he had to admit.

"Didn't think so. That's only one of the things that makes this whole sorry mess so peculiar."

Father James looked around. "But how did it get from George reporting a vision to all this?"

"Hell, Father, that ain't no mystery. You've lived here long enough to know how this town gossips. George told Father Keene. Father Keene rushed in and saw it, too. Then the Father told Mrs. Norris who called her niece and there you have it. People started making phone calls to relatives, friends. Then a television crew showed up and soon hundreds of folks started pouring into town. I had to call two of my old deputies out of retirement just for traffic control."

From somewhere off in the distance, a horn blared.

The sheriff straightened, looking over the line of cars. "Hill, you let the Father through, but keep everyone else waiting. I want to see who's in such a big hurry."

Father James said a quick prayer for protection for whoever the impatient driver might be.

Bromley took a few steps, then turned and walked back. Leaning into the car window he said in an uncharacteristically quiet voice, "Listen, Father, I'm not saying that I believe or don't believe in all of this, but I would appreciate any information you might uncover. Talk to Father Keene. Find out exactly what he *thinks* he saw."

Father James hedged. "I'm afraid that lately Father Keene isn't always himself."

"I know. I've heard. But you can understand my predicament. Having George Benson say he saw a vision is one thing. Definitely unusual, but containable. Having a priest—someone the town has known and respected for all these years—say he's seen a vision, now that's another thing entirely." Bromley lowered his voice further, then turned his ear toward Father James as one would in the confessional.

"I heard that you were going to put Father Keene into a nursing home. That true?"

"Not by choice," Father admitted sadly.

The sheriff nodded.

"He's never shown any signs of delusion, if that's what you mean. Forgetfulness, yes. But I feel he knows the difference between real and imagined."

"Okay. For now, I'll take your word on that."

"Listen, Sheriff, as soon as I straighten things out, I'll give you a call. I'm as anxious as you are to get to the bottom of this."

Father James put the Jeep in drive and carefully maneuvered through the traffic, wondering how does one begin to sort out a vision?

Chapter 18

As soon as Father James crossed the rectory threshold, Mrs. Norris rushed over, spewing news like a popcorn popper.

"Father James! Am I *so* glad to see you! You'll never guess what's happened." She grabbed his coat, peeling it off as quickly as a banana skin.

"I think I just might." He reached up to remove his hat, but Mrs. Norris had already snatched it off of his head and hung it on a peg.

She took his arm and steered him toward the kitchen table. "The Virgin Mary herself has appeared in our blessed St. Cecilia's." She pulled out a chair and nearly pushed him into the seat.

"Now slow down, Mrs. Norris. Start from the beginning," he said, watching the housekeeper sail to the counter, gather a handful of cutlery and sail back, rambling en route.

"She appeared in the sanctuary. Father Keene and George Benson saw her. People have been pouring into town ever since the news got out. Did you see the crowds when you drove down Main Street?"

"Couldn't miss it. Is there any coffee?" he asked hopefully. Mrs. Norris ignored him, retracing her steps back to the counter where she began to measure flour into a bowl. He sighed like a martyr. "I want to talk to you about all this, but first I want to know why no one called me? I left the phone number where I could be reached."

"We tried to phone."

"When?"

"Right after it happened the news crew left, but there was no answer at the number you gave us." She headed toward the back door and the tin milk box outside. "Oh, good. He's remembered my cream." She stacked two quarts of milk and a pint of heavy cream in her arms and kicked the door closed.

Father James swiveled in his chair. He wished she'd sit still. He was getting a crick in his neck. "Speaking about answering machines, why was ours on last night? I tried to call."

"Oh, that was my idea," she said without remorse, lifting the paper tab off a quart of milk and pouring a cupful into the biscuit mix. "The phone's been ringing off the hook ever since Our Lady first appeared. Poor Father Dennis and Father Keene couldn't get a wink of sleep, so before I left for the night, I turned the machine on and lowered the volume so they wouldn't be disturbed." Before Father James could protest, she held up a hand covered in flour. "I know. I know you'd rather the priests answer in person at night, but I thought there'd be no harm done, just this once."

He looked longingly at the cold coffee pot. He wondered if she'd bite his head off if he tried to make it himself. "I understand," he said, feeling a caffeine withdrawal headache coming on. "It was just that I needed to contact Father Dennis. I have some bad news."

Mrs. Norris looked up anxiously.

"Harriet Bedford's son, Peter, died last night," he told her.

For a moment she was speechless. "Peter Bedford, dead? Oh, no . . . poor Harriet." She wiped her hands on a nearby terry cloth towel. "But how did you come to know about Peter's death? No one in town has seen him for more than twenty years."

"As strange as it might seem, Jeff Hayden's fiancée turns out to be Harriet's granddaughter." Father James further explained what had transpired while he was in New York.

"I'll make some calls, especially to Sam," she told him. "Then I'll call the other folks in town. They'll want to offer their condolences." She returned to her biscuit making. "My heart goes out to Harriet. How awful not to be able to say a final good-bye, especially after all those years of separation. But at least she and Allison will be reunited. They will, won't they, Father?"

"Yes. Jeff is driving her here. She'll be arriving later. Allison wants her father to be buried in Dorsetville and the service held at St. Cecilia's."

"At least that should give Harriet some comfort." She placed the pan of biscuits in the oven, then reached for the coffee canister. "I'll hurry your breakfast along. You'll need to break the news before Harriet leaves for Mass. This is such a shame. It's such a terrible thing to happen in the midst of this great miracle."

"I don't think you should be bandying the word *miracle* around," he warned her.

She ignored the warning. "Imagine the Blessed Mother deciding to honor *our* St. Cecilia's with her presence."

He threw up a cautioning hand. "Let's verify some of this before we make unsubstantiated statements." He straightened his collar and noticed that his sleeve bore a jelly stain. He had polished off half a box of Dunkin' Donuts donut holes on the ride back.

"Unsubstantiated?" she scorned. "How can you say that? Why both George Benson and our saintly Father Keene saw the vision."

So, Father Keene was *saintly* now, was he?

The phone rang and Mrs. Norris picked it up on the second ring. "Good morning. St. Cecilia's Catholic Church."

"It's the archbishop's assistant," Mrs. Norris whispered, cupping her hand over the mouthpiece. "He's been calling since six o'clock this morning. Apparently, the entire archdiocese saw last night's news broadcast."

Great! Just great! He took a deep breath.

"I'll put on a pot of coffee while you chat." She handed him the phone.

"Hello, Richard. Yes, I've seen it, too. No, I really don't have anything to report. I've only just got back. I might be able to tell you something by the end of the day. Yes, I know the Church's position on these matters. I agree. No, I haven't had the opportunity to speak with Father

Keene. Yes, I'll tell him that the archbishop has ordered him to refrain from making any more statements about the apparition until he has spoken to you. Yes, I understand. I'll try to decipher everything quickly and get right back to you. No, tell the archbishop that I will not sanction anything without his consent. Thank you, Richard. I'll be in close touch."

Father James felt winded, as though he had jumped onto a fast-moving treadmill without benefit of a warm-up. Pulling out a kitchen chair, he patted the table, signaling Mrs. Norris to join him. "We need to talk."

"Let me start your coffee. You go ahead and begin. I can hear you from over here."

"Where is Father Keene?" he asked and reached in his pants pocket for a Tums. Now he had an acid stomach *and* a headache. Hopefully, the coffee would be coming soon.

"He's in the living room with Father Dennis. They're preparing tomorrow's sermons."

Sermons?

"When did we begin to say more than one daily Mass?" Was he to find nothing the way he had left it?

He popped four Tums into his mouth while Mrs. Norris filled his coffee mug before sitting down on the opposite side of the table.

She explained. "Father Keene decided to increase the number of daily Masses to accommodate all the people who have been piling into the church since Friday."

"I see," he said, not seeing at all.

A sound like an iron beam dropped against the cellar floor, shaking the kitchen table so hard it made coffee slosh onto his pants leg.

"What in blazes is that?" Father jumped up. He could already feel the hot liquid burn his inner thigh.

"Oh, that's just George," Mrs. Norris said, smiling as though George were her newest best friend. "Someone has donated a new furnace to St. Cecilia's. George is setting it up downstairs."

"Someone's *donated* a furnace?" he said, eyeing the dark stain right by his crotch. Good grief! "Who?"

"A couple from Manchester. They were here on Friday." Mrs. Norris was heated up again, spewing out words at a lively clip. "Lovely couple. In their early forties. I think the husband used to work for the First Federal, that was before it changed names to . . ."

"Mrs. Norris, please!" He knew from experience that if he didn't immediately steer her back on course, he would be obliged to ride out the infinite, unrelated details of the story along a scenic route that had absolutely nothing to do with the furnace.

"All right, I'll get to the point," she said indignantly, then didn't get to the point at all. "As I was saying, they had drifted away from the Church and hadn't been to Mass in years. Their personal life wasn't doing well, either." She lowered her voice as though someone might overhear. Father James worked feverishly to bridle his impatience. "I think they were about to get a divorce."

Father James nodded. "And then . . ." If he couldn't redirect her thoughts, perhaps he could help prod her along.

"Her aunt, Ethel Johnson's first cousin, told them about the visions. So they decided to visit our church. They were so moved by Father Keene's rendering of what he had seen that they insisted on making a donation to St. Cecilia's.

"Now, George just happened to be seated in the next pew, so when he overheard their discussion he turned around and introduced himself. Said he had worked on the furnace for years and how a new one was desperately needed. And the couple agreed to purchase one."

Father James didn't know what amazed him more—the fact that George had attended a Catholic service or that he had become a champion for St. Cecilia's restoration. He stared into his coffee mug as though it could portend the future and asked, "Tell me about this reported apparition." He could see Mrs. Norris bristle at the word *reported*. "You said that George was the first to see it."

But before she could defend either the vision or the visionaries,

George appeared at the top of the cellar stairs reeking of oil, his coveralls stained with soot. He had a huge lug wrench in his hand which he slipped into his back pocket.

"Hello, Father James. Nice to see you back from the city," he said with uncharacteristic civility.

Father James nodded, feeling more and more like Alice in Wonderland on the reverse side of the mirror.

"Who called for a new tank of oil?" George asked the kitchen at large. Not waiting for a reply, he continued, "I was just about to remove the feed line from off the old furnace when I heard the Jenson's oil truck outside and see the oil gauge start to rise. I called them yesterday and spoke to Pete Jenson, the owner's son. I told him that we had to remove that old tank and would be doing it today. State law says any tank over twenty years old has to be removed and, as fire marshal, I am duty-bound to see that through."

"Of course you are," Father James agreed, not at all certain where this line of conversation was headed, but from experience, knowing that he had to let it run its course. He'd question George about the apparition as soon as he was through.

"Not that I haven't overlooked a few things over the years. For the church's sake, of course," he added with benevolence.

Why, George has lost his thunder! Imagine! Father was stunned. No expletives. No caustic remarks. Had everyone gone through a personality change while he was gone? First Mrs. Norris, now George. Scenes from *Invasion of the Body Snatchers* ran through his mind.

"This morning I had the subcontractors pump out the tank so we could remove it this afternoon," George continued. "We've been digging all morning. We've just about got it out so we can cut it up and take it up the outside cellar stairs. Now Jenson comes along and tries to fill up the tank. Oil starts pumping out all over the cellar floor. What a mess."

For the first time since meeting George Benson three years ago, Father James felt compassion for him. "Here, sit down, George. Have a biscuit." Mrs. Norris had just pulled them out of the oven.

That seemed to help perk him up. "Don't mind if I do."

Mrs. Norris placed a wicker basket piled high with hot, steaming biscuits in front of George. He grabbed two with fingers hidden beneath a black casing of oil and quickly lathered them with butter and homemade strawberry preserves.

"Would you like a cup of coffee or a cup of tea?" asked Mrs. Norris.

"Either one would be nice, Mrs. Norris," George said between mouthfuls. "If it's not too much trouble."

"Trouble? Not at all!" Mrs. Norris pushed back her chair. "I was about to make a batch of pancakes. Are you hungry, George? What a stupid question. Of course you are! You've been here since the crack of dawn working on that furnace. And on a Sunday to boot!"

"Sunday, Monday, makes no difference," George said. "It's my job."

"Would one stack of pancakes do? Or would you like more?"

"I think two would fill 'er up," George smiled, exposing a gold front tooth.

I didn't know George had a gold front tooth, Father James thought. But then he hadn't ever seen George smile. George took a pocket knife and began to pry dirt from underneath his fingernails, an action Father James suddenly found comforting.

"George, I need to ask you about this alleged sighting of the Blessed Virgin Mary." He caught Mrs. Norris pursing her lips in displeasure at his choice of words. "As you know, the entire town has been turned upside down by this report."

"You mean the visit of Our Blessed Mother to St. Cecilia's?" he asked, like he had been a Catholic all his life.

"Yes. *Our* Blessed Mother." Father took a swig of coffee, trying to adjust to George as a proponent of the Catholic faith. It was especially hard, since George had always gone out of his way to criticize anything Catholic. "I heard you were the first to see her?"

Mrs. Norris set a mug of steaming coffee and a small pitcher of cream in front of George, then pulled up a chair alongside. "Go on," she urged. "Tell Father what you saw."

George hesitated, intermittently peering up from his coffee mug, shyly, uncertain as to how to continue. Father James watched him intently, then with the enlightenment that comes from years of counseling, realized George was fearful that the story he needed to tell would not be believed. Father James rushed to assure him otherwise.

"George, I'm not here to judge what you've experienced. I simply need to know what happened. Both the archdiocese and the sheriff have asked me to investigate and get back to them with a report."

George continued to stare silently at the checkered tablecloth.

Father James leaned closer. "And as St. Cecilia's pastor, I want to understand this event so I might better act on God's behalf. Please, George. Won't you share with me what you saw?"

George looked hard into his face as though deciding how much he was willing to tell and how much Father James might be willing to accept. He took a slow sip from his mug, then hesitantly began.

"I was in the sanctuary that afternoon."

"Thursday?"

"Yeah. Several parishioners complained during that morning's Mass that the radiator on the north side of the church, up by the front . . . what do you call that? You know, where the statue of Mary used to be."

"The niche," Father James offered.

"Yeah, the niche. Anyway, your church folks said that the radiator wasn't working, but you know how that is, them being so old and everything. Most of the time the heat is working just fine."

Realizing that he was veering from the main subject, George cleared his throat and realigned his thoughts.

"Anyway, I thought I'd take a look, just in case. I bled the radiator, that sometimes helps increase the pressure so the hot water can circulate better, and I spilled some of it on the floor. I didn't want any of the folks slipping on that puddle, you know how slick that marble floor gets when it's wet, so I took a rag out of my back pocket and began to mop it up.

"I was down on my hands and knees with the rag when I caught a movement out of the corner of my eye up at the front of the church. That's when I saw her, Father."

George lowered his head, tears copiously falling, dropping onto the kitchen table. Embarrassed, he swiped at them with the back of his sleeve.

"It was like I'm seeing you right now," George said, his eyes still shining with amazement. "She was real, flesh and blood. Like you and me. Not some kind of a ghost or anything like that. A real, live person. But she wasn't exactly standing or anything. She seemed to be, I don't know, floating above the niche.

"At first, I thought I was imagining things. Thought maybe it was the way the afternoon sun was coming through the windows. Thought maybe it was reflecting through one of those stained-glass windows." George looked up earnestly into Father James's eyes. "I tried to reason it out, you know. I'm not some kind of nut case that goes around seeing things that aren't there."

Father felt his struggle. "I'm sure it gave you quite a start."

"It sure as *hel* . . . er . . . it sure did." George smiled weakly, his face showing relief that Father James was not questioning the validity of his story. His confidence bolstered, reflections of the old confident George began to emerge. "I knew it was her right away. Looked just like the pictures you always see of her at Christmastime. You know, in the robe and all.

"I knelt there for several minutes, not sure what I was supposed to do. After all, I'm not Catholic and I don't know the proper way to greet the Blessed Mother. Was I supposed to kneel, or bow my head or say some kind of prayer?"

"So what did you do?" Father James smiled, imagining the scene.

"I made the sign of the cross. I know you Catholics do that sort of thing a lot, so I figured I couldn't go wrong."

Father James's smile broadened. "And what did Our Lady do when you did that?"

"I'll be darned if she doesn't look right at me and smile!" He slapped his knee. "Just like she was happy to see me. Can you imagine that?"

In fact, he could. "Then what happened?"

"I heard Father Keene in the rectory and I said, 'Excuse me your High Holiness of all Mothers,' I wasn't quite sure what name she goes by these days—Blessed Mother, Holy Virgin or such—then I edged myself along the side wall, past where she was kind of levitating above a bank of candles and fetched Father Keene."

"I see. Did she say anything to you, George?"

He shook his head. "No. Just stood there, looking down at me and smiling." He leaned over the table and whispered, "I got the feeling that she was kind of happy that I had been the first one to see her."

Neither Father nor Mrs. Norris could refrain from laughing. George didn't take offense.

"And Father Keene saw her, too?" Father asked.

"Sure did. And boy, was I glad. Made me feel that I hadn't lost my mind, or that I was suffering from some kind of brain tumor or something." George leaned farther forward and asked with great earnestness, "What do you think it means?"

"To the Church?"

"No, to me." He leaned back. "Why do you think she chose me to, well, you know, to appear to first? Must be there's some special reason she singled me out. I've been reading up on these appearances," he pulled a notepad out of his breast pocket and read off names of places. "Like in Fatima, Lourdes, Guadeloupe." He flipped the pad shut. "It says she always appears first to the one given the role of sharing her message."

"But you said she didn't say anything to you, am I right?"

George sat back in his chair and studied the ceiling for a second. "Not yet. But she might just be waiting for the perfect time. So what do you think it means?"

"I wish I could answer that, George. But I guess that's something you'll have to pray about."

George reached into his pants pocket and brought out a black pair of rosaries and placed them reverently on the table. "I've already started. Joined the Rosary Society last night."

George, a member of the Rosary Society?—it *had* to be a miracle! Father James rose, feeling a sudden well of emotion. He placed a hand on George's shoulder. "I will pray that God will reveal His plan for your life, George, and whether it be through a visit of Our Holy Mother or a simple whisper of His will upon your heart, the important thing is that you are being led back to God's grace."

"Thanks, Father."

"If you'll excuse me," he said. "I think I'll go and find Father Keene. Please hold my calls, Mrs. Norris."

"Father," George called after him. "I've been . . . praying." It was a new word, one that still didn't roll easily off his lips. "I want to convert."

"Convert?"

"Yeah. I figure now that Our Blessed Mother has chosen me to deliver her message . . ."

"But George, we're not clear about that yet."

With the zeal of a new convert, George waved his caution aside. "She'll reveal her plan. All in good time. But I figure that since she's a Catholic, I expect I should be one, too."

"Our Lord's mother is not a Catholic. She's Mother to us all," Father James tried to explain.

"Yeah, but she never appears to Baptists, or Lutherans, now does she?"

"Well, no . . ."

"Nope. She's definitely partial to Catholics. So I figure that if it's good enough for her, then it's good enough for me."

"We'll talk about this later," Father James said, reaching deep into his pants pocket for another Tums. He'd grab a Tylenol later.

Chapter 19

F ather Keene felt as exuberant as a young seminarian as he sorted out his vestments, checked the supply of sacramental wine and reviewed the roster of altar boys for daily Mass. There were now four services—6 A.M., 8 A.M., 9:30 A.M. and 5 P.M.

There had also been an increase in baptisms, several new marriages (Catholics were flocking in from out of town to be married in the church where the Virgin Mary had appeared) and one funeral—Peter Bedford's. Father Keene had presided over the ceremony just as he had for Peter Bedford's wife and daughter. Fortunately, this time, Harriet would find comfort in the company of her granddaughter.

Father Keene fished in his pocket for his reading glasses, wondering who was on the roster as altar servers for this morning's Mass. He riffled through the schedule, happy to note the Gallagher twins, Rodney and Dexter, had been assigned. He had been meaning to talk to them. It seemed the two were recently in a fight with some Protestant boys who had said that the visions of the Virgin Mary were nothing more than a bunch of lies (sentiments Father Keene was certain were carried from home like their brown paper lunch bags). Whatever the origin, the boys had no right to get into a fight. He would insist upon a good confession and some community service. This should help curb their tempers.

Father Keene took a small skeleton key from his pocket and opened the cabinet where an earthen chalice stood on the first shelf. Once two intricately carved gold and silver vessels had stood in its place but they had been sold several months ago to pay a delinquent oil bill. Father James had pined over their loss, but not Father Keene. He believed that had the Lord been given a preference, he would have chosen this. The elderly priest carefully took one down and set it on the counter.

Soon the church would be filled to the choir loft with a mixture of parishioners and pilgrims. It had been that way every Mass since the news of the apparition had been made public. How long had it been since St. Cecilia's pews had been filled? he pondered. Ten, maybe fifteen, years?

He poured the sacramental wine into a glass cruet, water into another, then walked through the archway which lead from the sacristy to the altar and placed them on the side table near the sacristy's door.

Father Keene walked out into the sanctuary, bowed ever so slightly at the foot of the cross, then turned toward the altar to review the day's readings, marking off specific prayers with the thin colored ribbons embedded in the spine of the prayer book.

After satisfying himself that all was in order, he looked out over the church amazed to see it was already nearly full, yet Mass was more than forty-five minutes away. Even more amazing were the two confessional lines, which snaked down the center aisle, dividing at the front of the altar, then winding back again, like ribbons at the end of a bow, to continue their course along the opposites sides of the church. Quite a difference from the past when few if any came to confession, a fact which had once prompted Father Keene to state, "The good people of Dorsetville should sleep easy in their beds at night knowing that there are no sinners at St. Cecilia's."

His flock had laughed, but he had never meant it as a joke.

For several minutes, Father Keene stood silently, still in awe of the transformation that had taken place; the very air seemed to be charged with a new energy. Gone was the feeling of heaviness that had once permeated the church, replaced by a sense of hope and renewal. People were now attending Mass *expecting* to experience the joy of God's presence, not just to fulfill an obligation. Gone was the look of boredom, eyes staring blankly into space, as people fully participated in the liturgy.

Father Keene's gaze shifted to the empty niche. Flowers were strewn in a huge semicircle around the floor, reaching to the pews, their fragrance mingling with the sweet smell of incense and burning candles. Prayer cards and messages scribbled on pieces of paper imploring Mary to intercede on the writer's behalf spilled over a worn rush basket.

With a warm flush of excitement, he remembered the vision of the Blessed Virgin Mary that both he and George had seen just days before. Like a comet's tail, this memory was quickly followed by another—two angels who had been sent to save him from a raging blizzard and certain death.

There's something else God wants you to do, they had said.

Father Keene was certain that that "something" was to be his testimony that lent validity to the Blessed Mother's appearance. They might not believe George Benson, but who would question the word of a priest? And with that validation, Father Keene felt certain the archbishop would have to rescind his plan to shut St. Cecilia's down.

Father Keene stood gazing quietly up at the empty niche, the memory of Mary's apparition still fresh in his mind.

He had been in the rectory, enjoying his midafternoon biscuit and tea when George had charged in—his face as white as the sheets used to cover summer furniture on the side porch—babbling on about something. It sounded as though he was saying that the Virgin Mary had appeared in the sanctuary. The man was daft.

Father Keene had long suspected George Benson of taking a little nip during the day. He had even confided his suspicions to Mrs. Norris.

"I don't believe it's only fuel oil I'd be smelling whenever George comes upstairs from fixing the furnace," he'd often said.

So when George came bursting into the rectory, Father Keene gave little credence to his preposterous tale. But George would not go away, so to placate the man, he followed him into the sanctuary, confident that whatever George had seen could be explained. He was, therefore, totally unprepared for the life-size image of the Virgin Mary that greeted him as he entered the sanctuary.

"Dear Blessed Mother of God, 'tis really you," he exclaimed, hardly believing his eyes. First a pair of angels, now the Blessed Virgin Mary. Was there no end to God's grace? He fell to his knees. George knelt beside him.

The Blessed Virgin Mary looked like a girl of fourteen or fifteen years old, her earthly age when the Archangel Gabriel had appeared, proclaiming her chosen to become the Mother of God. She stood approximately five feet three inches tall and had chestnut hair, several strands of which had escaped her head covering and were framing her face.

She was the most beautiful girl Father Keene had ever seen and the smile she wore instantly put the elderly priest at ease. From his pants pocket, he pulled the strand of black rosaries given him by his saintly mother at his ordination and began to pray. George ineptly prayed along.

"Hail Mary, full of grace, the Lord be with you . . ."

"Hello Mary . . . of graceness . . . God is near you . . ."

Then the apparition was gone. Vanished. Both men remained silent, searching for an understanding of what they had seen.

"George, my son." Father Keene was the first to break the silence. "You and I have been chosen by Our Lady to help save St. Cecilia's."

"We have?" George looked at the ceiling of the sanctuary which was brown with water stains, paint peeling in the corners. "How?"

"We're simply going to tell a few people what we have just seen."

Chapter 20

S ixty years ago, if Timothy McGree and Ben Metcalf hadn't tried to hide from St. Cecilia's old pastor, Father Fanny, after a fistfight with a gang of Congregationalist boys in front of St. Cecilia's, they might never have known the secret room existed, hidden off to the right of the choir loft at the top of the stairs.

Dorsetville's faith community consisted of three denominations, two of which had built structures perched on opposite corners of the town green like heavyweight contenders on opposing sides of the ring. Separating the two churches lay a small town park and a gazebo. It was here that the third denomination, the Salvation Army, which over the years had grown adept at acting as referee, gave free concerts every Wednesday evening at seven o'clock throughout the summer.

The Dorsetville Congregational Church, resplendent in traditional New England white clapboard charm, sat to the north of the green, amidst a grove of sugar maples. St. Cecilia's, looking more like a fortress imported from medieval times than a church, sat to the south of the green, in full sun, totally obscuring the Congregationalists' view of the Connecticut River below and adding to their chagrin.

The Congregational church was the first to be built on the town green. It was founded in 1772 by Reverend Obadiah Wheeler, a suspected British sympathizer. Wheeler suffered considerable harassment at the hands of the inspection committee and avoided incarceration by hiding from Monday through Saturday. The law forbade arrests on Sunday, which most fortuitously allowed him to reappear and concentrate fully on his meticulously prepared six-hour sermon.

In 1775, the inspection committee decreed that Wheeler be "put on limits" and forbidden to leave Dorsetville, and defended its decision to the General Assembly by stating that the minister had

> . . . publicly and contemptuously uttered and spoken many things against the doings of the General Assembly . . . and in derision and contempt of the same . . . hath by means thereof evidently showed therein his inimical temper and unfriendly dispositions . . . for the defense of the American cause.

Later summoned to answer these charges, Wheeler confessed to his political leanings, but gave his word that he would "in no way interfere with the defense of the United States." Apparently, the General Assembly had complete faith in his word. They allowed him to return to Dorsetville and his church, where he died the following year of consumption.

Within six months of his death, Wheeler was replaced by Titus Grey, a nineteen-year-old minister who had been the first seminarian to graduate from Bethany Theological School in Bethlehem, Connecticut. The Congregationalists were greatly enamored of this fiery young preacher who loved to extol the rewards of sin with such vivid word pictures of hell that it put Dante's *Inferno* to shame. But Grey was also a zealous patriot, which meant that many of his sermons were interrupted by a call to arms when British troops were sighted plying the Connecticut River.

Fortunately, Reverend Grey was as zealous for souls as he was for the cause for freedom and under his direction the Dorsetville Congregational Church grew and flourished. By the end of the war, a smart white, pillared church was erected on the north side of the town green where it had stood ever since. It was reported to be the second oldest church in New England.

The church and its history were a source of great pride to its parishioners who polished, painted and maintained the structure as lovingly as one would a precious family heirloom; and the gardens that surrounded the little church, like a cluster of precious jewels, outrivaled the famed Gertrude Jekyll gardens that encompassed the historic Glebe House in the neighboring town.

The meticulously manicured lawn was the backdrop for myriad gardens and pathways edged with an assortment of breathtaking perennial and annual flowerbeds all carefully orchestrated with blossoms that ebbed and flowed in concert with the seasons, providing a steady medley of color and beauty.

Although those on the selection committee for the current pastor, the Reverend Frederick L. Curtis, would never have admitted it, the fact that he was an avid gardener and twice president of his past community's garden club had weighed heavily on his behalf.

The church's parsonage—a white clapboard Victorian cottage—was set back about fifty yards from the road. The original 1791 structure burned down in 1895 and was replaced by this "modern" structure. It was a little jewel of a house swathed in a wraparound porch that from early June to late October sported flower boxes and hanging baskets filled to profusion.

Much to the Congregationalists' great delight, people came from all over the state to photograph this picture-perfect postcard setting. The church had even been honored by the state tourism board twice and included in their 1987 photo calendar sold in rest stops across the state. Dorsetville Congregational Church was June.

In stark contrast, neighboring St. Cecilia's architectural style, or as some would say, lack of it, caused hot debates from the very beginning. No sooner had the first foundation stones been set in place when the Dorsetville Historical Society led a movement to have it banned from the town green.

"If this type of . . . of . . . *style* . . ." the society president stammered with contempt, "is allowed, it will set a dangerous precedent. Can any of us truly imagine our beloved town filled with similar architectural horrors?"

Those in attendance sat back in their chairs in an effort to physically distance themselves from such a horrific vision.

"Allow St. Cecilia's to be built here and Dorsetville's natural charm will be forever lost," the president imputed to rousing applause. Emboldened by this show of support, the president convinced the members to sound the alarm.

The Congregationalists were their first group of adherents, interpreting the historical society's strong opposition as an act of divine intervention. They, too, had seen the drawings of the Catholic's pseudocathedral; had shaken their heads as they tried to imagine it stuffed onto its allotted postage-stamp-size plot of land, and had concluded that if it was allowed to be built on the same town green as their sweet clapboard church, its sheer hideousness would forever cast a dark shadow upon their beloved little town. The Congregationalists quickly banded with the historical society in petitioning the town to withdraw its offer of the land to the Catholics.

The Catholics would not take this skullduggery lying down. Oh, they knew that their style of building was cumbersome, bordering on horrific, but to be openly accused of defacing their town, well! So they tucked their true opinions inside their Irish pride and fought back.

The Catholics maintained that the architectural style of their church was a fitting edifice in which to house the teachings of the "true" Church. Of course, this line of defense only increased the ire of the Congregationalists.

Wanting to put these architectural bigots clearly in their place, the Catholics brought a lawsuit against the town, the historical society and the Congregational church.

And while the matter was being considered inside the brick façade courthouse by a district judge, ninety or so combined members of both the historical society and the Congregational church walked—arms linked in righteous indignation—along Main Street with banners held high that proclaimed AESTHETIC PURITY FOR NEW ENGLAND VILLAGES. It was Dorsetville's first staged protest march.

Of course, the march was rather short since Main Street is less than a mile long. But this fact did not daunt the protesters' zeal as they settled along the town courthouse's front steps to await the judge's verdict. They didn't have to wait long. The district judge sided with the Catholics and demanded the town make good on its original offer of land to St. Cecilia's.

"This is America," the judge reminded them. "And although you may not like the looks of the Catholics' choice of architecture, the Constitution assures everyone the right to the full pursuit of happiness and liberty under the law and explicitly denies any municipality from showing prejudice in the dispersal of public land."

And so a rift was born between these two Christian communities, which over the years grew like a tall hedge, casting a shadow of darkness where sunlight had once shone. And from this darkness came accusations, petty lies, small deceits all aimed at proclaiming the same evil myth that *they* and *they alone* were God's favorite children.

The war waged on between the two factions. Civil pleasantries were practiced in public but battle lines were drawn at home and children were subjected to proper architectural propaganda. Later, armed against what they perceived to be a holy war, the children marched into the Dorsetville schools with their quivers dipped in the poison of bigotry and took aim.

At least twice a week, boys from the Congregational Church and St. Cecilia's met to hurl insults and whatever else was available—soda bottles, spit balls and an occasional fistful of sand. Timothy McGree and Ben Metcalf always seemed to be in the thick of the melee, which was really more about their pubescent quest for power than the honorable defense of their Catholic faith. There was certainly nothing that made a boy feel more like a man than a good brawl.

Most likely, nothing would have been done about these weekly disputes between the boys of St. Cecilia's and the Dorsetville Congregationalists if the fights had remained just boyhood riots filled with wildly aimed punches. But, unfortunately, the fights escalated to include rock throwing, though none of their lobs ever hit their opponents, even though most of the boys were on the Dorsetville Little League and by rights should have been possessed of far better aim. Instead, these wild pitches were more likely to hit panes of glass. Recent fracases had resulted in two broken stained-glass windows at St. Cecilia's. The boys had been caught and their shame-faced parents had agreed to help around the church as restitution since none could afford to replace the expensive glass. Money was taken from the church coffers for that.

Then one day a rock sailed through Reverend Cross's cottage picture window, nearly crowning Mrs. Cross as it whizzed by. Both sides were warned that if another fight broke out charges would be filed.

This particular summer afternoon, both Timothy McGree and Ben Metcalf were walking home after having lost another softball game to these archrivals and needed no further provocation to start a fight.

"Hey, McGree," yelled ten-year-old Joey White as Timothy and Ben walked past.

Joey was an evil child, a master of manipulation who took delight in elevating himself by stepping on the backs of others. Unfortunately, he was also a born leader who knew exactly how to create allegiance within his group. He simply made them believe they were superior to others.

"What happened out there today, eh? You pitched like a girl," he taunted.

There were snickers from his crowd of boys.

"Maybe you'd better stop off at that church of yours and ask one of those saints for a miracle. You're going to need one if you think you can beat us this summer."

"Yeah, McGree. You don't have a chance at beating us," the others taunted.

Bolstered by his peers' support, and reveling in center stage, Joey fell on his knees and pretended to pray. "Oh, please, Saint What's Your Name, send me a new pitching arm."

"Shut up, White!" Ben yelled.

"Who's going to make me?" the boy countered.

"Yeah, who's going to make him?" the others echoed.

"I am!" Timothy said, and charged, like a wild bull, tackling Joey White to the ground.

The rectory's housekeeper at that time was Mrs. Shaeffer, who possessed two astonishing attributes. First, she was the most meticulous woman in all of New England, even carried a turkey feather in her apron to dust keyholes, and second, she had exceptional hearing.

Mrs. Shaeffer was polishing the woodwork in the upstairs guest room when she first heard the sounds of a fight breaking out. Laying her polishing rags aside, she parted the sheer draperies and stuck her head out the upstairs window, then gasped. A motley gang of boys were pummeling each other by the Reverend Cross's cottage while a second group stood at the ready to hurl an assortment of things—cans, sticks, rocks—at their leader's first command.

"Saints preserve us! We just fixed the last window those hooligans broke. There's no money left in the treasury for another."

Mrs. Shaeffer backed her 250 pound body inside the room and waddled down the stairs, shouting for the rector.

"Father Fanny! Father Fanny! Those boys are at it again!"

The priest had been sound asleep on his office sofa.

"Is the house on fire, woman, or are you just trying to give me a heart attack?" the priest yelled, swatting at her arm as she tried to yank him off the couch.

"It's those neighborhood ruffians, Father. They're fighting again." She pulled him to his feet.

"Which side of the green are they fighting on?" he asked, straightening his cassock.

"The Congregational side."

"Then it's not that much of an emergency, now is it, old woman?"

Outside on the lawn, Ben had seen Mrs. Shaeffer poke her head out the window and knew it was only a matter of minutes before Father Fanny would come charging out. He grabbed Tim's arm and yanked him free from the pile of boys.

"Tim! Tim! Mrs. Shaeffer saw us. We gotta get out of here. Come on. Before she tells Father Fanny!"

"Not until I beat the pants off Joey White." Timothy threw a wild punch into the crowd.

"Come on! You can beat him up later. If Father Fanny catches us fighting again, he won't let us make our confirmation. We'll be outside the sacraments of the church!"

"What's that mean anyhow?" Timothy asked, shoving a boy to the ground.

"I don't know," Ben conceded, "but our religion teacher always makes it sound awfully bad."

The rectory door flew open and a furious Father Fanny (more furious at having been disturbed from his afternoon nap than at the vandalism that threatened to be done) marched down the front stairs. Seconds later, Reverend Curtis also appeared. He, too, had been napping; imprints from the chenille bedspread he'd been lying on were etched alongside the right portion of his face.

"You boys stay where you are!" the reverend shouted.

Ben and Timothy frantically looked for an escape route.

"Inside the church!" Tim tugged at Ben's arm.

The two boys raced inside, propelled by a panic devoid of all logic. They had forgotten that once inside, the only way out was through the same door they had come in, or through the side door that led directly into the rectory and, no doubt, right into Mrs. Shaeffer's waiting arms.

"Now what?" Ben asked, breathing hard. It was hopeless.

"Up here!"

Timothy sprinted up to the choir loft. Ben followed close behind. The boys made a quick circle of the room but there was no place to hide.

"Well, this is great," Ben hissed, feeling the whole thing was Timothy's fault.

Timothy said nothing. He just wiped at the blood that still trickled down his nose. Wait until he got his hands on Joey White.

Outside, the Reverend Cross yelled across the green. "Hold on to them, Father Fanny. Don't let them get away!"

"None will be getting away," Father Fanny yelled back. "Including the two I saw run into the church."

"Oh, man," Ben moaned. "We're in for it now."

"Yeah, there goes the new fishing pole my dad promised me for confirmation," Tim said, pushing his bangs out of his eyes.

"I was supposed to get my dad's pocketknife."

"The one he took off that German soldier?"

"Yeah."

"What a mess," Timothy moaned.

Below, Father Fanny yelled from the outside of the church's front door.

"I'll be right back, Reverend Cross. I'll get the two who ran in here. They can't go far."

The sound of the heavy oak doors closing off all hope echoed below.

"All right, you two devils. Come out."

The priest's footfalls beat against the marble floors.

"Come out and take your punishment like men."

"Should we go down?" Timothy whispered, the high color on his cheekbones from the excitement of the chase had faded.

"I just wish I'd never been born. I wish I could just . . . disappear," Ben lamented.

He leaned his body heavily against the wood panel at the top of the stairs and slid down its chestnut planks. Halfway down to the floor, the wall behind him gave way, instantly propelling him backward into a mysterious black hole.

"Holy cow! Look at this!" Ben whispered excitedly, scrambling to his feet. "It's a secret room."

"I hear you up there," Father Fanny called.

The sound of the heavy shoes changed direction. He was headed toward the choir loft door. Ben reached for Timothy's shirt and pulled him inside, then hastily closed the secret panel door. The boys were now sealed inside the hidden room.

Father Fanny clambered up the stairs. "Now where the devil did they go?" he asked, standing just outside the wall from where the boys stood frozen like marble statues.

"Now if that ain't a puzzle," the priest said. "I could have sworn I heard them up here."

He started back down the stairs while the boys held their breath until the last echo of Father Fanny's footsteps resounded in the sanctuary below and the door to the rectory banged behind him.

"Boy, that was close," Ben said.

"I thought we were goners for sure," Timothy added.

"Isn't this great?" Ben asked.

It was a small octagonal room, roughly eight feet across. Scattered debris lay everywhere, including several wine bottles bearing an Italian label. Apparently the men who had been imported to work on the church had secretly used this space as a private social club. Even the mill owners who had funded the church's building hadn't known of its existence.

"Hey, look at this!" Timothy knelt down and pointed to a small metal grate in the floor directly above the confessionals, giving full access both to the two penitents and the priest below.

The boys looked at each other, their thoughts aligning. Wouldn't this make an interesting diversion for a Saturday afternoon?

"This place is great!" Timothy said, peering through an opening in the wall. Later inspection would reveal that the opening aligned with the mouth of a plaster cherub mounted on the outside wall.

Timothy turned back and looked around.

"Let's not tell anyone else about this room, okay?" he insisted. This was too great a place to share with anyone.

"Yeah. We'll make it our secret place. Like a clubhouse," Ben agreed.

"Only better," Timothy said, swatting at a cobweb.

"Let's make a pact," Ben suggested eagerly, kneeling down and taking out his pocketknife. "We'll swear it in blood. Neither of us will ever tell another living soul about this place."

"Deal," Timothy agreed, rolling up his sleeve.

And for more than sixty years, both had kept that pact. In fact, they had almost forgotten about its existence until the day they realized what a perfect place it would be to test the hologram of the Blessed Virgin Mary.

Chapter 21

During the blizzard, while the town had searched for Father Keene, Matthew Metcalf had been hard at work in his parents' basement with his friend Dominic Costello, designing a holographic image of the Blessed Virgin Mary. In fact, it would be several days before either realized that Father Keene had been missing.

The two teenagers hardly gave the weather a passing thought. Their attention was riveted on the arsenal of machinery secretly "borrowed" from the university where Dominic was enrolled as a sophomore. The only time they seemed to be dimly aware of the raging storm outside was when a sudden brown-out disrupted an online conversation they were having with a holographic technician. For all these two cared, it could go on snowing for weeks. They had plenty to keep them entertained.

Although neither Dominic nor Matthew had ever created a hologram before, they had every confidence they could and together they made a perfect team. If one boy lacked a particular skill, the other possessed it. If one reached an impasse, the other was able to reevaluate the problem and provide a new route. They worked easily and in tandem, using the power of the Internet and high-tech chat rooms to fill in the blanks, speaking in a language even more advanced computer programmers might find highly intimidating.

For forty-eight hours, high on chocolate and mugs of coffee heavily laden with sugar and Coffee Rich, neither slept more than a few hours nor had any idea if it was day or night. Their complete and undivided attention was focused on the equipment—lasers, photographic emulsion, beam splitter. To the side of the room sat the vibration-free tabletop and several mirrors that completed their needs.

Although both Matthew and Dominic had begun with only an elementary understanding of holographic imagery, through dogged determination they quickly succeeded.

The theory was relatively simple. A hologram records patterns of infinitesimal lines called an interference pattern. This is created by the interaction of two beams of laser light, which are recorded on a special light-sensitive material chemically similar to a photographic emulsion.

Applying that knowledge was somewhat harder, especially the need to reproduce the *exact* angle used in the original reference beam. Correctly reinstalled, the second beam should intersect at the precise coordinates in order to redirect the image and thus form a 3-D image. If it was off by even a breath, the process would not work. It was a problem that Matthew would have to consider when moving the equipment to St. Cecilia's.

The boys worked methodically, slowly improving both their understanding and their skills until by the end of the second day, they were able to create a three-dimensional image of a statue of the Blessed Virgin Mary that had been borrowed from the garden equipment stored in the garage. Technically, this meant that the boys had now completed their original goal. But surrounded with state-of-the-art holographic equipment and having nothing left to do was too taunting. They quickly devised another challenge.

"Let's try creating a spectral image," Matthew suggested, a process used to create life-like three-dimensional images capable of movement.

Matthew needed to say no more. Dominic grabbed another chocolate chip cookie and began to ply the Internet.

It only took a few hours until they had gathered the information needed for their newest experiment. The Metcalfs' cat, Samson, became their first test subject. He was more than willing to oblige as long as he was allowed to lie intermittently undisturbed over the heating vent. By the end of the third day, the boys had successfully created a holographic cat and now looked for new high-tech frontiers to conquer. This time Dominic provided the challenge.

"Wouldn't a live image of the Blessed Virgin Mary be a lot more interesting than that old plaster statue?"

Seeing a spark of interest ignite in Matthew's eyes, he quickly continued. "What if we use my sister dressed up in a costume? You know, like the Virgin Mary?" Dominic continued with growing excitement. "We could film her moving, but not too much. We don't want her walking back and forth along the altar or anything like that. But maybe we could just tilt her head a little. Or raise her arms in a blessing. Like this," he demonstrated. "What do you think?"

"That would be way cool!" Matthew's creative processes were launched like missiles.

Stephanie, who had developed a secret crush on Matthew, was only too happy to oblige. She stood quietly waiting as Matthew searched through closets, a trunkful of old choir robes and his mom's sewing supplies in order to create a plausible costume. Stephanie played along, eager to gain Matthew's attention, shyly tucking her long brown hair underneath a white linen tablecloth and cinching her waist with a navy blue drapery cord. Matthew, however, hardly noticed her hopeful smiles. He was much too intent on the technical process.

Dominic finally cast his sister's holographic image across the other side of the room. All three teenagers let out a small gasp of surprise.

"If I didn't know that was my sister, I'd swear it was the Blessed Virgin Mary standing right here in the room," Dominic said with enormous satisfaction.

On the following Wednesday morning at six A.M., Timothy, St. Cecilia's head usher—a position that came with a ring of church keys—quietly led Matthew and Ben up the choir loft stairs. The three were laden with a laptop computer, battery packs and the university's two five-hundred-thousand-dollar lasers, which Dominic had assured them would not be missed. "Everyone's left for spring break," he had said.

Ben carefully placed the box containing the lasers at the top of the stairs, then ran his hand along a side panel. Suddenly, the panel moved inward, revealing the secret room.

"Wow! How cool, Grandpa!" Matthew said. "I didn't know this was up here."

"Neither does anyone else except Tim and me."

Ben moved the boxes into the room, then motioned his grandson to inspect the front wall. "See this opening? It gives you a clear view of the entire sanctuary below. Thought you could run that laser beam through here."

"This is *great*, Grandpa. Perfect," he said, peering through. Matthew could hardly contain his excitement.

"We have to get out of here before people start showing up for morning Mass," Ben told his grandson. "Tim will leave the stairwell unlocked so you can come back later and set it up. If it works, we'll show Father James when he gets back from New York and see if he thinks it might be a good substitute until we can afford to replace Mary's statue."

It had seemed such a simple plan.

That afternoon, Matthew walked unnoticed into the back of the church and quietly slipped up the choir loft stairs and into the secret room. It was imperative that the equipment be properly aligned for the hologram to take form and he had come to perform one final test before officially unveiling the plan to Father James.

Matthew slipped out of his shoes to muffle his footsteps and quietly closed the panel door behind him. Switching on the battery light pack that illuminated the equipment sitting on two folding tables imported from Sam's garage, Matthew began to reposition the reference beam to the exact calibration used in the original exposure. It was a complicated and tedious procedure especially since he had to angle the beam through the inside opening of the cherubic figure along the outside wall. Forty minutes later, the reference beam was in position and the second beam was aimed directly at the empty niche in the sanctuary below.

He threw the toggle switch. Pencil thin beams of light threaded across the room and out through the opening in the wall. Unable to view the full effect of the image through the small opening, Matthew bounded out of the secret room, down the stairs and out into the sanctuary. What he saw couldn't have pleased him more.

The image of Stephanie Costello dressed like the Blessed Virgin Mary hovered inside the niche looking so lifelike that it seemed as though she were actually standing there. Dominic had been right. If they hadn't created the hologram themselves, Matthew might have believed that it was really the Blessed Mother.

"Wow," he said softly, watching the image move and turn slightly. The church setting, with its soft candle glow and stained-glass windows, only intensified its look of authenticity.

Matthew's thoughts surged with new holographic ideas. He could beam images of Sam's car into parking spaces and reserve them especially for him; he could create police car holograms and place them all over town. People passing by wouldn't know if they were real or not. What an ingenious way to stop speeders! Who knows, Matthew thought, the idea might even earn him some brownie points with the sheriff.

He was so caught up in his thoughts that he didn't notice George Benson until something moved over to his left. Matthew gasped. It was George, kneeling and gazing at the hologram, looking really ill. Seconds later, the fire marshal rose to his feet and began to make little bows as he headed toward the rectory's connecting door.

Matthew froze in place. What should he do? While he tried to think, George returned with Father Keene. Matthew hid behind the back pews.

"Look! Over there," George pointed toward the hologram.

"Dear Blessed Mother of God! 'Tis really you," Father Keene exclaimed and fell to his knees. George followed.

Both men began to say the rosary.

"Oh no," Matthew moaned softly. They thought the image was real. Now what? Should he try to explain it was just a hologram? If he did, would his grandfather and Mr. McGree get into trouble? Matthew knew they had set it up without Father James's permission. The church echoed with Father Keene and Mr. Benson's prayers. Matthew peeked over the back pew. The two men were staring transfixed at the holographic image of Stephanie Costello.

Matthew scrunched down again, his heart racing like a jackhammer. What if somebody walked in off the street, saw the image and thought it was real? They could have a heart attack. Did that mean he would be charged with murder? An image of Sheriff Bromley—as real as any hologram—played out in his mind. The sheriff had handcuffed him and was leading him to the police station. A prison cell loomed in the future.

Matthew lowered his head into his hands. Oh, why . . . why . . . hadn't he thought about any of this *before* he had suggested this experiment? Once again, his obsession with technology had landed him in deep dog-do.

Voices sounded outside on the street. He couldn't risk anyone coming in and seeing this. Hunching down close to the floor like a combat soldier under attack, he made his way to the choir staircase, quietly opened the door and slipped through. He tried to quell the rising sense of urgency in his chest as he stole up the stairs, afraid of making noise, but as he reached the landing, he could contain himself no longer. Hitting the spring to the secret panel, he raced through the portal before it had time to swing completely open, his stockinged feet skidded on the bare wooden floors, propelling him across the room like a hockey puck. He waved his arms wildly, regaining his balance just inches before crashing into the folding table laden with equipment. He threw the switch on the electrical panel, shutting everything down.

He could hear Father Keene speaking downstairs through the grate in the floor. Matthew lowered himself to a sitting position and listened.

"George, my son. You and I have been chosen by Our Lady to help save St. Cecilia's."

"We have? But how?"

"We're simply going to tell people what we have just seen."

Matthew sat back. What had he done? What would he tell his grandfather? He was only sixteen and already his life was over. First suspension from school. Now this. They'd probably excommunicate him from the Catholic Church, too, and God would probably bar him from heaven as well.

He'd really stepped in it this time.

Chapter 22

Father James awoke Good Friday morning feeling like his brain was coming undone. He couldn't possibly juggle anything else.

There were three days of Lenten services to conduct, which were the most important in the Church's calendar year. Preparations that needed to be made to physically close the church and rectory, and he'd yet to find a nursing home for Father Keene. Plus both the archdiocese and the sheriff were waiting for him to conclude his investigation into the Marian visions that had turned the quiet town of Dorsetville into a three-ring circus. How was he ever to get it all done?

He mentioned this to Mrs. Norris when he came down for his morning coffee.

"Now you know what it feels like to be a woman," she said, pulling a stack of dishes from the cupboards.

She was in the throes of packing the remains of the kitchen cupboards. Everything had to be out by Monday morning.

"Yes, I imagine it must," he sighed. "Any coffee?"

It was Good Friday, a day of fasting. The thought further depressed him. No food until after sundown but if he could just get a cup of coffee. . . .

"I'm waiting for George. He's going to carry these boxes out to the garage. No use making two pots." This morning Mrs. Norris's temper was as sharp as the kitchen knives she'd packed earlier. As far as she was concerned, there was no reason for the archbishop to close St. Cecilia's, especially with the advent of the Marian visions.

"I still can't understand why the archbishop insists that St. Cecilia's be closed." It was a comment she had made at least two dozen times each day over the past week. "The church is bursting out at the seams. Why, there isn't an empty seat at any of the Masses. Even some of our regular parishioners have to stand along the side walls."

Father James closed his eyes. He felt as though he needed an extra ten hours of sleep. "The archbishop feels that nothing really has changed. There are still less than a hundred parishioners registered."

Mrs. Norris began to wrap the salad plates. A box marked KITCHEN lay open on the table.

"I thought St. Cecilia's was being closed because there wasn't enough money to keep the church open. I didn't know the parish had to meet a quota of parishioners."

"No ... well ... yes ... but ..."

"I called Mike Harris, the church treasurer, at home last night. And do you know what he said? He said we've collected over twenty thousand dollars just this past week."

"Yes ... but ..."

"It seems to me that if the church is kept open, we'd collect enough money in a few months to be able to pay all of our bills and make some necessary repairs." She sighed heavily. "I don't see why we just can't go on as always?"

Father James understood Mrs. Norris's disappointment. He felt it, too. He had hoped the archbishop would reconsider, delay the church's closing in light of the throngs of people who filled every pew and lined the walls of the church each day.

But the archbishop felt that the present state of the church's disrepair was that much more reason to close it. Someone could get seriously hurt. Father James had to admit those fears weren't unwarranted. Two days earlier a large piece of plaster had fallen from the ceiling, barely missing a small Asian woman and her three-year-old daughter, Hope.

Father James began to feel weak at the knees from lack of food and sat down across from Mrs. Norris. "But what happens when all those folks go home? The apparition that Father Keene and George said they've seen has not reappeared. How long do you think people will stick around before they grow tired of waiting and go back home? Then who will take care of the church?"

Mrs. Norris crumpled packing paper into tight balls and stuffed them down the sides of the box. "You *still* aren't convinced that Mary appeared, or that she'll appear again, now are you?" She ran a two-inch strip of gray packing tape expertly along the box's seam, sealing it shut.

My kingdom for a cup of coffee, he thought. "Mrs. Norris, what I believe or don't believe is not the issue."

Mrs. Norris glared at him from behind the packing box. "So you think that both Father Keene and George are lying?"

"I didn't say that and you know it," Father James snapped.

He was tired. Tired of the whole mess—visions, nursing homes, church closing, painful good-byes, his last sermon in St. Cecilia's looming in front of him. He needed a walk.

He rose, ending the conversation, picked up the sealed carton and placed it alongside the long row of packing boxes by the pantry door. Then grabbing his black woolen coat from the row of wooden pegs by the door, he fled the kitchen.

Walking outside he stuffed his hands deep into his coat pockets, a habit he had formed since realizing the cuffs were badly frayed. The tips of his fingers grazed an oval-shaped metal object, which he pulled out. It was a medal of St. Anthony given to him by Monsignor Casio.

Oh, St. Anthony, if ever we needed a miracle it is now, he prayed. *And since you are the patron saint of miracles, would you kindly offer up a prayer on our behalf?*

A cold wind began to blow off the river, instantly turning the tips of his ears an angry red. But he hardly felt the cold as he headed toward Main Street and the Country Kettle spurred by one thought: Perhaps if he could just get his caffeine levels back up, he'd feel a little less depressed.

⁓❧

Father James waited for his coffee as he watched Harry's growing frustration with his new short-order cook, a man of uncertain ethnic heritage who spoke in short, broken phrases while jabbing a stubby finger at the orders clipped above the grill.

"It say egg. I cook egg. Lots of egg."

Harry pointed with his spatula at the same order. "Look, it says *two* orders of scrambled eggs, one well done with sausage and the other soft with bacon. You've got"—Harry pointed to the mound of eggs with pieces of home fries and brown, charred specks—"Hell . . . I don't know *what* you've got there!"

"Harry, I need that stack with blueberries," Lori Patterson insisted. "The guy's been waiting for nearly twenty minutes."

Two new waitresses hovered close behind, one of whom Father James recognized as the wife of a former church deacon. What was her name? Jillian? No, Barbara. Or was it Geraldine?

"I've been waiting for two omelets—one's a western, one egg white," she said.

"I know, I know," Harry's patience had waned. "Tell them to hang on or go over to Dunkin' Donuts in Manchester."

"Now, Harry," Lori placated. "Why don't you let me in there and send Peppy to help the dishwasher in the back."

"Well . . . I suppose you couldn't do any worse."

Harry grabbed Peppy's spatula and motioned for the little man to go in the back and help with the dishes. Peppy threw his hands up and stomped away while rattling in his native tongue. Lori took over his place behind the grill.

What has happened to my quiet, laid-back town? Father James wondered as a new waitress delivered his coffee. "Thanks," he murmured gratefully, then closed his eyes. He took a long, long sip and nearly gagged.

"Hazelnut?" he yelled as though he had been poisoned. Where was the regular coffee? The plain old everyday coffee he had savored for nearly three years?

"You like it?" Harry asked walking over, his spatula dripping oil all over the counter.

"Truthfully, no. What's wrong with just plain coffee?" he asked petulantly.

Why did everything have to change? The sound of saws and hammers behind the side walls only intensified his lament. Harry had decided to expand the restaurant and had rented the two empty buildings on either side of his building.

"Get Father a new cup, will you?" he yelled to one of the new girls.

"It's not that I don't . . ."

"No need to explain," Harry said, dumping the mug into a dishpan under the counter. "I prefer a good old plain cup of coffee myself. But this new crowd," he said, looking around, "they like the flavored kinds and those herbal teas. The kinds that are made with sticks and twigs. Tried a cup last night. Tasted like sh . . ." He cleared his throat. "Let's just say it wasn't Lipton."

The waitress placed a new mug of coffee in front of Father James. He sniffed it warily before taking a sip. Ah, at last, he sighed with relief.

"Come on, Harry, you're falling behind," Lori yelled, flipping several eggs in rapid succession.

"Gotta get back."

Father James watched them move mounds of home fries, buckwheat pancakes, bacon and ham around the grill. The aroma was tantalizing on a normal day, but on a day of fast . . . it was hellish. His stomach rumbled so loudly, the customer seated beside him at the counter looked his way and smiled.

"Catholic priest?"

Father nodded.

"Thanks for dropping by to see Bob," Lori yelled, pouring pancake batter onto the hot grill, which sizzled and snapped.

"Bet he can't wait until the month is over." Father James moved in a little farther to inhale the smells.

"That's for sure. The isolation period is really grating on his nerves. The only thing that keeps his spirits up is the doctor's reports. They say he's really doing great."

Her spatula paused in midair. "Just imagine, Father. When this is all over, Bob will be able to resume a normal life." She looked at him over her shoulder. "Isn't that a miracle?"

"It sure is, Lori. And I can't think of anyone who deserves it more than you and Bob."

She turned back to the grill, but Father James could sense the tears in her eyes.

"I still can hardly believe that a donor was found who matched Bob's bone marrow *exactly*. We had nearly given up hope."

Lori expertly flipped a stack of buckwheat pancakes onto a plate that had been warming on a shelf above the grill.

"Gladys, come pick up your stack."

Gladys. Her name is Gladys, Father James reminded himself.

Lori moved another order along the metal clipboard, quickly scanned it and broke three eggs into a bowl. "The doctors say they've never seen a patient respond as well as Bob." She paused briefly before giving the final egg a hard tap. "God really does answer prayers."

"Yes, He does." Father James said with a smile. *For He is able to do exceedingly, abundantly more than we could ever ask or imagine.* Then remembering his own prayers, silently added, *and sometimes He elects to say no.*

How he yearned to linger, but time was a commodity he no longer possessed. There was a list of things on his desk back at the rectory that needed to be finished before the three o'clock service. He finished his coffee with one last swig, stood and fished in his pocket for some change.

"Coffee's on the house," Harry yelled as always, spearing several pieces of bacon with prongs and placing them on an order of scrambled eggs.

"Harry!" Lori wailed, "that bacon was for *my* order!"

Father James smiled and walked toward the door.

"Father James," Ethel Johnson called out.

Father James walked back over. "Good morning, everyone. How are you, Honey?" He bent down to scratch Honey behind the ears.

Ethel's golden retriever cast a quick look his way, thumped her tail twice, then went back to studying her mistress. Ethel had a spoon and was feeding Honey the food scraps Harry had saved from the grill.

"Good morning, Father," Ethel said, enjoying how Father James always greeted her beloved pet. The spoon paused in midair. "Eating on Good Friday isn't a sin for a dog, is it Father?"

Honey waited expectantly, eyes locked on the food hovering several inches away from her snout. Not a muscle moved.

"No, Ethel," he smiled. "I think dogs are exempt from fasting."

"I thought so. Here you go, girl."

Honey seemed to inhale the spoon's contents, then tensely waited for more.

The morning regulars were circled around their usual table, including Harriet Bedford. Father walked over and gave her a kiss on the cheek.

"I didn't know you were back in town. How are you doing?" he asked, taking her hand. He and Father Keene had presided over her son Peter's funeral just a few weeks ago. Since that time, Harriet had been with Allison in New York as together they sorted through Peter's things and closed up his apartment.

"I'm as good as can be expected," she said, grief still fresh in her eyes.

"I've been praying for you," Father said.

She smiled. "And I could feel your prayers. Thank you, Father. It's been a hard couple of weeks, but I try to keep ahead of the grief by focusing on the blessings. I have my granddaughter back in my life and she's even asked me to help with her wedding plans."

"Allison's a wonderful woman," Father said. "My best friend is a very lucky man."

"I'd have to agree," Harriet said with pride. "Jeff and his family are joining Allison and me for Easter dinner. You, Father Keene and Father Dennis are invited, of course."

"We'll look forward to it."

She turned to the nun dressed in a blue habit seated to her right. "Have you met my sister, Mary Veronica? She's with the order of the Daughters of Mary of the Immaculate Conception. Their convent is in Burlington. Mary Veronica is their mother superior."

"Hello, Father," Mother Mary Veronica said, peering over the rim of a pair of wire, half-moon reading glasses.

"Nice to meet you." He added, "So, you're here for Easter?"

"That and sort of a busman's holiday," Mother Mary Veronica said.

"Oh?"

"Our order wants to create a retirement home for the religious."

"And you're considering Dorsetville?" he asked hopefully.

She nodded.

Heart be still, he ordered. What a perfect answer to his prayers for Father Keene.

"Some of the mansions across from the town green might do nicely," he offered eagerly. "In fact, several are for sale."

"Yes, I know. I've been in contact with John Moran. He's shown me several."

And? he wanted to ask.

"They'd be just perfect except for just one thing."

His hopes paused on their ascent. "Which is?"

"Harriet tells me that St. Cecilia's is closing on Easter Sunday. Is that correct?"

Disappointment moved in. "I'm afraid so."

"I see." The nun frowned. "Of course, that would be a problem. Our residents will need the support of a local parish. They can hardly be expected to travel by bus to another town for daily Mass, nor can we rely upon outside priests to minister to our home-based needs."

"No. Of course, you can't," Father James admitted, trying not to let his disappointment show. "I'm sorry. Your facility would have been warmly welcomed, and I'm certain that your residents would have found a great home. I don't know of a better place to spend one's last years than among the people and beauty of Dorsetville."

Mother Mary Veronica smiled softly. "Yes, I know. It was my childhood home."

"Of course," he said, feeling somewhat foolish.

"I've placed it in God's hands," Mother Mary Veronica said, then concluded with a twinkle in her eyes, "Perhaps He's not had the last word?"

"Perhaps," Father admitted with little enthusiasm. There was no sense in letting his hopes get dashed again.

Father James was reminded that his computer needed to be dismantled and packed when he spied Matthew seated next to his grandfather.

"Matt, do you think you could come over to the rectory and help me pack up my Compaq?"

"I've given up computers and high-tech equipment, Father," Matthew said, slumping deeper into his chair.

"Oh, why is that?"

"I don't see much future in them for me."

"He's just feeling a little blue," Ben said, affectionately patting his grandson's knee while the equally sober faced Timothy and Sam sat silently alongside. "Good Friday affects some people like that."

"I know what you mean," Father agreed.

Father James walked back to the rectory, grabbed another mug of coffee and headed toward his desk which someone had shoved in the corner next to the pantry to make room for several large packing boxes. After clearing away rolls of tape, scissors and packing labels, he looked around for his swivel desk chair. It was missing. Not wanting to waste precious time hunting it down, he grabbed a kitchen chair and sat down, deliberately turning his back to the barren room, and faced the window that looked out on the green.

He'd once heard an artist say that of the four seasons, winter was the most difficult to paint with any sense of hope. Spring, summer and fall, on the other hand, begat a landscape filled with the soft curves of leaves, tufts of grass and flowering plants that encouraged the eye to travel into the distance (a metaphor, the artist had said, for hope in things not yet discovered). The winter landscape stripped bare of all foliage, however, often filled a viewer with despair, for the sharp vertical lines of the hardwoods imprisoned the eye.

A winter landscape, that's how the room behind him felt now with its tall packing boxes. Also gone were the yellow checked curtains, hand-embroidered tablecloths and the row of neatly placed wine goblets that once lined the top shelf of the oak hutch. Even the pantry, which up until yesterday had been filled with homemade preserves, jars of canned tomatoes, cucumber relish and pickled beets all lined like soldiers ready to ward off hunger, had been packed away or given to the community food pantry now temporarily housed in Sam Rosenberg's garage. Only a few jars remained. In their place were the tall vertical boxes that echoed the winter landscape.

There was no time for self-pity or recrimination—*what ifs*. Much too much needed to be accomplished in the span of a few hours. He pulled out his list. He had walked around with it stuffed in his shirt pocket for weeks. He placed the paper on the desk and smoothed it out.

With uncommon efficiency, he scanned its contents rather quickly, and within twenty minutes had contacted both the electric and telephone companies (thank goodness their offices remained open until noon). He made arrangements to have the services disconnected on Tuesday, the day after the move.

Next, he left a message on Chester Platt's answering machine, reminding him to board up the windows of both the rectory and the church late Monday afternoon. Father James paused after the phone call to remember their last conversation.

"I'll do it, but I have to tell you that boarding up those windows will be like placing copper pennies on the eyes of the dead," Chester had said in an uncharacteristic display of emotion.

It took Father James the longest to track down the town selectman, Roger Martin. Martin was at home preparing to meet with the director of public works for a round of golf. Father James, feeling the selectman's impatience not to be late for his tee-off, quickly advised him that St. Cecilia's would like to relinquish its lease for the land on the town green. Could they sign the papers late Monday afternoon before Father James was scheduled to leave?

Martin, a thirteenth-generation Dorsetville Congregationalist, immediately canceled his golf plans—something he had never done before in more than twenty-five-years—and called his church. Within the hour, several Congregational members—including one to oversee the wrecking crew—stood gathered outside St. Cecilia's front door, enthusiastically taking measurements and arguing where the best place would be to put the Dumpsters.

Although his spirits had momentarily been boosted by Mother Mary Veronica's retirement home plans, Father James realized that it was too late for anything to save Father Keene from being sent away. He made repeated calls throughout the state but the responses were all the same: no openings. He widened his search.

At two thirty-five that afternoon, Father James finally located a facility that had an opening. It sat forty miles outside of Pittsburgh, Pennsylvania and was called Misty Manor. The administrator said it was a new facility that had opened last month. They still had one room left. Did Father James want it?

No! He didn't want it. Didn't want any part of sending Father Keene hundreds of miles away from the only home he had known for more than forty years. Away from his friends and those who loved him. But instead he asked, "To whom do I have the archdiocese make out the check?"

Chapter 23

Good Friday services began at three o'clock and the interior of St. Cecilia's sanctuary had been stripped bare. The altar stood naked, a cold, gray slab of marble. The large wooden crucifix behind the altar was shrouded in black, as were all the statues, and the gold tabernacle that housed the Host now stood open, like an empty tomb.

Not a candle flickered. Not a single flower graced the barren sanctuary. Even the organ was silent as hymns were to be sung a cappella.

In contrast to the soberness of the sanctuary, the pews had begun to fill by noon with people whose low conversations filled the air with a hum like that of a high-revolution motor. By one-fifteen there was standing room only. By one-thirty the ushers had started to turn people away at the door.

Harriet Bedford, her sister, Mother Mary Veronica, Ethel Johnson and her dog, Honey, arrived a little before three o'clock and nearly died from shock at the length of the line of people that wound its way around St. Cecilia's, many still hoping to be allowed inside the church. The women continued on toward the church's front door, past the horde who glared in open hostility.

"Hey, you!" someone shouted. "No cutting in front! Get to the back of the line."

Mother Mary Veronica turned to stare into the crowd and wondered when people had become so rude. Had they forgotten that she was a nun, a servant of God? She steadied her gaze then slowly made the sign of the cross in blessing over the crowd. People looked away embarrassed. No one said another word.

Fred Campbell met them as soon as they stepped over the threshold.

"Harriet! Ethel! I'm so glad you're finally here." He escorted them inside, then quickly closed the door. "Father James has been looking for you for nearly an hour. You were supposed to go over today's readings."

"I'm sorry, Fred. We had no idea the church would be so mobbed," Harriet said, slipping out of her coat. "We had trouble finding a place to park."

"You and all our other parishioners," Fred laughed. "But you're here now and that's what counts. I saved you a place up front."

"Thank you, Fred."

"But there's only one small problem."

"Oh?"

"Two women sneaked in about an hour ago and took over the entire pew. They said they're saving it for some friends. I tried to explain that you and Ethel need to be up front because you're the readers for today's service, but no matter how much I pleaded, I couldn't get them to move."

"Imagine!" Ethel said, in a huff. What made these out-of-towners think they could just charge in and take seats away from longstanding parishioners?

"Want me to move some people outside, ladies?" the sheriff asked. He and Deputy Hill had been leaning against the confessional when the women walked in. Although neither was Catholic, the sheriff had insisted they come to help control the crowds.

Mother Superior sighed wearily. What had happened to the respect once shown the Church? "Let me have a go of it, Sheriff. I think I might be able to persuade them to leave."

"All right, but if they give you any trouble just let me know."

She nodded without comment then quickly set off down the aisle followed by her small retinue. As Fred had warned, two super-size ladies had commandeered the pew, strewing along its length a plethora of shopping bags, empty film boxes and assorted snack food wrappers.

"Ladies, you seem to be in the wrong seats," Mother Mary Veronica began. The woman nearest the aisle barely gave her notice.

"Sorry, Sister, but we got here at noon so we could save these front seats for our friends."

Mother Mary Veronica peered over her metal frames. "This is not a movie theater, ladies, where one saves seats. This is the Lord's house and these two women are part of the proceedings."

"I'm sorry, Sister, but we're not moving. We've driven all the way from New Jersey. It took us four hours, and we plan to have front row seats in case the Blessed Mother shows up again. Maybe you can get those people over there to scrunch up a little."

Honey began to growl.

My sentiments exactly, Mother Mary Veronica thought. If this was the only reason these women had come to church, she wondered why they had come at all. She grew more determined to move them out. "I don't think you ladies understand. This is not a request. You are to move and move now!"

A flicker of confusion raced across the woman's face. She was not used to being challenged, the main reason her friends had sent her to commandeer the seats. "And if we don't?"

"I will have you physically removed by the nice sheriff, who is standing at the back of the church."

The woman turned around. Sheriff Bromley, who had been keenly watching the exchange, met her gaze with a hand motion saying, *move it outside.*

"Well! Of all the nerve! Asking us to move *now* just as the service is about to begin," the woman scowled. "Come along, Shirley. And we were told that this town was supposed to be a friendly place. Ha!" The two women quickly snatched up their shopping bags, murmuring under their breath.

"Make sure you pick up all those candy wrappers, too," Mother

Mary Veronica said. "It looks like you have also confused the Lord's house with a food drive-in."

The women turned to glare but did as they were told, then stepped out into the aisle. Honey snarled as the women left, exposing two-inch-long fangs.

"Get that mad dog away from me!" one woman said, hurrying past. "Imagine letting a dog in church while chasing people out!"

"This *dog* has been going to St. Cecilia's all her life," Ethel said defensively. "And I might add, she's better behaved than some people." Ethel stepped in front of the women and slid into the pew next to Honey.

"Well, I never!" the woman said in a huff. Then with as much indignation as she could muster considering the situation, she added, "Come on, Shirley. This is just the kind of attitude that has made so many people leave the Church."

The women lumbered back down the center aisle as fast as their piano legs could carry them, trying to ignore the veiled smirks of seated parishioners as they passed. Sheriff Bromley opened both of the large oak doors and personally ushered them outside.

While Harriet and Ethel whispered quietly, Mother Mary Veronica knelt to pray the rosary.

"I hope the others can get through the crowds outside," Harriet said.

"I do, too," said Ethel. "I'd hate for any of our friends to miss St. Cecilia's last Good Friday service."

Minutes later, George Benson and Mrs. Norris emerged from the rectory door just as Harry, Lori Peterson and her daughter, Sarah, raced up the side aisle. Harriet motioned them over.

As the congregation began to rise, Harriet reached over and grabbed Lori's hand. "I'm so glad you found us," she whispered.

"So am I. With Bob in the hospital, I hate sitting alone at Mass," Lori said, watching her daughter squeeze in next to Honey.

The congregation grew silent as Father James, Father Dennis and Father Keene walked out of the sacristy, their red vestments in stark contrast to the somber surroundings. They paused in front of the altar, bowed deeply, then prostrated themselves on the hard marble floor. The church descended into reverent silence.

Finally, Father James rose as both he and Father Dennis cupped their hands underneath Father Keene's arms, helping the elderly cleric to his feet. In unison, the priests stepped up to the altar, then turned to face the congregation.

Father James raised his hands in prayer.

Lord, by the suffering of Christ, your Son, you have saved us all from the death we inherited from sinful Adam. By the law of nature we have borne the likeness of His manhood; may the sanctifying power of grace help us to put on the likeness of our Lord in heaven, who lives and reigns forever and ever. Amen.

Bodies thundered against the hard wooden pews as Harriet and Ethel took their places at the altar to begin the reading of the Passion.

Harriet cleared her throat, willing herself not to cry, wondering if she should have asked Arlene Campbell to take her place. Her emotions were still raw with grief over Peter's death, but she had stubbornly insisted on coming. This would be the last time this text would be heard at St. Cecilia's and, as a reader for nearly thirty years, she had wanted to be the one to have read it.

She glanced nervously at Ethel and noted that her eyes were also wet with tears. Harriet swallowed hard against the rising lump in her throat and forced herself to begin.

Twenty minutes later, toward the end of the recitation, Ethel repeated the words of Jesus as he hung on the cross. "Woman, this is your son."

Acting as narrator, Harriet responded, "In turn, He said to the disciple . . ."

Ethel concluded, ". . . this is your mother."

Harriet had just taken a breath, ready to recite the next line when a woman at the back of the church screamed. Harriet looked up. The woman was pointing toward the empty niche.

"Look! It's the Blessed Virgin Mary!"

"Oh, my God! Have mercy on our poor souls!" another shouted.

"What in heaven's name?" Father James jumped out of his chair. Father Keene rushed forward.

The service was thrown into chaos. People began to weep. Some cried out. Others fainted into the aisles.

"Our Holy Mother, you have returned," Father Keene proclaimed, falling to his knees.

Had everyone gone mad? Father James wondered, moving out into the aisle. Then he glanced up.

"Dear Lord," he whispered. The Virgin Mary was hovering several inches above a bank of candles, appearing just as Father Keene and George Benson had reported. Father James watched her bow slightly, then lift her head and smile at the congregation.

He stood alongside Father Keene and a sobbing Father Dennis who kept repeating, "Oh, Mother of God, I can *really* see you. I can see you!"

Father James fell to his knees, his eyes locked on the unearthly vision. *Wait until I tell the archbishop!*

Chapter 24

In the upstairs church behind the hidden panel to the secret room, Timothy, Ben and Matthew had been quietly waiting since noon to dismantle the holographic equipment in hopes of finishing before the church began to fill for the three o'clock service, but they had forgotten, of all things, a Phillips head screwdriver.

Sam had been sent to Stone's Hardware Store. That had been over three hours ago. The delay, however, was not his fault. What had started as a simple errand had grown increasingly complicated.

It began when he decided to drive his car down to Main Street rather than walk, figuring it would be faster. That assumption would have been true several weeks ago, but now, with hundreds of people flooding into the town for a glimpse of where the miracle had taken place, there wasn't a parking space to be found.

Thirty minutes later as Sam cruised Main Street for the twentieth time, he gave up. Even the side streets were packed with cars. There was nothing left for him to do but return to the church, park in the lot and walk back down to Main Street.

This plan, however, didn't fare any better.

St. Cecilia's parking lot was filled, as were all the parking spaces along the green. The other side of the street was also filled with cars, some having been driven onto the front lawns of the empty mansions.

Even the parking lot of the Dorsetville Congregational Church was filled—which really irked their head Sunday school teacher, Mrs. Phillips, who had been planning to spend the afternoon sorting the costumes for the Easter play and needed a parking space close to the church's side entrance so she might tote the heavy cases of costumes into the downstairs basement community room. She resolved to get the church council to have signs installed, PARKING FOR DORSETVILLE CONGREGATIONAL MEMBERS ONLY. ALL OTHERS WILL BE TOWED AWAY AT OWNER'S EXPENSE.

Sam had finally driven a mile out of town, parked his car, then walked back into town to Stone's, which, as luck would have it, had run out of the size of Phillips head screwdriver that Sam needed—another forty minutes wasted. Knowing he had the one they needed back home in his garage buried somewhere inside his red metal tool chest, Sam walked the mile back to his car, where he wasted more time trying to maneuver his Plymouth Duster out from the parking space that was now hemmed in by a Cadillac and a rusted Chevy Malibu. It then took thirty *more* minutes to drive the four miles to his home and back.

By this time, it was nearing three o'clock and Sam still had to navigate the crowds outside St. Cecilia's who were not about to let anyone get inside the church's door before those who had been on line since noon. Sam tried to explain that he had been sent on an errand by one of the church officials, but this explanation only fell on deaf ears.

"Sure, and the pope sent me to see if the church has enough candles," one man said.

The crowd was still upset about the three women who had previously sneaked inside.

What could Sam do? *Not a thing,* he concluded, until the crowd went home. He found a park bench across the street and sat down to wait it out.

Sequestered upstairs in the hidden room, Matthew, Ben and Timothy grew impatient.

"What's keeping Sam?" Timothy complained, loosening his tie. "We asked him to get a screwdriver, not a gas-powered generator."

The poorly ventilated space had grown hot and stuffy and added to their general discomfort and mounting anxiety. Timothy watched Ben take out a handkerchief and mop his face. "You all right?" he asked.

"Yeah, it's just hot in here. I could use some fresh air." At least that's all he hoped it was. His heart was racing like a runaway train and he was having trouble breathing. Dr. Hammon had recently warned him that his blood pressure was getting high, and his cholesterol readings were always over 250. Could this be the beginning of a heart attack?

He glanced over at Matthew, who looked at him with worry. Ben smiled and patted the boy's arm. "I'll be fine," he said. Ben didn't want to scare the boy even though his owns fears were mounting.

"Are you sure, Grandpa? You don't look so . . ." Matthew froze in midsentence. Footsteps sounded along the staircase outside.

Timothy raised a finger to his lips, indicating they were to be quiet.

Ben closed his eyes and willed himself to breathe normally, but his breathing only grew more labored and a tightness was spreading around his chest. He swallowed hard against the rising panic. It was all this worrying, he thought. It was making him sick.

Ben had ridden a crest of rising panic ever since Matthew's friend Dominic had called the night before with the news that the university had finally discovered the laser equipment, which they had "borrowed," was missing. College officials had called in Sheriff Bromley to make out a report for stolen goods. Now, if any of them were caught with this stuff, they would be charged with grand larceny. What a mess!

Choir members shuffled outside the room.

Ben tried to focus on their new plan. If it worked, all of this would be behind them in a few hours. If not . . . well . . . he didn't even want to think about the consequences.

They were scheduled to meet Dominic at five P.M. outside the college science building. The kid had managed to somehow get a key from a friend who was to leave for spring break at five-thirty P.M. Ben looked again at his watch. It was nearing three. This was their last shot. If they missed it, Ben figured they'd all be wearing prison garb by the end of the week. Now he felt nauseous.

Maybe if he stood up, he'd feel a little better. He rose to his feet, his arthritic knees nearly buckling under the pain, but finally he was erect. He slipped off his shoes and began to pace.

"I just need to stretch my legs," he told Matthew.

How did things get so out of hand? Ben pondered. What had begun as a simple plan to help save St. Cecilia's had turned into a full-fledged disaster, which now included a cast of pilgrims bigger than a Cecil B. De Mille production, a Main Street-turned-carnival, dozens of television crews, an arrest warrant issued for stolen property and the prospect of all of them being charged with grand larceny.

Ben massaged the back of his neck with a liver-spotted hand. He was too old to do time. His hands began to shake. They were never going to make it out of here before five o'clock.

"We might as well get comfortable," Timothy whispered, as the rest of the choir members clambered up the stairs. "Sam's probably gotten caught in the crowds."

Ben nodded, then slowly lowered himself to the floor, the pain in his knees increasing beneath his weight.

Matthew reached for his grandfather's hand. "It's going to be all right, Grandpa."

"I know," Ben said, trying to reassure himself as much as the boy.

Below, people rising from their pews sounded like thunder. The service had begun.

Inside the chamber all remained quiet. Ben continued to try and divert his attention. The pressure tightening around his chest was mounting. Be calm, he told himself. Maybe it's just a little indigestion. He shouldn't have eaten that bacon and egg sandwich for breakfast. He began to silently recite the Sorrowful Mysteries of the rosary. It didn't help. In his mind, he listed the batting averages of baseball's Hall of Famers. This didn't work either. The pain increased. Should he tell Timothy to go get help?

Ethel's and Harriet's voices wafted up through the floor grate as they read the Passion. Those sequestered in the tiny room shifted uncomfortably, knowing it would be another thirty minutes before the women were through.

Timothy, who was wedged directly beneath the equipment table, felt the first twinges of a muscle spasm along his shoulder blades. Ever since he turned sixty, these painful spasms had plagued him. Lack of potassium he had read somewhere.

He raised his left shoulder slightly and slowly rotated his arm. Halfway into a revolution, the muscle locked. A hot, lancing pain flamed across his entire back. He tried not to scream out as he scrambled to his feet, swinging his arm in a full circle although not certain why. He only knew that he had to do *something* to release the muscle spasm. The pain was blinding.

Ben and Matthew looked on from across the room.

"You having some sort of fit?" Ben whispered sharply, momentarily forgetting his own discomfort.

"Got a charlie horse in my shoulders," he said in a stage whisper.

Timothy flailed his arms, bent at the waist, then righted himself in what appeared to be some strange native dance. Nothing was working. Matthew giggled.

Timothy stretched his arms out straight, parallel to the floor. *Ahhhh . . . that was better.* If only he could stretch the muscle a little more, it might release. He closed his eyes and stretched farther. Still farther . . . farther. His fingers hit the toggle switch on the console.

Instantly, a laser beam appeared, bounced off a mirror to merge with another, sending a perfect holographic image down into the sanctuary below.

"Ohhhhh." The congregation sounded in unison.

Downstairs someone shouted, "Look! It's the Blessed Virgin Mary!"

"Oh, man," Matthew groaned, burying his head in his hands. "Not again."

Someone else screamed, "Oh, my God! Have mercy on our souls!"

"What's happening?" Ben tried to get up again.

"The hologram," Timothy said. The muscle spasm was ebbing. "I accidentally hit the switch."

"Sweet Mother of Jesus," Ben said.

Downstairs, several people loudly sobbed.

"Turn the blasted thing off!" Ben hissed.

Matthew rushed to the console and flipped the switch.

"Oooohhh . . ."

Timothy raced to the opening in the wall and peered below. "Well, that about cinches it. Everybody's kneeling. Some are saying the rosary. They think the vision is real." Timothy leaned back. "Of all the times for this stupid muscle to freeze up. Now they'll never go home. We're probably stuck here 'til midnight."

Timothy turned just as Ben clutched his chest. "Ben? Ben, are you all right?"

Ben fell to the floor with a thud.

"Grandpa! Grandpa!"

"Ben! What's wrong, Ben?" Timothy shouted, so loud he could hear Alan Dambrowski, the choirmaster next door ask the choir, "What was that?"

"Please don't die, Grandpa. Please!" Matthew knelt down and cradled his grandfather's head in his lap. "This is all my fault."

Timothy flew to the panel door and swung it open. Two women choir members nearly collapsed with fright as he stepped through the opening.

"My God, Timothy! Where did you come from?" asked Alan.

"Never mind. Ben Metcalf's in there and I think he's having a heart attack. Call an ambulance."

Chapter 25

It was nearly midnight before Sheriff Bromley made his way back to the police station. He was bone tired and should have gone directly home but delayed, knowing that his wife would be working in the kitchen until dawn as she did every Saturday before Easter, coloring hundreds of eggs for the egg hunt sponsored by the Dorsetville Women's Club.

Like the first crocus, the town's Easter egg hunt was a sign of spring and was eagerly awaited by all the townspeople. The event took place in the park on the green between the two churches and was traditionally a time spent in fellowship with neighbors and friends, many of whom hadn't been seen since Christmas. A time to catch up with all the local news—who had caught the flu this winter, who had visited Florida, their opinions on snow removal. This year, however, the sheriff wagered that those topics would pale compared to the happenings over at St. Cecilia's.

Bromley settled in, deciding to make his nightly cup of hot chocolate at the station rather than go home and try to find a space among the dye cups, drying racks and boxes of colored eggs. Besides, he liked working late. He liked the silence. Liked having free run of the place without interruptions. It was easier to think here late at night. Sort things out. In fact, it was only a week ago, on a similar late night alone in the station, that he had pieced together how the university's missing laser equipment fit in with the reported Marian sighting at St. Cecilia's.

After interviewing the university's science department head and making out a report, he decided to spend some time at the college library reading up on lasers; it might give him some insight into who would want to steal that type of equipment. Among his reading was an article on holograms which stated that the three-dimensional images they created were so lifelike it was impossible to discern the original solid object from the hologram when placed side by side.

That night, alone in the station with only the company of his thoughts, the recent Marian sighting aligned itself with what he had read about holographic images. Suddenly . . . bingo! He knew he was onto something.

Two lasers had been stolen from the university along with some high-tech camera equipment, all of which was needed to create a hologram; yet other more expensive equipment—which had been in the same room as the lasers—had gone untouched. In the beginning, this had mystified him. But if the equipment was stolen for the specific purpose of creating a hologram, then that explained why.

Suddenly the stolen laser equipment and the Marian image connected. He remembered college sophomore Dominic Costello and his sister en route to Matthew Metcalf's house stranded on the side of the road during the blizzard. He had clearly seen the Middlebury College parking sticker on the driver's window and heard Dominic state that he and Matthew had met at a computer fair.

Bromley had a gut feeling that this kid and Matthew were behind both the missing equipment and the apparition at St. Cecilia's.

Convinced he was on the right track, Bromley scoured the church for any signs of wires or high-tech equipment. He even had the janitor get him a twenty-foot ladder to check the chandeliers, thinking that something might be hidden in their bases. Nothing.

He had to admit he was stumped. How were these kids pulling this off? But then Ben Metcalf had collapsed and the room hidden at the top of the choir loft stairs had provided the "how" as well as the "where."

He looked at his watch, one-thirty A.M, then stretched. He should go home and get a good night's sleep. Tomorrow was going to be a killer. Hundreds of kids and parents, forty Dorsetville Women's Club members giving him the evil eye as he tried to keep a town full of strangers from horning in on what Dorsetville folks felt was an exclusive town event. Still . . . he wanted to get everything that happened today written down in his report before he forgot any of the details.

Pulling a blank report from the right-hand bottom drawer of his desk, the sheriff fed the paper into his manual Smith-Corona typewriter. The town council had been badgering him for the last five years to take computer classes. They offered to pay, saying within the next five years the entire town would be linked by computer—fire station, police, town clerk, tax assessor. The town fathers had not been able to convince him.

He took a sip of his hot chocolate, which now had a dollop of fresh cream floating on top, scraped off of Deputy's Hill birthday cake in the refrigerator. Hill's birthday was tomorrow and the sheriff would catch the devil from Betty, the dispatcher and self-appointed birthday coordinator; however, that was tomorrow's problem.

He aligned the blank report, then set the margins and cranked the carriage return until the keys aligned with the body of the document. The names, addresses and such at the top of the sheet he'd fill in tomorrow.

He leaned back in his swivel chair, its tired springs groaning under his weight, and folded his hands in his lap, allowing his thoughts to drift back to the afternoon, which had proven to be the most exciting episode in his entire thirty-five-year career.

When the apparition of Mary had appeared above the niche by the front altar complete pandemonium broke out. People screamed. Some fainted. Others rushed forward in a crushing surge. Even more tried to rush in from outside. Only Mother Mary Veronica's quick action had prevented injury. Quickly slipping out of the pew, she stood in front of the advancing crowd, held up her arms and commanded everyone to kneel. To the sheriff's sheer amazement, everyone obeyed.

The apparition had only lasted a few moments before it disappeared, but it was time enough for Bromley to recognize the face of Stephanie Costello, Dominic's sister. This confirmed his suspicions. Apparently, Dorsetville's infamous teenage computer hacker, Matthew Metcalf, was at it again. Unfortunately, the image hadn't lasted long enough for him to ascertain its source.

Bromley tried to make his way through the center aisle, which was packed as tight as a can of sardines when Alan Dambrowski shouted over the choir railing.

"Someone call an ambulance. Ben Metcalf is up here and he's just collapsed."

"Call it in," Bromley shouted to Hill, then trundled up the stairs.

A group of people hovered at the top of the landing in front of what appeared to be an open panel. Bromley pushed his way past.

"He's in here," Timothy said and motioned for the sheriff to follow him into a room hidden behind a secret panel.

"Let me through," Bromley said, elbowing his way in.

"Go back to your seats," Allan urged. "Let the sheriff get by."

In the center of the floor lay Ben Metcalf as Matthew cradled his head. The teenager looked up, his face tight with fear.

"How are you doing, Ben?" Bromley asked, kneeling down beside the old man.

"Not too good," Ben whispered.

"Well, you just hold on. The ambulance is on its way." He gave Ben's hand a reassuring squeeze.

"He's going to be all right, isn't he?" Matthew asked, tears gathering in the corner of his eyes.

"We'll get him to the hospital and they'll fix him right up," Bromley said with as much confidence as he could muster. Ben's skin tone had turned a sickly gray.

"This is all my fault," Timothy moaned. "I was the one who cooked up this scheme."

"Well, once we get Ben, here, safely taken care of, I want you and Matthew to tell me all about it," the sheriff said. Nodding toward the table in the far corner and the two lasers bearing Middlebury College stickers, he asked, "Those the missing lasers?"

Ben's breathing grew more rapid.

"Hold on, Ben. Try to calm down," Bromley said.

"We didn't steal 'em," Matthew said. "Honest. We just . . . borrowed 'em."

Bromley didn't bother to look up. "You ask to borrow them?"

Matthew looked away. "No."

Ben clutched his chest. "My heart is racing so fast I can hardly breathe."

"A few more minutes, Ben, and help will be here." Bromley said. Several minutes passed in silence before he asked Timothy, "How did you find this place?"

"Ben and I discovered it by accident when we were kids," Timothy answered.

"Anyone else know it's here?"

Timothy thought about Sam. "No. Just Ben and me."

Sirens sounded in the distance.

"They're almost here," Bromley told Ben. "Just a few more minutes. Hold on."

They could hear Deputy Hill downstairs shouting to the crowd of people. "Move back, let the emergency crews by. We don't want the man upstairs to die."

Ben gripped his chest, his eyes wide with fear.

Damn, stupid, horse's . . . , Bromley thought. He managed a calm smile for Ben's sake. "It's all right, Ben. You're not dying. My deputy likes to exaggerate."

Minutes later, the ambulance crew and paramedic clambered up the stairs; they quickly assured Ben that he was not on the brink of death.

"Pressure's elevated and pulse rate is rapid, but you're not in immediate danger," the paramedic told Ben. "We're just going to give you some oxygen and start a saline drip. You seem a little dehydrated. Once that's in place, we'll get you to the hospital where they'll fix you right up." He patted Ben's shoulder reassuringly, then added, "Our only problem is how are we going to get a stretcher up that staircase."

"We have a stair chair in the ambulance," his partner said.

"You'd better radio and have them send it up," said the other attendant, opening a bag of saline.

Ben was finally carried down the stairs and rushed to Mercy Hospital's emergency room in Woodstock, where he was diagnosed with an acute anxiety attack. His heart, they assured him, was fine. It was his nerves that needed treatment. Apparently, being in possession of stolen property had taken its toll. The doctors loaded him down with tranquilizers and placed him in a room two floors above Bob Peterson.

Back at the church, Bromley had his men gather up the university's equipment and take it to the police station, where, after hearing Timothy and Matthew's story and the series of events that had turned their quiet town into a circus, he decided that there was no real malice or intent to commit grand larceny. It was a simple case of good intentions turned bad.

Later, the sheriff called Father James to accompany them to Judge Peale's home on the edge of town. Peale was a district court judge who also sat on the board of directors at the university. Bromley planned to call in a favor. But as he was ushering Timothy and Matthew into the back of his Chevy Blazer, Sam Rosenberg showed up to make a confession.

"I'm just as much to blame as the others," Sam said. "I want to turn myself in."

The sheriff leaned into the back seat of the SUV and stared at Timothy. "I thought you said that there was no one else involved?"

"I'm no stoolie," Timothy answered.

Bromley hid a smile as he told Sam to get in the back with the rest of his gang. It was like rounding up the Sunshine Boys.

Seventy-two-year-old district court judge, the Honorable Jeremiah F. Peale, lived in a 175-year-old farmhouse that sat on a two-hundred-plus-acre parcel of land down by the river. It was the most beautiful tract of land in the county, with expansive river views to the east and a backdrop of mountains to the west. The land had been in the family for five generations.

The property included a marker commemorating the original campsite of Pierre Dorseaux, Dorsetville's founding father. This was also the site of the town's annual Fourth of July picnic and fireworks display, a daylong event that included inner-tube races on the river, horseshoe contests, barbecue ribs cooked by the fire department and strawberry shortcake made by the Friends of the Dorsetville Library and (up until two years ago when the Platts' field horse had been spooked and trampled nearly an acre of Mrs. Peale's prize dahlias) there had also been hayrides. No one ever planned a vacation the first week of July. No one wanted to miss this event.

Judge Peale was a well-loved citizen of Dorsetville, as was his father and his father's father before him. To show the town's great respect for this family, the stonemason hired to cut the late Peales' gravestone had carved the following epitaph underneath the death date: A PATRIOT AND AN HONEST MAN. There could be no higher praise.

The Peales, although a wealthy family, never lorded their money or status over other townspeople. Instead, they humbly insisted their blessings came from God and they were merely stewards of His grace. No Dorsetville family was more deeply revered.

And so it was that when the judge's four headstrong and rambunctious sons became teenagers and fell into trouble as often as young boys fall into spring-fed ponds, the judge insisted upon no special treatment. But the sheriff, who had the utmost respect for the judge, often tried to spare him as much embarrassment as he could by quietly intervening in his sons' litany of pranks.

During their teenage years, that meant intervening about once a week. There were numerous incidents, some funny, some not. One Halloween night, the boys had spread Limburger cheese along the fan belts of the police cruisers, then called in false reports. Then there was the time two of the boys filled garbage-can tops with gasoline and floated them to the center of Platts' pond, then proceeded to pitch lighted matches until they exploded, which in turn, ignited the surrounding woods. It took two full days to put out the fire, which leveled nearly forty acres of forest.

Throughout those trying years, the sheriff personally visited the judge before releasing information to the press, and although Bromley never lied, he felt the press didn't need to know all the intimate details.

The judge had always been grateful and said, "If you ever need a favor, Al, and I can grant it, you come and see me."

It was nearing ten o'clock that night when the five elderly men and one frightened teenager entered the judge's study. The judge met them wearing a flannel bathrobe, leather slippers and a weary smile. It was already an hour past his bedtime. He would have preferred to wait until morning to sort this out, but the sheriff had insisted, saying they needed to resolve the matter before the press got wind of it tomorrow.

"Coffee, gentlemen?" the judge asked, holding up a silver coffee pot.

"Nothing for me, Your Honor," the sheriff said. Timothy, Sam and Matthew just shook their heads no.

"How about you, Father James? You look like you could use a little warming up."

"No thanks, Judge. It's going to be hard enough to get to sleep tonight."

A bottle of Jack Daniel's stood on the tray; the judge liberally poured some into a cup, then followed it with a stream of hot coffee. He smiled rakishly. "This is how I offset the effects of caffeine." He extended the bottle of whiskey toward Father James. "Sure you won't reconsider?"

"Well . . . maybe I will," Father James said, taking a cup. "It's been an awfully long day."

The judge poured a liberal amount of Jack Daniel's, topping it off with some coffee, and handed it to the priest, then recapped the whiskey before settling in behind his desk. "Won't you all sit down?" he asked.

The sheriff and Father James found a set of chairs by the wall of bookcases. Sam, Timothy and Matthew remained standing in front of the desk.

"Al, you want to tell me what's so important that it couldn't wait until morning?"

"It has to do with the university's stolen laser equipment," the sheriff offered.

"Yes, I know about the stolen items," the judge said. "Have you found who took them?"

Timothy, Sam and Matthew cast their eyes toward the carpet.

"It was these three here, Your Honor, plus another man, Ben Metcalf. A university student, Dominic Costello, was also in on it."

"I see." The judge looked up at the three who were standing.

"Your Honor," Father James began, "I know what these men did was wrong. They took expensive pieces of equipment and used them without the university's permission. But in their defense, sir, they never intended to keep the equipment. They only wished to test an idea to replace a broken statue of Mary in the belief that it would somehow help St. Cecilia's from closing. And since they couldn't afford a new statue, they cooked up this scheme to use a hologram instead."

The judge looked at Matthew. He knew of the boy's previous prank. "May I assume that you were the technical genius behind this great plan?"

"Yes, sir," Matthew said.

"And this university student . . . what's his name?"

"Dominic Costello," Matthew answered.

"Mr. Costello—he was the one who actually took the equipment from the university and delivered it into your hands?" The judge wrote his name on a yellow legal pad.

"Yes, but he was just trying to help us," Matthew said, interceding for his friend. "He never intended to keep the equipment. We figured with Easter break and the college closed, we could get it back before anyone noticed it was missing."

"We never meant to create this much trouble," Timothy added. "We just wanted to help save our church."

"And this hologram is the image reported as a Marian apparition in all the papers?" the judge asked.

"Yes, sir," the three accused answered in unison.

He covered a smile with a hand. It certainly was the damnedest thing he had ever heard, an entire town turned upside down by three old coots and a teenager trying to save their church. Although what they had done was definitely against the law and could not go unpunished, it was apparent that their actions were conceived without malice and, as they said, they had intended to *borrow* the equipment—not *steal* it. How often had his owns sons *borrowed* football gear or computer programs when they attended the university?

Of course, the judge had to admit that the value of what his sons borrowed could not be compared to the hefty price tags attached to the two lasers Matthew and his friend had appropriated. But he knew a criminal when he saw one, and these three standing in his library did not fit that profile.

"If the university should decide to drop these charges, I fear that it might give others the wrong impression," the judge said, hoping to scare them a little while instilling a sense of the seriousness of their actions. "Others might think that they were free to 'borrow' from the university with impunity. We just can't have that."

Matthew, Timothy and Sam looked up, eyes wide with fear.

"On the other hand . . ."

The men waited apprehensively.

"I can see that none of the parties involved intended to steal property from the university, or to use it in any way that might bring them profit." He sat forward in his chair and placed his hands together on the top of his desk. He let several moments of silence fall for effect before continuing.

"Gentlemen, I believe I can speak to the university officials in this matter and suggest that the charges be dropped if I have your solemn oath that nothing like this will ever happen again."

The accused vigorously shook their heads.

"Judge, you have our word that we will *never* do anything like this again," Timothy declared.

"That goes for me, too, Your Honor," Sam added. "I'm too old to do hard time."

"And you, young man?" the judge asked. "Can I have your word as well?"

"Yes, sir," Matthew said earnestly. "In fact, I think I might give up all this high-tech stuff for a while. It only seems to land me in trouble."

"I am going to recommend that you each be given thirty hours of community service. Agreed?"

"Agreed."

"Then it's settled," said the judge, rising. "And if I may borrow from your text, Father James," he added, "go and sin no more."

Chapter 26

Easter morning dawned clear, soft sunlight gently enfolding the small river valley town like a silk scarf. Daffodils lined the river bank, reflecting off the lumbering waters, and a gentle breeze wafted up toward the mountaintops, carrying two hot air balloons that rose like bubbles in a glass of champagne against a crystalline sky. And the woods, long silenced by the bleak winter, were now filled with birdsong.

Saturday morning, Father James shut off his alarm clock before it rang. There had been no sleep for him last night. After the visit with Judge Peale, he had accompanied Timothy, Sam and Matthew back to the police station while the sheriff had finished the paperwork involved in closing the case. Afterward, still charged and restless, Father James drove the back roads to Mercy Hospital to leave a note for Ben Metcalf, stating that he was no longer a wanted man.

While there, he had also checked up on Bob Peterson, whose doctors had just given him the results of the most recent tests on the bone-marrow transplant. According to the night nurse, everyone was amazed at how well Bob was doing. The prognosis for a full recovery was highly favorable. Father James told her it proved the power of prayer.

When Father James had finally arrived back at the rectory, it was well past two A.M. He took off his shoes at the bottom of the back staircase and silently trod upstairs, careful not to awaken Father Keene or Father Dennis. The hall light, which had been left on awaiting his return, illuminated a note tacked to his bedroom door.

I had to promise Mother Mary Veronica that you would read her enclosed letter as soon as you arrived. So, don't go to bed until you've read what it says.

Mrs. Norris

P.S. This nun is the bossiest woman I have ever met!

He smiled. Apparently Mrs. Norris had finally met her equal.

He walked into his room, threw his keys on his dressing table, emptied his pockets, then sat on the edge of his bed and read the front of the envelope. "Extremely important. For Father James's eyes only." Per Mrs. Norris's instructions, Father James opened the envelope before changing for bed.

Dear Father James,

By permission of the archbishop, I am informing you that our order has been given approval to procure property here in Dorsetville to be used as a retirement facility and nursing home for the religious.

The archbishop has also decided that in the best interest of our project, St. Cecilia's must be allowed to stay open. To this cause, he has allotted $325,000 from the Archbishop's Annual Appeal for the church's repair, and he has assured me that he stands ready to offer whatever other assistance is needed.

I look forward to working with you as Christ's ambassadors to our community and will be staying at my sister Harriet's to oversee the completion of our project should you need to contact me.

Yours in Christ's Service,
Mother Mary Veronica

P.S. I understand that you are in need of a nursing home facility for Father Keene. If you can make arrangements for his care until our project is completed, we would most gladly consider him our first resident.

For several seconds, he remained still, unable to react. Just moments before, he had felt a heaviness weigh upon his soul as he pondered the burdensome task of saying good-bye at tomorrow's Mass to the parishioners he loved so deeply. But now this.

While he had fretted and worried these last few weeks about who would feed his flock, who would take care of Father Keene and where his parishioners might find another church they loved as dearly as St. Cecilia's, God had been busy working it all out behind the scenes.

God began by giving Mother Mary Veronica the dream to build a nursing home in Dorsetville so Father Keene wouldn't have to leave his friends. And in providing for the elderly priest, God had created the need for St. Cecilia's to stay open. Only God could have worked out such an incredible plan!

Father James's spirit began to soar. His heart beat with a new rhythm, a new song. Deliverance had come, although not in a way Father James would have expected. But wasn't that just like God, whose ways were beyond a mortal's understanding?

"Praise you, Father," he shouted. "Praise you, for you have seen your people's sorrow and have replaced their tears with songs of gladness!"

Next door, Father Dennis woke with a start at the sound of Father James's shout. In his haste to scramble out of bed, he fell to the floor with a giant thud. Seconds later, he burst through the door, his eyes wide with excitement. "What is it now? What's happened?"

Since his arrival at St. Cecilia's, Father Dennis had learned to live in a state of great expectancy. At this parish, one never knew from moment to moment what new and amazing event might occur. In the past few weeks, there had been Marian visions, media frenzies, hordes of pilgrims, secret rooms, holograms and near panic in the sanctuary.

Whatever parishes Father Dennis would be assigned to in the coming years, nothing would ever be as exciting as this first assignment at St. Cecilia's.

"The Lord has sent a miracle for St. Cecilia's," Father James cried with laughter.

"God has sent a miracle," Father Dennis repeated with absolute certainty that there had been one.

Father James patted him on the back. "My dear brother priest, God has found a way to save St. Cecilia's."

"Save it?" he asked incredulously. "You mean . . . you mean the church isn't going to close? Easter Sunday is not to be the last Mass? But how?"

Father James handed the letter to Father Dennis, who eagerly read its contents as Father James looked out his bedroom window into the dome of stars and proclaimed, "Your path has led through the sea, Your way through the mighty waters, though your footprints were not seen."

Father Keene came racing into the room. "What in heaven's name is all the racket about in here," he asked, tripping over the belt of his bathrobe and falling into a startled Father Dennis's arms. The young priest helped Father Keene untangle himself.

"Saints preserve us!" he admonished, repositioning his wire glasses, which had fallen to the tip of his nose. "You two were making so much noise I thought for certain our blessed Lord had come to rapture His Church."

Father James laughed out loud. "No, Father Keene, that's not the case, but He has come to give us back a church here on earth."

❦

Easter morning, St. Cecilia's choir members tried valiantly to sing Handel's "Hallelujah Chorus" with as much elation as they could muster considering this would be the last time these strains would ever be heard inside this church. Alan Dambrowski avoided eye contact, fearful he might break into tears.

But standing in front of the altar, Father James was all smiles, knowing what his parishioners did not. God had resurrected St. Cecilia's, like the Lord, from an empty tomb. With childlike impatience, he could hardly wait to begin the homily so he could share God's great miracle.

The church was packed from floor to rafter with hundreds of faces, both new and familiar. The discovery that the Marian apparitions had been a hologram did little to reduce the number of people who still surged daily through St. Cecilia's sanctuary to get a firsthand look at where the Blessed Mother was reported to have appeared. In fact, few were convinced that Mary's apparition had been a hologram. Most believed it was a church cover-up to avoid sanctioning her appearance.

Realtor John Moran had caught Father James earlier that morning to say he had received several inquiries into home sales and rentals in the area. It seemed many of St. Cecilia's pilgrims were considering making Dorsetville their permanent home. "A real boon to the downtown economy," John predicted.

"Glory to God in the Highest," Father James sang and the choir entered into the response.

Father James sang with a heart nearly bursting with joy as he looked out into the sanctuary. The sun's rays, like golden streamers, flowed through the stained-glass windows, adding a high luster to the intricately carved woodwork. The altar guild had rubbed and polished the entire sanctuary with the same zeal as a housewife expecting the in-laws. The church smelled of a unique mixture of Murphy's Oil Soap, Lemon Pledge and fresh-cut flowers.

Harriet Bedford had always been in charge of the flowers, but she had certainly outdone herself this year. A dozen varieties of tulips, daffodils and hyacinths adorned every window sill; bundles of fragrant Easter lilies surrounded the altar and exotic flowers in a riot of color were packed to profusion in every nook and cranny. Parishioners felt as though they had entered a tropical paradise.

Father James motioned the congregation to be seated as Ethel Johnson stepped up to the podium to begin the first reading.

Peter addressed the people in these words: "I take it you know what has been reported all over Judea about Jesus of Nazareth, beginning in Galilee with the baptism John preached; of the way God anointed Him with the Holy Spirit and power. He went about doing good works and healing all who were in the grip of the devil, and God was with Him. . . ."

Father James looked out into the sanctuary with love. The entire congregation looked as though it had been scrubbed and polished. Everyone, it seemed, had made a special effort to dress in their best Easter finery. Several women wore large pastel hats swathed in netting and soft-colored bows. Older women clutched black patent leather bags, small girls held white ones, and boys sat with faces and necks scrubbed pink, trying not to squirm in starched white shirts and constricting ties. Even the men were carefully attired; they appeared stiff and uncomfortable beside their brightly smiling wives.

Father James noticed the ushers looked rather dapper in an assortment of finery that was the height of fashion when they had retired some twenty-five years ago. All the suits were freshly pressed and shirts neatly starched. Hair neatly trimmed. Even Timothy McGree had on a new pair of white socks underneath his suit pants. This morning, George Benson had joined their ranks, adding his own fashion statement with a four-inch white patent leather belt and Road Runner tie.

George was one of the many who believed in the conspiracy theory concerning the apparitions. He wasn't buying the hologram story. And he made it his business to tell everyone who would listen (and there were a lot of people who wanted to hear his firsthand account) that what he'd seen was real.

"You know how the Church is about these things," he would explain, sounding like he was privy to inside information. "They don't want the word getting around that Mary chose our church and risk other Catholic folks bailing out of their own parishes to come here and deposit their money in our collection basket. Nope, the Church likes to spread its money around. Got to keep up all that prime real estate they own."

Sarah Peterson smiled at Father James, then shyly waved. He waved back, thinking she looked the perfect picture of little-girl innocence in her pink dress and coat with white hat and gloves, acting very well behaved although there appeared a glint of excitement in her eyes. Lori, seated alongside, was just as excited. Today Bob's thirty-day isolation period, since the bone-marrow transplant, was over.

Harry Clifford, with wet comb tracks still evident in his hair, was seated between Sarah and her mother. Beside them sat Ben Metcalf and Matthew. Ben had insisted on being released early from the hospital. His health took an immediate turn for the better once the nurse delivered Father James's note stating that he and his friends were no longer outlaws. His son and daughter-in-law, seated farther down the pew, were unable to convince him to go home and rest. Ben insisted that there was no way he was going to miss the last Sunday Mass at St. Cecilia's. He needed to pray within its walls one last time.

Ethel Johnson's dog Honey—a garland of pastel silk flowers around her neck—was seated beside Matthew, curled into a tight little ball of fur, unconcerned for her mistress's absence. From experience, Honey knew she would be back once she had finished the readings.

Ethel continued with the responsorial psalm.

"This is the day the Lord has made; let us rejoice and be glad . . ."

The congregation responded as Ethel looked over to her sleeping pet. She wondered if the priests at St. Bartholomew's would allow her Honey to attend Mass. Probably not, she thought sadly. She pushed the thought and the tear it evoked aside and continued the reading.

Father James smiled as his eyes rested on a beaming Harriet Bedford, flanked by her granddaughter Allison and Jeff Hayden. Jeff's parents were seated beside him. In fact, the entire Hayden family—brothers, wives, grandparents—had come to share this Easter morning at St. Cecilia's. When they saw Father James look their way, the whole row gave him the thumbs-up.

They were scheduled to meet at the rectory after the service to discuss Jeff and Allison's upcoming wedding. Father James could hardly wait to tell them that it could be celebrated here at St. Cecilia's, now that it was no longer slated to be closed.

Ethel began the second reading.

> *Since you have been raised up in company with Christ, set your heart on what pertains to higher realms where Christ is seated at God's right hand. Be intent on things above rather than on things of earth . . .*

Father James watched Mother Mary Veronica and several nuns from their order of the Daughters of Mary of the Immaculate Conception of the Blessed Virgin Mary seated in the front pew to the left of the altar. All were attired in royal blue habits with Miraculous Medals on slender silver chains around their necks. Mother Mary Veronica had her eyes closed behind her wire-rimmed glasses, appearing to be in meditation.

The choir sang a response.

Sam Rosenberg joined in, singing slightly off-key yet looking as though he attended Mass every Sunday. He was seated behind the row of nuns. Earlier that morning, Sam had called Rabbi Polokoff to ask if there were any rules against a Jew attending Easter Mass with a friend. Sam expressed his desire to support his friends as they said a final goodbye to St. Cecilia's. The rabbi had given Sam his blessing.

The Mass moved toward the gospel reading. Father James rushed to the podium like a child eager to deliver a gift. He adjusted the microphone as he looked out into the congregation, his heart nearly exploding with joy.

Funny, a few days before, he had sat laboring over a sermon, searching, praying for just the right words that would help his flock relinquish their hopes for a miracle without losing their faith in God's love. But now the hoped-for miracle had arrived and with it a new song. A song of celebration of the wondrous love of God.

Father James had sat up until dawn trying to pen just the right words to adequately explain not just the gift, but the Giver of this miracle. The story he wished to tell was not about saving a building, but of God saving a people.

But the right words would not come; and now, standing behind the podium, looking out into the sea of faces turned expectantly in his direction, Father James realized that there was only One who could adequately express what was in his heart. He lifted his eyes heavenward, trusting the Holy Spirit to convey what he could not, then opened his heart and allowed Him to begin.

Dear Friends:

Six weeks ago, on Ash Wednesday, I stood at this same pulpit and told you all that St. Cecilia's was about to close, that through a decline in parishioners and the church's most desperate need of repairs, the archdiocese had decided it could no longer financially support our small parish. The archbishop then decreed that this Easter Mass would be the last given here in our beloved church.

Several parishioners reached for their handkerchiefs.

I have to tell you that as a priest, that message was the hardest one that I have ever had to give, not just because St. Cecilia's—the building—would be closed, but because our spiritual family was about to be broken, scattered among outlying churches.

As Christians, we are called to believe that all things work together toward good. But it's hard to believe that any good could come out of St. Cecilia's closing, now is there?

Two men seated in the center rows shook their heads no.

It's hard for us to reconcile because we so often walk by sight and not by faith.

The cancer that has come into your life, the relationship that has dissolved, that monetary need that seems so great that you can't possibly see how it can be filled.

And when these things happen along, our first thought is . . . why has God elected to punish me?

But God is not punishing you.

Things like this just happen in life. Even our Lord suffered. But God's response when trials or tragedies enter our lives is this, "Give it over to me and use it as an opportunity to strengthen your faith."

"Faith" is an action word. Faith is always growing, always changing, enlarging, until someday you, like Christ, can say to whatever mountain is blocking your path, "Be thou removed" and watch it disappear.

Ah, but you want that to happen immediately, now don't you? You want to say to that trial, that pain, "Be gone in the name of Jesus," and see it dissolve right before your eyes. But God doesn't work that way, now does He? God's not a magician. You can't say "Abracadabra" and pull your blessings out of a hat.

A wise man once told me that God allows trials to prove His faithfulness. God wants us to have faith in His love regardless of the storms that rage around us. He wants us to believe . . . to have faith in His ability to keep us—no matter the circumstances.

Pharaoh's chariots might be bearing down on us and there's no place to go but into the Red Sea . . .

. . . but God wants us to believe in His deliverance.

We've traveled for forty years in the desert with still no sight of the Promised Land . . .

. . . but God wants us to believe in the dream He has placed upon our hearts.

You've just been diagnosed with cancer, you've lost a child, or at age fifty-three you've lost your job . . . God asks us to trust Him. He wants us to believe with every fiber of our being that He will never leave us nor forsake us. He wants us to practice absolute faith in His Word—even though everything around us might say otherwise.

Let's go back to that first Easter morning two thousand years ago. Imagine the disciples' fear, their despair. They had left everything to follow Jesus because they believed with all of their hearts that He was the Messiah. And hadn't He verified their beliefs hundreds of times as He fed the multitudes, healed the sick? They'd even seen Him raise the dead.

There was no doubt, when Jesus walked among them in the flesh, that He was the Son of God. As long as they could reach out and touch Him, lean against His breast, look into His eyes and hear His voice, they had absolute faith.

But that was before Good Friday. That was before they saw their beloved Master beaten, spit upon and brutally crucified.

What they had seen with mortal eyes was not what they expected. Their mortal senses told them Jesus had failed. Their faith wavered.

But the apostles had missed it. They missed the most important lesson Jesus had brought . . .

. . . man was to live by faith and not by sight.

Hadn't Jesus proven that when He asked Peter to walk on water? As long as Peter kept his eyes on Jesus—the Word made flesh—He was able to suspend natural laws. He entered into the supernatural, the miraculous. But once he allowed his mortal eyes to govern his reasoning, he became fearful and began to sink.

But on that first Easter morning, God's plan was finally revealed. You see, while the disciples were fleeing in fear, based on the events they had witnessed with their human senses, God was busy working behind the scenes, behind the rock rolled across the face of the tomb.

In a flash of brilliant light and power, the Holy Spirit transformed Jesus' lifeless mortal body into the risen Lord. The gateways of heaven had been opened. The powers of hell had been banished. Jesus had broken the chains of death to free man from fear, a fear that Jesus said, "had bound men all of their lives."

God's plan from the beginning has been to reconcile us to Him. And through faith in His only Son, Jesus Christ, we are raised by the same power of the Holy Spirit from death to eternal life. From having to rely upon our own resources, to depending upon God to provide a way no matter the need or the trial.

St. Paul writes in Romans, "If God is for us, who can be against us? He who did not spare His own Son, but gave Him up for us all—how will He not also along with him, graciously give us all things?"

God continues to ask us to trust . . . wait in hope . . . in earnest expectation even when things around us say otherwise. Trust that He has a plan, even though we may not see it or that the answer may not be what we want. Trust that He has heard your prayer. Believe that He has the very best in mind for you. That as soon as your prayer was uttered, He set into motion all the events, people and circumstances needed to bring about your highest good.

We all have been praying for St. Cecilia's to stay open—but as the weeks passed without an answer, many of us—including me—began to despair that God would not answer our prayers. Our faith wavered because we could not see with these natural eyes the unseen miracles that were taking place all around us in answer to our prayers.

Seated here among us this morning is mother superior, Sister Mary Veronica, and several nuns from her order, the Daughters of Mary of the Immaculate Conception of the Blessed Virgin. Mother Veronica has just informed me that her order has chosen to open a retirement home for the religious here in Dorsetville. And since they will need the support services of a church, Mother Mary Veronica has also convinced the archbishop to allow St. Cecilia's to remain open!

The parishioners were stunned. They stared at the pulpit with expressions of disbelief.

"*St. Cecilia's is not going to close,*" he repeated, now laughing. "*The archbishop has decided to keep the church open. God has sent a miracle for St. Cecilia's!*"

"A miracle . . ." several whispered.

"Bless the name of Jesus."

"A miracle!"

Father Keene rushed into the aisle and grabbed hold of the reticent mother superior and planted a huge wet kiss on her check. The startled nun pulled back.

"Bless you, my darling. You're truly an angel sent from heaven!"

"Father Keene! Control yourself!"

The congregation howled with laughter. Even the nuns couldn't help themselves from joining in.

Suddenly people were scrambling to their feet, rushing across aisles to embrace friends. The ushers looked to Timothy for direction, but he had raced to the front of the church to find Sam and Ben.

Parishioners surged upon Mother Mary Veronica, who tried unsuccessfully to get them to return to their seats. "Please, please. You must sit back down," she implored. "The Mass hasn't ended."

The people ignored her, pumping her hand in gratitude, tears glistening on their cheeks, gushing with offers to help with the retirement home.

"My quilting bee would love to make quilts for all the beds."

"The garden club would like to volunteer to plant your gardens."

The ushers had joined the celebration to shake hands along the outside aisles. Even George Benson beamed brightly, knowing that he had somehow played a role in God's plan to save the church.

"I knew Our Lady would work it out somehow," he exclaimed to no one in particular.

Ethel Johnson's Honey, who had been napping during the homily, now awoke with a start and began to bark. People laughed. The church rang with celebration and from the choir loft were heard the first strains of "How Great Thou Art." The congregation joined in tearful refrain as Father Keene stepped back onto the platform by the altar and motioned for everyone to return to their seats.

People began to find their pews as their voices rang out in glorious adoration. Father James waited until the last refrain had been sung; then he motioned for those still standing to be seated.

I have had time to ponder the many miracles that God has sent to St. Cecilia's during these last few weeks. Not only has He saved St. Cecilia's from closing, but as I look around I see Lori Peterson, whose husband Bob will shortly be returning home from a successful bone-marrow transplant.

Lori clasped her daughter's hand and smiled at Father James with tears in her eyes.

I see Harriet Bedford seated with her granddaughter—returned to her after many long years, and I am amazed at the set of "coincidences" God used to bring that about.

Harriet beamed as Allison leaned over and kissed her on the cheek.

I marvel at how God has miraculously provided a home for Father Keene here among us—and at the complexities of all the decisions and events that took place to bring that to pass.

Father Keene nodded, smiling, his bald head shining like a polished apple in the bright morning sun.

So may this Easter, and every one that is to follow, remind you of God's infinite love, as He has demonstrated here through His people. And when trials come your way, may you walk by faith and not by sight. In doing so, you will come to experience the miracles God has fashioned just for you.

After Mass, Father James felt as though he were filled with helium, ready to drift up into the air as he walked down the aisle of St. Cecilia's and out the front door. His stomach rumbled, but he hardly noticed, even though it was well past his lunchtime and he'd still not had his Easter meal. No matter. Sam was outside in his Plymouth Duster, Father Keene and Father Dennis seated in the backseat, all waiting to be taken to the Bedford's, where tables would be laden with hams, roast leg of lamb, new potatoes roasted in garlic and rosemary, fresh asparagus, pots of fragrant, rich coffee and enough savory desserts to send even a nondiabetic into a coma.

Father stood outside the church and looked across the green to the park, whose yellow daffodils and beds of pastel tulips bore the first gentle colors of spring. The Reverend Curtis and his wife were taking a leisurely stroll after lunch. Father waved and the Curtises waved back without enthusiasm. No doubt the gossip mill must have already delivered the news. St. Cecilia's was not closing.

Sam pulled his Plymouth in front of the church and Father James walked over, casting a quick glance at the Norton's old mansion across the street, the future site of Mother Mary Veronica's retirement home. It would be a wonderful addition to their community. He had already overheard several working mothers discuss their intention to approach Mother Mary Veronica with suggestions to annex a child-care facility alongside. Father James couldn't think of a better place for children to grow and blossom than under their care.

"You'd better get in," Sam said, leaning across the passenger seat. "Harriet wants us there by one-thirty for a toast."

"Sorry, Sam. I was just thinking about all that's happened," Father said, sliding into the car.

"It's sure been something!" Sam said. "Amazing how everything has worked out, isn't it?"

"It certainly is," Father said, leaning his arm outside the car window. "But then, when man gets out of God's way, things have a way of doing just that. In Ephesians, Paul says, He is able to do exceedingly, abundantly more than we could ask or imagine."

Sam put the Plymouth in drive. "We Jews have a saying, too."

"What's that?"

"God created man because He likes a good story."

Father James laughed. "Could be, Sam. But either way, it's going to be a story that people around here will be telling for years to come."

Acknowledgments

In 1999, I prayed for a miracle. My husband, Paul, was quickly nearing retirement age yet there were no retirement funds. What we had managed to save over a thirty-year marriage had disappeared five years before when Paul was hurt on a construction job. We had no health insurance. It had always been more than we could afford. Consequently, we were forced to sell our home and cash in most of our savings in order to pay the medical bills. Then in a tragedy that far surpassed anything I had ever endured, our precious three-year-old granddaughter, Marissa, was killed in a tragic accident. What little money we had left was used for her funeral expenses.

People often ask how I got through that period. It certainly was the hardest trial I had ever had to endure, tougher than my bout with cancer twenty years before. Although I possessed a strong faith forged by years of adversity, at times the heartache seemed more than I could bear and I was often tempted to give in to self-pity and despair. But God's presence is never nearer than in adversity and in His compassion He sent friends with outstretched arms and words of comfort; allowed me to feel His physical presence close at hand; and in my darkest moment sent a choir of heavenly angels to lift my spirits. As He had promised, He never left me nor forsook me and for the next five years, with few resources of our own, Paul and I became dependent upon God for so many of our needs. I can testify that God never once failed us.

But no matter how great one's faith or how great God's faithfulness has been in the past, as long as we are mortals we are subject to doubts. And on the morning of Paul's sixty-fourth birthday, as I took an early morning walk, I wondered if God had forgotten our needs. There were only twelve short months until Paul turned sixty-five. Where would we get the money for him to retire and would we ever know the security of owning our own home again? In response, God sent me the idea for this book and the assurance that its sale would abundantly answer my prayer.

When I think of all that has transpired since I first took pen to paper I stand amazed because I felt that the idea for this novel was solely an answer to a personal prayer. Now, however, in light of the recent terrorist attacks on our beloved country, I can see that the Lord had a larger plan. He wished to use the stories in this novel—parables of His faithfulness, His miracle-working power—to bring healing and hope to a wounded nation.

Along the way He sent others to help me fulfill His plan. Carolyn Carlson, my editor, whose gentle touch and expert skills have helped to make this a work that both the Lord and I can be greatly proud of. He also sent readers, friends and advisers who cheered me along, including my beloved daughter Heather Valentine, Marilyn Moffo, Maddy Orsillo, Rita Reali, Anita Naiss, Patti Struski and all the wonderful women of the Southbury Public Library—Jacqueline Hoffman, Valerie Oakley, Carol Webster, Pat Standish and Ellie Noll. And most precious, He sent me two of His dearest priests, true shepherds, who supported me with their prayers, Monsignor Reagan and Father Joe Keough.

May the Lord Jesus Christ be given all the glory.